Mr. Darcy's Proposal

Susan Mason-Milks

Grove Place Press
Seattle

Mr. Darcy's Proposal

Copyright © 2011 by Susan Mason-Milks
Edited by Will Mason
Cover design by Newman Design Illustration
    (http://newmandi.com/)
Cover image: *Portrait of a Lady*
    by Henri Francois Mulard, ca 1810

This is a work of fiction. Any resemblance to real persons, living
or dead, events, or places is entirely coincidental and not
intended by the author. Further, the author wishes to
acknowledge Jane Austen, upon whose characters this book is
based.

Grove Place Press
mrdarcysproposal@groveplacepress

ISBN-13: 978-0615529721
ISBN-10: 0615529720

Quotations used in this book are from the following sources:
Paradise Lost by John Milton: Books 5.17–19, 8.364–66, and 8.619
Sonnet XVIII and *Sonnet CXVI* by William Shakespeare

DEDICATION

For my mother who taught me to love books

ACKNOWLEDGMENTS

My everlasting thanks to...

My brother, Will Mason, for spending endless hours with me skyping from Australia so we could discuss ideas and review edits. This book would never have happened without him.

My dearest friend, Mindy Woll, for helping me cultivate my imagination when we were kids.

My friend and business partner, Beth Hannley, for letting me bounce ideas off her and for listening when I read chapters aloud to her in the car while we were driving to work.

Friends (especially Ramona, Barbie, Carol, Denise K., Dorothy, and Denise A.) for encouraging me, reading drafts, making suggestions, and most of all, for believing in me.

Jane Austen for creating such amazing characters who continue to live in our hearts and stimulate the imagination.

And last but not least, to my husband, Norm Milks, for his patience which has allowed me to pursue my dreams even when I know he thought I was a little crazy.

PREFACE

This is a *Pride and Prejudice* "what if" story. It starts with the same basic plot and asks "what if" events did not happen the same as in the original?

Elizabeth Bennet is visiting her friend Charlotte for the Easter holiday. Also a guest in the neighborhood is Mr. Darcy whom she had met the prior fall. His haughty, unfriendly behavior left her with a very low opinion of him, and she's quite certain that he dislikes her, too.

To make matters worse, she has just inadvertently learned that Darcy influenced his friend, Mr. Bingley, to cease his attentions to her beloved sister Jane. This has confirmed to Elizabeth that she was right in thinking him a proud and disdainful man.

Meanwhile, Darcy has been unable to deny the feelings he developed for Elizabeth when they met last fall. He has decided to forget the differences in their stations in life and the improper behavior of some members of her family and propose to her. Completely unaware that she knows about his interference with Bingley and her sister, he is confident she will welcome his declaration. This is where the two stories diverge.

ONE

Elizabeth sat on the edge of her chair in the parlor at Hunsford parsonage. She was stunned and outraged, scarcely able to believe what she had just learned. Apparently, that haughty man, Mr. Darcy, was the one responsible for nearly ruining her beloved sister's life!

This afternoon, Elizabeth had been out walking with Colonel Fitzwilliam when he had told her the story of how Darcy had saved his friend, Mr. Bingley, from making a terrible mistake. According to the colonel, Bingley had been quite smitten with a young lady who lived in the neighborhood near his Hertfordshire estate. Darcy had interfered by convincing Bingley this lady was completely unsuitable to be his wife. Of course, Colonel Fitzwilliam, who was Darcy's cousin, had no idea that Bingley's love was actually Elizabeth's sister Jane. Even though four months had passed since these events, her sweet Jane's heart still ached at the loss.

Elizabeth's head pounded as she turned these revelations over in her mind. How could he? How dare he? If Mr. Bingley did not mind their family's lack of connections and fortune, then what was it to Mr. Darcy? She jumped up from her chair and commenced pacing about the room as if she could keep her tears from flowing by staying in motion.

If she could just give Mr. Darcy the verbal thrashing he so

richly deserved, he might think twice about meddling in affairs that were of no concern to him. Finally, she collapsed into a chair and the tears she had struggled to keep behind a dam of self-control began to overflow.

What a relief it had been this afternoon when Charlotte and Mr. Collins had accepted her excuse of a headache as reason to stay behind when they called upon Lady Catherine and her nephews for tea. Under the circumstances, Elizabeth was not sure she would be able to keep her temper under control if she were in the same room with Mr. Darcy, the proud and disdainful man who had caused her sister such unhappiness.

Just at that moment, she heard someone at the front door. Attempting to make herself presentable, she reached for a handkerchief to dry her eyes, but discovered that as usual, she had none. Instead, she was forced to pat her face with the corner of her shawl. A few moments after she heard the front door, the maid appeared in the parlor with a letter in her hand.

"An urgent post for you, miss. The messenger is going up to Rosings now and will return in half an hour to take your reply."

She thanked the girl and turned her attention to the letter. Recognizing Jane's handwriting on the letter, she wondered what could be so urgent that her sister would expect an immediate reply.

Dearest Lizzy,

I hardly know how to tell you the dreadful news. Our dear father was taken ill last night quite suddenly. It is his heart. The doctor says his condition is quite grave, and he is not optimistic that Papa will recover. Please come home, Lizzy. I know that we would all be comforted by your presence at this dreadful time. I have asked the messenger to wait for your reply and pray I will receive the good news that you will soon be with us.

Your loving sister,

Jane

Elizabeth's mind flew in a hundred different directions all at once. If she could find a way to return home to Longbourn immediately, perhaps her father would still be alive by the time she arrived. At that moment, she heard sounds at the front door again. It was too soon for the messenger to return. Surely, he could not expect her to pen an answer in so short a time. Just as Elizabeth was rising to go write a hasty note to her sister, the maid announced that Mr. Darcy had arrived and asked if she might show him in.

Elizabeth wondered what he could possibly be doing there. She was mortified that he of all people should see her in such distress. Before she even had a chance to tell the maid to send him away, Mr. Darcy appeared in the doorway. Forgetting all pretense of a proper greeting, she stood clutching the back of a chair for support. Darcy entered giving her a polite bow. When he looked up, his face instantly changed to concern.

"Miss Bennet, what is it? Are you ill? Should I call the maid back to attend you? Please, you must sit down at once," he stammered.

"No, no. Do not call anyone. Just give me a moment."

"Would you like a glass of wine?" he asked.

Elizabeth was silent as she considered what explanation she could possibly give for her state. Eventually, despair made her forget all propriety, and the story began to tumble out.

"I...I have just had the most distressing news from Longbourn. My father is gravely ill and not expected to recover. If you will please excuse me, I must make arrangements to return home immediately to be with my family." In the silence that followed, Elizabeth began to regret her outburst. "I am so sorry, Mr. Darcy, I should not have burdened you with my problems."

"Perhaps there is something I can do to assist you, Miss Bennet. Colonel Fitzwilliam and I are planning to leave early tomorrow morning. If you accompany us as far as London, I will have my driver take you on to Longbourn directly."

Elizabeth was stunned and puzzled, unsure how to respond. Why would cold, proud Mr. Darcy want to help her? Moreover, how would she tolerate riding all that way in the same carriage with him?

"Surely, this would be a great inconvenience to you and your cousin. I could hardly impose on you for such a favor." As much as she disliked accepting his help, she nonetheless found herself hoping he would not change his mind. Time was of the utmost urgency and traveling in Mr. Darcy's private coach would be most expedient. When her thoughts turned to her father and the possibility of never seeing him again, tears began to well up and spill over. Knowing Mr. Darcy was witness to this emotional display made her even more distraught. What would he think of her? But then, how could his opinion be worse than it already was?

As soon as she began to cry, Darcy fumbled in his pocket and offered his handkerchief. When she reached out to take it, their fingers accidentally touched, and for a moment, neither of them moved. Her eyes flew up, and she saw that he looked a little startled, too. For a moment he lingered, and then suddenly, as if he remembered himself, he withdrew his hand.

"I am so sorry, Miss Bennet. I did not mean to..." his voice trailed off as he looked away.

For a moment, Elizabeth was unable to form a coherent word. Then she recovered herself.

"Do not trouble yourself, Mr. Darcy. You have been more than kind. I am the one who should be apologizing to you. I am sorry you have been forced to see me in this condition. I must look frightful," she said keeping her eyes cast down so she would not have to meet his again. Even though she did not like him, she did not want him to think ill of her.

"You look lovely as ever, Miss Bennet," he said quietly almost to himself. "I should be returning to Rosings to make the arrangements. We will also need one of my aunt's maids to accompany us as your escort. Would you like me to ask Mrs.

Collins to return to the parsonage?"

"Yes, thank you. That is most thoughtful of you." Elizabeth knew she should have left it there, but her nature would not allow it. "Mr. Darcy, I must admit I am at a loss as to why you have made such a generous offer. I am afraid my tears have made you feel obliged to help me." Elizabeth thought it was most certainly out of character for him to be concerned with someone other than himself. Her feelings still stung with the injustice he had perpetrated upon her sister.

Darcy hesitated. "You do not understand?"

Nothing in their past interactions had led her to think he would ever behave in such a chivalrous manner.

"Mr. Darcy, I am astonished you would concern yourself over the problems of my family. I hardly know what to think. I told you before when we danced at Netherfield that I cannot make out your character as I have heard such differing accounts of you as to puzzle me exceedingly. Your actions now have only added to my confusion."

Darcy looked at her blankly. "I do not comprehend your meaning, Miss Bennet."

"Most of the times you have spoken to me have been to criticize or find fault. I can only guess at what you are thinking as you rarely give much away," she said betraying some irritation.

"So you have been under the impression that I somehow disapprove of you?"

She knew her comments were inappropriate, but she could feel her emotions rising and could not stop herself as she plunged recklessly ahead without regard for the consequences.

"When you were in Hertfordshire, you seemed to disapprove of *everyone* you met. We were not up to your high standards for proper society." As she spoke, she could hear the edge to her voice but could not control it.

Darcy turned pale and then red but did not speak to defend himself. Elizabeth's feelings were so raw and tangled that her usual self-control abandoned her completely.

"After seeing your selfish disdain for the feelings of others, I am astonished that you would deign to go out of your way for me—especially after you ruined the hopes of my sister Jane! I know you took it upon yourself to exert your influence upon Mr. Bingley to ensure he did not return to Netherfield. She has been devastated ever since." Interpreting the look on his face for denial, she pressed on. "Surely, you do not deny that you separated your friend from my sister because you did not think her good enough for him."

"I did attempt to influence Bingley, but you have misunderstood my motives."

"Oh, I think I understand all too well. Does your experience tell you that every young woman is a fortune hunter? You cannot imagine that a young woman of good character with no connections and little fortune could care for a man for himself alone and not just his material worth? You must judge everyone by your own experience, sir. Or perhaps it was her family? Were we so much of an embarrassment that Mr. Bingley would be forever disgraced by such an association?"

Although his face had returned to its normal color, the tips of his ears remained red. "Miss Bennet, please. I must say in my defense that I observed your sister most carefully. I did not think she showed any real interest in Mr. Bingley beyond the temporary pleasure of a few country dances."

"Jane is shy and modest. She only shows her feelings to those close to her. She is reserved even with me."

"I was concerned that my friend not make a loveless match as so many men are apt to do when their heads are turned by a pretty face. I am sorry if I have misjudged your sister's feelings. If what you say is true, perhaps there is something I can do to make amends."

"I think you have meddled enough already!" she snapped still trembling with the emotions that had been stirred up. His face remained unreadable.

"Elizabeth, I mean Miss Bennet, your first concern must now be for your father's health. Surely, we could continue this topic at a later time. I would not want either of us to say something in anger that would do irreparable harm."

His calm and reasonable words surprised her, and though she remained distraught, she was also exhausted by the exchange. Taking a deep breath and swallowing the lump in her throat, she struggled to regain her composure. Elizabeth finally recognized that her worry about her father had made her speak imprudently.

"I have forgotten myself. Please accept my sincere apology for my inappropriate outburst. I hardly know what came over me," she said. "Under the circumstances I would understand if you withdrew your offer to assist me tomorrow."

"Let me assure you that my offer still stands, but could I please suggest, that during our journey, you refrain from reprimanding me for my numerous faults." A hint of a smile played across his lips. "I think I can bear up under the strain, but I fear you may distress Colonel Fitzwilliam."

Was this an attempt to ease the tension between them with humor? She shook her head. "You truly are a most confusing man. I do not think I will ever be able to make out your character."

"Well, Miss Bennet, you will have a very long coach ride tomorrow to see what you can discover." With that, he excused himself to go make the arrangements for their travel.

TWO

By the time Charlotte returned to the parsonage, Elizabeth had almost completed packing her trunk.

"Oh, Lizzy, I am so sorry about your father!" Charlotte said embracing her friend. "Is there anything I may do for you?"

Elizabeth burst into tears dabbing her eyes with the handkerchief Mr. Darcy had loaned her. "I only wish I could be home this minute. It is so difficult being here and not knowing if my father is still living or if I am too late."

Charlotte squeezed her hand. "I will start making arrangements for your travel."

"Thank you, but that will not be necessary. Mr. Darcy is taking care of everything. He has offered to assist me in traveling to London and then on to Longbourn using his carriage. He is also arranging for a maid from Rosings to accompany me."

Charlotte looked surprised. "Mr. Darcy offered to take you in his carriage? That is generous indeed, Lizzy. He must think very highly of you to make such an offer. I have suspected as much ever since the ball at Netherfield when he singled you out for a dance."

"Oh, no, Charlotte, you must be mistaken. I think Mr. Darcy just felt sorry to see me crying so," said Elizabeth trying to downplay his offer. "He arrived to call just as I finished reading Jane's letter. I am certain he made the offer without really thinking. Perhaps he was hoping that it would stop my tears. You know how men hate to see a woman cry."

"I believe there may be more to it than that," said Charlotte. "He has called at the parsonage many more times than required by courtesy, and I have seen the way he looks at you. I think he may very well be in love with you, Lizzy."

Mr. Darcy in love with her? It was simply too preposterous. Again, Elizabeth denied that he could feel anything romantic toward her. She quickly changed the subject and began thanking Charlotte for her generous hospitality during her visit.

�֍

When Elizabeth went to bed that night, she was unable to sleep in spite of how exhausted she felt. Her mind whirled with thoughts of her family. As much as she wanted to see her father, she dreaded the scene that her mother would surely create. Then, there was the new complication of Mr. Darcy. Was Charlotte right—did he have some sort of romantic feelings for her? It could not be true. After the disdainful way he behaved toward her friends and family, he could not possibly care for her. Accepting his offer of help did put her in his debt, however. Would he expect something in return? These thoughts kept her awake for a good bit of the night.

The next morning she found herself alone in the dining room with Mr. Collins for a few minutes before Charlotte appeared. He took the opportunity to express effusively—as only he could do—his appreciation that she had come to stay with them. Of course, he could not resist telling her one more time how he and Charlotte were so well suited for each other and lived in perfect marital harmony. Having exhausted that subject, he began to offer his condolences as though her father had already died. Elizabeth could not imagine how Charlotte could have married this odious little man. Last fall, Mr. Collins, who was to inherit the Bennet's family estate through an entail, had proposed to Elizabeth. There had been quite a family uproar when she declined. Immediately, Mr. Collins had switched his attentions to her friend, Charlotte.

Just as she was wondering if she could tolerate another word, Charlotte appeared to rescue her. Elizabeth was sad for her friend, but reminded herself that Charlotte had accepted this man with her eyes open. If Charlotte was happy with her life here, then Elizabeth was genuinely glad for her. On the other hand, this visit had only served to reinforce to Elizabeth that she had made the right choice in refusing him.

As they waited for the carriage, Mr. Collins continued to prattle on so mindlessly that at one point Elizabeth was sure she was going to scream. Biting her tongue, she tried to smile, but she was certain Charlotte knew exactly what she was thinking. Finally, Mr. Darcy and Colonel Fitzwilliam arrived. She made sure her trunk was loaded as quickly as possible so they could depart before the little parson could find some new way to offend.

THREE

Both Elizabeth and Darcy were very quiet as they rode in the carriage toward London. Although Colonel Fitzwilliam tried to engage them in conversation to lighten the trip, he had been unsuccessful so far in soliciting much of a response from his traveling companions. Even as bored as he was, he certainly could not talk to the maid from Rosings accompanying them.

Miss Elizabeth's preoccupation could be attributed to worry about her father, but he was not sure what was on his cousin's mind. He sensed a strange tension between Darcy and their guest, but he could not make out the cause. Even though the colonel had suspected for some time that his cousin was partial to the lady, Darcy had never indicated any preference for her. It was mostly the way Darcy seemed to look at her that made him wonder.

Colonel Fitzwilliam took this opportunity to watch Miss Elizabeth. He found her to be one of the most remarkable young women of his acquaintance. She was beautiful, but more than that, she was gifted with a lively, intelligent mind that made her brilliant in the art of conversation, an activity he very much enjoyed. If only she had possessed even a small fortune, he would have seriously considered asking for her hand. But such was not the luck of a second son who must marry his fortune.

Darcy tried to focus his attention on the passing scenery in order to prevent himself from looking at Elizabeth. She evoked such a range of feelings in him that he could not help but be confused. He was baffled as to how she could have misunderstood his attentions these last few weeks. Or more to the point, how could he have so misunderstood her? Worse than just simple indifference, it had become clear that Elizabeth seriously disliked him, blaming him for interfering with Bingley and her sister. She had also accused him of being prideful and unconcerned with anyone but himself. How could this be? If she did not return his regard, why had she spoken to him in that teasing, flirtatious manner over the months of their acquaintance?

Based on these new revelations, he began to wonder if many of the comments he had taken as flirtatious had actually been double-edged. Darcy went over each of their conversations in detail, and finally, he understood. She had been cleverly disguising her disdain for him with her witty banter. How could he have been so blind? Something about Elizabeth Bennet had made him let down his guard, and this was his reward. She did not feel affection or love for him—she felt contempt. Did others truly see him as she had described—haughty and disdainful?

As he thought about how she had mocked him without his even being aware of it, his blood began to boil. Then he glanced across the carriage and saw her sitting quietly with her hands folded in her lap. She was so beautiful, so clever. Immediately, he knew he was helpless in her presence. He could not hate her—he could only love her.

Darcy realized he had an important decision to make. He could help Elizabeth return home and then retreat to nurse his wounded pride thus removing himself from her life forever. This would probably be the most appropriate course under the circumstances. His other choice was to find a way to show her he had taken her opinions of him to heart. To do this he would have to address the faults she had described and prove to her that he was a better man than she had judged him for. It would be so much easier to brush off what she had said as the foolish talk of a prideful woman who, by the way, was as guilty as he of judging people too quickly. He recalled that day at Netherfield when he had told her that his good opinion once lost was lost forever. She had called it a failing she could not laugh at. The other side of that same coin was that he knew himself to be incredibly steadfast and loyal to the people he loved, going to any lengths to help or protect them regardless of the cost to himself.

No, he loved her, and for some reason he knew that would not alter. She was now such a part of him that he could not give her up. Taking the more difficult course of trying to change her opinion of him was the right choice. He resolved to find a way to win her love no matter how long it took. The question was how to do it. In taking on this challenge, he knew instinctively that he might have to put aside his pride. He only hoped that she might do the same.

Elizabeth and her family would be in great difficulty if her father died. A picture formed in his mind of that toady Mr. Collins to whom the family estate was entailed going to Longbourn to throw them out. He closed his eyes and let out a long, slow breath at the horror of that image. While he did not especially like Elizabeth's family, he knew their predicament would cause her pain—and that was something he would do anything to prevent. Elizabeth, her mother, and sisters would be forced to rely on the generosity of any relative who could pro-vide financial assistance and protection. What would happen to Elizabeth? What choices did she have? All of her options were too unbearable for him to contemplate. Would she live the rest of her life in reduced circumstances? Seek employment as a governess? Or worst of all, marry someone like Collins for security.

Darcy knew her well enough to be certain it would be against all her principles to marry simply for money. Also, he thought about Mrs. Collins who had married that foolish little parson when she had seemed like such a sensible young woman. Would Elizabeth do the same and marry for security? She would not do it for her own benefit or convenience, but for her family she would undoubtedly make any sacrifice no matter the personal cost. There was no doubt this was a weak moment because of her family's situation. If she were going to marry to save her family, why should it not be to him?

Looking at her across the carriage, he promised himself that if she accepted him, he would court her properly. He would take things slowly and not force himself on her in spite of the fact that the temptation she presented was almost too much to bear. Darcy blushed as he contemplated how he longed to touch her, kiss her, hold her, and have her in his bed. For some reason, he was certain that with patience he would be able to change her mind about him, and she might even come to love him. He refused to believe he had been entirely wrong in thinking there was an attraction between them. In his heart, he knew that his own future happiness depended entirely on securing Elizabeth as his wife. Her lightness of spirit and love of laughter and life seemed to draw him out and balance his more serious nature.

Darcy was jolted from his reverie when the carriage hit a rut in the road. Looking out the window, he realized they were nearing the small inn where they always stopped to rest and take some refreshment on the way to London.

When their driver pulled up in front of the inn, a boy came running to take care of the horses. Obviously the lad recognized the coach, and he seemed eager to assist probably in hopes of a large tip from the rich gentlemen. Darcy stepped down from the carriage and turned to offer Elizabeth assistance.

Once her feet were on the ground, Darcy was reluctant to let go of her hand fearing she would refuse if he offered her his arm to walk in. So instead he simply tucked her hand under his arm and guided her toward the inn.

�֍

The Wild Swan was small, but neat and cozy, and the food was above the usual quality available on the road. They ate some light fare with Elizabeth barely touching anything except her tea. Fitzwilliam, always eager for conversation, talked easily with the innkeeper as he was still getting little encouragement from his companions.

It was clear to Elizabeth that the gentlemen stopped here regularly. She half-listened as they talked of the weather, changes in the small town since their last visit, and Colonel Fitzwilliam's opinions about the possibilities of war. Darcy mainly remained silent.

After picking politely at her food for a while, Elizabeth excused herself and wandered out through the wide double doors into the little garden at the side of the building. There was a certain satisfaction in stretching her legs after being confined to the carriage for several hours. Seeking the warmth of the sun, she followed a small stone pathway further into the garden. Even in her distress, she could not help but notice how someone lovingly attended the plants and trees in the walled garden. It was spring and a small fruit tree near the door was beginning to bloom. Being near nature always eased her mind. *All I have to do is breathe in, breathe out, and I will get through this*, she thought.

"Are you feeling unwell, Miss Bennet?"

She almost jumped when she heard his voice. Turning, she saw Darcy looking at her with real concern.

"You did not touch your food. Perhaps I could ask the cook to pack a small basket in case you should become hungry later," he offered.

"Thank you, that is very thoughtful of you, sir."

"I remember how I felt when I lost my own parents. It was a very dark time for me."

Elizabeth was surprised that he would reveal anything of such a very personal nature to her. Indulging her natural curiosity, she inquired, "How old were you when your father passed?"

"I believe I was a little older than you are now. Are you and your father very close?"

"Oh, yes. We love to talk about books and often enjoy a game of chess. Of all my sisters, Father and I are the most alike in our interests and the turn of our minds. I only hope I am in time to speak with him and give him some comfort in his illness," she said.

"Forgive me for being too personal, but I understand from my aunt that your family estate is entailed to Mr. Collins."

She knew she should be upset that he had knowledge of this very personal information. She certainly should have been appalled that he had mentioned it to her, but her need to talk to someone at this moment took precedence over propriety. After all, she would never see Mr. Darcy again after today.

"We shall all be at the whim of Mr. Collins. I am sure he will want us out of the house *post haste* once it becomes his. I always knew it would come to this. I just did not think it would be so soon. What a great irony!"

"Irony?" said Darcy looking puzzled.

Elizabeth hesitated for a moment wondering how much to say. What was it about this enigmatic man that made her feel as if she could confide in him when she did not even like him very much?

"The morning after the ball at Netherfield last fall, Mr. Collins made me an offer of marriage, and I refused him. If I had accepted, my family's security would now be ensured."

"Surely, you have no regrets," said Darcy.

"No regrets," she said with half a smile, "especially after spending time at Hunsford. Charlotte made her choice, and I made mine. Let us just say I am easily amused by the twists and turns that life can take."

"Perhaps something will happen to change your family's fortunes after all," he said looking at her intensely.

Elizabeth held his gaze, but could not quite grasp what he was implying. The only thing she could think of that might save them would be an advantageous marriage by her or one of her sisters. As it stood, there was no possibility of that happening any time soon. Jane had already lost her chance with Bingley thanks to Darcy's interference.

As she tried to form a polite response, she saw that he continued to look at her in that impenetrable manner of his. It occurred to her that maybe he was truly sorry he had come between Bingley and her sister. Could he be planning to attempt to somehow correct the situation? Suddenly, the garden began to swim before her eyes. "I believe I am more tired that I realized. I need to sit," she said.

Darcy took her arm, eased her down onto a garden bench, and sat beside her. Elizabeth put her head in her hands, and although she had promised herself not to cry in front of Mr. Darcy again, she could not control her tears. This time they were more tears of frustration than anything else.

Darcy immediately offered a clean handkerchief from his pocket. "Of course, if this continues, I shall have to order more from my tailor," he said quietly.

Elizabeth looked up at him in astonishment. This was the second time he had attempted to ease the situation with a small bit of humor.

"Yes, quite soon I shall have a whole collection," she replied. Darcy smiled at her, and for the first time, she saw how truly handsome he was.

"Mr. Darcy, just when I think I have reached an understanding of your character, you say something that takes me completely by surprise."

"I wish I knew some way to relieve your pain, Miss Bennet,"

he said looking away. As he turned his head, Elizabeth noticed that the tips of his ears had turned a little red, and she remembered that had happened before when he was embarrassed. Her immediate reaction was to try and ease his discomfort.

"Perhaps the best you can do right now, sir, is to see that we start off for London again as quickly as possible."

"Yes, yes, of course," he said. "I will call for the carriage to be brought around." Rising, he offered his arm. This time, Elizabeth took it without thinking and allowed herself to be guided back inside.

FOUR

That evening at Darcy's home in London, the gentlemen relaxed over brandy in the library after dinner. Georgiana was in London but staying with her aunt and uncle so they had the house to themselves. Finally, Fitzwilliam decided he could wait no longer for an explanation of Darcy's recent behavior.

"What is this between you and Miss Elizabeth Bennet? You are being terribly generous in helping her. I am not saying she is not deserving of your aid. Still it is not like you."

"Why do you say it is not like me? I am always helping people."

"Yes, for family, but you barely know this woman."

"It was nothing. She was desperate to return home, and we were already going in that direction."

"That is the official version, but I am your cousin. We have always been close. In fact, we are closer than I am with my own brother. You know that. Come, come, tell me what this is all about."

"There is nothing to tell."

"Very well," said Fitzwilliam raising his hand to signal he would cease this line of questioning. He decided to change to a more indirect campaign to extract the information. "Shall we have another brandy? This is really incredibly smooth stuff. Even better than what you had last time I was here."

SUSAN MASON-MILKS

After pouring more brandy for each of them, Darcy stood up and started to walk around the library, occasionally pulling out a volume, examining it, and putting it back on the shelf. Observing his cousin, Fitzwilliam was sure that Darcy would not be able to tell him the titles of any of the books he had pretended to look at. Something else was on his mind. Fitzwilliam decided to wait while the brandy did its slow work. Confident that he could out-drink his cousin, he knew it was just a matter of time and patience—both of which he had in abundance.

Darcy continued to prowl around the room, poking at the fire, examining the pictures on the mantle. He was generally very calm even in difficult situations, and this restlessness was a side Fitzwilliam rarely saw. After his grand tour of the room, Darcy settled back into his chair and his cousin filled his glass again.

"Are you maybe in more of a mood to talk now?" Fitzwilliam ventured.

"I am sorry I am not better company this evening. It has been a long day, and I am quite fatigued from our journey."

Fitzwilliam tried another approach. "It certainly made for much more pleasant scenery than usual today—having Miss Elizabeth in the carriage with us. She is a very handsome young woman. Have you noticed?"

"You know I have," Darcy said quietly without looking up.

Fitzwilliam was pleased to get this small admission. Usually, these conversations began with one small opening, and from there he was an expert at prying out the rest of the story. Continuing his battle plan, he remarked, "She is one of the handsomest women of my acquaintance. Not only that but she has a quick mind and a good sense of humor."

Darcy continued to stare at the floor, merely nodding.

"She is brilliant at conversation, and you know how much I love to carry on an intelligent discussion, especially when it is with a beautiful young lady." He watched for a reaction on Darcy's face and saw a small smile playing at one corner of his

20

cousin's mouth—another chink in the armor. "If she had any fortune at all, I would have been quite interested in her," he remarked with an air of studied casualness. "I might even have considered offering for her." He looked again for a reaction. At first, there was none. After a few moments, Darcy erupted.

"Stop! Enough. Very well, I admit it."

"You admit what?" Fitzwilliam asked, trying to look surprised.

"There is more to it than just helping a woman in distress."

"More to what?"

"Damn it, you know what I mean."

"Oh, such language for a gentleman," said Fitzwilliam feigning shock. "I do not know if this old soldier can stand to hearing such strong words!" With that, they both broke up laughing. Fitzwilliam always found a way to get what he wanted out of Darcy. It usually took a little time, a little teasing, and a few glasses of good brandy. He had triumphed again.

"Why do I always end up telling you everything?"

"Confession is good for the soul, Cousin. You will feel better for it."

"I am not sure about that, but at least you may stop tormenting me."

Darcy swirled the brandy around his glass, warming it with his hand, and then took another large swallow before he began.

"I am in love with her," said Darcy quietly.

"In love with whom?"

"You know very well whom—Miss Elizabeth Bennet!"

"Ah! I suspected as much. I have seen you in many moods—angry, frustrated, even happy—but I have never seen you in love. Tell me all about it."

"I am sure I told you how we happened to meet. I was in Hertfordshire visiting Bingley last fall."

"I seem to recall you did not have much good to say about your visit to the country. It was a little too rustic for your cultured taste."

"Yes, I found most of it quite tiresome. Every social situation was more tedious than the last. You know how difficult I find talking to strangers. I despise being the focus of attention and the object of gossip. I could just feel the target on my back as word of my situation made its way around. All those hopeful mothers pushing their daughters my way!"

"Knowing you, you must have been miserable."

"Bingley gets along with everyone, and he found it all quite delightful, especially a certain young lady—the one I mentioned to you before."

"You said you managed to save him from making a huge mistake with a local fortune-hunter."

Darcy winced. "There is more to that story than you know. The woman Bingley was infatuated with was Miss Elizabeth's sister, Miss Jane Bennet."

"Oh, no," said Fitzwilliam, slipping down in his chair. "I think I may have made a terrible *faux pas*, Darcy."

"Ah, so that is how she learned of my involvement."

"My sincerest apologies. I had no idea that story was in any way connected with Miss Elizabeth. I hope I did not make things too difficult for you."

"Oh, no," Darcy said sarcastically. "All it did was turn a bad situation into a near disaster, but that seems to be the course of my relationship with her almost from the very first evening we met."

"The famous Darcy charm! Let me guess—you managed to offend her somehow. You are so good at that."

Darcy shot him one of his disapproving looks. "Yes, and in the worst way. I cringe to even think about it. It is ironic considering how I feel about her now. Bingley was insisting I dance at the local assembly, but I was in no mood to make any effort at civility. He kept after me to dance, and when he suggested I ask Miss Elizabeth, I put him off by pronouncing her something like "tolerable but not handsome enough to tempt me", and of course, she overheard every word."

Fitzwilliam grimaced and rolled his eyes. "That will teach you to keep opinions like that to yourself."

"As I said, Bingley was quite taken with Miss Bennet. When his sisters, Miss Bingley and Mrs. Hurst, invited Miss Bennet for dinner one evening, she fell ill and had to stay several days to recover. Bingley was delighted, of course. Miss Elizabeth came to Netherfield to take care of her sister and ended up staying for several days, too. While she was there, I began to admire her, but I was cautious and did not want to show her too much attention. Despite my efforts, Miss Bingley, who has been following me around for several years now in hopes I would turn my attentions to her, managed to sniff out something of my interest in Miss Elizabeth. She was quite vocal in her criticisms of Elizabeth and her whole family. It was even worse after I admitted in a weak moment that I thought that the young lady in question had very fine eyes."

Fitzwilliam threw his head back and laughed. "Oh, Darcy, this gets better and better. You were quite cruel to have kept this little entertainment to yourself all this time. You must have known how very amusing I would find it."

"I am glad you see humor in it. I do not find it funny in the least. After being around her only a few times, I began to feel myself in danger of forming an attachment, and my good sense fought against it."

"Why was that a problem? In your position, you could have any woman you wanted. Miss Elizabeth is a lovely, accomplished young woman. Her father is a gentleman. Did you think she was not good enough for you, you old snob?" he teased.

"Fitzwilliam, Miss Elizabeth and her sister are both delightful, well-mannered young ladies. The rest of their family is altogether another story. It is true that her father is a gentleman, but their situation is frankly so far beneath my own that it made it almost impossible for me to consider her seriously. Their mother is so brash that she had Bingley and Miss Bennet practically engaged before we had spent more than a half dozen evenings in their company. Everyone in the neighborhood was talking of it."

"What did it matter to you, if Bingley loved her?"

"I have seen Bingley fall in and out of love a dozen times, but this time I began to wonder if he was not in real danger. I watched them together, and she did not look as if she loved him, so I tried to prevent him from making a big mistake. If they really loved each other, I suppose I could have overlooked her family's ill manners. Oh, yes, I forgot to mention there are three younger sisters who all behaved in very unladylike ways at several parties we attended. It was embarrassing to see. I finally persuaded Bingley that Miss Bennet was indifferent to him, that she was just after his fortune and he would be miserable married to her. I admit to having some help from Bingley's sisters in this. Charles is a very good man, but he is prone to being easily influenced. I may have taken advantage of that. He was not secure enough of Miss Bennet's affections so he took my advice and did not return to Netherfield. I thought I had saved him from an imprudent marriage. Also, I was spared from having to see Miss Elizabeth again."

"But you could not forget her?"

"I am embarrassed to admit I even dreamed about her for months after that."

"Not really a surprise. She is charming enough to induce any man to dream a bit."

"Behave yourself," Darcy said in mock anger. "She is spoken for."

Fitzwilliam flashed a wicked grin. "So when we arrived at Aunt Catherine's for our annual Easter visit, there she was."

"Yes, and it gets even more complicated. Mr. Collins, that obsequious little parson Aunt Catherine sponsors, is the Bennet's cousin. He was visiting Hertfordshire when I was there and had the temerity to come up and speak to me with no introduction. Can you imagine that?"

"He is an unpleasant fellow," Fitzwilliam agreed.

"Unfortunately, the Bennet's home, Longbourn, is entailed to Collins upon Mr. Bennet's death as there are no sons—just the five girls."

"I begin to see where this is going."

"Apparently, Collins was in Hertfordshire at our aunt's instruction to find a wife presumably from among his cousins. I learned recently that he proposed to Miss Elizabeth, but she had the good sense to turn him down. He married her friend, instead. That is how Miss Elizabeth came to be visiting Kent."

"I frequently caught you looking at her when she was at Rosings. At first, I just thought that our dear aunt was boring you more than usual, and you were entertaining yourself by watching a beautiful lady. After it went on for a while, I suspected you had feelings for her, but I never dreamed it was this serious. What are you planning to do now?"

"You remember the evening before we left, she stayed back at the parsonage claiming a headache—the one brought on by learning about Bingley and her sister from you!"

Fitzwilliam grimaced. "I seem to recall you disappeared for a while."

"I went to call on her to beg her to end my misery and marry me. When I got there, she had just received the letter about her father's illness. Understandably, she was quite distressed. In that moment of weakness, she told me everything."

"As usual, your timing is perfect!" exclaimed Fitzwilliam with a laugh.

"Once I knew she needed help, I offered my carriage. I admit at the time I was thinking that if I assisted her, she might be even more inclined to look favorably on my proposal."

"And she did allow you to help her. What is the problem? All you have to do now is follow her to Hertfordshire after an appropriate period of time and ask for her hand. No woman in her right mind would turn you down."

"There is one who most definitely would. In spite of my attempt at chivalry, Miss Elizabeth was more than a little angry with me—having it fresh in her mind about the role I had in ruining her sister's life. She let me know in no uncertain terms what she thinks of me. In addition to despising me for hurting her sister, she also thinks I am selfish, conceited, and disdainful of others—to name just a few of my many faults she enumerated that evening."

"A small complication, I am sure."

Darcy put his head in his hands. "I know I should be practical and let her go, but I find I cannot give her up that easily. She is not like any other woman I have ever met. She has never tried to gain my attention nor has she ever been impressed with my fortune or status. No, I believe the only course open to me is to prove to her somehow that I am a better man than she has taken me for. It will not be an easy task, but I believe she is a woman worthy of being pleased."

"So you are determined to mend your ways in hopes she will change her mind about you. That should prove interesting! How do you plan to accomplish this magical trick?"

Darcy sighed and leaning back in his chair, stretched his long legs out in front of him. "Her family is in a very difficult position. When her father dies and Collins inherits, he will most certainly want them out of the house as quickly as possible so he can take over. I know through other sources that the family will have a very limited income, so I am sure she must be concerned about how they will manage."

"I am surprised at you. You have always despised anyone you thought was just after your fortune. Now you are hoping she will marry you because of it?"

"I am ashamed to say it is true. I plan to entice her into accepting me by offering her mother and sisters my protection. Once we are married, I will somehow find a way to win her love. I think, in spite of what she says, there is an attraction there on her part, too. I had a hint of it when we were talking that evening at the parsonage and again when we stopped at the inn. I only hope I am right."

"I think you have lost your mind, Darcy."

He looked at his cousin and shook his head. "No, it is my heart that is lost."

"Very well. Get on your horse and ride for Hertfordshire tomorrow. If this is what you truly want, you best go after it whole-heartedly or else you will wonder later why you did not try hard enough."

"That is exactly my plan, but first, I have a call to make in the morning to correct the injury I have done my friend, Bingley. I know I am risking his friendship, but I cannot in good conscience leave this as it is. He has a right to know that Miss Bennet's feelings for him were real."

The cousins talked until nearly midnight and then retired. Darcy's dreams that night were filled with Elizabeth. He saw her at Pemberley walking the grounds with him, sitting across the dining room table, playing at the pianoforte in the music room. In each of his dreams, her eyes were bright with love as she looked at him.

FIVE

When Elizabeth finally arrived at Longbourn, she and Jane embraced giving each other comfort.

"I am so glad you have come home." As they walked into the house, Jane seemed to read the unspoken question on her sister's face. "Oh, Lizzy, I am so sorry to have to tell you this. The doctor says his heart has been so weakened that while he may live for a few weeks or possibly months, he will certainly never recover."

Elizabeth's heart sank. This could not be happening. How could she go on without her beloved father? What would become of their family? Elizabeth noticed how exhausted Jane looked and was glad she was now home to share the burden.

"Jane, you must be very tired from all you have had to bear by yourself, but I am here now, and we will manage together somehow."

"You cannot imagine my relief to have you home."

"I am almost afraid to ask about our mother."

"I think everyone from here to Meryton has heard her weeping. She is so irrational that she is no better than a patient herself," said Jane.

"Let me take over now so you can rest. I suspect you have barely slept these past few days."

"Do not worry about me, Lizzy. Let me take you to see Papa.

Mostly, he sleeps but occasionally he wakes and has been able to speak to us a little. He has asked for you several times."

Together, Elizabeth and Jane went up to their father's bedchamber where they found him asleep. Going immediately to his side, Elizabeth knelt down and took his hand in hers.

"Papa, I am here. Your Lizzy is home. Everything will be fine now." She laid her cheek against his hand, and tears formed in spite of her resolution to remain calm. Pulling a handkerchief from her pocket, she patted her eyes dry. As she was refolding it, she realized it was one of Mr. Darcy's, embroidered with his initials, FD, and a simple scroll-like design. She sighed and tucked it back into her pocket.

"The doctor says there is little hope he will recover, but I cannot believe it is so hopeless. Surely, the doctor could be mistaken," said Jane.

Elizabeth smiled at her sister's ever-present optimism. Pulling up the big chair next to his bed, she waved Jane away. "Now go and rest. I will stay with him."

Just as Jane reached the door, she asked, "Lizzy, was that Mr. Darcy's carriage you arrived in?"

"Yes, it was. It is a long story and I shall tell you later all about it. Now off you go." Elizabeth kept up her vigil throughout the rest of the day and into the night. Her sister Mary came to sit with them early in the evening. She read from Fordyce's sermons and the Bible, telling Elizabeth she was certain this would comfort their father. After an hour, Mary excused herself and went to bed. Elizabeth stayed, determined not to leave his side until she was sure he knew she was home again. Near midnight, her father opened his eyes and spoke to her for the first time.

"Lizzy, is that really you?" His voice was barely audible.

"Of course, Papa, I am here with you," she responded taking his hand. "Is there anything I can do to make you more comfortable?"

He gave her hand a small squeeze and answered, "Yes, my

dear, could you please ask Mary to stop reading to me. I find all those sermons and Bible passages quite tiresome." And after winking at her, he closed his eyes and went back to sleep.

SIX

Elizabeth dozed in the big chair by her father's bed through most of the night until Jane returned to relieve her. A few hours of sleep in her own bed revived her enough that she felt able to face the day.

After eating something herself, she took a tray to her father's room. She spoke softly to him a few times, and Mr. Bennet opened his eyes and looked at her. A small smile crept across his mouth.

"Good morning, Papa," she said kissing him on the cheek.

Elizabeth soaked some bread in beef tea and fed it to him slowly. Almost immediately after finishing, he fell asleep again. Elizabeth must have dozed off herself because the next thing she knew, she felt someone shaking her gently.

"Miss Elizabeth," said Hill, the family's maid.

"Yes, yes, I am awake," she answered although she really was not.

"You have a caller downstairs." As she pondered who could possibly have come to call, Hill said, "I have put him in the parlor."

Suddenly more alert, she asked, "Who is this caller?"

"Mr. Darcy, miss."

"Mr. Darcy?" He was the last person in the world she had expected. Trying to clear the cobwebs of sleep away, Elizabeth asked Hill to offer Mr. Darcy refreshments and inform him that she would be down in a few minutes.

Hill went off to see to Mr. Darcy, leaving Elizabeth to ponder this turn of events. In her room, sitting at the dressing table, she tried to shape her long hair into some semblance of neatness. Looking at herself in the mirror, she was dismayed at what she saw. Her face was tired and drawn, and her eyes betrayed sorrow and worry. Well, it did not matter anyway. She was certain Mr. Darcy had never thought her handsome, so why should she be concerned about trying to impress him now? She would greet him, spend a few minutes just to be courteous, send him on his way, and that would be that. The call must be merely a polite gesture on his part. She felt obliged to receive him as she was in his debt for the use of his carriage.

After she finished making herself presentable, she went slowly down the stairs, uneasy about the encounter. When she entered the room, he stood immediately and greeted her with a bow.

"Good afternoon, Miss Elizabeth."

"Mr. Darcy, I did not expect to see you again so soon."

"I have come to inquire after the health of your father. I hope the timing of my call is not inconvenient."

Elizabeth sensed him watching her every move. "Please sit down, Mr. Darcy."

He took a seat in the big wing chair near the fire and Elizabeth sat opposite. She was having difficulty meeting his gaze and found herself looking down at the floor where she saw a small tea stain on the carpet. As soon as he was gone, she would have Hill clean it up. What a strange thing to notice at this moment, she mused.

"May I inquire after your father, Miss Bennet?"

Elizabeth realized he was repeating the question she had been too distracted to answer the first time. As she described her father's condition, he leaned toward her, listening intently. Suddenly, the words caught in her throat and tears sprang to her eyes. She glanced at him in embarrassment but saw he was looking at her with only kindness and warmth. Darcy reached into his pocket and wordlessly extended his handkerchief.

"I am so sorry, again, Mr. Darcy. It seems that every time you have seen me recently, I have been in tears. I assure you this is not my usual state."

"You have been under an unusual strain these last few days. Next time, however, I will prepare in advance and bring several of those with me," he said, indicating the handkerchief she now clutched in her hand.

His comment caught her off guard, and she wondered again why he was being so kind to her.

"Would you like me to send to London for my personal physician? He could provide another opinion on your father's condition."

Elizabeth was so surprised he would make such an offer that she hardly knew what to say. It would not do to be any more in his debt than was already the case. "Thank you for your kind offer, but I believe everything that can be done for him is being done. The doctor tells us it is just a matter of time. We can only try to make him comfortable."

"I am truly sorry to hear that, Miss Elizabeth. It makes me think of my own parents, and how much it grieved me to watch them slip away."

Elizabeth was surprised again that Darcy had shared something personal about himself. The only time she could recall his ever speaking of his parents was yesterday in the garden at the inn.

Darcy rose and began pacing in front of the fireplace. Elizabeth sat in silence, too tired to attempt initiating any conversation. She hoped that maybe if she remained silent, he would leave. Then she remembered—Mr. Darcy had never been uncomfortable with silence.

As she watched him walk back and forth, she noticed that his boots had obviously been meticulously shined. In fact, she could not think of a time when any aspect of his personal appearance was less than perfect. Her eye went back to the tea stain on the carpet again, but she looked away quickly for fear that if she stared at the spot, it might draw his attention to it. For some reason, she could not bear the thought of his noticing the imperfections of her mother's housekeeping.

After what seemed like an hour, he stopped pacing. Thinking he was about to take his leave, she stood to thank him for calling. Much to her embarrassment by the time she was on her feet, he had crossed the room and was standing directly in front of her where they nearly collided. He caught her by the elbows to steady her.

"Excuse me, sir," she murmured looking down to avoid his eyes. Although he released her immediately, he did not back away but remained standing a bit closer than she liked. She caught the exotic scent of cloves and other spices and recalled noticing this several other times when he was nearby.

"Forgive me, Miss Elizabeth, if I speak too plainly, but I am very concerned about how you and your family will manage should your father..." he hesitated, "...not recover. When your cousin inherits Longbourn, you may very well be left in a precarious position. From what I have observed of Mr. Collins, I do not anticipate he will be generous toward you. If we were married, your mother and sisters would benefit from my protection. You would not have to worry about anything."

Elizabeth's cheeks suddenly felt hot. Had she understood him correctly? Was this his idea of a marriage proposal?

"You must forgive me for being a little slow, Mr. Darcy. Perhaps it is because I am tired, but I am not quite certain I understand what you are saying."

"I thought I was quite clear. I am asking you to marry me."

If he was asking for her hand, why had he said nothing of love or attachment? In fact, his words held no more warmth than if he had been making a business arrangement. Just as she opened her mouth to respond, Darcy put his finger lightly over her lips to prevent her from speaking. The intimacy of his action stunned her.

"Please do me the honor of hearing me out."

She nodded slightly. In spite of her irritation over what he had said—or failed to say—she was completely distracted by his close proximity and the tingling feeling that lingered on her lips where he had touched them. Dropping back into the chair behind her, Elizabeth's mind raced. She wondered what possible response she could give that would not bring offense. In spite of her low opinion of him, he had been most kind to her over the past few days, and she owed him something for that. She would be sorry to hurt his feelings by refusing him, but it was simply impossible to imagine being married to a man she hardly knew, let alone one who had insulted her before they were even introduced.

Darcy surprised her by sitting down on the footstool beside her chair. Because of his height, this brought them nearly eye-to-eye. Elizabeth thought he looked vulnerable, almost like a little boy sitting there with his knees nearly up to his chin. When he spoke, his voice was soft and gentle.

"I believe it would most certainly relieve your father's mind to know that you and your family will be financially secure."

"Mr. Darcy, I am more amazed than anything else. I simply cannot comprehend why you would wish to marry me." At this, she risked a glance in his direction.

Darcy wrinkled his brow in confusion. "As I have said, I am concerned about your family's financial situation, and I also believe you would be a very good influence on my sister. She is of an age where she needs the influence of a woman in her life."

"You have given me all the practical reasons why this marriage would be advantageous, but I am still unsure of why you have chosen me? Is this to be just a business arrangement?"

"No, that...that is not my intention," he stammered.

"Because if you are looking for a new companion for your sister, I am sure you could find someone suitable at considerably less expense to yourself than taking a wife."

He cleared his throat and took her hand in his. "I am sorry I was not more clear. Miss Elizabeth, I have admired you from the first time we met. You are not like other women of my acquaintance who are only concerned with my fortune and position in society. As we have spent more time together, my admiration has continued to grow. I hold you in the highest regard."

Elizabeth blinked slowly. This was certainly news to her. "You must forgive my shock at your proposal, Mr. Darcy. We hardly know each other, and until very recently, I had been under the impression you did not like me."

"Not like you?" he responded wrinkling his brow.

"In all of our acquaintance, we have only spoken a few times and when we have, we have always disagreed. You have also made yourself quite clear as to what you think of my family."

"Yes, well, your family is...interesting to say the least."

At this, she reclaimed her hand and folded it with her other so he could not pick it up again.

"You say you have admired me from the time we first met, but that is not entirely true. At the assembly in Meryton last fall, I overheard what you said about me—that I was 'tolerable, but not handsome enough to tempt you'. I believe those were your words. What do you have to say about that?"

Darcy blushed again all the way to the tips of his ears. "I owe you an apology for that remark. It had nothing to do with you."

"Nothing to do with me? You insulted me and yet insist it had nothing to do with me? I do not understand, sir. I heard what you said quite clearly. I was only a few feet away, and my hearing is most acute."

"Bingley was pressing me to dance when I did not wish to. The only way I could dissuade him from torturing me was to feign indifference."

"What about the disdainful way you treated almost everyone here in the neighborhood last fall? You barely deigned to speak to anyone."

"You have mentioned this before, and let me say again I am not comfortable conversing with people I do not know."

"You must tell me how you become acquainted with people unless you speak to them. You move in the highest circles of society, sir. I find it difficult to believe you have no skills in the art of conversation."

Darcy's eyes widened at her comment. "Miss Elizabeth, although I do not have first-hand knowledge of how marriage proposals are usually received, it would surprise me very much if young ladies take it as an opportunity to argue with the gentleman who is asking for her hand." His eyes were deep and intense, but there was a hint of humor around the edges. Now it was Elizabeth's turn to blush.

"But as I said, you are not like any woman I have ever met. I admire not only your beauty but your spirit and intelligence as well."

Elizabeth mumbled a thank you, but found she could no longer look him in the eye. Looking away, her gaze came to rest on the tea stain on the carpet again. Its presence irritated her now more than ever.

"I remember last fall when you walked three miles through rain and mud out of concern for your sister. I respected you for that. When I saw you again in Kent, I had to acknowledge that my feelings had not diminished, and I resolved to make you an offer of marriage."

"I had no idea," Elizabeth said softly.

"Surely, you must have known that I intentionally sought you out on your walks around Rosings Park. Did you think that our frequent meetings were merely by chance?"

"But you barely spoke to me."

"As I told you, I am not as adept in the art of conversation as my cousin, Colonel Fitzwilliam. I was enjoying the pleasures afforded by simply being in your presence. I thought you understood that."

"Clearly, I did not," said Elizabeth raising an eyebrow.

"I was foolish enough to think you returned my regard, but that evening at the parsonage, I discovered my error. I have taken your words to heart. I have been hoping my actions over the past few days might persuade you to think better of me. I hope you will agree to become my wife—if not for your own sake, then for the sake of your family."

"Mr. Darcy, how could you think I would even consider accepting you after the way you came between Mr. Bingley and my sister," she said feeling her anger and frustration rising again.

Although he looked surprised at her bluntness, he answered evenly, "If you remember, I told you that I would try to make amends for my error, In fact, when I call at Longbourn tomorrow afternoon, Mr. Bingley plans to be with me."

"Mr. Bingley, here?" She could not disguise her shock.

"He is escorting my sister and Mrs. Annesley, her companion, here. They will arrive this evening."

"I am quite astonished, Mr. Darcy. And you are certain he means to call on us?"

"Before I left London, I met with Bingley to confess that the advice I had given him about your sister's feelings was in error. I abhor deception of any kind. I had already carried some guilt for my part in those events, and after your words at Hunsford, I resolved to tell him the truth." Darcy's eyes seemed to challenge her. "I told him I had reason to believe that Miss Bennet still held him in high esteem and that he would be warmly received should he decide to renew the acquaintance. I hope you will forgive my revealing this to him. I did not tell him how I came to have this information."

"I thank you most sincerely, Mr. Darcy. My sister mentioned her regard for Mr. Bingley only just yesterday. His call will be most welcome."

"It was one the most difficult things I have ever had to do," he confided. "Bingley is a dear friend to me, in many ways like a younger brother. I knew I was risking the loss of his friendship by confessing that I had also kept your sister's presence in London from him this past winter. Fortunately, Charles has such an amiable disposition that he cannot stay angry with anyone for very long. He forgave me even before we had finished talking and immediately formed a plan to return to Netherfield."

"So you told Mr. Bingley all this even before you came to Hertfordshire and before you knew how I might receive your proposal?" she said with astonishment.

"Do you really think me so unkind that I would make your acceptance of me a condition of my telling Bingley the truth about what happened?" he replied somewhat indignantly.

Elizabeth blushed and fumbled for something to say.

"I consider it a matter of honor to correct my mistakes when I become aware of them," he added.

That he considered it so important to speak to Bingley about Jane gave her new insight into his character. He had known the importance she placed on her sister's happiness, and he had taken action without the expectation of anything in return. Elizabeth looked away wondering if she should feel flattered or offended by the unusual manner of his proposal, but her curiosity was definitely piqued. This speech and his behavior over the past few days were leading her to wonder if perhaps there was more to Mr. Darcy than she had first thought, but still, how could she say "yes" to him?

"Mr. Darcy, I thank you for your very generous offer, but I am not able to give you an answer today. Would you allow me some time to consider your offer?" Elizabeth was surprised that what came out as her response was not what she had intended to say. Her plan to refuse him then and there came undone somewhere between her head and her mouth. Somehow she could not bear to disappoint him when he was sitting there so like a vulnerable little boy. Turning away, she stared at the picture over the fireplace so she would not have to look into his eyes.

Darcy reached over and gently turned her face back toward

him. Elizabeth noticed his other hand had somehow come to rest on her knee, and she found herself staring at his long slender fingers. His touch was creating heat on her leg, heat that seemed to travel all through her body causing her cheeks to glow. She marveled how just his touch could create such unsettling feelings.

"Elizabeth?" He spoke very softly. Finally, she raised her eyes to meet his. He was so close she was certain he must be able to hear her heart beating. "Promise me you will give my offer serious consideration. I can take care of you. You would want for nothing."

Elizabeth bit the side of her lip as she thought about what to say. "I promise I will think this over very carefully before I give you my answer, but that is all I can agree to at present."

Darcy rose slowly as if he were reluctant to leave. "Very well," he said with a small sigh. "I will leave you for now and with your permission call again tomorrow morning to inquire about your father. Good-day, Miss Elizabeth."

The warmth of feeling she had seen in him a few moments before had been quickly replaced with his more familiar formal manner. Giving a small bow, he turned and walked out of the room. She heard the sound of his boots on the marble floor of the entryway, the front door opening and closing, and then silence. Still shaking from what had just transpired, she could not seem to get up from her chair.

Looking around the room, she noticed that someone had poured a cup of tea for her. With a shaky hand, she took a small sip. It was still a little warm. Darcy's visit—that had seemed an eternity—must actually have been quite brief.

SEVEN

After sitting for a while in shock, Elizabeth returned to her father's room and found Jane sitting at his bedside. "Do you think he has improved?" she asked putting a reassuring hand on Jane's shoulder.

"No improvement, but he does seem to be resting more comfortably now. Lizzy, was that Mr. Darcy in the parlor?"

"Yes, he came to inquire after Papa, but there is more to tell. Come to our room where we can talk. I would not want to wake him," she whispered.

As they walked arm in arm along the hallway, Elizabeth thought about what she would say. Part of her wanted to share all that had happened, and another part of her thought if she spoke of it out loud, it would become much too real. She knew she could not tell Jane about Mr. Bingley's return at this point, as she did not entirely trust Mr. Darcy yet.

Once in their room, they sat cross-legged on the bed facing each other as they had so many times before when sharing confidences. "Remember, I told you yesterday that Mr. Darcy's behavior recently has been quite puzzling to me," said Elizabeth. "I could not understand why a man so conceited and so self-absorbed would ever want to help me, but I think I finally understand."

"It was very kind of him. You see, Lizzy, Mr. Darcy is not as bad as you thought him to be. I have always said he has some very admirable qualities."

Elizabeth squeezed Jane's hand. "You always believe the best of people. I wish I had your goodness to see the world that way." Elizabeth was reminded again of Darcy's influence on Bingley, and how much that interference had cost her sister. Even if Mr. Bingley renewed his suit, nothing could erase the pain of these past few months. If Jane only knew, how might her opinion change?

"I have something to tell you that you may not believe. I hardly know how to think about it myself."

"What do you mean?" asked Jane.

Elizabeth hesitated for a moment and then took a deep breath. "Mr. Darcy has asked me to marry him."

Jane's eyes grew wide. "What? Mr. Darcy? Just now?"

"Your surprise is no greater than mine."

"But you always believed he did not like you. I still remember how upset you were with him after the Meryton Assembly."

"Not handsome enough to tempt him? Yes, his insult is etched upon my memory." Elizabeth rolled her eyes.

"I believe he was more pleasant to you later when we were staying at Netherfield."

"But still, he always looked down at everyone around him," said Elizabeth.

"You saw him again in Kent, I believe. Was he any different there?"

"In some ways, I suppose. I also met his cousin, Colonel Fitzwilliam. You could not find two gentlemen as different as they are. I very much enjoyed talking with the Colonel. He has all the charm and ease Mr. Darcy does not."

"So you liked his cousin, Lizzy?"

"He made my visit more enjoyable. We were invited several times to dinner and tea with Lady Catherine, her daughter, and nephews," said Elizabeth smiling and rolling her eyes. "I actually think Lady Catherine extended the invitations because she was bored and felt the need of some entertainment." Elizabeth went on to explain how she and Darcy had met several times on her walks around Rosings Park. At first, she had thought it a coincidence. Now, she realized he had been seeking out her company.

"He is not indifferent to me at all, Jane. In fact, it is quite the opposite. I do not know what I did to bring this on. I never desired his good opinion nor tried to win his affection. If anything, I mocked his prideful manners and haughty attitude."

"Maybe he was drawn to you *because* you treated him so differently than other women of his acquaintance," Jane observed. "Caroline Bingley's behavior was shameful as she tried to win his attentions."

Elizabeth shrugged her shoulders thoughtfully. "And, Jane, when I think of all the times I noticed him staring at me! I thought it was a sign of his disapproval."

"Have you given him an answer yet?"

"I asked for time to consider his offer, but I am finding it hard to think about anything at the moment. I cannot seem to focus my mind with all that has happened."

Jane watched her sister's face intently. So much had changed in a very short time. Elizabeth was finding it difficult to absorb all the implications.

"If—no, we must face the truth—*when* father is gone, everything will change for us. We have always laughed at Mama trying to find us wealthy husbands. Maybe she was wiser than we thought," Elizabeth said wryly. "If none of us marry before Papa dies, we will be in a very precarious situation. We will lose our home to Mr. Collins and have only a small income to live on, but if one of us is comfortably married, all the rest would benefit."

With that tears welled up in Jane's eyes. Elizabeth reached in her pocket for a handkerchief and offered it to her sister. When Jane refolded the handkerchief to hand it back, she noticed the embroidered initials—'FD'.

"Is this Mr. Darcy's?" she asked holding it out.

Elizabeth smiled. The fabric was very fine and clearly expensive—an indication of all that could be hers if she agreed to become Mrs. Darcy. "Yes, I have several now. I am embarrassed to report that over the past few days—nearly every time Mr. Darcy has seen me—I have cried, and he has given me another one of these. I have several more in my room. Do you think he proposed because he felt sorry for me or because he thought it was the only way he would get his handkerchiefs back?" said Elizabeth, her sense of humor returning.

"Oh, Lizzy, I do not know what to think about all this. It is too much to take in," Jane replied.

"He came to call today with the express purpose of asking for my hand. I now suspect that was the reason for his call on me at the parsonage the evening I received your letter. I had just read it when he arrived, and I was in such distress that I told him everything without thinking. The next thing I knew, he had offered his carriage to take me home. I didn't want to accept, but I really had no other choice. And so it seems, that may be the position I find myself in now. I have put myself in his debt in such a way that it will be difficult for me to turn him down."

"Surely, you do not think that was the sole purpose behind his offering assistance," asked Jane.

"It all happened so quickly. I find it hard to believe he had any motive other than genuine concern, but I cannot be sure. The most important thing is he has generously offered to take care of all of us if I marry him and that, Jane, is my dilemma. We both know that marriages of convenience are made every day. Although I have always vowed I would marry only for love, under these circumstances how can I refuse him?"

"Lizzy, you must not sacrifice yourself for the rest of us. Somehow, we will resolve this without your having to tie yourself to someone you do not love."

"Oh, Jane, I fear you are far too optimistic."

"Perhaps, but I refuse to believe our situation is so hopeless."

"And I find it hard to be hopeful! Oh, Jane, what should I do? I have so many reasons to dislike Mr. Darcy. On the other hand, marrying a very rich and handsome—though somewhat unpleasant—man might not be the worst thing that could happen to me. After all, I understand he has a very nice house in town and a rather large estate in Derbyshire," she said mischievously with a twinkle in her eye.

"Lizzy, be serious. You must decide what *you* want regardless of the affect on the family. We will all manage somehow if you choose not to marry him." Jane leaned toward Elizabeth as she continued, "At the same time, I have always said Mr. Darcy has many good qualities. He has also been incredibly kind and generous to you. Charles—I mean Mr. Bingley—regards him as his closest friend. That has to count for something."

Elizabeth gave her sister a questioning look.

"I know. I know," said Jane holding up her hands. "You are disappointed in Mr. Bingley, as am I, but I truly believe he is an honorable man. What happened between us does not change that."

"Jane, you are far too generous with regard to Mr. Bingley."

"Perhaps I am," she said.

"I think it would be best not to mention Mr. Darcy's proposal to Mama. I could not bear to hear her response. She would most certainly try to exert pressure on me to accept, and I think you are right—I have to make this decision on my own."

"We will not speak of it until you have decided," Jane assured her.

EIGHT

After a night of fitful sleep, Elizabeth awoke early and decided to venture out for a walk before the rest of the household was up. She still had no answer for Mr. Darcy, but fresh air often helped her think. Wandering along one of her favorite paths, she began to reexamine all of her previous beliefs about marriage. She recalled her skepticism when Charlotte had said she believed that her chance of happiness with Mr. Collins was at least as fair as most people could hope for upon entering into a marriage. After observing her friend on her recent visit, she could see that while marrying Mr. Collins had been more a matter of expediency than love or even respect, Charlotte did not seem unhappy. She enjoyed running her own home and managed to limit her time with her unpleasant husband very adroitly. Soon, it appeared, he would inherit Longbourn, and Charlotte's fortunes would improve even more.

Elizabeth now faced a similar decision. Could she marry a man she did not love, a man whose behavior was often offensive and at the very least a mystery to her? He had been quite solicitous toward her recently and had even shown a sense of humor, but his manner was still prideful and intolerant as often as not. Did she have a chance of happiness if she accepted him or was that too much to hope for?

She thought about his wealth and status and wondered why

he would want to marry someone whose circumstances he clearly perceived to be so far beneath his own. Although she had never seen Mr. Darcy's home in Derbyshire, she understood it was large and quite beautiful. Being mistress of such a great estate would have its compensations, but would it be enough to make up for the loneliness she would undoubtedly suffer?

The walk did seem to be helping clear her mind. Then just as she reached the top of a small hill, she saw Mr. Darcy striding toward her.

"Good morning, Miss Elizabeth," he said with a tip of his hat.

"Mr. Darcy," she said. Elizabeth tried to carefully arrange her face so as not to display her feelings of disappointment at his appearance.

"Has there been any change in your father's condition?" he inquired.

"No, he is much the same."

"I am sorry to hear that. May I walk with you a while?"

"Whatever you wish, sir." What else could she say? Guessing he had come out early specifically with hopes of encountering her, she imagined he must be anxious for an answer. She still needed more time and hoped he would not press her. As at Rosings, Darcy did not seem to feel the need to talk as they walked along. Elizabeth used the quiet to turn her choices over in her mind again. Perhaps there were some advantages to a man who did not try to fill every silence with useless talk.

"It is a very fine day for walking out, is it not?"

Elizabeth was a bit amused by his attempt at small talk. "Indeed, it is. I spent much of the evening at my father's bedside so it is very pleasant to be out of doors and in nature. As you know, walking is one of my greatest joys."

"Yes, you are a great walker."

Elizabeth gave a sideways glance at his profile and discovered he was smiling.

"I would like to ask your permission to introduce my sister to you this afternoon. She is a very shy girl, and I think she would benefit from making your acquaintance. As I told you, at her age she could use a woman's influence in her life."

Elizabeth was more than a little irritated that he was already assuming there would be a relationship between herself and his sister. Was he so confident of her accepting him? His presumptuousness did not make Elizabeth happy in the least. Keeping her feelings in check, she bit her lip. She decided the best course was to show an interest in Miss Darcy by inquiring politely about her.

"Tell me about your sister, her interests and pursuits. I have heard Miss Bingley and Mrs. Hurst talk about her but that is all I know."

"Georgiana is just sixteen and, as I said, very shy. I would say that music is her greatest love. She has been taking lessons on the pianoforte from a very fine teacher in London. Practicing keeps her occupied many hours each day. Although she generally does not find it easy to meet new people, she is very anxious to make your acquaintance."

Here Darcy hesitated for a moment, but then went on, "There is something I must tell you about Georgiana that is quite important in understanding her. It is one of the reasons I am hoping the two of you will become friends. I know I can rely on you to keep this in confidence."

"Of course you may," said Elizabeth. When she glanced at his face, she saw the pain he was trying to cover and wondered what could have affected him so deeply.

"Last summer, Georgiana and Mrs. Younge, who was her companion at the time, went to Ramsgate for a visit. While my sister was there, she encountered a man who had grown up near Pemberley and was often in the company of my family. This man is a rake and a scoundrel, but I had kept the true nature of his character from her over the years. With the aid of Mrs. Younge, whose character was not what I had thought, this man ingratiated himself to Georgiana. He used everything he knew about her from her childhood to charm her. Thinking she was in love, she consented to an elopement."

Elizabeth tried to keep the shock from showing on her face.

"When she was a child, he had always gone out of his way to appear the perfect gentleman in her presence so that when he flattered her, she could not see the insincerity of his proposal. She was only fifteen, and I suppose her youth offers some excuse for her imprudence. When I joined them unexpectedly a day or two before the intended elopement, Georgiana felt guilty at the idea of upsetting me, and so she told me of their plans."

Elizabeth observed that Darcy was clenching and unclenching his hands as he related the story. Her first thought was how he must have agonized over this incident and probably blamed himself.

"Fortunately, I was able to avoid any public exposure of the incident. As soon as he was aware that I knew of their plans, he left the area. Mrs. Younge was, of course, immediately removed from her post."

"But why would he do such an abominable thing?" Elizabeth asked incredulously.

"His chief reason for the elopement was unquestionably my sister's fortune of 30,000 pounds. These events have affected Georgiana in many ways, not the least of which has been to make her even more shy and mistrusting of people."

"Mr. Darcy, that was a narrow escape," said Elizabeth. "I am thankful you were able to keep her safe. You must have been very relieved that in the end she was sensible enough to confide in you so that you could prevent her from coming to harm. I can only imagine the anguish of losing a sister to such a man."

"Yes, we were very fortunate indeed. You must understand how important Georgiana is to me. With both my parents gone, she is all the more dear."

"So this incident has left her withdrawn and even more uncertain of herself."

"Both she and I already have a tendency to be uncomfortable with people we do not know well," he offered.

"You do remember what I told you that evening when I was playing the pianoforte at Rosings?"

Darcy furrowed his brow, and then one corner of his mouth turned up just a bit.

"When there is something you do not do well, you should practice," she reminded him. "If you do not take the time to talk to people, then you will never become more proficient."

"Of course, you are right. Although it is difficult, I have tried to take your words to heart," he said. "Now, I hope you will be able to impart similar wisdom to my sister."

"But you do not need me to speak with her. You could tell her yourself."

"Somehow I do not think it would carry the same weight coming from me," he told her.

"You flatter me too much, Mr. Darcy," she said, suddenly irritated that she was allowing herself to be drawn in. She stopped and pretended to examine a small patch of wildflowers at the side of the path.

"She is very curious about you."

"Curious about me?" she asked as she leaned over and picked a small purple flower.

"I have never spoken so highly of any young lady before, so naturally Georgiana wants to find out all about you for herself."

"Are you trying to intimidate me, sir?" she teased as she stood to face him.

"I have it on the best authority that you are not easily intimidated," he replied raising an eyebrow.

Elizabeth laughed to herself. She was beginning to enjoy their verbal sparring even more than before, which was both pleasing and disconcerting. Entering a small wooded section of the path, the sun, which had been very bright, became filtered, throwing everything into shadow. They walked in silence for a few minutes before she spoke again.

"I have something I must ask you, but it is of a most personal nature. I am not certain just how to speak of it to you without causing offense."

"As you know, I do not easily talk about myself, but I will try to answer whatever you request."

"It concerns some information about you and a certain gentleman," she said. Watching Darcy's face, she saw his jaw tighten.

"I believe you must be referring to our mutual acquaintance, Mr. Wickham," he said with some sarcasm in his voice. "I can only imagine the falsehoods he has presented to you as truth. No, if he has done anything to mislead you about our dealings, I welcome the opportunity to clear myself of his accusations."

"As you suspect, it is about Mr. Wickham. He has told me and others in the neighborhood that you are responsible for depriving him of the living your father promised him. As a result, he was forced to join the militia to make his way in the world. I believe you must explain yourself—if any acceptable explanation can be given." Although Elizabeth could see how her words had hurt him, her need for the truth outweighed any guilt she might have felt for causing him pain.

"This is not something I like to speak of, but I want to tell you what really happened. The story goes all the way back to my childhood," he began. Darcy related that George Wickham was the son of a very good and respectable man who had managed all the Pemberley estates for many years. Because Darcy's father had thought so highly of his steward, he made provisions to give the man's son a gentleman's education. In his will, Darcy's father had granted Wickham a legacy of 1,000 pounds, which Darcy paid to him immediately. Darcy's father had also recommended that he further assist Mr. Wickham by giving him a valuable family living should he follow through with his plans to take orders.

Elizabeth saw great sadness on Darcy's face and knew this could not be easy for him to speak of. Darcy explained that within half a year Wickham had written to indicate he had decided against taking orders and was planning to study law instead. In spite of Darcy's reservations that this would come to nothing, he gave Wickham three thousand pounds for this purpose. In exchange, he required that Wickham resign all future claims to the church living near Pemberley.

As he spoke, Darcy clenched and unclenched his fists. "I knew Mr. Wickham's nature far better than my father, and I admit to being relieved he had decided against the church. I have never known anyone so ill-suited to take orders. From boyhood, Wickham was very careful around my father, but he was more open with me. He hated me because he knew I saw him for what he really was. After the arrangements were made and the money delivered to him, I believed I had fulfilled my father's wishes and was finished with him. Unfortunately, I had not heard the last of Mr. Wickham."

Elizabeth listened intently still uncertain what to believe. He went on to explain that Wickham did not pursue the law but had quickly squandered all the money. After making inquiries, Darcy discovered Wickham had engaged in gambling and frivolous living until he was penniless again and in debt.

"At that point, he came to me saying he had changed his mind about the church and asked to have the living at Kympton or additional money." Darcy grimaced with the pain of recalling these events. "When I refused, he became unreasonably angry and hurled every kind of abuse at me such that I thought we might come to blows. Finally, I had to have several of my footmen escort him from my home. Then like a spoiled child who could not have his way, he vowed revenge and began to tell outrageous tales behind my back."

Elizabeth could not contain her shock at hearing this information. As she examined both their stories in her mind, she could see that Darcy's version matched most of what Wickham had told her. However, it was becoming clear that Wickham had conveniently chosen to ignore certain details that entirely changed the meaning of the events. Although she was reluctant to admit it, this new information also matched what Caroline Bingley had tried to tell her, and Elizabeth began to wonder if she had been too quick to believe Wickham's accusations.

After relating this information, Darcy was silent. Elizabeth could find no words to express her astonishment. At this point, Darcy stopped and turned to face her. "Miss Elizabeth, I am reluctant to reveal my most recent dealings with that man. The circumstances are simply too shocking, but I believe you must know. The man I told about earlier, the man who nearly ruined my sister, was George Wickham."

Elizabeth gave an audible gasp. First she felt her face drain of all color, and then she flushed with embarrassment. She closed her eyes against the rush of emotion that came with these revelations and felt herself wavering where she stood. When Darcy reached out to offer support, she pulled away, walking off a few steps where she stood with her back to him. Still unsteady on her feet, she put her hand out and leaned against a tree. Her disbelief was extreme, but she knew instantly in her heart that it all must be true.

Elizabeth felt shame and embarrassment that she could have made such a grievous error. She had always prided herself on being a good judge of character. How could she have been so wrong about Mr. Wickham? Was it because Mr. Darcy had wounded her pride with the comments she had overheard at the assembly that first evening? Darcy's generally cold demeanor toward people must also have been a factor. Apparently, when considering Darcy and Wickham, one man had all the goodness while the other all the appearance of it.

"Miss Bennet, I am very sorry to have caused you discomfort, but I am certain you must know the truth in order to better understand Georgiana."

When Elizabeth remained silent, he added, "If you do not believe me, then you have my permission to ask my cousin,

Colonel Fitzwilliam, to verify this story. He knows the particulars as he is joint guardian of Georgiana with me."

Elizabeth took a deep breath and exhaled slowly. When she turned to face him, she had tears in her eyes. Although he immediately offered his handkerchief, she waved it away. Searching his face, she saw concern for her but also fear that she did not believe him.

"I believe you, Mr. Darcy. I do not understand why he would have done that to your sister. I suppose it makes sense if you think that his actions at Ramsgate might have been a sort of revenge on you for refusing him any additional help."

"Revenge and the opportunity to gain control of my sister's fortune," said Darcy looking visibly relieved that she seemed to accept his word.

"Were you aware that when Wickham was in Meryton, I was not the only person he told that you had treated him so abominably?" she asked.

"It does not surprise me that he would try to turn me into the villain yet again. I am sure it allowed him the double pleasure of making people think ill of me and bringing sympathy to himself."

"If you suspected he was spreading falsehoods, why did you not reveal the truth about his past?"

"I am a very private person, and I decided his character and actions were no one's business but my own. There was also the risk that if one part of the story was revealed maybe someone might learn all of it. I could not take a chance that Georgiana would be hurt again just when she is beginning to recover a small measure of confidence."

Elizabeth continued to rearrange in her mind everything she had believed about the relationship between the two men. "I am ashamed to say I was taken in by his lies. I had thought myself a better judge of character," she said quietly.

"Do not blame yourself. George Wickham has always been very charming. My father was so taken in that he never saw him for the scoundrel that he is. When we were boys, he would lie and my father believed every word. There was always a hint of truth in his lies—just enough to make them plausible. Worst of all, Mr. Wickham has no conscience, and I am sure no remorse for the way he lives or the damage he caused Georgiana."

Elizabeth walked over to him and placed her hand on his arm. "Mr. Darcy, would you mind walking me home?"

"Yes, of course, if you wish."

She noticed that he looked calmer than he had a few minutes ago. Elizabeth was not sure if the relief came from simply unburdening himself of the truth or that she had believed him. As they walked together, Elizabeth considered what she had just learned. If she had been wrong about Wickham, what else might she have been wrong about? Everything seemed in question now. This new information did not make Elizabeth like Mr. Darcy more, but now she was at least beginning to see that there were many sides to him she did not know.

In her mind, she reviewed all of her objections to his proposal. He was attempting to make amends to her sister Jane by speaking to Bingley at no small cost to himself. His version of his interactions with Wickham rang true especially after hearing about Miss Darcy's near escape. There would be no advantage for him to lie to her about this and then offer his cousin to verify the truth of these events. Based on what he had just told her, it made even more sense that he needed her help with his sister. As for his behavior, he seemed to be making an effort to change in that area also, but there was no way to know if he would be successful in keeping his pride under control in the future.

Soon they emerged from the woods and continued on the path that ran along beside one of the freshly plowed fields of her father's estate. Drinking in the familiar earthy smell that mixed with the scent of wildflowers and new grass, she felt her mind slowly clearing. One final question remained. She took her time, choosing her words carefully. After walking along in silence for a full quarter hour, Elizabeth was finally ready to speak.

"Mr. Darcy, I have something I must ask you before I can give you my answer."

"You may ask whatever you wish."

Elizabeth knew that she could not enter into a marriage through any deceit. He would have to know her reservations and her true feelings. Taking a deep breath, she began, "I have considered your proposal very carefully as I promised you I would. Your offer to assist my family is more than generous, and it would certainly relieve my mind to know they would be taken care of. After your revelations today, I have a better understanding of your character, and my respect for you has grown as a result."

Glancing at him, she saw a hopeful look on his face and was not sure if it pleased or irritated her. "You have said you do not like deception of any kind, and the same is true for me as well. Some women in my position would try to deceive you with pretty but false declarations of love. I cannot do that. I believe, however, that marriages of convenience are very common in society. They are often entered into by people who do not know each other well with the hope that in time affection may grow. I have always said I would marry only for love, but it seems events are forcing me to be more practical. So now, knowing all this do you still wish to marry me?"

The question seemed to float in the air for a long time like an early morning mist.

"Elizabeth, I knew what your feelings were yesterday before I declared myself, but my offer has not changed. I have to say, however, that I appreciate your honesty," he said almost sounding relieved.

"I do not want you to find later that you have regrets," she told him.

"My only regret would be if you were to walk out of my life forever. But I am hoping for more than just your respect."

At this point, Elizabeth made the mistake of looking at him. His eyes were dark green pools of intensity. Her heart pounded in her chest, and she felt as if she were about to walk off a very steep cliff. She had to take a deep breath to stop herself from shaking. "Very well, I accept your proposal, Mr. Darcy. I cannot promise you how my feelings might change after we are married, but I will endeavor to be a good wife to you and sister to Georgiana. I only hope I can live up to your expectations as the Mistress of Pemberley. There are many who will not agree with your choice of a wife."

Darcy's smile was so wide that for the first time, she could see both of his dimples. Quickly, she looked away.

"The only person whose blessing I require is my sister's, and I am confident of her approval."

Darcy took her hands in his and even through her gloves she could feel the warmth emanating from him. Since she did not have the courage to look him in the eye again, she continued to study his hands as they held hers. She knew that once a couple was engaged, some favors were deemed acceptable, but what would he expect? Would he want to kiss her? She supposed he must be hoping that at least she would look at him. After what seemed like forever, she finally risked a glance and found he was staring at her as if he thought she might disappear.

"You have made me very happy, dearest Elizabeth." Darcy raised her hand to his lips and kissed it lightly as if to seal their bargain and then tucked it under his arm. As they walked back to Longbourn, he told her he would apply for a special license so they could be married immediately. He outlined his plan for a small private ceremony with only a few family members present out of respect for her father's illness.

Elizabeth listened with very little comment amazed that he never once asked her opinion. For a moment, she thought of pointing out to him she had not given him permission to use her first name, but she did not have the energy to protest. She also noted that Darcy seemed to assume it natural that he would make all the decisions and arrangements.

He told her he would like her to come to Netherfield early in the afternoon on that very day to meet Georgiana. Their plans for later in the afternoon and evening would depend upon her father's condition and her mother's nerves. Elizabeth was certain her mother's state of mind would improve immeasurably once she learned of their engagement and the security it would bring.

"I know your father is very ill, but will it be possible for me to speak with him today?"

"He was awake for a short period this morning, but you must give me some time with him first so he will not be so shocked when you meet with him. I am sure he would say you are the last man in the world he would ever have expected to be asking for my hand."

If Darcy was surprised at this, he hid it well.

"I would also like to be the one to tell my father about Wickham. I do not think other members of the family need to be privy to what happened to Georgiana."

Darcy nodded in agreement. "I remember your mentioning an aunt and uncle in London. When I go to obtain the special license, would you like me to carry a letter to them inviting them to the wedding?" he asked.

Elizabeth brightened at his thoughtful suggestion. "That would be wonderful! They have been like second parents to me all my life, and I would very much like them to be here."

Elizabeth was unsure how to explain her apparent sudden change of heart about Darcy to friends and family. She suggested they tell people they had begun to form an attachment while they were in Kent, but had chosen to keep it a secret until now.

Just before reaching Longbourn, they stopped. It was an awkward moment in which she sensed he would like to kiss her, but she did nothing to encourage it. He relieved some of the tension by asking, "You will have to help me learn to get along better with your mother. I confess I am always at a loss as to what to say to her."

"Oh, you probably do not have to worry. She will either be too awed to speak to you or will carry on the entire conversation by herself. In either case, all that will be required of you is an occasional nod," she said with a grin.

"It is good to see you smile, Elizabeth."

"I hope I never lose the gift of finding humor in all sorts of situations."

"Now that we are engaged, would you consider calling me by my first name?" he asked.

Elizabeth was not at all comfortable with this idea as he still seemed like a stranger to her, but if it was important to him, she would try.

"Although my first name is Fitzwilliam for my mother's family, those close to me call me William to avoid confusion with my cousin the Colonel.

"Very well, William. I shall say good-bye until this afternoon."

Darcy took her hand and raised it to his lips again. "Until later, my dearest Elizabeth."

NINE

As she walked the last few yards to the house, Elizabeth felt light-headed. Had she really said "yes" to Mr. Darcy's proposal? The idea of being "Mrs. Darcy" was not something she could even imagine. Oh, what have I done, she thought.

After searching the house, Elizabeth finally found Jane in the garden cutting flowers. Standing for a moment in the doorway that led out to the garden, she saw Jane with a basket and clippers searching through the roses to find just the right ones for her bouquet. Elizabeth watched her, admiring the graceful way she moved as she bent to her work. Just then, Jane looked up and waved.

"Lizzy, how was your walk?"

"It was lovely. Oh, yes, and while I was out, I happened to encounter a certain gentleman whom I had been hoping to avoid."

"So Mr. Darcy was up early, too?"

"I suspect he was out walking in hopes of seeing me. I wanted to be alone to think, but as it turns out, it was a most advantageous meeting. He shared some very interesting information with me about a certain militia officer of our mutual acquaintance."

Elizabeth related all she had learned about the character and ungentlemanly behavior of Mr. Wickham as it related to Mr.

Darcy. Jane was truly shocked at these revelations.

"How could we have been so taken in by Mr. Wickham?" Jane said with astonishment.

Elizabeth loved that Jane always believed the best of people. "His past actions show he is very skilled at this kind of deception. His good manners and handsome demeanor make it hard to believe any ill of him, but I think we must. I am certain what Mr. Darcy shared with me is true."

"How bold Mr. Wickham was in telling those terrible stories!" said Jane.

"If you think about it, he waited until Mr. Darcy was no longer in the county before spreading his version of the truth very widely. He knew just how to take advantage of the fact that most people, including me, were already predisposed to dislike Mr. Darcy because of the way he had acted here. Nevertheless, I am ashamed of myself for being so quick to believe the worst of him. You know I have always prided myself a good judge of character. I do not understand how I could have made such a grievous mistake in judgment!"

"Do not be too hard on yourself, Lizzy," Jane told her sister. "We were all taken in by Wickham's charms."

"It still does not make it easier for me to bear. I should have been more discerning."

Jane turned her attention back to cutting flowers and asked casually, "So, Lizzy, have you decided what your answer will be to Mr. Darcy? Has this new information made any change in your disposition regarding his proposal?"

Elizabeth hesitated for a moment, biting her lip. "Yes, as a matter of fact, I have made up my mind. I told Mr. Darcy just a few minutes ago that I would marry him."

Jane looked up at her with wide eyes.

"But I felt obliged to tell him that I am uncertain as to my feelings for him. As long as he was willing to accept me on those terms, then I could agree."

"Oh, Lizzy, I hope you did not wound him too much with

your honesty. At times, your manner can be a little too direct."

"I think in some ways he appreciated that I did not try to flatter him as some women might, but I do believe he is hoping that with time my opinion of him will improve."

"And do you think it will?"

"I cannot say what will happen although I do have more respect for his character after what I learned this morning."

Jane hugged her. "Let me be the first to wish you joy. You certainly deserve all the very best. When will you be married?"

"Mr. Darcy will have to obtain Father's permission, but I do not think that will be an obstacle. I am planning to inform Papa so he will not be too shocked when Mr. Darcy calls on him. Then, we will be married once he has obtained the special license."

"Oh, Lizzy, so soon!"

"Yes, we thought it best to be married immediately in a small private ceremony."

"Have you thought about what might happen if Father recovers? Would that make you regret your choice?"

"I cannot think about that. The fact remains that someday— be it now or in the future—our family will need the kind of support and protection he has offered. I believe I must be practical. One of us has to marry well to ensure security for rest."

Jane looked at her sister sadly. "Oh, Lizzy, it should have been me as the eldest. I wish you would not make this sacrifice for all of us."

"Dearest Jane, do not say that," she reassured her. "I have made my decision, and we will speak of it no more. Now, I have some news that I hope you will find more pleasing."

"News for me?"

"Your Mr. Bingley returns to Netherfield this very day, and I have it on the best authority he plans to call at Longbourn this afternoon."

Jane's eyes grew wide. Though she tried to contain her excitement, Elizabeth knew her well enough to be sure this unexpected news cheered her greatly.

"He is not 'my' Mr. Bingley," said Jane casting her eyes down.

"Yes, but I think that will change very soon," Elizabeth reassured her.

Jane blushed, but quickly regained her composure. "It is very kind of him to think of paying his respects to our family under the circumstances."

"I am sure he is concerned about Father, but Jane, he is coming expressly to see you."

Jane put her hand to her heart and drew in a sharp breath as her bright blue eyes widened. "How did you discover he is coming today?"

"Mr. Darcy told me that Mr. Bingley is escorting Miss Darcy and her companion here from London. I am to go to Netherfield this afternoon to meet my future sister, and Mr. Bingley is planning to call on you here at Longbourn."

Suddenly, Jane threw her arms around her sister and hugged her tightly. "I hardly know what to think. I cannot believe that after all these months of silence he still thinks enough of me to call."

Elizabeth placed her hands on her sister's shoulders. "It is true, Jane. He is coming to see you."

"In that case, I think I should cut more flowers."

Elizabeth found her father propped up on pillows dozing a little while Mary read from her ever-present book of sermons. After opening the window a little bit to let some fresh air into the sick room, she sat down by the bed.

"Mary, I must to speak to Papa alone. Would you mind?"

Mary picked up her books and retreated from the room with a sour look on her face. As soon as she was gone, her father opened his eyes.

"You promised to ask Mary to stop reading to me, Lizzy, but still she goes on and on. I am so tired of hearing sermons that I am forced to fall asleep to stave off boredom."

Elizabeth patted her father on the hand. "Well, I guess you are feeling well enough for a little chat," she said with a laugh.

"Just a short one."

As she helped him sit more upright against his pillows, she tried to plan what she would say. She took a deep breath to begin but found that no words would come.

"Are you feeling well, my dear child?" asked Mr. Bennet looking at his favorite daughter with concern.

"I am fine, Papa, but I do not know quite where to begin."

"This must be very serious indeed. You rarely have trouble expressing yourself."

"Do not worry. What I have to tell is good news I think."

"I am in need of some cheering up."

"Papa, I have just received a proposal of marriage, and I have accepted on condition of your blessing, of course."

"A proposal?" asked her father looking surprised. Then he recovered himself. "I do not mean to imply I am surprised that someone would want to marry you, only that I was unaware anyone in the neighborhood has been courting you."

"It is not someone from the neighborhood. I fear when you hear from whom the proposal has come you may not be pleased at first. Promise me you will reserve judgment until I have told you the entire story."

"I am now in such suspense that you had better get on with it," he told her.

Before she spoke, she put her hand on her father's arm. "I have received a proposal of marriage from Mr. Darcy."

"Mr. Darcy?" Mr. Bennet made a face. "Lizzy, dear, please enlighten me on exactly how this came about."

Elizabeth calmly went on to explain how they had met again in Kent and how Darcy had been a great help to her in returning to Longbourn expeditiously when she learned of his illness. She also told him about Wickham's deceptive behavior and how they had all misjudged some elements of Mr. Darcy's character. Most importantly, she told her father of Mr. Darcy's offer of help for the family and how it would ensure the security of her mother and sisters should that become necessary.

"But he is still a very proud, unpleasant fellow, Lizzy. How can you be happy with such a man?"

"I have come to know him a little better, and I am convinced he is a good man," she said.

Mr. Bennet looked at his second oldest daughter with a frown. "That is not what I asked."

"I believe I shall be content as his wife," she told him hoping that she sounded more convinced than she actually felt.

"I do not want you to go through life with a partner you cannot respect, Lizzy. We have all seen the sorry results of that sort of marriage. I want more for you, my dear."

"Papa, we must be practical in this matter. Mr. Darcy's offer would provide security for everyone, and you could rest easy knowing all of us would be taken care of most comfortably."

"Is this truly your wish, Lizzy?" he asked, his eyes searching her face.

"Yes, it is," she said calmly. "I have discovered in the past few days that he has more kindness and compassion than I had imagined. No one can deny that he loves his sister very much. He has been a good friend to Mr. Bingley, too, and at times, he has even displayed a sense of humor." She grinned. "Surely, that must count for something."

Her father took her hand. "Very well. You may bring Mr. Darcy to me this afternoon. Although I still have reservations, if it is truly your desire, I will give my consent. I certainly know better than to oppose you when you have made up your mind about something."

"Thank you, Papa."

"Now who is going to tell your mother? My illness has been hard enough on her nerves. I fear that news such as this may send her over the edge." He raised an eyebrow and Elizabeth heard an unmistakable note of mischief in his voice. They looked at each other and began to laugh.

TEN

After leaving her father, Elizabeth enlisted Jane's help, so she would not have to face their mother alone. They found Mrs. Bennet just where they expected—in her room sitting with her feet up. Kitty was nearby doing some needlework. When they reached the doorway, their mother waved in their direction.

"Girls, girls, come here. I have been telling Kitty I am not feeling well enough to go downstairs to eat. She was just leaving to get me a tray." When Kitty did not jump up to do her bidding, Mrs. Bennet gave her a disapproving look and motioned toward the door with her head. "Off you go now, Kitty. Tell Cook not to forget that orange marmalade I like."

Kitty reluctantly set aside her sewing and went off with a frown on her face. Jane settled down in a chair next to her mother's and took her hand to comfort her. Elizabeth decided she preferred to remain standing to deliver her news.

"Mama, I have something I must speak to you about."

"I hope it is something entertaining. My poor nerves could not survive any more bad news."

"It may not be entertaining but I pray you will find it cheers you." Elizabeth noticed her mother's attentions waning.

"Well, out with it, Lizzy. Has Mr. Collins decided to let us stay on here after your father is dead? Now, I would find that good news indeed."

SUSAN MASON-MILKS

"No, this is not about Mr. Collins. It is about Mr. Darcy."

"Mr. Darcy, that disagreeable friend of Mr. Bingley's?"

"He came to call yesterday morning to inquire about Father's health. I believe you were resting at the time." Putting her hand in her pocket, Elizabeth nervously fingered Darcy's handkerchief.

"He called? That is a surprise. Well, I suppose it is only right that he pay his respects to our family, but I would not have believed him to be so courteous. I am sorry that you had to entertain him. He did not stay too long, did he?"

"No, it was just a short visit. He was very solicitous and asked that I convey his regards to you for your health. I believe I told you how kind he was in assisting my return home from Kent to be with all of you."

"Yes, yes. I was a little surprised to hear he put himself out for you. Perhaps he is more of a gentleman than we first believed him to be." Mrs. Bennet absentmindedly plucked at some lace on her dress as she spoke.

"I have come to know a little more of Mr. Darcy's character and find that he is much more agreeable than we first thought. In fact, my respect for him has grown significantly."

"Oh, if only his friend, Mr. Bingley would return. Now that would truly lighten my heart for our dear Jane," said Mrs. Bennet patting Jane's hand. The sisters exchanged a look.

"Mama, you may be surprised by what I have to say. I only hope it will not be too overtaxing for your nerves." Elizabeth stalled for a few more moments while she braced herself for her mother's inevitable reaction.

Mrs. Bennet fanned herself with her handkerchief and looked a little more interested now that the conversation was coming around again to the subject of her nerves. "Well, out with it, child," she urged her daughter.

Unable to delay any longer, Elizabeth plunged in. "Mr. Darcy has made an offer of marriage to me, and I have accepted him. He will speak with Papa this afternoon."

Mrs. Bennet's eyes grew wide and her mouth froze in a perfect "O" but no sound came out. For a few moments she was completely silent as if she could not comprehend what her second daughter had just told her. Then she erupted calling out in her high shrill voice. Elizabeth secretly prayed that they would not be able to hear her all the way to Netherfield. "Mr. Darcy has offered for you? Oh, but this is indeed good news. One of my girls married to a man of such wealth and status! But Lizzy you did not like him—no one liked him. He is always so unpleasant." Mrs. Bennet wrinkled up her nose.

"I believe we may have been wrong about him," offered Jane trying to give her sister support.

Mrs. Bennet took a deep breath as if she was going to say more about her dislike of the man, but then she must have thought better of it and continued, "Oh! Lizzy dear, how rich you will be! The best of everything! Ten thousand a year and possibly more—a great estate and a house in town!" Their mother fanned herself even more vigorously as two bright circles of red appeared on her cheeks.

"Come here and let me congratulate you, my dear. I had always thought it would be Jane who married first, but at least you have done very well for yourself. Maybe this will prove to be advantageous for all of us. Do you think Mr. Darcy can be prevailed upon to help our family should your father...well, you know what I mean," she said, thoughtlessly waving her handkerchief in the air.

Elizabeth was astonished that her mother's thoughts had taken such a selfish turn so quickly. She was glad that no one else was present to hear. "Yes, Mr. Darcy is well aware of our situation and has expressed his wish to be of assistance."

"Ah! What a relief to hear! We shall not find ourselves living in the hedgerows after all! I do hope he will overlook my disliking him so much before. Do you think it necessary for me to apologize to him?"

"I do not think so, Mama," Elizabeth responded with a sigh.

"Well, if it comes up, you must smooth things over for me." Her mother smiled sweetly.

Elizabeth threw her sister a look, but Jane only smiled back calmly as if nothing at all were amiss. "I have more to tell you," added Elizabeth. "This concerns Jane."

"My dear Jane. My darling girl! So beautiful! So sweet," she said clutching her eldest daughter's hand tightly.

"We are going to have a caller this afternoon so you might want to dress after you have finished eating."

"Oh, dear! Is Mr. Darcy coming to call?"

"Yes, but it is another gentleman to whom I am referring. Mr. Bingley has returned to Netherfield and will be calling on us," said Elizabeth brightly. She was very happy that she had apparently been successful in redirecting her mother's attention.

"Oh, my goodness! Mr. Bingley coming here? Oh! Oh! This is good news! I must get dressed immediately. Hill, Hill! Where are you? Come here right now! I need you."

"Do not worry, Mama," Jane told her patting her hand. "I will help you get ready. But first, you should have something to eat. I will go see what is keeping Kitty with your tray."

Jane went off in search of their younger sister, leaving Elizabeth and her mother alone in the room. Mrs. Bennet eyed her daughter suspiciously. "You are very sly, my dear. Is there something you have not told me?"

Elizabeth was confused. "What do you mean, Mama?"

"There has not been some impropriety between you that has forced this wedding to be so rushed?"

Elizabeth could not believe her ears. She felt the heat of embarrassment and anger rising in her face. "How could you say such a thing? I cannot believe you would ever think that I would..." Elizabeth stammered.

"Ah, well, never mind. It does not matter now. If you are to be wed to such a man, we must plan a grand wedding for you. Oh, so much to do!" Mrs. Bennet clapped her hands together in excitement just like a child.

"Mama, I do not think a large wedding would be appropriate given Father's health. Mr. Darcy is planning to obtain a special license in London, and we will be married here very quietly as soon as possible."

"Oh, a special license! But Lizzy, Mr. Darcy will expect a large wedding, will he not? I want to show him we can put on as fine an event as anyone. I do not want him to think we are not good enough."

"Mr. Darcy will be very well pleased with a small wedding. His only wish is for us to be married."

Mrs. Bennet's face fell in disappointment, but brightened again almost immediately. "Oh, very well, I suppose you are right, but I still think you should have a large wedding celebration. At least, you will be married! And to such a rich man! Oh, I cannot wait to tell everyone about it, especially Lady Lucas. You know she was quite proud of Charlotte stealing Mr. Collins away from you. Now, she will be the one who is envious of me."

Elizabeth could see that her mother had already rewritten events to her own liking, and it was no use trying to correct her. "You must not say anything until Mr. Darcy has spoken with Papa."

The pout returned to Mrs. Bennet's face. "Oh, very well, Lizzy. You say he will speak to your father this afternoon?"

"Yes, and then you may tell whomever you wish. Now, I am sure you want to be ready to receive our guests so I will go see what has happened to your tray," said Elizabeth rushing off before her mother could think of another excuse to delay her.

ELEVEN

As promised, Mr. Darcy called early that afternoon. Accompanying the carriage on horseback was Mr. Bingley. His stated purpose was to call on the entire Bennet family, but from the moment he entered the house, he only had eyes for Jane.

Elizabeth greeted their guests and took a few minutes to speak with Mr. Bingley in order to ascertain her sister felt comfortable with the meeting. Seeing Mr. Bingley again was a little awkward for all, but his easy manners and genuine enthusiasm for renewing his acquaintance with the Longbourn family quickly helped everyone relax.

Mr. Darcy's manner toward her mother and sisters was so markedly different that Elizabeth could only wonder at the change. He politely inquired after Mr. Bennet's health, complimented Mrs. Bennet on the refreshments and even attempted to smile a few times. Elizabeth's surprise was complete when she heard him tell Mary he had mentioned her love of music to his sister and that Georgiana was looking forward to meeting her to discuss their favorite pieces. Was this change for her benefit? She hoped it was the case but could not trust it entirely.

Mrs. Bennet's behavior was also a surprise to Elizabeth as she noted her mother did not 'ooh' and 'ahh' over Mr. Darcy or make inappropriate remarks about their impending engagement or wedding. She honored Elizabeth's wishes and said not a word about the purpose of Mr. Darcy's visit that day until their guests had been there for almost a quarter of an hour.

"Does Mr. Darcy not have some important business with your father, Lizzy?" Mrs. Bennet asked, inclining her head toward the doorway. "You may show him up to your father's room. I believe he is expected."

Elizabeth blushed and looked to Darcy to see his reaction. Instead of cringing, he rose and gave a formal bow toward Mrs. Bennet.

"I promise to keep our discussion as brief as possible, Madam, so as not to fatigue Mr. Bennet."

With that, he and Elizabeth left to go upstairs to her father's bedchamber. The stairs were wide enough so they could ascend side by side, and part way up he caught her hand and held it.

"Mr. Darcy, please," she said, attempting to pull her hand away.

"Please what?" He grinned at her, still refusing to release her hand. Seeing his dimpled grin and the way he looked at her nearly undid Elizabeth, and she blushed deeply.

"Please release my hand, sir. We are not yet formally engaged, and someone might see us."

"May I not hold your hand to give me courage to speak with your father?" he said with mock seriousness.

"I really think you must give it back to me as it is not yet yours."

"But now is when I need it."

"So let me see if I understand," said Elizabeth boldly teasing him back. "You need my hand in order to ask for it, but you may not have it until you have asked. Now that is something of a conundrum, sir."

Before Darcy could respond, they reached Mr. Bennet's door and Elizabeth knocked. "Papa, Mr. Darcy is here to speak to you. Are you feeling well enough?"

"Yes, my dear. Show him into my lair." Although his voice was weak, at least his sense of humor was still intact.

When she opened the door, Darcy who still had not relinquished her hand squeezed it gently and walked past her into the room closing the door behind him. Elizabeth stood in the hallway wishing she could hear what they were saying, but she did not want to be caught listening. After pacing in the hallway for a few minutes, she reluctantly made her way back to the parlor to wait.

�֍

Darcy opened their interview by expressing his sincere wish that Mr. Bennet would soon be feeling better. After these formalities, he found himself at a loss as to how to begin one of the most important conversations of his life. Even though he was accustomed to dealing with people in many different types of business situations, this was the first time he was going to ask a father for his daughter's hand in marriage—let alone a favorite daughter. Darcy fought the urge to pace, which he sometimes did to help him to think more clearly.

"Please sit down, Mr. Darcy," said Mr. Bennet indicating a chair near the bed.

Darcy cleared his throat nervously. "I believe you know why I am here today," he said.

"Lizzy and I have talked, but I would like to hear what you have to say in your own words."

"I know you do not think much of me, Mr. Bennet. Last fall, when I was in Hertfordshire, I gave no one reason to like me and for that I am sorry. I am not a man who is comfortable in society."

"It seems we may have something in common after all, Mr. Darcy."

"When I first met your daughter, I did not make a good impression. In fact, I believe I was generally disliked in the entire county partly because of my demeanor and partly because of what Mr. Wickham told people about me. I am now convinced if I had behaved differently in the beginning, Mr. Wickham's stories about our dealings would not have been so easily believed. It was entirely my own fault. Elizabeth has told me she related the truth to you about that man's character and his dealings with my family."

"Yes," said Mr. Bennet, "Lizzy has told me about that, but what I would like to hear is just how you came to fall in love with my daughter."

Darcy was a little surprised at the question, but his desire to win Mr. Bennet's good opinion encouraged him to answer. He related how he had enjoyed Elizabeth's wit and intelligence, not to mention her beauty, almost from their first acquaintance last fall, but had done nothing to forward the relationship before it was time for him to leave the neighborhood. When he arrived in Kent, he was very much surprised to find her there visiting. After spending time together, he became convinced that their feelings of attachment were mutual. He had resolved to ask for her hand, but things had not gone as he had planned.

"I know now if I had proposed that evening, she would have rejected me out of hand. In the process of offering to help her return to Hertfordshire expeditiously, I discovered her true feelings toward me. At first, I was crushed as I had every belief that she would welcome my addresses, and I was angry with her for being so blunt about what she perceived as my failings."

"Yes, my dear Lizzy can be quite direct," Mr. Bennet told him. "No one who has been caught on the sharp end of her wit has much chance of coming away unscathed."

"I know that well, sir. Her words pierced my soul, but after I got over being angry, I began to examine what she had said more carefully—I tried to see myself through her eyes however painful it might be. I did not know nor even care very much how I appeared to others until that day."

"I would have wagered that you would have simply withdrawn to London and forgotten her quickly," said Mr. Bennet. "With your fortune, you would certainly have no trouble finding any number of beautiful women willing to marry you."

"I admit that was my first inclination, but I realized it would not be possible for me to forget her. She was already too much a part of me. So after I admitted to myself there was a certain truth to what she had said, I resolved to do something about it."

"And that brought you to Hertfordshire," said Mr. Bennet.

"I have promised Elizabeth that if we are married and something happens to you, I will provide for the well-being of Mrs. Bennet and your other daughters."

"Frankly, sir, I am concerned you have taken advantage of our situation to bring pressure to bear on my daughter to accept you," Mr. Bennet challenged.

Darcy was uncomfortable with the direction this conversation was taking. As he looked deeply in to the older gentleman's eyes, he considered the idea that Mr. Bennet might be testing to see how he would react and decided to be more forthright than he might normally have been with someone he scarcely knew. "Elizabeth's happiness is my primary concern, but yes, the timing of all this has been to my advantage. That does not change the fact that I can give her what she most needs right now—peace of mind."

"And what would you do if I told you I would not consent, even with all you have offered?" asked Mr. Bennet.

Darcy paused for a moment to consider his response. "Of course, I would use all my powers of persuasion to convince you to change your mind. I have realized that I must make certain changes in my life, and I cannot envision a future that does not include Elizabeth by my side to guide me. In the short time I have known her, she has brought me more happiness than I have known for a very long time."

Mr. Bennet painfully adjusted his position on the pillows. Darcy patiently awaited an answer although a few moments began to seem like forever as he was suspended in anticipation. "Mr. Darcy, I believe what you have told me, but I am still reluctant to agree to this marriage."

Darcy remained silent contemplating how to convince Mr. Bennet of his sincerity.

"Are you aware Lizzy has entreated me to give my consent?" asked Mr. Bennet.

"She did not say so explicitly, but I had hoped she would," said Darcy.

"I do not want her to trade her chance at happiness in life for material advantages for herself or her family," said Mr. Bennet, "but she has asked me to agree to your proposal, and I must admit I have been moved by the sincerity of your declarations. Given your station in life, coming here and explaining yourself to me in this manner could not have been easy. I give you credit for your efforts. It tells me much about you." He grimaced as he took a deep breath.

Darcy felt awkward, unsure what to do for his comfort. He hoped that their discussion was not causing Mr. Bennet's health to suffer. "Are you uncomfortable, sir?" Darcy asked. "Is there anything I can do? Should I call for someone to help you?"

"No, there is nothing anyone can do. I fear I shall never recover my health although the doctor and my family try to sound encouraging for my benefit. I do not wish to leave this world uncertain about how my family will be cared for. I know I should have planned better, saved more money, but by the time I gave up hope of fathering a son, it was too late," said Mr. Bennet regretfully. After a minute of silence, he continued. "I still have my reservations, but I am inclined to give you my blessing. I believe you are a man of your word, sir, and I am going to trust you will see to it my girls are secure when I am gone."

Darcy took a deep breath. He had not realized he had barely been breathing while waiting for Mr. Bennet's response. "I give you my word I will do everything in my power to make your daughter happy and will attempt daily to deserve her."

Seeing that Mr. Bennet was tiring quickly, Darcy offered to return the following day to outline the financial arrangements.

Darcy also told Mr. Bennet of his plan to go to London to secure a special license so that they could be married as soon as possible. Mr. Bennet was amenable to the plan, as he wished nothing more than to live long enough to see his Lizzy married.

When all was settled, Darcy reached out and shook Mr. Bennet's hand. For some reason, he felt the need to add his other hand on top in an uncharacteristic gesture of warmth. Their eyes met, and for a moment, the two men seemed to understand each other and were united in their love for Elizabeth.

�֎

It was nearly half an hour before Darcy returned to the parlor to find the others still taking tea. Nearly every face turned to him expectantly as he entered.

"Miss Elizabeth, may I speak with you a moment in private?" he asked.

Elizabeth rose and followed him out into the front hallway.

"Before we make a formal announcement to everyone, I want to tell you how very happy you have made me. Your father has given his permission for us to marry as soon as possible. I hope this news is as pleasing to you as it is to me."

"You were upstairs a long time," she said.

"Your father was not willing to give you up so easily, but we discovered we have more in common than either of us realized."

"You do?" said Elizabeth wrinkling her brow.

"We did not complete discussing the particulars of the financial arrangements because he was growing tired. I will meet with him again tomorrow morning before I leave for London. Now enough of these details. Shall we go in and share our news with everyone?" he asked.

Elizabeth took his offered arm, and they went in together to make their announcement and receive everyone's good wishes.

TWELVE

After announcing their engagement and receiving congratulations from all, Darcy and Elizabeth took their leave to Netherfield so Darcy could introduce his new fiancé to his sister. As they were leaving, Elizabeth heard Mrs. Bennet suggest that Mr. Bingley and Jane walk out with Kitty to chaperone them. Thus far the reunion between the couple had been successful, and she only hoped that the attraction between the two was still as strong as it had been last fall. She could not bear it if Mr. Bingley changed his mind and disappointed Jane yet again.

Once on their way to Netherfield, Elizabeth worried about what she would say to Miss Darcy when they met. She also wondered how much Mr. Darcy had told his sister about the circumstances of their engagement. Would Miss Darcy be a sophisticated and accomplished young woman, or would she be more like her brother—quiet and watchful? Suspecting that Georgiana might be shy and uncertain of herself, Elizabeth resolved to do her best to put the girl at ease and engage her in conversation. She knew Mr. Darcy had high hopes of a strong, sisterly relationship developing between them and did not want to disappoint him. She might not have wished for this marriage, but having said yes, she resolved to do her best to please him.

Part way to Netherfield, Darcy stopped the carriage and presented her with a small jewelry box. "I hope you will wear this now we have your father's blessing."

Elizabeth opened the box and gasped at the beauty of the ring inside. It was a large square-cut emerald with a cluster of small diamonds on either side. She was so surprised that all she could say was, "Oh, my!"

Darcy took the ring from the box and slipped it onto her finger. The fit was perfect. Extending her hand to admire the ring, Elizabeth was amazed at how it sparkled in the sun. She was overwhelmed. Somehow the ring made their engagement more real than she was ready to acknowledge.

"I do not know what to say."

"You do like it?" he said looking a little worried.

"Of course! I am just overcome by your thoughtfulness and by the ring itself. I have never seen such a beautiful emerald."

"It belonged to my Grandmother Darcy. If you are not satisfied with the way it fits, I will have the jeweler adjust it to your liking."

"No, it is perfect, but you do not have to give me an engagement present," said Elizabeth feeling a little self-conscious about the elegance of the gift.

"I hope it will be the first of many."

"I do not want you to think I expect lavish gifts. My tastes are simple and I..." she hesitated.

"I believe I am beginning to know something of your preferences."

"You are?" she asked, curious as to what he might say.

"I know you like daisies, lily of the valley, and the color yellow. You take milk and sugar in your coffee but only sugar in your tea. You tend to avoid most sweets, but you cannot resist anything with strawberries—which by the way, we grow in the hot house at Pemberley."

Elizabeth was astonished at his recitation. "What else have you observed?"

"I know you do not like to be late, so I think we should continue on our way."

MR. DARCY'S PROPOSAL

As they rode on to Netherfield, Elizabeth pondered all of this and then began to wonder if she knew as much about him. She resolved to be more observant of his likes and dislikes in the future as it would be part of her job as his wife to notice these things and to help arrange their lives for his comfort.

When they reached Netherfield, he helped her down and placed her hand on his arm in a possessive way to lead her into the house. Going up the steps, Darcy complimented her on how well she looked that afternoon. Although Elizabeth was more nervous than she had expected to be, she gave him a warm smile she hoped would please him. Darcy told her that Mr. Bingley's sisters and Mr. Hurst were still in London. This information pleased Elizabeth, as she would not have Miss Bingley's critical eye constantly on her when she was introduced to Miss Darcy.

Upon entering the drawing room, a tall, slender young woman stood to greet them. Although little more than sixteen, her figure was womanly and graceful. There was a certain sweetness in her manner that won Elizabeth over almost immediately. She was also introduced to Mrs. Annesley, Miss Darcy's companion, who immediately excused herself to see to the refreshments.

Much to Elizabeth's surprise, after their formal introduction, Miss Darcy began by asking after Mr. Bennet's health. She also expressed her concern for Elizabeth's entire family and the anguish they must be experiencing. Her sincerity and thoughtfulness touched Elizabeth's heart. While Miss Darcy's reception of her was all that was proper, Elizabeth quickly confirmed that she was indeed quite shy and reserved. Some people might mistakenly consider her demeanor as proud or disdainful, but Elizabeth saw her reserve for what it really was and resolved to begin by engaging her on subjects she knew would be of interest.

"Miss Darcy, your brother tells me that music is your greatest love and that you play the pianoforte exceedingly well."

Georgiana blushed slightly and gave her brother a sideways glance. "Yes, music is my greatest joy, but I have heard from my brother that you also play and sing very well, too. In fact, he told me that he has rarely enjoyed hearing anyone play and sing as much."

Elizabeth was caught unawares by this compliment and raised an eyebrow in Darcy's direction. "Your brother greatly exaggerates, I fear, Miss Darcy. I play very ill indeed. I am surprised he could listen to me with any pleasure after hearing you so often."

"Oh, Miss Bennet, my brother never gives compliments that are not fully deserved. I hope to have the pleasure of hearing you very soon."

"Perhaps we could attempt something together—you could play while I sing?" Elizabeth suggested.

Georgiana blushed and stammered a little but finally agreed. "I will play, but only if it is just the three of us in the room. I do not usually perform in front of anyone but my family and my music master. My brother is always telling me I must work to overcome my shyness."

While they talked about their favorite music pieces, Darcy simply sat back and listened. Their tea arrived, and as hostess, Miss Darcy poured although she was clearly not comfortable in the role. Elizabeth observed that the refreshments included fresh strawberries and cream. Glancing over at Darcy, she saw he was smiling at her. Returning the look, she wondered in what other ways she had misjudged this man. Over the past few days, he had been more than kind to her. Even though he sometimes lapsed into his old ways, he had made very real attempts to be more genial around people.

After they finished their tea, Georgiana said, "Miss Bennet, as we are to be sisters, I would very much like it if you would call me 'Georgiana.'"

Elizabeth saw the girl exchange a look with her brother and suspected that Georgiana's suggestion of using her first name was a signal to her brother of her approval. Darcy's look in return was so warm and engaging that it left no doubt of how much he loved his sister and of his joy in her acceptance of Elizabeth. For a moment, Elizabeth was lost studying his face observing again how handsome he looked when he smiled.

"I would consider it an honor. You must call me 'Elizabeth.' I hope very soon to introduce you to all of my sisters. Jane is the oldest and considered by everyone to be the most beautiful. Lydia and Kitty are about your age, and Mary who is just a little older has almost as great an interest in music as you do although she is not nearly as accomplished, I am sure."

"I will look forward to it. I see my brother has given you Grandmother Darcy's ring. He sent to Pemberley for it while he was still in Kent," said Georgiana.

Elizabeth turned to Darcy and said in a teasing voice, "You were so sure of me you sent for this ring even before you proposed?"

Darcy blushed. "I only hoped," he replied softly.

Georgiana looked a little uncomfortable that she might have made an error in speaking, but when Elizabeth continued to smile at her brother, she relaxed. "I understand you are a great walker, Elizabeth. Maybe you would like to take a turn around the gardens with me? After some hours in the carriage coming from London, I would find a walk very refreshing."

It was agreed that since the day was indeed very fine that they should all three go outside to enjoy the afternoon before Elizabeth returned to Longbourn. Darcy seemed content to let the two women walk beside each other so they could continue to converse while he proceeded just behind them. Elizabeth could feel his eyes on her as he followed making it difficult for her to concentrate on conversation. Finally, she invited him to walk beside her, as the path would just accommodate three abreast through most of the formal part of the garden.

By the time they were to leave for Longbourn again, Elizabeth found she genuinely liked Georgiana and had high hopes for a true friendship with her soon-to-be sister. Darcy suggested that Georgiana rest from her journey while he took Elizabeth back to Longbourn. She was fairly certain that part of his motive was to have more time alone with her.

Elizabeth exchanged good-byes with Georgiana, and Darcy kissed his sister on the cheek assuring her he would return soon. After helping Elizabeth into the carriage, he sat beside her and took her hand. "It seems you have already won my sister's complete approval. You do not know how happy that makes me. I had to marvel at the way you drew her out and made her feel comfortable. I knew you would be a good influence."

"She is very easy to like. I can see that the two of you are similar in many ways. You both share that same reticence in talking to strangers. I must say though I have noticed you have taken my advice—impertinent as it was—and have been practicing the art of conversation with people you do not know very well."

She raised an eyebrow as she looked at him.

"Yes, I took that suggestion and some of your others to heart. Thank you for noticing."

"Georgiana seemed a little uneasy when I was teasing you. Does no one else torment you the way I do?" she asked.

"That is the one fear I have in bringing the two of you together. She is very quick to learn, and I believe it will not be long until she follows your lead and begins to tease me as well."

The rest of the way back, they talked about his plans to leave on the next day for London to obtain the special license. He expected to return in a day or two, and the wedding would be held as soon as possible after that. As it would be a small, private affair, it would not be too difficult to arrange quickly. Darcy reiterated his plan to call on the Gardiners to apprise them of Mr. Bennet's condition and invite them to return with him for the wedding.

Darcy told her he had already obtained Bingley's permission for them to move into Netherfield after the wedding, as

Longbourn would be very crowded. It would also give them a little more privacy, as Netherfield was quite a large house, and they could have an entire wing to themselves.

Elizabeth found it nearly impossible to think about the fact that she would be married in just a few days time and would be moving out of the home she had grown up in—the only home she had ever known. It was even stranger to think of herself as 'Mrs. Darcy' and all that title entailed. She resolved to take things one step at a time and not to let her mind jump ahead too far.

As they drove along, Darcy continued talking about plans for after the wedding. Listening to him, Elizabeth began to grow uncomfortable. Clearly, Darcy was a man who was accustomed to making decisions for everyone around him. He had great responsibilities but also great freedom to arrange his life and the lives of those around him in any way he chose.

As he continued telling her his plans, Elizabeth became more and more uneasy. She began to wonder why he did not think to ask about her wishes. Then she remembered that when they were in Kent, Colonel Fitzwilliam had once said he was entirely at Darcy's disposal. At the time she had replied that she wondered Darcy did not marry so as to secure a lasting convenience of that kind. How ironic! Now here she was—at his disposal—and he was arranging things as he thought they should be. As she continued to ponder the implications, she must have ceased listening to him, as she was brought back to the present when she heard him asking, "Elizabeth, are you well?"

"I am sorry. My mind was occupied with thinking about my father," she told him unable to face telling him the truth about her concerns.

"No, I am the one who is sorry. You have much more serious matters on your mind at the moment. We can discuss our plans for after the wedding later."

There will be the rest of my life to talk to this man, she thought. And what would they speak of over the dinner table?

During the long winter evenings? She knew he loved to read, so possibly they would talk about books. As he had a more formal education, perhaps their discussions would expand her own haphazard one. Eventually she supposed they would talk about their children. After that thought, she tried to focus on the beautiful spring scenery instead of examining her future life as Mrs. Darcy.

The rest of their journey back to Longbourn passed quickly with only a few words spoken between them. Darcy did not seem to notice her unease nor mind the silence. As she thought about it, she realized that he was certainly more comfortable with silence than she. Since his return to Hertfordshire, he had talked more to her than he had in all of their previous meetings put together. Contemplating the complexity of this man, she thought of how little she knew him.

Was this how it happened to everyone? How well did people generally know each other before they married? As she considered it, she wondered how well any married couple—even those married for many years—really knew each other. Her parents certainly were not great examples of marital harmony. But of course there were exceptions such as her Aunt and Uncle Gardiner. They seemed to be quite in tune with each other. Could she possibly hope that her relationship with Darcy would grow to be as harmonious as theirs? She may not have wanted this marriage, but now it was up to her to try and make the best of it. Elizabeth knew she should speak to him about taking her wishes into consideration before he made decisions that would affect her, but she was reluctant to bring it up. Perhaps there would be another opportunity later.

✷

Just before Longbourn was in sight, Darcy stopped the carriage and turned to her. "I was hoping you would allow me to kiss you now," he asked somewhat formally.

MR. DARCY'S PROPOSAL

In some ways, Elizabeth was not surprised by his request. In fact, she had been expecting it. Looking into his eyes, she saw a hopefulness she could not deny and so gave permission for the kiss. Her heart was beating quickly and her hands shook a little in anticipation. Not having been kissed before by a fiancé, or any man for that matter, she was unsure what to expect.

Darcy gently lifted her chin. Then he leaned closer and briefly touched his lips to hers. Although she had nothing to compare it with, the kiss seemed very sweet indeed, and she found herself quite breathless as he pulled back. Risking a quick glance at his face, she found he was still watching her intently, his eyes dark. She blushed and looked away.

"Thank you," he said quietly and took up the reins again. As soon as she sensed he had turned to face forward to drive the carriage, she risked another look. His face seemed relaxed and happy. Unsure if she was trying to please him, or perhaps just please herself, she placed her hand on his arm. When Darcy saw what she had done, one corner of his mouth turned up again revealing a dimple in his cheek. She spent the rest of the journey contemplating how handsome he looked when he smiled.

THIRTEEN

Elizabeth arose early on the day of her wedding in order to have some time with her father. She knew he would be feeling sad not to be with her for such an important event. Together they reminisced about her childhood and all the trouble she had created with her curiosity and high-spirited ways. Of all the girls, she was the one who loved to run with the boys and climb trees—things a proper young lady should never do. By contrast, Jane had always been a model of deportment and modesty just as she was now. Elizabeth took comfort that her father seemed slightly stronger today and was able to sit up long enough to take some nourishment.

"Are you certain about this wedding, Lizzy?" asked her father. "It is not too late to change your mind."

"Papa, this is what I must do—for all of us. Mr. Darcy has been very generous in his promises. I believe he will keep his word and I must keep mine."

"It grieves me to be such a burden to all of you. If I had been better prepared, this would not have happened," he said regretfully. "I want you to know that I would never have given my blessing if I did not believe he is truly a good man."

Elizabeth kissed her father's cheek tenderly. "Please do not worry about me," she said. "Now I must be off. It would not do for the bride to appear in her dressing gown, would it?"

"You will look beautiful no matter what you wear, my dear."

"Just before I leave for the church, I will return so you can give your final approval." On her way back to her room, she hoped that she had sounded confident when she told her father not to worry. Inside, she was not feeling nearly as certain about her choice.

�֍

The Gardiners had returned with Darcy to Longbourn for the wedding although they could not stay more than a few days. While Elizabeth did not mind having a small celebration, she was very glad for her aunt and uncle to be in attendance. Elizabeth wondered what Charlotte would think when she received the note informing her about their marriage. Of course, Charlotte had been the one who had suspected some partiality on the part of Mr. Darcy toward her although at the time, Elizabeth had not given much credit to the idea.

Darcy had written to his aunt, Lady Catherine, but waited until the day before the wedding to send it via regular post. Anticipating she would not be pleased, he did not want her to have time to send her disapprovals or worse yet, come in person to interrupt the proceedings. Elizabeth was concerned about causing a rift in his family, but Darcy seemed optimistic that given a little time his aunt would come around to accepting his decision. He assured Elizabeth that he would not tolerate any one, including Lady Catherine, treating her with any less deference than was her due as his wife.

Jane had almost finished putting up Elizabeth's hair when Mrs. Gardiner arrived to assist. Together they carefully wove yellow satin ribbons into Elizabeth's upswept curls. Next they helped her into her new dress. Miraculously, Mrs. Bennet had cajoled one of the local seamstresses into making a new gown for Elizabeth in only two days. It was white with tiny yellow stripes woven into the fabric. The dress also had delicate yellow flowers decorating the neckline, sleeves, and hem.

When Jane left to go help her other sisters, Mrs. Gardiner stayed. "Lizzy, why is your mother not here helping you prepare for the wedding?"

"She is busy checking last minute details for the wedding breakfast. I believe she is hoping the event will go so well that she will make a favorable impression on Mr. Darcy and Mr. Bingley and his family. You know how she is. Once she had helped choose the dress, she seemed to lose interest in me."

"Your mother should think more about you and less about herself on a day such as this," Mrs. Gardiner replied.

Elizabeth smiled and hugged her aunt. "I do not mind. I would rather have you and Jane helping me. Mama would just make me nervous with her endless talking and flitting about." To change the topic, she asked for her aunt's impressions of her fiancé.

"Mr. Darcy had your letter delivered to us along with a request to call the next morning. I do not think I have ever been so surprised in all my life as I was to learn you and Mr. Darcy were engaged and that the wedding would take place so soon," said her aunt. "Everything you had told us about him before had made him sound so disagreeable, but your letter gave quite a different view."

"Yes, I have learned more about him," answered Elizabeth.

"We were shocked to discover that Mr. Darcy had been wronged by Mr. Wickham rather than the other way around so we were prepared to give him a chance. Then when we met the gentleman himself, we were most pleasantly surprised to find him so amiable."

"And now after spending more time with him," asked Elizabeth curiously, "what is your opinion?"

"I must say that your uncle and I have been most favorably impressed. Rather than being silent and taciturn, as you had described him before, he seemed quite at ease with us on the journey from London."

"I do not understand him very well at all. He is still something of a mystery to me. Sometimes he is so silent that I cannot imagine what he is thinking."

"Oh, Lizzy, dear," said her aunt, "that is true even for couples who have been married a long time. Perhaps you are expecting too much. Has it occurred to you that sometimes when he is quiet, he might be thinking about you or wondering what is on your mind?"

"I had not considered that," said Elizabeth thoughtfully. "You grew up near Pemberley. Tell me, what is it like?"

"I was born in Lambton, which is only a few miles away. Pemberley is one of the greatest estates in all of England. I think you will be surprised when you see your new home."

"And what do people who live near Pemberley say of the Darcy family?"

"I do not know them personally, of course, but your fiancé's father had a reputation for being a concerned and generous landlord. I have heard nothing from my friends in the area to indicate *your* Mr. Darcy is any different."

"I hope you are right," said Elizabeth.

"I believe you are very fortunate indeed to have won his affections," said Mrs. Gardiner.

"I hardly know how it happened. I did not seek to impress him," said Elizabeth. "I cannot imagine how he came to love me."

"My dear Lizzy, it is so very easy to see how any young man would love you. You are not just beautiful, you are also intelligent, clever and level-headed," said her aunt touching Elizabeth's face affectionately. "I think Mr. Darcy is showing very good sense falling in love with you instead of some empty-headed young lady of the Ton who has superficial accomplishments but no substance."

Elizabeth moved over to the window while her aunt continued to fuss over her dress.

"Lizzy, your mother may have already spoken to you about

this, about the relations between a husband and wife. I know this is not an easy subject, but if you wish to talk or ask questions, I will do my best."

Mrs. Gardiner looked calm enough, but Elizabeth was certain it must have been difficult for her aunt to bring this up. She trusted her Aunt Gardiner in a way she had never been able to trust her mother, and she did have questions.

"Well, it is just that what she said was confusing and made no sense."

"Yes, that is what I feared. And what did she say?"

"Aunt Gardiner, this is so difficult..." Elizabeth knew she must be completely red, but took a deep breath and continued. "She said I must lie still, let him push up my nightdress, and take his pleasure, and it would be over soon."

Mrs. Gardiner put her arm around her niece. "Oh, you poor child. No wonder you are confused."

"I understand the physical mmm...mechanics of what will happen. As I was growing up, I was always around the farm after all, but..." Elizabeth hid her face. Mrs. Gardiner gently took her niece's hand and held it.

"Lizzy, what happens between a man and a woman is a very natural thing. It can be wonderful if you both...how should I say it...participate? The physical joining is not the whole experience. What happens before and after is even more important."

"Now I am truly confused."

"Has Mr. Darcy kissed you?" Elizabeth groaned in discomfort. "I will take that as a yes. And how did it feel? Did you like it?"

"It was pleasant. He was very gentle."

"Is that all that has happened between you?"

"Our engagement is of a very short duration! How much more *could* have happened?" Elizabeth reddened again this time from her chest up to the tips of her ears.

"I know, my dear, but surely, there is something else," her aunt insisted.

Elizabeth sighed. "When he proposed, I started to interrupt, and he put his finger over my lips to silence me. My lips continued to tingle where he had touched me." At this, she put her own fingers to her mouth as if reliving the experience. "And later as we were sitting together, his hand came to rest on my leg. Here," she said, showing her aunt what she meant. "I could feel the heat of it travel all through me." She quickly added, "He was not trying to take liberties. It was just an accident."

"I understand. So it was pleasurable?"

"Well, yes, I guess I liked it."

"That feeling, the heat, it is just the beginning. If he shows you his love in these ways, you will feel that only much more so. You will want to be as physically close to him as possible."

"Oh, I see." For the first time during their discussion, Elizabeth smiled.

"Yes, my dear, I think you do," said Mrs. Gardiner. "Your Mr. Darcy may be quiet, but I believe there is a great depth of feeling behind his calm demeanor. What he cannot say in words, he may communicate in other ways. Just trust him and follow his lead in this. He certainly loves you. I see it when he looks at you across the room or talks about you."

Before either could say more, they heard a knock on the door and Jane entered. "Lizzy, you must hurry if you want to have a moment with Papa. The carriage will be here soon."

As Mrs. Gardiner embraced her niece, she whispered in Elizabeth's ear, "I wish you every happiness, my dear. I think you may be more fortunate in this marriage than you realize right now."

"Thank you, Aunt," said Elizabeth and then mostly to herself she added, "I truly hope you are right."

※

Elizabeth was with her father only a few minutes before Hill came to let her know that the carriages had arrived. Elizabeth said her farewells and promised to attend him again when they returned for the wedding breakfast.

"Be sure to bring your husband with you when you come next time. I want to congratulate him on his fine choice of a wife," said Mr. Bennet with a twinkle in his eye.

"Of course, I will bring my...my husband," she said finding the words awkward to say. "But you must promise you will rest until I return."

Mr. Bennet smiled, slipped down a little in the bed and closed his eyes. After a second, he opened one eye and peeked at her slyly.

"Papa! Do not joke about this. You must rest!" she scolded him, partly teasing and partly serious in her admonition.

"Off you go, child," he said with a wave of his hand. "I will be just fine."

❈

Reluctantly, Elizabeth left her father and descended the stairs to the front hall where Lydia and Kitty fairly bounced around the room with excitement. Elizabeth worried, not for the first time, about how her sisters might act at the wedding and the breakfast that would follow. When she asked her mother to speak to the girls about their behavior, her request fell on deaf ears.

"You are being very selfish, Lizzy. Lydia and Kitty are feeling left out and want to have some fun, too. It is only natural when everyone else is paying attention to you that they would want their share of society as well," twittered Mrs. Bennet as she swept out the door and into the awaiting carriage.

Jane and Elizabeth exchanged a look. Once in the carriage, Jane did her best to distract Lydia and Kitty by engaging them in conversation about their new dresses. This gave Elizabeth a few moments to gather her thoughts before they arrived at the church.

FOURTEEN

"You look beautiful!" Jane exclaimed. The sisters had found a few moments to be alone before the service started.

Elizabeth sighed. "This is not the way I had thought my wedding would be, Jane, but I am determined to make a success of this marriage. I will do my best to be a good wife to Mr. Darcy although I hardly know what he expects."

"He has many good qualities, Lizzy, and I am certain he will treat you well."

"Yes, I suppose I should consider myself fortunate," said Elizabeth looking away unable to meet her sister's eyes directly.

"I think Mr. Darcy is the fortunate one," said Jane with such feeling that it brought tears to both their eyes.

Just then, Mr. Gardiner came into the room and announced it was time for him to escort Elizabeth inside for the ceremony. Jane kissed her sister and left to go take her place inside. Mr. Gardiner offered his arm and guided Elizabeth into the church.

Going up the aisle, she saw the faces of her sisters, her mother, Aunt Gardiner, and the Phillips on one side of the church with Georgiana, Miss Bingley, and the Hursts on the other. When Caroline Bingley looked arrows through her, Elizabeth merely smiled back as sweetly as she could.

From the time she entered the sanctuary, Mr. Darcy watched her with such open admiration that it had made her feel uneasy.

With great effort, she forced herself to smile back at the man who in just a few minutes would be her husband. Elizabeth barely heard the words at the beginning of the ceremony. Although she tried to pay attention, her mind was too consumed with thoughts of her father and all the dramatic changes in her life.

How different her life was from just a few weeks ago. When it came time to repeat the wedding vows, she tried to focus on the words as she spoke them and determined that no matter how little she had desired this marriage, she would take the promises she was making this day very seriously indeed. When Darcy put the ring on her finger, she noticed his hand shaking slightly. Without thinking, she squeezed his other hand. He answered with a look that made her heart beat faster.

Suddenly, it was over and everyone was congratulating them. At that moment, Elizabeth was very glad they had decided to have a small wedding. It was difficult enough to maintain a happy countenance with family and close friends. With a larger circle of people, it would have been impossible.

FIFTEEN

The wedding breakfast at Longbourn was also a small affair. Mrs. Bennet basked in the glory of all the attention and compliments she received for her efforts at planning the meal. Elizabeth had to give her mother credit for at least attempting to display modesty and humility at all the praise she received, but it did not last very long.

All through the rest of the morning, Elizabeth smiled and talked to everyone. Looking back on that day later, she could not remember much more than the toasts to their health and happiness. Pretending to look happy proved to be very taxing. Soon her face began to hurt from the effort. Several times she caught Darcy watching her intently and she wondered what he could be thinking. Why did she find his gaze so disconcerting?

While the party continued to linger over coffee, Darcy and Elizabeth slipped away to visit Mr. Bennet. Once alone in the hallway, Darcy pulled her to him and kissed her. Once he released her, she laid her head on his chest in hopes of avoiding more kisses. She could hear his heart beating loudly. Wondering what he would want her to do next, she tentatively put her arms around him. Darcy exhaled heavily and held her even more closely, resting his cheek on top of her head. Inwardly, she was quite shocked to find herself standing there in the arms of a man she hardly knew, but she counseled herself to remain calm.

This would certainly be just the first of many demands her husband would place upon her.

So far she had been successful in keeping thoughts of the wedding night from her mind, but as she stood there, she could no longer deny that she was terrified. In spite of her best efforts at bravado, she began to tremble. Darcy looked into her eyes with obvious concern.

"Are you feeling unwell?" he asked.

"I am very well, thank you. Perhaps a little tired from all of the excitement of the wedding preparations," she replied hoping that this explanation would suffice. "I think we should go up now."

"The last time we were on this stairway you would not let me hold your hand. Will you give it to me now?" he asked in a teasing manner, holding out his own to her.

"Of course, sir," she said, laying her hand in his. As he looked deeply into her eyes, the stairway seemed to tilt beneath her feet, and she had to reach out to gasp the banister to steady herself. Elizabeth's mind went blank for a moment. Finally, she recovered enough to move without stumbling, and they proceeded to her father's room.

When they entered Mr. Bennet's room, Darcy still had her hand in his. "You are holding my little girl's hand, Mr. Darcy. I assume that means you two are married now," said Mr. Bennet observing them with sharp, discerning eyes.

"You know we are, Papa," Elizabeth responded. "You should not tease like that. Mr. Darcy is not accustomed to your little jokes."

"Mr. Darcy, I am entrusting my precious Lizzy to you. You best take great care of her."

Darcy took Mr. Bennet's hand. "You may depend upon it, sir."

Mr. Bennet continued to hold Darcy's hand and with his other reached out for his daughter. Taking Elizabeth's hand, he joined hers and Darcy's together in a manner similar to what the minister had done in the church. "It is up to the two of you to care for each other now. I do not believe I will live to see my grandchildren although it is my fondest wish to hold a child of yours in my arms."

Elizabeth began to protest but her father silenced her.

"No, you must allow me to say this, my dear. I am glad that I lived long enough to see you wed."

"Papa, do not..." she interrupted again.

"Let me finish, Lizzy. Please, I may not have another opportunity to share what little wisdom I have gained over nearly twenty-five years of marriage."

Elizabeth sat down on the edge of the bed.

"Your mother means well, and I must say that I was quite taken with her charms when we were first wed, but that is not enough to make a good marriage as you know. Ultimately, our temperaments were not well suited. Still, if I had not married Mrs. Bennet, I would not have had the pleasure of knowing you, my dear Lizzy. You have always been my greatest joy."

"Papa, please do not tire yourself."

Mr. Bennet held up a hand yet again to silence her. "I believe that, unlike your mother and me, you two may do very well together. Your strengths and weaknesses compliment each other."

He turned to Darcy who seemed to be listening intently. "Thank you for indulging an old man, Mr. Darcy. I give you both my warmest blessings as you begin your life together." With that, he leaned back farther into his pillows and closed his eyes. "Now you have quite worn me out. I think it is time for you to go and let me rest," he said.

Elizabeth was certain he did not want them to see how emotional he had become. Tears welled up in Elizabeth's eyes, but she managed to keep herself from breaking down. Putting her arms around her father, she whispered, "I love you, Papa, with all my heart."

Although reluctant to leave, she kissed her father's forehead gently and promised to return the next day to read to him. Darcy shook Mr. Bennet's hand and then led Elizabeth out into the hall. Once the door was closed, Elizabeth shocked herself by putting her arms around him. Burying her face in his chest, she let out the tears she had been holding back all day. Darcy eased her away from the door so that Mr. Bennet would not hear. Without comment, he simply held her and let her cry. From time to time, she heard him whisper words of comfort and felt him kiss the top of her head. They stayed like that for some time until she recovered herself with a little help from another of Darcy's handkerchiefs.

Patting her eyes, she said, "I have been wondering if you married me to ensure that all the handkerchiefs you have loaned me are returned."

Darcy tenderly brushed a stray lock of hair back off her face. "You have found me out," he said quietly. "I have been running short and have had no time to order more." The corner of her mouth turned up just a tiny bit in response and he added, "Do you think anyone would notice if we disappeared instead of returning?"

Elizabeth sighed and tried to smooth some imaginary wrinkles from her gown. "I have had enough of crowds today, too, but I suppose we must go back," she replied, trying to smile.

Darcy took her hand and led her down the stairs. When they reached the door to the parlor, he looked at her as if to ask if she were ready. Elizabeth squeezed his hand, and they went in to their guests.

❈

Most of Elizabeth's belongings had already been moved to Netherfield where she and Darcy would live until they were more certain of Mr. Bennet's health. Jane had been invited to dine at Netherfield that evening so she went along in the carriage with Mr. Bingley, his sisters, and Mr. Hurst. Georgiana was also to ride with the Bingley's so that the newlyweds would have a few moments of privacy.

As they were taking their leave from Longbourn, Mrs. Bennet hugged her daughter and then stood back, dabbing her eyes with her handkerchief. "Oh, my darling daughter Lizzy married and maybe another engaged very soon," said Mrs. Bennet looking at Mr. Bingley and Jane.

Elizabeth flushed with embarrassment at her mother's inappropriate comments, but Mr. Bingley did not seem to hear. She was sure, however, that those hints had not escaped Mr. Darcy's notice. Elizabeth held her breath when she saw her husband turn to address her mother.

"Mrs. Bennet, please allow me to compliment you on the lovely wedding breakfast you hosted in our honor. I know you have much on your mind these days, but you seem to have outdone yourself, and we thank you." He took her hand and made a show of kissing it.

"Oh, Mr. Darcy," said her mother fluttering and waving her hands in the air. "You are too kind."

"Not at all, Mrs. Bennet," he replied. "Now if you will excuse us, I believe it is time for us to go. Thank you again for your most excellent hospitality."

As if on cue, the footman opened the carriage door, and Darcy took Elizabeth's arm to help her inside. Once she was seated, he joined her, taking his place next to her on the cushioned seat. Elizabeth was not sure what to expect now that they were alone again. If he wanted to kiss her, she could hardly refuse. They rode for a while in somewhat awkward silence until Elizabeth felt compelled to speak to break the tension.

"Thank you for your kind remarks to my mother. I am sure she is entirely in your power now after your compliments."

"You do not need to thank me for giving her the respect and courtesy she is due as your mother."

Elizabeth smiled. "Still, I thank you, sir.'

Darcy took her gloved hand and held it in his. As she watched in stunned silence, he pulled gently on the end of each of her fingers until her white kid glove was loose enough to be removed easily. Once the glove was off, he raised her hand to his lips and kissed it gently. Although she wanted to reclaim her hand and return it to safety, she found herself unable to hurt his feelings and so left her hand in his for the remainder of their journey to Netherfield.

SIXTEEN

As a pleasant evening in the company of Mr. Bingley and Jane drew to a close, Elizabeth asked her sister to her rooms to assist in changing out of her wedding clothes. She did not want one of the maids helping her tonight. It was a special time for the sisters. Jane would want her to do the same when she married.

Elizabeth was wearing a new nightdress and dressing gown decorated with small yellow flowers. Mrs. Gardiner had brought this beautiful ensemble from London for her as a wedding gift. Elizabeth examined at herself in the full-length mirror and was satisfied. Her hair was down but held back with a matching yellow ribbon. With all the hurried preparations, there had been little time to contemplate all the implications of the wedding night. Elizabeth had no idea what her husband was expecting. Even though she was a reluctant bride, she would let him take the lead in whatever he wished to do. She was, strange as it seemed, his wife now and promised herself she would act the part.

Jane hugged her and said, "Lizzy, I believe you are very fortunate to be married to Mr. Darcy. He has certainly shown himself to be kind and honorable beyond anything we had expected. I know he loves you very much."

With that, Jane left her. Alone now, Jane's words brought tears to her eyes. That he loved her was well and good she thought to herself, but the more important question was how did she feel about him. At least she was learning to respect him. Fumbling around for a handkerchief to blot some dampness from her eyes, she found one of the several she had collected from Mr. Darcy over the past week. A knock on the door made her heart jump up into her throat.

"Elizabeth, would you please come into the sitting room whenever you are ready," Darcy requested.

"Yes, I will be just a moment," she answered nervously as she continued to try and erase all signs of tears from her face. Paused with her hand on the doorknob, she pushed back a curl and took a deep breath. When she opened the door, she saw Darcy sitting in a chair near the fire still fully dressed except he had removed his jacket and neck cloth. He had that look on his face that she found a little unnerving. He stood immediately. "You look beautiful, more beautiful that I could even have imagined."

"Thank you, sir," she responded.

"I thought you had agreed to call me William."

"Thank you, William," she said, struggling to get his name out.

"Please, sit down. It has been a very busy day, and I think we have a few things to discuss."

Good, she thought to herself, anything to postpone what she believed to be inevitable. Making her way across the room to another chair near the fire, she sat down pulling her legs up underneath her so she felt a little less vulnerable. Darcy came over and sat down on the footstool in front of her chair. She was reminded of how he had done this same thing a few days ago when he had proposed. He took her hands.

"You are trembling, my dear. Are you cold?"

Should she answer truthfully—*No, I am just terrified?* "A little cold."

"Let me find something to wrap around you. Do you have a shawl nearby?"

"I think I left it on the bed." And then she felt awkward at having mentioned the bed.

Darcy disappeared for a moment and came back with her wrap. Placing it gently around her shoulders, he kissed the top of her head and then sat down again. For a while he was silent as if making up his mind what to say and then he took both of her hands again and looked deeply into her eyes. "I have loved you for a long time although I hardly know how it happened. As I told you before, I think it may have begun at Netherfield when you walked three miles on muddy roads to come to the aid of your sister." He smiled and added, "Then, of course, it could also have been when I realized we had more in common than just a love of books."

Elizabeth gave him a questioning look. "And what is that?"

"Neither of us can abide Caroline Bingley, of course!" With this they both laughed, breaking the tension between them a little. Then he grew serious again. Reaching into his pocket, he took out a flat velvet box. "I think most women enjoy receiving small gifts from their admirers, and while you are certainly not 'most women,' I thought you still might appreciate a token of my affection for you."

Elizabeth's eyes met his, and she saw how earnestly he looked at her. "I hardly know what to say. You do not have to give me gifts." Elizabeth opened the box carefully and inside found a beautiful necklace made of gold with a small perfectly round pearl hanging from each link. It looked exactly like something she would actually wear and certainly not the kind of ostentatious jewelry she might have expected he would choose to impress her. "Mr. Darcy, I am speechless."

"It was my mother's. I thought it looked like you."

"It is very beautiful, and it means so much more to me that it belonged to your mother. I would have thought Georgiana would have inherited all of your mother's jewelry."

"My father left it to my discretion as to what would be done with the family jewelry. Some has already gone to Georgiana, and others will pass to her when she is of age. Some I kept for my wife. This particular piece has always been one of my favorites. My mother wore it more often than any other necklace she owned. I sent to Pemberley for it as soon as you said 'yes' to me."

"Will you help me with it, please?" Elizabeth asked holding it up. Turning her back slightly to him, she could feel his fingers brush her neck as he fastened the clasp. His soft touch sent a shiver through her. Turning around to face him, she saw that he glowed with satisfaction at the sight of the necklace at her throat.

"You look more beautiful wearing it than I had even imagined. I hope you like it."

"How could I not? You may know me better than I thought,' she said giving him a genuine smile of pleasure. "This looks like something I would have chosen for myself."

"Good, good," he said quietly and then he added as if unsure how to proceed, "I thought maybe we could sit together for a while before we say good-night?"

He took her hand and led her over to the settee. Settling in beside her, he put his arm around her shoulders and began to tell her about Pemberley. As he talked about the place he clearly loved more than anywhere else on earth, she could hear the excitement in his voice. Much to her surprise, she found being close to him more pleasant than she had imagined although her hands continued to shake.

As Darcy talked, he played with her hair, occasionally wrapping a curl around his finger. Several times his hand brushed the exposed skin on her shoulder and her heart jumped. Elizabeth detected a hint of the exotic scent she was beginning to associate with being close to him—bay leaves, cloves, and some other spices she could not identify. It was pleasant but not overpowering.

"There is a place where the road turns and suddenly Pemberley appears," he told her. "It always takes my breath away. Every time I return home, I stop there for a moment to appreciate the beauty of the view. I cannot wait to show it to you."

"If it is half as lovely as Rosings, I shall think it wonderful," she told him sincerely.

"Rosings cannot even compare, but you will see it very soon and then you may decide for yourself," he told her.

She asked a few more questions about Pemberley and the grounds as she tried to envision herself there. Finally, Elizabeth's eyes began to grow heavy.

"Elizabeth?"

"Yes," she said sleepily.

"I think it is time to retire. It has been a long day for us both." As they walked toward the door to her bedchamber, he kept his arm lightly at her waist. When they reached the open door way, he stopped. She turned and smiled up at him. Darcy put his arms around her, pulled her to him, and kissed her—gently at first and then with more urgency. Elizabeth did not resist—in fact, she found herself kissing him back. She had not expected his lips to be so soft. When he released her, she could feel her heart pounding in her ears. She noticed that Darcy was as breathless as she was. His eyes were dark and intense. Confused for a moment, she was unsure what to do next. Thinking perhaps this was her cue to go into her room, she turned assuming he would follow.

"Goodnight, Mrs. Darcy," he said.

Then she heard the door close, and there was nothing but silence. She whirled around expecting to see him just behind her but instead she found herself alone. This was not what she had anticipated would happen this evening. Her cheeks were warm, and she felt a little dizzy. She wondered if he was planning to join her later and she was unsure what to do.

Crawling under the covers, she stretched lazily. The big bed felt warm and delicious. Elizabeth assumed he must be changing into his nightshirt and robe, so she waited patiently thinking about the events of the past few weeks. She stared at the ceiling for a long time until finally she could not stay awake any longer.

�֎

In his room, Darcy undressed quickly without calling for his valet. Sleep did not come easily. Still shaking with the passion Elizabeth had stirred in him, he realized how difficult it was going to be to keep the promise he had made to himself to give her time. Never in his life had he wanted anything as much as he wanted her right now. He groaned softly. Trying to imagine her warm body next to him in bed caused even more agony. He told himself to be patient. She was still like a skittish colt—one unexpected move and she would bolt.

He knew this was the right course—giving her time to grow more comfortable with the whole idea of being married. She was not his property, and he would not treat her as such. Many men in his position would merely take what they wanted, but he could not do that. He simply loved her too much, but he knew his patience would have its limits. Finally, he fell asleep dreaming of holding her in his arms.

SEVENTEEN

About a week after the wedding, Mr. Bingley and Jane announced their engagement to the family. Although Mr. Bennet's health continued to decline, he rallied long enough to receive Mr. Bingley's request for Jane's hand with great joy and give his blessing to his eldest daughter and her fiancé. After Bingley had departed for Netherfield, promising to return that evening, the family assembled in Mr. Bennet's room to celebrate the news.

"Jane, I congratulate you. You will be a very happy woman," pronounced Mr. Bennet as they gathered around his bed. Jane kissed her father and thanked him for his good wishes.

"I have great pleasure in thinking you will be so happily settled," he said. While he had the old, familiar twinkle in his eye, he looked exhausted.

Jane blushed and looked down at the floor.

"My dear, dear Jane," said Mrs. Bennet. "I am so happy! I do not know how I will sleep tonight after such good news. I was sure you could not be beautiful for nothing! I knew this would happen. Did I not tell you so when he first came into Hertfordshire last year? I thought it very likely then that he would marry you and I was right. He is the handsomest young man I have ever seen."

As she listened to her mother, Elizabeth could feel the flush of embarrassment spreading across her face at what Darcy must be thinking of this outburst. She wished desperately he was not there to hear it. Looking around, she noticed he had walked to the window and was staring out—one of the things he tended to do when he wished to ignore what was going on in the room.

The moment Mrs. Bennet stopped to draw a breath, Mr. Bennet interrupted. "Yes, yes, he is very handsome indeed, but he would have to be much more than just handsome or even rich to deserve our Jane," he said with a smile, giving Jane's hand a squeeze. "I believe he is a very kind and caring man and will take good care of you, my dear child. Now I believe I have had enough excitement for one day. Perhaps you would all leave me to rest."

"Yes, yes, Papa, we will go now. I did not mean to tire you out," said Jane sweetly.

"Seeing you happy was well worth the effort it cost me. Come, give me another kiss, my dear," said her father. As everyone began to filter out of the room, Mr. Bennet called to his daughter. "Stay for a moment, Lizzy, I would speak with you." When the others including Darcy had left, Elizabeth sat on the edge of the bed.

"I understand you had another game of chess with Mr. Darcy this afternoon," she said, fluffing the pillows behind her father's head to make him more comfortable.

"I have enjoyed our games. Although he does not have much to say, he has proven a formidable opponent."

"You know he is not comfortable with making small talk," said Elizabeth.

"The true measure of a man is not what he says—it is what he does," replied Mr. Bennet.

"And after spending more time with Mr. Darcy, what do you think of him now?"

"Has he treated you well?" asked Mr. Bennet.

"Yes, he has been kind and thoughtful."

"Then it does not matter what I think of Mr. Darcy. It only matters what *you* think of him," her father said.

"Are you asking me?" said Elizabeth.

"No, I believe that is now a very personal matter between the two of you."

Elizabeth was surprised at her father's response and relieved he did not require more of an answer. "I will return after supper to read to you if you are feeling well enough," she said, kissing her father on the cheek.

"I will have to check my extensive social calendar to see if I have an opening this evening," he replied.

Elizabeth laughed, amazed that in spite of how ill he was he could still tease her. "Until later, then," she said moving to the door.

"Lizzy?"

"Yes, Papa."

"You seem to be spending quite a bit of time here with me. Are you certain you are not neglecting your husband?" asked Mr. Bennet.

Elizabeth bit her lip as she often did when she was thinking. "I believe he understands," she answered. "Now you promised to rest."

"Ah, that is all people ever say to me these days—rest! No one ever asks me to go to a party!"

They both laughed. No one despised social gatherings as much as her father—except perhaps Mr. Darcy. As Elizabeth went downstairs she was thinking that it did not matter to her if Darcy thought she was spending too much time here at Longbourn. The excuse of her father's illness relieved her of the necessity of having to feign interest in anything or anyone. Instead, she was able to focus all her attention on the man who was still more important to her than any other. As much as she wanted to hope for his recovery, she could tell that her father was not getting stronger.

❇

Georgiana continued to stay at Netherfield and often accompanied Elizabeth to Longbourn. While Elizabeth attended to her father, Georgiana visited with the other Bennet girls. At first, she was very quiet and did not say much. Instead, she watched intently as if she was conducting a scientific study of an entirely new species. Elizabeth suspected Georgiana had spent very little time around girls her own age as she was growing up. It was not long before Georgiana began to join in their conversations, tentatively at first and then with more confidence.

EIGHTEEN

Just a few days after a small engagement supper for Jane and Mr. Bingley, Mr. Bennet slipped away in his sleep leaving a dark pall over Longbourn. Mrs. Bennet was wild with grief and had to be sedated most of the time leaving Elizabeth to make most of the arrangements with help from Darcy. The Gardiners came from London as quickly as possible, and Elizabeth appreciated their presence and support. Mr. Gardiner was one of the only people besides Jane who could have a calming effect on Mrs. Bennet.

The day of Mr. Bennet's service was cool and cloudy. First, there was to be a service in the church and then the one graveside. Mrs. Bennet was, of course, too distraught to leave the house, but Elizabeth insisted on going to the church. After much discussion, Darcy finally conceded. Mary went along to the church, too, but the rest of the girls stayed at home to comfort their mother and help prepare for the neighbors to visit after the service. As was the custom, none of the women from the immediate family would go to the graveside.

As the minister spoke, Elizabeth looked around the church filled with friends and neighbors from Meryton as well as those who lived on the Longbourn estate. She had attended this church all her life. Most of the time she had sat in this very pew with her father, but now it was Darcy who was at her side.

Elizabeth found it difficult to focus on the minister's words, and her mind began to sift over all that had happened in just a few short weeks.

She was married, married to a man she barely knew. Much to her surprise, Mr. Darcy had made no demands on her—time or otherwise—but lent emotional support in every way he could over the painful days she was suffering through, and for that she was very grateful. She could not understand why he had not demanded his rights as her husband, but she had been too preoccupied to give it much thought until now.

Elizabeth observed he was making a continued effort to become more acquainted with her family and had even attempted conversation with her mother. However, she still felt more comfortable keeping them as far apart as possible. On more than one occasion she had seen him wince at one of her mother's thoughtless outbursts.

On the other hand, Darcy's relationship with her Aunt and Uncle Gardiner was a pleasant surprise. She had observed their interactions with curiosity to see what his manner would be a-round her relatives from Cheapside. In the past, he had always disdained people like her uncle who were in trade. In some ways, times were changing, but there was still a decided stigma around anyone who worked for a living regardless of how successful they were.

After just a short acquaintance, Darcy treated Mr. Gardiner as an equal, and they had actually discovered some common interests they could talk about such as fishing. Elizabeth had been quite shocked one day when she overheard Mr. Darcy inviting her uncle to visit later that summer in order to take advantage of Pemberley's fine fishing streams.

Her sister was now engaged to her beloved Mr. Bingley. Giving his permission for Jane to marry had been one of the last things her father had done, and Elizabeth knew it had brought him great happiness. In spite of Jane's sadness over their father, she seemed to glow from within whenever she was around her fiancé. Seeing Jane so content brought Elizabeth joy, but she also envied the love she could see growing daily between the engaged couple. Suddenly, her own future seemed very bleak indeed. Contemplating the inevitable separation from Jane in the coming weeks filled her with a sadness that weighed heavily upon her heart.

Hovering nearby over the last few days had been the unpleasant Mr. Collins. She detested being around her cousin almost as much as she loved having Charlotte there. And there were changes in that family, too. Charlotte had told her in confidence that a new little Collins would make an appearance next winter. Elizabeth wondered how long it would be now before Mr. Collins began to urge what was left of the Bennet family to move out of Longbourn so he could take up residence. Every time he was nearby, Mrs. Bennet made sure to loudly bemoan the entailment that was driving her out of her home. Elizabeth tried to ignore her mother's rude behavior, but her patience was sorely tried.

To relieve Mrs. Bennet's mind and keep her from coming to blows with their cousin, Darcy and Bingley had found a local agent who assisted them in locating a comfortable house in Meryton for Mrs. Bennet and the girls. They had been fortunate enough to find one, available immediately, that would do quite nicely. It was not nearly as large as Longbourn, but it was very pleasantly situated in easy walking distance to her Aunt Phillips' house.

Looking at Darcy, she wondered what he could be thinking at the moment, but as usual his face was unreadable. Did he already regret the bargain he had made? He had taken on a significant amount of the responsibility for her family—although Mr. Bingley would now share in that—in exchange for what? For her? Why had he been willing to give so much for so little in return? Was it a reflection of how much he cared for her? She knew that many men treated their wives as another possession to be shown off and disposed of as they chose. If he had wanted a bauble for his arm, he could have married any one of a hundred young women who were more socially acceptable to his status in life and would also bring a large fortune to the match. No, he must truly love her, but what did love mean to him?

�֍

Once back at home after the service, Elizabeth had almost no time to herself before their friends and neighbors came to the house to pay their respects and partake of some light refreshments. As Elizabeth observed the faces of her friends and neighbors, she had the odd feeling of being suspended between her old life and the new one she was about to begin.

Elizabeth observed her mother and sisters with interest. Each of the Bennet women grieved in a different way, one that was consistent with her personality. Mrs. Bennet fluttered and wept and generally kept everyone running here and there taking care of her.

Jane spent most of her time thinking about others. She comforted her mother, held Mr. Bingley's hand tightly, and acted as the gracious hostess to their guests. Mary sought comfort in her Bible and her music. She kept mostly to herself finding some relief in quietly playing hymns on the pianoforte. Much to Mary's delight, Georgiana asked to join her at the instrument.

Lydia's range of behavior went from tears to laughter—at a moment's notice. Like her mother, she seemed to be enjoying the attention and sympathy she was receiving from their guests. Elizabeth was certain that if propriety did not forbid it, Lydia would have been quite glad to dance or play cards and forget all about dreary funeral rituals.

Kitty was the surprise. Elizabeth had expected she would run wild with Lydia. Instead, Kitty concerned herself with the comforts of their visitors. She made certain their guests were taken care of and generally acted the part of a proper young lady.

Darcy quietly stayed by Elizabeth's side until she sent him off to talk with the Gardiners while she sought out Charlotte and some other family friends. As he left, he put his hand on the back of her elbow and gave it a little squeeze. It was a very intimate gesture, and she had to admit it had sent an unexpected shiver of pleasure through her.

After visiting with nearly everyone, Elizabeth excused herself and escaped upstairs to the bedroom she and Jane had shared since childhood. It was very strange to think that she had lived in this room for more than twenty years and now it was no longer hers. While she might come back to visit, it would never be the same. In a few weeks, Longbourn would no longer belong to her family but would become home to Charlotte and Mr. Collins.

Elizabeth's things had been packed up and removed to Netherfield long ago. Sitting at her dressing table, she thought how sad and bare the room looked without the clutter of her hair ribbons, pins, and combs. Although Jane's belongings remained, most were in the process of being packed into the large trunk that would be used to move them to the little house she would share with her mother and sisters until her marriage to Mr. Bingley.

From this room, Elizabeth could hear the sounds of people's voices below. It was almost impossible to pick out any one person's voice although a few times she distinctly heard Lydia over the low hum of the crowd. Elizabeth laughed to herself. Her father had called Lydia "one of the silliest girls in England," and she definitely had to agree.

Elizabeth examined her face in the mirror at the dressing table. Except for the sadness around her eyes, she looked much the same as she had just a few weeks ago, but so much had changed. Her mind was whirling with thoughts of her father and Darcy. Her feelings about her father were clear—his death was a wound she feared would never heal. Her feelings about her husband were much less defined. She hardly knew him. In fact, she could barely bring herself to call him by his first name.

In spite of this, the response she frequently had to Darcy's physical touch was profound and therefore confusing. She had expected that she would only feel this way with someone she really loved. Was that just a romantic and childish notion?

While she was coming to respect Darcy, the idea of ever feeling a deep love for him was so foreign that she could barely think of it. Elizabeth let out a long sigh. What madness had caused her to tie herself irrevocably to a man who was not much more than a stranger? What would they talk about on those long, cold nights in Derbyshire?

Finding no answers in the mirror, she wandered over to the window to look for the last time at the view of the garden and the fields beyond. She would miss this perspective. Perhaps there would be a window at Pemberley that she could claim as her own special view just as this one had been hers as she was growing up. As she stood before the window, she heard footsteps coming up the stairs. It was the sound of a man's boots, not the quiet padding of her sister's slippers. Glancing over her shoulder, she saw it was Darcy.

"No one seemed to know where you had gone so I was concerned."

At first, she bristled at how closely he was apparently watching her every move. Before sharp words came out, she got hold of herself and answered in an even voice. Sometimes, she found his solicitousness a bit unnerving.

"I was just looking out at my favorite view across the garden and the fields. It may not be the very best view from the house, but I feel somehow it belongs to me. I am going to miss it."

Darcy walked over and stood behind her. He was so much taller that the top of her head just barely reached his chin. She could see the reflection of his face in the glass as he looked out over her head. When he placed his hands on her shoulders, she reacted involuntarily to the heat on her bare skin. Standing this close to him, she detected his now familiar fresh, spicy scent.

Glancing up at their reflections in the windowpanes, she saw he was watching her face intently. Her next thought was how improper it was for them to be alone in her room. One corner of her mouth turned up in a half smile.

"You are smiling," he said.

"A thought crossed my mind of how improper it would be for anyone to find us alone in this room together. Then I remembered we are married. I find that oddly amusing for some reason."

"I like being alone with you," he responded, gently touching one of her curls that had escaped from the pins and was trailing down her neck.

As they continued to stand together looking out, the dark clouds that had been rolling in across the fields finally gave up their burden, and large raindrops began to hit the window glass.

"A part of me wants today to be over while another part of me does not want it to end because it means that my father is really gone. It is much too final," she confided. Then she relaxed and leaned back with a sigh. Darcy put his arms around her and held her closely against him. For a moment, she allowed herself to enjoy the secure and solid feel of his body supporting her.

Darcy kissed her neck just below her ear as they stood in silence watching the ominous beauty of the storm. There were definitely times when Elizabeth appreciated that he was a man of few words. As more and more raindrops obscured the view out the window, it seemed a signal that it was time to go.

"I think we had best go down to our company," she told him. "I would like to spend a little more time with Charlotte. It may very well be quite a long time before we have a chance to visit again."

Elizabeth took his arm and as they walked out of the room together, she looked around one last time to say good-bye to a part of her life that was already fading into the past.

NINETEEN

When Darcy returned to their suite that evening, he found Elizabeth slumped on the settee staring into the fire. Darcy sat down and held her hand lightly in his. When she turned to him, her eyes looked hollow and lost. "You look quite exhausted," he said.

"These last few days even my bones feel tired," she told him as she leaned over and rested her head on his shoulder. He thrilled at this little affectionate gesture. Although he wanted desperately to kiss her, he contented himself with gently running his thumb across the back of her hand as he held it.

"Mama likes the house you and Mr. Bingley found in town. I overheard her talking about it to her friends as if it were actually a big improvement over Longbourn—less to take care of and worry about," Elizabeth told him.

His heart melted even more as she looked up at him with her beautiful, sad eyes.

"Thank you. It has been a great relief to have someone else take care of it," she added. She rested her head on his shoulder again. "I do not know how I would have managed these last few days without you," she told him.

"I am happy to do anything that will be of help to you," he said. Just knowing that she was beginning to let him take care of her even a little brought him great joy. Without thinking he began to massage her shoulder lightly. At first, she stiffened but did not move away. Finally, he could feel her beginning to relax. "You are learning all of my weaknesses very quickly. How did you know I love to have my shoulders rubbed?" she asked.

He turned her so her back was to him and began to gently massage her neck and shoulders, which were full of knots. After a few minutes, she reached up and put her hand on his as it lay on her shoulder.

"Thank you."

With that, he leaned over and kissed her hand. Next he kissed her lightly just below her ear. Noticing she had given a slight shudder, he asked, "Are you cold?"

She shook her head. When she turned around, he could see her eyes were filled with sadness. Darcy put his arms around her waist and pulled her onto his lap. Again, there was a moment when he thought she might run, but she stayed. In fact, she put her arms around his neck and rested her head on his shoulder. He inhaled deeply taking in the sweet scent of the lily of the valley perfume she often wore.

"My father used to hold me on his lap like this when I was a little girl. It always felt very comforting and safe," she said.

Darcy was not sure exactly how to interpret her comment. His feelings for her were anything but fatherly. Perhaps what she most needed right now was a physical connection to a pleasant memory from the past. Maybe he should be grateful and just enjoy the feeling of having her against him. He wanted to tell her that she was safe, that she could trust him, but he did not know how to begin.

They stayed like that on the settee not talking, listening to the crackle of the fire. From time to time, he kissed the top of her head or tucked back a curl that had fallen across her face. After ten or fifteen minutes, her breathing slowed, and to his relief, she fell asleep in his arms. As Darcy watched her, he noticed how her face seemed much more peaceful in repose. When he tightened his arms around her slightly, she unconsciously snuggled closer to him. His feelings were a mixture of protectiveness and desire. He sat like that for almost half an hour, simply holding her as he watched the fire burn down.

When he was certain she was sleeping deeply, he carried her to her bed. Laying her down gently, he was unsure of what to do next. At first, he thought about calling for her maid to help her finish undressing, but then she would surely wake. She was wearing just her nightdress, dressing gown, and slippers so he reasoned he could take care of those himself. When he pulled off her slippers, he became fascinated with her feet. They were so small and perfect, delicate but strong. Darcy could feel his pulse in his ears.

As he was pulling the blanket out from underneath her in order to cover her up, her dressing gown and nightdress edged up showing the pale white skin of her ankle and calf. His breath caught. Despite feeling a little guilty, he admired the perfection of her leg—slender and feminine yet strong from all the walking she did. Darcy sighed audibly.

Finally, he was able to pull the blanket over her. He found himself wishing he didn't have to leave her, but he could hardly crawl into the bed beside her. She might wake up and be startled to find him there. It might erase all the progress he seemed to be making. Instead, he found a comfortable chair and footstool, pulled them over next to the bed and settled down to keep watch in case she woke in the night and needed something.

TWENTY

After the funeral, life settled into a routine for Elizabeth. Each morning, she had breakfast with Mr. Bingley, his sisters, Mr. Hurst, and Mr. Darcy. Then she either walked or took the carriage to Longbourn depending on the weather. Frequently, Darcy walked with her and over time, she began to grow accustomed to his continual presence. Sometimes while walking, he would hold her hand, and she found, much to her surprise, that she rather enjoyed the security she felt in his care.

One afternoon after her daily visit to Longbourn, Elizabeth was returning to Netherfield on her own after sending Darcy back early in order to attend to his correspondence. As she approached the house, she was surprised to see a carriage with what she thought might be Lady Catherine's crest heading up the long drive to Netherfield. Watching to see if it was really Darcy's aunt who emerged, she speculated what might be the purpose of her visit. From a letter Charlotte sent, she had learned Lady Catherine was most aggravated with her nephew's marriage. It must have been quite a blow to her plans when she learned that Darcy had married someone other than her daughter—especially someone like Elizabeth. She could be coming to congratulate them or more likely show her displeasure. Either way, the new Mrs. Darcy felt it was an honor she could do without today, so she lingered outside awhile, enjoying the afternoon. Then she began to feel guilty for trying to avoid Lady Catherine and decided she to go in and face her new aunt. It would have to happen sooner or later. It might as well be now.

Upon entering, she could hear raised voices coming from Mr. Bingley's study—one was a shrill female voice and the other she recognized as Darcy's. At exactly that moment, Caroline Bingley drifted out of the main drawing room with a sour look on her face.

"Mr. Darcy is in the study with Lady Catherine, and Miss de Bourgh is in the drawing room. I would appreciate it if you would go entertain her, as she is your relation after all. I have other more important matters to see to."

With that Caroline floated away, leaving Elizabeth standing in the front hall alone. Unsure what to do, Elizabeth decided to act as if nothing was amiss and go greet Miss de Bourgh. After all, they did have a previous acquaintance from Elizabeth's stay in Kent just a few months ago. She and Anne had never exactly had a conversation, but Elizabeth felt confident she would be able to find something they could discuss to pass the time. Her only concern was how Anne would receive her under these awkward circumstances. When she entered the drawing room, she found her new cousin standing at one of the windows looking out over the grounds.

"Welcome to Netherfield, Miss de Bourgh. I did not know you were planning to call or I would have been here to receive you."

Although Anne seemed a little embarrassed, her good manners took over as she attempted a smile that showed more warmth than Elizabeth had ever seen her exhibit before. "It is very nice to see you again, Mrs. Darcy."

"Are you enjoying our scenery here in Hertfordshire?" Elizabeth inquired.

"I am finding Hertfordshire very lovely indeed. I am so rarely away from Kent, or from Rosings for that matter, that every place I go is an exciting experience for me."

Elizabeth smiled and joined her at the window. Together they looked out at the sun-drenched gardens ablaze with flowers of all colors.

"I understand the home you grew up in is not very far from here," said Anne.

"Yes, I walk over frequently to help my mother and sisters. They are currently engaged in packing up to move into their new home in Meryton. As you are no doubt aware, Mr. Collins will be taking over Longbourn very soon."

Anne turned and put a hand on Elizabeth's arm catching her completely off guard. "I was so very sorry to hear about your father. I know what it is like to lose a parent, and it is never easy to bear. I was only a little girl when I lost my father, but I still miss him." Anne's sincerity touched Elizabeth deeply. "When my father was alive, he used to take me around the Park in his curricle. Sometimes, when he thought Mother would not know, he allowed me to drive," said Anne almost smiling.

"So you enjoyed that?" Elizabeth asked.

"Oh, yes, very much."

Elizabeth thought for the first time that with a change in Anne's hair and a little more color in her cheeks she could be an attractive young woman rather than the pale shadow she always appeared.

"My father's first love was reading. He allowed me to read almost anything I wished—over my mother's objections," said Elizabeth. "Nearly everything I know about literature, history, and philosophy I learned with my father's help and encouragement. When I was younger, my mother used to despair that I would rather have a new book than a new dress."

"And did you inherit your love of observing people from your father?" she asked taking Elizabeth by surprise.

"Did you?" responded Elizabeth without thinking, and then she wondered if she had overstepped the bounds of propriety with her cousin. Instead, Anne startled her by laughing out loud.

"I must apologize for being so..." Elizabeth began.

"So what? So honest?" asked Anne still smiling. "Your honesty and outspokenness are what I noticed about you when you were in Kent. Oh, yes, I observed you most carefully when you verbally fenced with my mother. Believe me, when I say that most people do not speak to her so boldly. I only wish I could be as brave."

"I am told that sometimes I can be a little too outspoken," Elizabeth confessed.

"You should not change that for anyone."

Elizabeth was surprised to find that her cousin was turning out to be nothing like the sickly young woman she had met in Kent. "I have forgotten my manners. You must be tired from your journey, Miss de Bourgh. Would you like me to ring for some tea?"

"I would enjoy that very much," Anne replied, "And please, call me Anne. We are cousins now, are we not?"

Elizabeth was surprised at this gesture but acknowledged it warmly. "Of course, Cousin Anne. And you must call me Elizabeth."

While they waited for tea, Elizabeth told her she hoped someday she would be able to visit Rosings and enjoy its beauty again. Then they talked about the Park and the way it changed over the seasons.

"Mostly, I watch the turn of the seasons from my window as I am not often allowed out of doors. There is one particular view from my sitting room that is a favorite with me. On sunny days, it is almost as though I can see all the way to the next county."

"I had a special window at my home, too, where I used to sit and contemplate the world. I am hoping to find such a place at Pemberley," Elizabeth confessed feeling an unexpected kinship with Anne.

"You have never been to Pemberley before?"

"No, but we will be traveling there in a few weeks. Everyone talks about how beautiful it is. I am anxious to see for myself."

Anne turned to Elizabeth and said, "I am glad we have had some time to talk. I believe I understand why my cousin married you. You are not at all the fortune hunter that my mother has taken you for." And then as if she remembered herself, she added, "Please forgive me for speaking so plainly. I hope I have not given offense."

Elizabeth realized she had no idea how Anne might be feeling about their marriage. He had told her Lady Catherine still stubbornly clung to the belief that he would marry Anne although that had never been his intention.

"I suspect you have been wondering if I was distressed because William chose to marry you?"

Elizabeth nodded.

"Let me put your mind at ease. You need not worry about my feelings. My cousin and I reached a special understanding on that topic long ago, and it never included being married in spite of what Mama may have said. The engagement was always her wish, never mine, and certainly never his."

"Oh, I see," said Elizabeth relieved to be learning this directly from Anne. "So the two of you have talked of this in the past?"

"Yes, and we understand each other perfectly. Mama and I had quite a disagreement before we came here when I told her I was happy about your marriage. She was very angry with me, but I think she will recover." She leaned over toward Elizabeth and said quietly, "I would just love to be a fly on the wall right now so I could hear what they are saying in the other room."

They both laughed and looked at each other with a new understanding. Just at that moment, the door to the drawing room opened, and the great lady herself swept in dramatically with Darcy close behind. Elizabeth rose to greet Lady Catherine and gave a curtsey as she approached. Checking Darcy's face, she thought he looked very composed considering what must have occurred in the other room. He walked over and stood beside her, putting a proprietary arm around her waist.

Lady Catherine would neither look at Elizabeth nor address her. In fact, she acted as if she were not even in the room.

"Anne, come along. We must depart. Darcy, you have not heard the last of this from me," she said, shaking a boney finger at him. And with that, she left the room without even the courtesy of a farewell.

Anne rose and turning to Elizabeth, she took both her hands. "Remember what I have told you," Anne said very softly. "This storm will pass."

When they were alone, Darcy kept his arm around her waist in a protective manner. "I believe I would like a drink before supper after that experience," he said. "Will you join me?"

Darcy kissed Elizabeth on the forehead and then went to the cupboard where Bingley kept his liquor. She was not sure if she was more surprised that he had kissed her or that he had offered her a drink. Still a little stunned, she agreed something fortifying might be just the thing at that moment. Darcy poured Elizabeth some sherry and a brandy for himself. Sherry was not her favorite but after a few sips, the warmth from the golden liquid had traveled all through her body, and she finally thought herself brave enough to ask about the substance of his encounter with his aunt.

"What did Lady Catherine have to say that was so important it brought her all the way to Hertfordshire?"

Darcy reached over and squeezed his wife's hand. "There was quite a list," he confessed. "I married without her permission or approval; I married you when Anne and I have been engaged since childhood; you were not the right sort of person for me to marry—shall I go on?"

Darcy leaned back and took another sip of his drink. "Anne and I never intended to marry each other. We made a pact when we were quite young that we would never be forced into something we did not want. Everyone treats my cousin as if she was not even in the room, but she is an intelligent and sensitive young woman. I feel very sorry for her having to put up with a mother like that."

"I do not think Anne feels sorry for herself," said Elizabeth. "We had an opportunity to talk this afternoon while we were waiting for you. Much to my surprise, I liked her, and I think she liked me, too."

"That pleases me very much."

"Do you really think Lady Catherine will continue to be angry with you?"

"Nothing I said made the slightest difference. I doubt she even heard me. She only gave up because she saw I was not about to back down to her. I suppose she will either get over it or find some other way to irritate me. Now enough about my family. How is your mother doing today? Is she almost ready to move?"

Elizabeth was surprised by his question but welcomed the opportunity to change the subject nonetheless. "I think she may be ready to move to the new house by Saturday."

"So we will be able to leave for home by next week, then? I am very anxious to show you Pemberley," he said, smiling.

"Home. How strange that sounds," said Elizabeth. "I have been without a real home for weeks now since we have been living at Netherfield. I am very ready to be away from here. I have been wondering how long it will take before Pemberley feels like home to me."

"Do not worry. I am certain that in a very short time you will love it as much as I do."

Elizabeth hoped he was right.

TWENTY ONE

As Elizabeth walked along the path, she attempted to calm herself. She had been helping with the preparations to move from Longbourn to the new house in town but her tolerance for her mother was wearing very thin. Her mother was being so indecisive that almost nothing was getting done. The walk back to Netherfield was a welcome respite and a chance to clear her mind.

Just as she was leaving the road to take a short cut across a field, she saw a rider approaching in the distance. Hesitating for a moment to see who it might be, she was uncomfortable when she recognized the horseman as George Wickham. Her next thought was she was very thankful Darcy had urged Georgiana to return to London so there would be no chance of an encounter between them.

Although dreading the idea of having to speak with him, he was close enough that she could think of no polite way to walk on without at least acknowledging his presence. As she waited by the road for him to pass, Wickham waved in greeting. Then he startled Elizabeth by dismounting beside her.

"Well, well, Mrs. Darcy, what a delight to see you again," he said tipping his hat to her politely.

"Good afternoon, Mr. Wickham," she answered rather stiffly. "I had been under the impression that your regiment had already removed to Brighton." Elizabeth kept her hands clasped tightly together to prevent Wickham from seizing one of them and kissing it as he had done several times in the past.

"Yes, but I had to return for some...um...shall we say unfinished business in the area, but that is of no consequence. I was very sorry to hear about your father. Please convey my condolences to your mother and sisters. I was hoping to call on them, but I am afraid urgent business takes me elsewhere today."

"Thank you for your kind words. Now if you will excuse me, I am expected at Netherfield." When she started to walk away, Wickham continued to address her.

"I have not had the opportunity to congratulate you on your marriage to my old friend Darcy," he said with a bit of sarcasm. "What a surprise! You certainly underwent a remarkable change in your attitude toward the man, but then your circumstances have changed significantly since we last met."

Elizabeth hesitated, unsure how to respond. Uncomfortable with the man's underlying innuendo, her every thought became focused on how to leave his company as quickly as possible. "He has not changed. I have simply come to know and understand him better," she said.

"Indeed!" cried Wickham with a look of mock surprise.

"I have found him to be the most generous and honorable man of my acquaintance," she replied defensively.

"I wondered if perhaps given how your circumstances have altered that you were the one who had changed."

"My circumstances have nothing to do with it," she said in an attempt to signal that the subject was closed.

Wickham's face betrayed a moment of alarm, but quickly his charming manners returned. "Well, then you are very fortunate indeed to be so happily married," he said dryly. "And when are you going to Pemberley? I declare it is the most beautiful estate in all of England! I do so wish to see it again, but that will surely never happen."

"Of course, I am very anxious to see my new home."

"When you go by Kympton, think of me. It is the living I ought to have had."

"And how would you have liked making sermons?" Elizabeth asked, incredulous that he should bring this up as if she would not have learned the circumstances from Darcy by now. Was he testing to see if she knew what had happened or did Mr. Wickham believe his own stories?

"I am sure giving sermons would have been one of the best parts of that position," he said confidently. "A quiet life in a country parish would have been very satisfying, but some people had other ideas. Ah, well. It was just not to be." His geniality sounded forced.

"If I am not mistaken, there was a time when you declared you would never take orders. In exchange you received generous financial compensation in order to pursue the law as a career instead. What happened to that plan? I suppose it was just not to be either."

Wickham became a little flustered at her comments but attempted to smooth over the rough place by applying the full force of his charms. After this exchange, however, Elizabeth only talked about the weather, and finally, seeing she was not inclined to say much more, he began to lose interest. After making his excuses, he mounted his horse, and with a dramatic flourish of farewell with his hat, went on his way.

Elizabeth stomped her foot in fury at Wickham and also at herself for ever believing a single word he had said those many months ago. Now that she knew him for what he was, it was so easy to see through his false and ingratiating manners. She was embarrassed to think she had ever believed him amiable or admired him in any way. Elizabeth walked along briskly and by the time she had reached Netherfield the exertion of her walk had at least partly wiped out her irritation at the encounter.

One concern that weighed upon Elizabeth's mind was whether she should acquaint Darcy with the circumstances of meeting Wickham. Finally, she concluded that to keep it from her husband would be worse than the reaction it might elicit. That evening as they were walking to their rooms, she broached the subject as delicately as she could.

"As I was walking back from Meryton today, I was quite surprised to see George Wickham riding along the road. I had no idea he was in the neighborhood."

Darcy froze. "Wickham? Still in the area? I certainly hope you did not speak to him."

"Since he had already seen me, I did not feel I could escape at least greeting him, although I tried to keep the conversation as brief as possible."

"The militia has left Meryton. What was he doing here?" snapped Darcy.

His reaction startled Elizabeth. She had never seen him this upset. "He did not volunteer much except to say he had returned to take care of some business in the area. I am certainly glad Georgiana has gone back to London. It would have been very uncomfortable for her to have somehow encountered him."

Darcy took her by the arm and abruptly pulled her into a nearby unoccupied guest room closing the door after them. His eyes were bright with emotion. "I do not want you ever to speak to that man again, do you understand?" he hissed.

His intensity made her uncomfortable. Although she had no intention of ever finding herself in Wickham's presence again, she did not appreciate Darcy telling her what she could and could not do. She had never responded very well to ultimatums. Neither did she appreciate the way he was holding on to her arm.

"It was an awkward situation, and in my best judgment I did not believe it would be proper to just walk off and ignore him. It would have been unforgivably rude of me. Now please let go of me," she said sharply, trying to pull away from him.

Darcy looked down as if he had not realized what his hand

was doing and then promptly released her. "I do not care if you are rude to him. He does not deserve any consideration at all, and you are not to speak to him if your paths somehow cross again. As I think about it, you should not be walking alone in the neighborhood. You will have to start taking the carriage from now on."

Although she bristled at his comments, she tried to maintain an evenness in her voice. "Very well. If I see Mr. Wickham again, I will not speak to him. That is easily done, but I am not prepared to give up walking," she said defiantly.

Darcy's eyes narrowed. He looked as if he could not believe she would ever consider disagreeing with him. Elizabeth felt a shiver pass down her spine. First, he had held on to her arm a little too tightly, and now the look on his face was so intense it could have melted ice. Then suddenly his look softened.

"Elizabeth, I am only thinking of your safety. Obviously, he knows we are married. I am concerned he might decide to injure me by harming you in some way."

When he reached out to take her hand, she pulled away in irritation. "I do not believe he would ever touch me. He is certainly a scoundrel, but he has never been violent," she said rather pointedly.

"I know better than anyone the kind of unpleasant mischief he can cause. You must at least agree to take the carriage until I have been able to discover he has left the county again? I am only concerned for your welfare and safety."

Although she was angry at what she saw as his attempt to control her, she had to weigh just how far she was willing to go to defy him. Finally, she acquiesced to his request but made it very clear that she would resume walking to Meryton and Longbourn again as soon as they could ascertain Wickham was no longer in the area.

Later in her room, Elizabeth mulled over the events of the evening. Part of her wished she had never told Darcy about crossing paths with Wickham. Reason told her that he had every right as her husband to tell her what to do, but in her heart, she could not accept his tendency to command rather than ask. She knew he was only thinking of her safety, but in some way she felt he did not trust her yet, and that was a much stickier problem.

※

That night Darcy lay awake unable to sleep as visions of a smiling Elizabeth talking to Wickham played through his mind. He wondered if the shadow of Wickham and his treachery would follow him for the rest of his life. Darcy recognized that his reaction that evening was partly the protectiveness he felt for his wife, but it was also born of the fear that somehow Elizabeth still held that disreputable man as a favorite or that she somehow regretted him. Darcy could tell from her reaction that she was not pleased when he insisted she take the carriage instead of walking. He was probably being overly cautious, but he could not take the chance that Wickham might endanger anyone in his family ever again.

TWENTY TWO

"I cannot comprehend what is taking your mother so long to prepare for her move. We have provided assistance in packing. She was to be ready by last Saturday, and now it is stretching into another week," said Darcy setting his book aside with a thud. Elizabeth winced involuntarily. They were alone one evening in their private sitting room when Darcy surprised her with this outburst about Mrs. Bennet's glacially slow progress in her moving preparations.

"My mother does everything in her own time. It is just her way," answered Elizabeth quietly looking up from her book.

"I know you want to see her settled before we leave for Pemberley, but I am most anxious to go home," said Darcy. "I have been away longer than usual, and I have much estate business waiting for my attention."

"You may leave any time you wish, and I will follow as soon as things are settled here," she offered. 'I cannot leave it all for Jane to manage." Her words earned a scowl.

"No, I want to be with you the first time you see Pemberley." he said gently. "It is very important to me."

"I know you do not like my mother very much..." When he opened his mouth to respond, Elizabeth held up her hand to stop him from speaking. "...and I agree she is taking too long, but I wish you could be more sensitive to her situation," she added, feeling suddenly defensive about the whole issue of her family.

"Insensitive? Just who is being insensitive?" he asked, his irritation increasing again. "I wish she were a little more concerned about anyone but herself. That would be a change!" With that, he rose, walked over to the window, and stood looking out with his hands clasped behind his back.

"I know you are not pleased with the current situation but try to understand how difficult all this is for her."

"Try? All I know is that she is trying my patience exceedingly."

Elizabeth joined him at the window putting her arm through his. The delays must be bothering him a great deal for him to be so adamant. "Try to imagine yourself in her place for a moment. Suddenly, she is alone in the world and must face reduced circumstances. I know my parents did not have an ideal marriage, but at least she had protection and security. Now she must rely on the good grace of others for most of her support. Longbourn has been her home for more than half her life. Can you not see why she would want to delay leaving it as long as possible? Surely, anyone in this situation would react the same way."

Darcy said nothing in response but continued to look out at the night sky.

"Think what it would mean to you if you were forced to leave Pemberley. Would you not want to take your time and enjoy every last day you could?"

He took a deep breath and gave a long exhale. "Of course, you are right, but I still wish to return home as soon as possible. And I will not go by myself and leave you here! That is final. I beg you to do something to persuade her to move a little more quickly."

"I will do everything in my power, but as you know, I am not her favorite daughter."

"Elizabeth, my admiration for your father grows almost daily," said Darcy with a sigh. "I do not know how he managed to live with her for so many years."

"In spite of her protestations and attacks of nerves, my mother had no choice ultimately but to accept Papa's decisions. I admit he did pick his battles, and when he made a decision she did not like, he had a tendency to remove himself to his study for long periods of time so he did not have to deal with her flutterings and spasms." Elizabeth waved her hands in the air in a good imitation of Mrs. Bennet in the throws of one of her spells. Darcy could not help but laugh at Elizabeth's pantomime, and this seemed to break the tension that had been building between them.

"Very well," he sighed. "I will be more patient, and you will urge your mother to move a little faster. Are we agreed?"

"We are agreed," she answered. Darcy kissed her on the top of her head, and they both silently returned to their chairs and took up reading again.

After about ten minutes, Darcy excused himself for the night. Elizabeth tried to go back to her book but all she could do was stare at the pages. She felt some regret that her family had come between them yet again.

In spite of his efforts to disguise it, Elizabeth had seen Darcy gripping his book tightly with shaking hands just before he excused himself for the evening. She took this as a sign that he was still angry. While chiding herself for feeling she must always come to her mother's defense, she was also upset he could be so insensitive and unfeeling toward her family's plight. Elizabeth wondered if she would ever understand him. First he had showed concern for their welfare by coming to their aid. Then he was insensitive to their feelings—what a contradiction!

Suddenly, it occurred to her that perhaps he might already be regretting his decision to marry her. Surely, that would explain his recent impatience. She still could not say she loved him but knew she was coming to rely on his presence in her life. Somehow the idea that he cared for her was reassuring in this time of grief over her father. If Darcy stopped caring, what would happen to her? She knew many men treated their wives in an off-hand, careless manner, but he did not seem like one who would do that. Still, how well did she really know him?

At times, she knew she saw real emotion on his face, especially when he talked about Georgiana, his parents, and Pemberley. Also, there had been a certain tenderness in the way he had treated her after her father died. Several times she had felt sure she was seeing the real man behind his cool demeanor. Although she was usually good at reading people, she still found him elusive.

�֎

After excusing himself to retire for the night, Darcy sat in his room thinking about what Elizabeth had said about her mother having to accept Mr. Bennet's decisions. Darcy had always assumed that a man had the right, as well as the responsibility, to decide things for the members of his family. Fortunately, they had not yet come to a situation in which they disagreed and could not reach a resolution, but he was certain it was inevitable. Elizabeth could be very stubborn when she felt strongly about something.

Over the past few weeks, she had been growing warmer toward him. At first, he had rejoiced and then he began to wonder if the underlying reason for the change was that she thought it was what he expected of her. Was Elizabeth just showing more affection because she thought it was her duty to her husband? Or was it gratitude for what he was doing for her and her family?

Even after nearly a month, he could not believe that she was really his wife. He had to admit he was completely bewitched by her. To his eye, she was the most beautiful creature in the world—even more lovely than her sister Jane whom everyone always considered the beauty of the family. He also greatly admired his wife's intelligence and wit, the way her eyes flashed, and how she arched her brow when she teased and joked with her friends and family. No one excelled more at making people feel comfortable and important than she. Elizabeth's skill at helping Georgiana forget her shyness was nothing short of miraculous.

Being so close to her physically day after day and yet unable to take her into his arms and possess her completely was driving him to distraction. Just a few minutes ago as they sat together, he had realized his hands were shaking with desire. He had gripped his book more tightly in hopes she would not notice. Ultimately, the only way he knew to cope with these feelings was to leave the room.

He had read poems about the tortures of the heart but had never felt it himself—until Elizabeth. Now he understood what the poets were talking about when they described the intense, unbearable longing for someone. This was not intellectual—it was an actual physical experience in his heart and stomach and much to his amazement, he perceived it as both a lightness and a weight.

Almost all his life—and especially since his mother had died—he had kept his heart safe and guarded. He realized with a pang of guilt that often he kept even Georgiana at a distance. Now that he had risked everything in opening his heart, he had so much to lose. He did not want to think about how he would go on if Elizabeth never returned his love. The thought that she might someday look at him with the same longing he felt for her caused his heart to beat more quickly.

Darcy had wanted to express his love for her earlier in that quiet moment when they had been sitting together. He longed to tell her all that was in his heart, but feared that if he opened his mouth to speak, he would be unable to stop from making a fool of himself. Even a small opening in his reserve would have caused everything to come pouring out, and he did not want to embarrass either of them with the strength of his passions. So here he was alone with his thoughts. Even though she was just in the next room, she might just as well have been miles away.

TWENTY THREE

Elizabeth preferred to spend as little time as possible in the company of Caroline Bingley, minimizing their contact by visiting her mother and sisters as frequently as she could. She also chose to spend most evenings in the small sitting room she and Darcy shared upstairs. He seemed to enjoy their evenings together and never objected when she suggested they retire early. Maybe the others thought this was natural for a newly married couple to prefer each other's company, but Elizabeth was thankful no one ever commented on it.

Miss Bingley's flirtatious manner toward Darcy was less obvious than it had been before, but Elizabeth sensed there was still a decided undercurrent, which made her uncomfortable in Caroline's presence. Her attitude toward Elizabeth was something just short of contempt although she kept it more or less in check in Darcy's presence. As soon as Elizabeth was alone with her, Caroline often let her true feelings show.

Caroline Bingley was an attractive, well-educated young woman who would have had no trouble finding a husband if she were not so unpleasant. Elizabeth hoped she would decide that country life was too boring and return to London to her friends, but Caroline showed no signs of relinquishing her position as Mistress of Netherfield. In fact, she seemed to be enjoying her last days in this role before Jane replaced her.

MR. DARCY'S PROPOSAL

Elizabeth did not envy her sister having to deal with Caroline and only hoped that after Jane moved in Caroline would have an added incentive to marry and make a life of her own.

❈

Elizabeth found herself alone with Caroline one morning in the dining room as they both finished their morning coffee. Sensing Caroline watching her, Elizabeth kept her nose buried in her book even though it was probably not the most polite way to treat her hostess. Finally, Caroline addressed Elizabeth.

"So you will be going to Pemberley soon. It is such a lovely place, but then I am sure you have heard all about it from Mr. Darcy."

Elizabeth felt trapped and had no choice but to respond as politely as she could. "Yes, I am looking forward to going home," she replied and then added, "I am sure you will be glad to be relieved of the duty of entertaining guests. Your hospitality has been most gracious although I am afraid we have imposed upon you much longer than we should have."

"I am glad we could be of service to you. There is nothing that Charles would not do for Mr. Darcy. And after all, it is only right as we have been guests of Mr. Darcy so many times over the years," she said rather pointedly so that Elizabeth could not mistake her meaning. "Of course, you will be anxious to assume your duties as Mistress of Pemberley. Such a great estate—you will have so much to learn in order to manage a household of that size. It is quite different from what you have been accustomed to, but then you can always rely upon dear Mrs. Reynolds. I am sure you will manage somehow."

Elizabeth felt the sharp sting of her comment and tried not to react in anger. Reminding herself that soon Jane would be part of the Bingley family, she knew it would be best to avoid irritating Caroline any further. She would never forgive herself if Caroline decided out of spite to take it out on Jane later.

Letting the comment go unanswered, Elizabeth proceeded to gather up her things in order to leave before the conversation escalated to a truly unpleasant level.

"When we were all here last fall, who would have thought that you of all people would become Mrs. Darcy," said Caroline apparently unable to let go of her resentment at not being able to claim that title herself.

"Yes, it was most unexpected," replied Elizabeth evenly.

"How convenient for you that Mr. Darcy always waits upon his aunt every year at Easter. That must have been a pleasant surprise for you to have him all to yourself in Kent—or did you know he would be in the neighborhood when you accepted Mrs. Collins' invitation?" Caroline kept her eyes on the napkin she was folding. Elizabeth did not like the implication that she had somehow contrived to be in the neighborhood at the same time as Darcy so as to lure him into marriage.

"I often find that life is full of unexpected turns," she replied leaving Caroline to give her comment whatever interpretation she chose. Weighing whether to speak further or let the matter drop politely, she finally decided to have one last word on the matter. "Miss Bingley, I must thank you again for your generous hospitality to my husband and I during this difficult time for my family. It has been most kind of you. I hope to return your kindness in equal measure when you visit us next at Pemberley," she said as sweetly as she could. With that, Elizabeth excused herself and left Caroline sitting there alone with her resentments and regrets.

TWENTY FOUR

On the second day of their journey to Pemberley, Elizabeth gave up trying to talk with Darcy. Instead, she began to contemplate how she would manage her new responsibilities as mistress of such a great house.

Then just as she was getting accustomed to silence, he asked, "Are you worried about something, Elizabeth?"

"No, not at all. Why do you ask?"

"You have a particular way of wrinkling your brow and biting your lip when you are thinking deeply or worrying about something," he replied.

"I do?"

"Yes, you do. So?"

"Excuse me?"

"So what is worrying you?" he asked.

"Oh, it is nothing."

"Mmm. Nothing?" His gaze was penetrating.

She decided he was not going to let this go. "Very well, I have been concerned about how I will ever learn my responsibilities as mistress of such a great house."

Darcy leaned forward taking both of her hands in his. "First of all, I have every confidence in you. I have observed you are quick to learn new things, and even more importantly, you have a way of making people feel at ease. I know everyone will love you. Do not forget, you will have a great deal of help. Mrs. Reynolds has been managing things almost entirely on her own for years now, only consulting me when she felt it was required. She will teach you everything you need to know."

"Thank goodness for Mrs. Reynolds," she said wryly.

As he spoke, he began to rub the backs of her hands with his thumbs. At first, she had the urge to pull her hands away, but she forced herself to allow him to continue this intimacy. We are married, and he has every right to touch me in whatever way he chooses, she thought. This led her to puzzle over why, after all this time, he had still not come to her bed.

After a few more hours of travel, Elizabeth could see Darcy's anticipation growing, which she took as a sign they were near their destination.

"Come, look out this window," he told her. "It will not be long now."

Turning in at the lodge, they drove slowly through a beautiful woods which thinned as the road began to ascend a hill. They proceeded slowly until they reached the top where she saw a large open area. Almost immediately Pemberley appeared in the distance. At her first sighting, she involuntarily gasped and reached out putting her hand on her husband's arm. She could sense Darcy watching her face intently as she took in the splendid view.

It was a large, handsome stone building, standing on the top of a gentle rise and backed by a ridge of high, tree-covered hills. In front, a stream wound gracefully into a beautiful lake that had been left in its natural state. It was everything Darcy had said and more. Elizabeth had never seen a place where such natural beauty had been so undisturbed. To be Mistress of Pemberley she realized was going to be beyond anything she had even imagined.

"So you are pleased with what you see?" he asked hopefully.

"I am..." she paused, weighing her words as she knew what she said next was very important to him. "I am more than pleased. I am in awe. Now I understand why you were so anxious to be at home. I cannot imagine ever wanting to leave this place!"

Darcy's face glowed at hearing her enthusiastic approval. Once the carriage began to move again, they descended the hill, crossed the bridge, and in a few minutes arrived at the front of the house. Peering discretely out the window of the carriage, she could see that the entire cadre of servants had lined up in front of the house to greet them. To think that the sole purpose of all these people was to see to the comforts and needs of the Darcy family! What had she done? The house, the staff—everything was beyond what she had imagined.

At the time, she had totally discounted Caroline Bingley's derisive remarks about her ability to manage the house, but now as she prepared to emerge from the carriage, she wondered if Caroline had been right after all. Shaking off her fears, she resolved to meet this challenge as she had met others in the past—with patience, intelligence, and a bit of good humor.

Darcy descended from the coach and offered her his hand. As she stepped down, his eyes never left her face. The idea that he wanted to share all of this with her was overwhelming, and she could not help being caught up in the moment. Holding Darcy's arm tightly to bolster her courage, she ascended the impressive steps to the house.

Darcy acknowledged the servants and thanked them for coming out to greet their arrival. He introduced Elizabeth and announced that each one would have the opportunity to meet Mrs. Darcy very soon. Elizabeth stood in amazement as she observed that Darcy did not seem to be at all self-conscious speaking to such a large group of people. Apparently, some things would be different about him now that he was at home. Here people knew and respected him.

Mrs. Reynolds, the housekeeper, had a warm, friendly face. Elizabeth knew that how well she was able to get along with this woman would determine at least in part her success in her new role. She saw Mrs. Reynolds looking at her politely, but looking her over, nevertheless. As they stood conversing, she thought she noticed the elderly woman's smile becoming more genuine as if Elizabeth had achieved at least a first approval.

Observing Darcy and Mrs. Reynolds, she was surprised to see the true warmth shared between them. It was a side of Darcy she had not seen before. This gray-haired woman may have been his employee, but it was clear that he respected and cared for her very much. Elizabeth could see by his face that he was hoping she and Mrs. Reynolds would like each other, too.

"Everyone on the staff is anxious to make you welcome. If there is anything you require, you have only to ask," Mrs. Reynolds told her.

After the housekeeper had excused herself, Darcy took her arm to show her around the house. First he led her through the hall and into a large parlor. Next they walked through the music room and the formal dining room. Everywhere they went she was taken with how handsomely the house was decorated. The rooms themselves were large, lofty, and full of light. Much to Elizabeth's delight the furniture was tasteful and elegant, not gaudy or pretentious as it had been at Rosings. Her respect for Darcy grew as she admired and appreciated his refined taste as reflected in what she had seen so far of the park and house. Darcy joined her as she stood at a window in one of the smaller parlors.

"You seem to be enjoying the views. Are you thinking about the view from your own window at Longbourn?" he asked.

Elizabeth smiled, surprised and pleased he had remembered their discussion. "I could hardly compare the two," she said.

"Come, there is much more to see!" He took her arm and almost pulled her along in his eagerness to share it all with her.

"I think it will take me days to see everything in the house. It is much more..." she hesitated trying to find the right word.

"More what?" he asked, looking a little apprehensive.

"I do not know—just 'more' in every way. I never imagined it would be like this. The park, the house, all of it—words fail me when I attempt to describe it."

"It is praise indeed when you are left speechless. That almost never happens in my experience," he replied with a laugh.

Elizabeth arched her brow, responding to his humor with amusement.

"I am overjoyed that you are here at last. In my mind I have seen you walking these rooms for many months now," he told her.

Elizabeth felt him fixing her with one of his intense looks. She was sure he wanted to embrace her, but propriety prevented him from making any show of affection lest Mrs. Reynolds or any of the servants see them. She reached over and touched his arm again.

"Be assured, I love everything about Pemberley." As soon as she had said it, she realized the double meaning that could be inferred, and she blushed. Wondering which way he had taken her statement, she studied his face and saw that he looked back at her with a certain softness in his eyes. Hoping to cover her embarrassment, she turned away and began to examine a small statue.

Darcy made no comment but led her down the hallway to the picture gallery decorated with some very handsome paintings including family portraits. When she reached the one of Darcy, she paused to contemplate it for a moment. It was a very good likeness. She recognized the smile on his face as the one she had sometimes noticed when he looked at her. Darcy came over as if he were uneasy at the idea of having his likeness examined too closely and began to point out the portraits of other family members including his parents.

Elizabeth wondered if he planned to commission one of her or possibly one of them together as was often done. The idea of her own likeness staring back at her every time she passed through this part of the house was a little unnerving, and she began to understand why Darcy had been so eager to move her attention away to other paintings in the room.

After viewing more rooms than she could remember, they finally reached the wing of the house in which their private suite was located.

"I asked for your room to be thoroughly cleaned before we arrived, but the furnishings and draperies have not been changed for many years. I thought you would like to redecorate it to suit your personal taste."

As she looked around, she was taken with the sheer size of the room, much larger than any room at Longbourn including the family dining room and parlors. Her dressing room attached on the right was nearly as large as the bedroom she had shared with Jane. Double doors to the left opened into a cozy sitting room furnished in a slightly less formal manner than the rest of the house. As they entered, she noticed an arrangement of fresh flowers had been placed on one of the tables to welcome her.

"Of course, you may make any changes you wish in here also," he told her.

"The room is so lovely as it is. I am not sure I could improve it."

"I am hoping we can spend some time here in the evenings," he said.

"It looks very comfortable."

"My room is through there." He indicated another set of double doors opposite the ones leading to her bedchamber.

She did not want to think about his room at the moment and so pushed it out of her mind by focusing on the sitting room. In fact, she was feeling awkward with the entire conversation. As Elizabeth tried to cover her discomfort by examining the furniture, the pictures, and views from the windows, she could sense his eyes on her as she moved about the room. Finally, he walked over and took her hand cradling it gently in his own.

"I suspect you would like to refresh yourself and rest after our journey today. We will have dinner around 6:30. Until then, if you will excuse me, I have some business requiring my immediate attention."

"Yes, thank you. I had not realized until this moment how fatigued I am."

"I have asked Mrs. Reynolds to assign one of the maids to take care of you for a few weeks until we can find just the right person to fill that role permanently. I hope she will meet with your approval. Mrs. Reynolds said her name was Margaret."

"I am sure she will be just fine," Elizabeth responded.

"This evening after dinner, I will show you the library. I think you will be very pleased with all it has to offer."

Elizabeth sensed the intensity of his emotion and was certain he would have liked to kiss her now they were alone. She was unsure how she might react if he did. Before she could make up her mind, he lifted her hand, but instead of kissing the back of it as he had done many times before, he turned it over and kissed the tender inside of her wrist. The intimacy of it caused her to emit a slight gasp.

"Until this evening, Mrs. Darcy," he said. Elizabeth stared at his back as he walked away. Her heart was beating so loudly that she was sure it was competing with the clock on the mantel.

TWENTY FIVE

Elizabeth entered her bedchamber looking around in disbelief at its size and elegance. Before she had time to begin investigating, she heard a knock. Mrs. Reynolds was at the door with a young woman who was staring uncomfortably at the floor.

"Please excuse me, Mrs. Darcy," said Mrs. Reynolds. "This is Margaret. She will be acting as your lady's maid for the first few weeks. She is a good girl and has been in service here for several years. Most recently, she assisted Sally in taking care of Miss Darcy as well as seeing to many of our visitors."

The young woman curtsied to Elizabeth and spoke in a soft voice, "Pleased to meet you, Mrs. Darcy."

Elizabeth looked Margaret over and saw a shy young woman who was more nervous about her new role than Elizabeth was about her own. Being the lady's maid for the mistress of the house—even temporarily—was a major responsibility, and she must be worried about how she would perform. Elizabeth resolved to put Margaret at ease if she could.

"Margaret will unpack your trunk and see to it if you wish a bath," said Mrs. Reynolds.

"I would like to lie down and rest for a while before bathing," Elizabeth told her.

"Yes, mistress." The young girl excused herself past Elizabeth and went into the dressing room.

"Thank you. Mrs. Reynolds, I would like to meet with you first thing tomorrow morning to begin learning about how this house runs."

"Of course, Mrs. Darcy. This evening, if there is anything I can do for you, anything you need, please let me know. We are all at your service. The staff is very anxious to make you feel comfortable and welcome here."

After shedding her traveling dress, she lay down on the big bed and began thinking about Pemberley. As her mind drifted over all she had seen, she began to wonder just what she had gotten herself into. It was difficult not to feel overwhelmed. The next thing she knew, someone was gently touching her shoulder. Although she felt a little awkward about being dressed and bathed by a servant, Margaret seemed to know just how to make her feel at ease. Clearly, she had been well trained, and they quickly began to feel comfortable with each other.

That evening, they took their meal in the small family dining room where the setting was more intimate. Darcy seemed in a pleasant mood but as usual, he said very little. After asking him a few questions about Pemberley, he began to open up. She discovered he was happy to talk at length about his home or about the history of the house.

One thing led to another, and he began to tell her about his first pony, a birthday gift from his parents when he was a boy. Whenever Darcy talked about his childhood, he seemed to grow lighter in his speech and manner as if recalling a time when he was more relaxed and possibly less formal than he was now. Elizabeth wondered what he had been like as a child and resolved to ask Mrs. Reynolds about that tomorrow.

After dinner, Darcy took her to the library. The room was enormous, easily four times the size of her father's library with floor to ceiling shelves almost completely around three walls.

The other wall was filled with tall windows to let in the maximum amount of light during the day for reading.

As they walked around the room, Darcy talked about how the books were arranged so that later she would be able to find what she was looking for at any time. He explained that he had recently employed a young man studying at university to catalog and organize the entire library.

"My family has been building this collection for many generations," he said proudly, "and I am always looking for books worthy enough to be added."

"I believe this room has the largest number of books I have ever seen in one place except for a few of the shops in London. It will happily keep me busy reading for years."

"I have it on the best authority that you are a great reader," he said smiling.

Thinking of her conversation at Netherfield with Darcy and Miss Bingley, she said, "Based on the number of volumes available here, I should be able to meet at least one item from the list of accomplishments you once told me that a lady should have."

"Accomplishments?" Darcy asked.

"Surely, you must remember Miss Bingley's list of requirements a lady must have in order to be considered truly accomplished. Her list included singing, drawing, dancing, and speaking modern languages. You added one particular item to her list as I recall."

"I said that a lady should add something 'more substantial by the improvement of her mind through extensive reading.'"

"Yes, that was it."

"I did not like the way Miss Bingley treated you, and I was attempting to come to your defense."

"Oh, yes, Miss Bingley took great delight in being as unpleasant as possible to me at every opportunity. You were much more patient with her than I could ever be. She was constantly trying to capture your attention and show herself off in what she thought was a favorable manner."

"She did not realize that her efforts had quite the opposite effect. My comment about reading was made in the hope of letting you know that I respect women who are intelligent and have a liveliness of mind much more than those who have just superficial accomplishments to their credit. I hope you took it as a compliment," he said.

Elizabeth blushed. "I was uncertain what you meant. At the time, I thought you took no notice of me at all except to disapprove."

Darcy turned and took her hands in his. "Whenever you were in the room, I could hardly notice anything else."

"If that was the case, why were you so often silent?"

"I was occupied with watching you, of course," he said wryly.

"I left you speechless then," she teased, giving him a flirtatious glance that was rewarded by a brief glimpse of one of his dimples. Darcy continued to gaze at her until she became uncomfortable and looked away.

"My father would have been quite delirious over just being in a room with this many books. If he had come to visit, we would never have seen him at all. I would have been sending all his meals to the library," she said, moving over to one of the bookshelves. She ran her fingers along the spines of the books and found their beautiful leather covers delicious to her touch.

"I am sorry not to have known your father better. He was a very good man," Darcy responded.

"He was, but I admit at times I thought he loved being with his books more than with his family."

Walking over to the big table that served as a desk, Darcy picked up a small package wrapped in white paper and tied with a pretty ribbon. "I wanted to give you something to mark your first day here at Pemberley. Having discovered you do not value fancy gifts as much as some women do, I decided this might be more appropriate."

Elizabeth could not help but be touched by his gesture.

"Thank you," she said, giving a genuine smile. "You seem to know me quite well."

"As you recall, I now have many months of observation to guide me," he replied. His smile was almost shy.

Removing the ribbon and paper wrapping, she found a slim volume of poetry bound in very fine leather. It was a collection of romantic poems. While she was familiar with many of the poets included in it, she had never seen this particular anthology before.

"I took the liberty of marking a few favorites," he said.

Elizabeth found her heart softening to Darcy whenever he allowed this more thoughtful and gentle side of himself to come out, and she wondered if he knew the affect it had on her. Opening the book to one of the poems he had marked, she saw it was one of her favorite sonnets by Shakespeare.

"Thank you very much. This is the perfect gift. I will treasure it always," she said quietly blushing as she scanned the familiar lines of the sonnet—'Let me not to the marriage of true minds Admit impediments' it began. She turned quickly to another poem he had marked. 'Shall I compare thee to a summer's day...' Elizabeth prayed he would not see the color that had risen on her face.

"Is something wrong, Elizabeth?"

"I am deeply moved by the thoughtfulness of your gift," she said. On impulse, she went over to him and standing on tiptoe kissed his cheek lightly. Now it was his turn to blush.

"I am still fatigued from our journey and would like to retire now if you will excuse me," she said, stepping back.

"Yes, of course. I have kept you too long while I carried on about the library."

"No, no. I enjoyed every minute of seeing it for myself after all the times I have visited it in my imagination."

"I believe I will stay here for a while unless you need me to escort you back to the suite," he said.

"I think I can find my way," she told him. She was a little relieved she would be spared the awkwardness of saying good-night to him at the door to her bedchamber.

"Good-night and thank you again for my gift." Reaching the door, she stopped and turned back to him. "And thank you for making me feel so welcome here."

"This is your home," he replied.

"No, not quite yet, but I believe it may be in time."

TWENTY SIX

On her first morning at Pemberley, Darcy sent a message asking her to join him in the small dining room that the family often used. When she arrived, he was already seated at the head of the table sipping coffee. He stood immediately as she entered the room. Peeking in several of the silver covered serving dishes, she was amazed that so much food had been prepared for just the two of them. As she began to put some food onto her plate, she noticed that he remained standing.

"Please sit down. Do not wait for me." He sat but did not pick up his fork again until she had joined him at the table. "I have some business with my steward this morning. I left many things in his hands since we had to be away for so long, and now there are a few items I must attend to immediately. I am sorry to leave you alone this morning, but perhaps I could show you more of the house this afternoon. Would you like that?"

"Yes, thank you. I planned to spend time with Mrs. Reynolds this morning to start going over the running of the household. I do not want to make any changes until I learn more about how things are being done now. Mrs. Reynolds has taken very good care of you and of Pemberley for many years, and it is going to take some time for me to grasp it all."

"You could just rest this morning. We were on the road for the better part of two days."

"Yes, but it is something I want to do."

He smiled, and for a moment she began to think that being married to this man might be more pleasant than she had first thought.

✄

"Mrs. Darcy, I want to welcome you again," began Mrs. Reynolds when she met with Elizabeth later that morning. "Mr. Darcy has instructed me to tell you anything you wish to know about the running of the house. He has also said that over time you may wish to make some changes in various areas. Of course, all you have to do is ask, and we will carry out your wishes."

"I know you have been doing an excellent job of managing the house for a very long time. Even though I had heard about the grandeur of Pemberley, I was not prepared for the sheer size of the house and the staff. I am not sure how long it will take me to even begin to understand the way things are done here. I hope you will be patient with me."

"We will take all the time you need. I would like to say I am very pleased the master has finally decided to marry. I did not think he would ever find a young lady who was good enough for him, but it was worth the wait. I think he has made a very fine choice."

"Thank you very much, Mrs. Reynolds. I appreciate your gesture."

"Oh, no, mistress, it is no gesture. It is what I truly believe."

"Well, then I thank you for your encouragement. I hope you will always speak frankly with me. I value your insight and experience." They talked for an hour or so as the housekeeper acquainted her with the staff and their duties. Finally, Mrs. Reynolds offered to take Elizabeth below stairs to view rooms such as the kitchen, pantries, and laundry. Although these were areas Elizabeth would seldom visit in the future, they were vital to the smooth running of the house. Generally, Mrs. Reynolds would be her link to the staff who tended to the daily needs of family and guests of this vast estate.

As they walked, Elizabeth decided to take advantage of the housekeeper's long acquaintance with her husband in order to learn more about him and his temperament. "You have known Mr. Darcy since he was a small child, have you not?"

"Oh, yes. The master was just four years old when I came to work here."

"And what was Mr. Darcy like as a child?"

Mrs. Reynolds smiled as if recalling a pleasant memory. "He has not changed much at all. It is my experience that good-natured children remain so when they grow up, and he was always the most sweet-tempered and generous boy in the world. In all the years I have known him, I have never had a cross word from him. My only concern over the years has been how serious he was for one so young."

"He can be very intense at times," remarked Elizabeth. She was amazed that Mrs. Reynolds had described Darcy as good-natured, but then there was much she had learned about him since their marriage that had proved a surprise.

"And what do you think of Pemberley?" asked the housekeeper.

Elizabeth noted how Mrs. Reynolds made no comment on her description of Darcy. "It is not exactly as I had imagined. I thought it would be more like Rosings." Elizabeth saw the concern on the older woman's face and hurried to reassure her. She reached out and put her hand on Mrs. Reynolds's arm. "Oh, no, do not be concerned. I think Pemberley far superior to Rosings in every way. The house and furnishings here, as well as the grounds, are much more to my own taste. I would have to say that Pemberley has exceeded my expectations in every way."

Mrs. Reynolds looked relieved and pleased. "Most of the furniture and decoration in the house was done by Lady Anne. She had impeccable taste. Many things have been left just the way she arranged them before she died, and that was almost fifteen years ago now. I am afraid change does not happen quickly here."

�֍

On their first Sunday at Pemberley, they attended services in the parish. Elizabeth, anxious to make a good impression on their neighbors, took what for her was an unusual amount of time deciding what to wear. Once they entered the church, all eyes turned to watch as Darcy led her to the family pew. During the service, she was aware they were the focus of everyone's attention so she tried to set a good example by listening attentively to the readings and homily and by adding her clear voice to the singing of the hymns.

After the service, they stood on the steps of the church while Darcy introduced her to people as they went by. In addition to calling each man and woman—and most of the children—by name as he greeted them, he also included significant little details such as "Mr. Small is a town elder" or "Mrs. Jacobson is a very fine seamstress" to help her remember who they were. Elizabeth was amazed that a man who generally did not seem to notice other people—let alone care enough to learn about them—should know so much about everyone here.

Elizabeth turned her full attention to remembering as many names as possible but quickly became overwhelmed by the task. The men looked at her admiringly while the women sized up her complexion, figure, and clothing. Regardless of what they might have thought of her at first, by the time they left that day, Elizabeth had charmed nearly everyone with her sincere interest, unaffected manner, and friendly smiles. The children were the easiest to win over as she had the foresight to put some sweets in her reticule to give out.

"You did very well today, my dear," said Darcy as they were riding home in the carriage. "You charmed everyone, but of course that does not surprise me." He took her gloved hand in his and gently set it on his knee.

"You knew each person's name there today," Elizabeth said in amazement. "I have never heard you speak so much at one time."

"Of course, I know their names. I have known many of these families all my life," he replied.

On the way home and for most of the remainder of that day Darcy did not say much. It was as if he had a daily limit on his words, and having used them all up with introducing people, he preferred to be silent.

TWENTY SEVEN

There was no doubt—Elizabeth was awed by Pemberley. Never had she seen both beauty and elegance on such a grand scale. The realization that Darcy and Georgiana had lived in all this splendor and comfort their whole lives caused her to ponder the multitude of ways they were shaped by the experience. It shed new light on many of Darcy's attitudes and behaviors.

There was much to learn, and Elizabeth threw herself into it with her whole being. Rather taking Mrs. Reynolds for granted as the days went by, she grew to appreciate her even more. Elizabeth was amazed to find that this kindly, intelligent woman was often able to anticipate her needs and desires even before she knew she had them.

It became Elizabeth's habit to meet with Mrs. Reynolds every morning to review menus and schedules, discuss the needs of family members and guests, hear special requests from the servants, and keep abreast of what was going on among them. Sometimes she was called upon to settle disagreements among them. In a very short time, Pemberley's staff began to respect and trust the new Mrs. Darcy as she always considered every side of the story and worked to resolve each situation with an even-handedness that was becoming well known.

Little by little with patience and Mrs. Reynolds' excellent help, Elizabeth's competence grew and so did her confidence.

She knew that most women who managed great houses did not do it by themselves. They relied heavily on the housekeeper and the butler to keep things running smoothly on a day-to-day basis. Nevertheless, it was a source of pride for her to be as involved as possible.

❈

"Mrs. Reynolds tells me you are a very quick study," Darcy casually remarked one evening at dinner. "She says you have developed quite a grasp of household procedures."

Although Elizabeth had been feeling pleased with herself at how much she had learned, suddenly, she felt uncomfortable. Had Darcy been checking up on her? Had he been talking with Mrs. Reynolds behind her back? His comment set her teeth on edge.

"I hope my progress is pleasing to you," she said, trying to keep her voice as smooth as possible. Picking up her wine glass, she took a sip to give herself something to do, but found she was gripping the glass a little too tightly. Realizing there was a real danger of snapping the stem of the very delicate crystal, she set it down quickly. Darcy went on without comment apparently unaware of the waves of tension flowing from her.

"She also tells me you are doing a splendid job of learning about the management of the servants. You already know them all by name. She says everyone seems to like and respect you, but then that is no surprise to me."

"I am glad you are pleased," was all she could manage.

Darcy went on to discuss the events of his day. As he talked, she barely listened. Her mind raced as she tried to understand what had just happened. Was he checking up on her? If he had married her to have someone to manage the house, then why did he seem to mistrust her? Had he realized too late that she had so little experience?

"Elizabeth?" said Darcy.

"Yes," she replied, returning abruptly from her far away thoughts.

"I asked if you have decided what changes you would like to make in your bedchamber and in our sitting room."

"Mrs. Reynolds and I have gone over everything and sent for some fabric samples. I will be happy to show them to you when they arrive. You may want to approve my choices." Elizabeth looked down at her plate as she spoke.

Darcy set down his fork and leaned back in his chair. He wrinkled his brow and fixed her with an intense look. "I do not need to be involved. I am leaving his matter is entirely in your hands. Whatever you decide will be satisfactory to me."

"Very well." Elizabeth's appetite had vanished, and she began pushing the food around on her plate hoping Darcy would not notice.

"Are you feeling unwell this evening?" he asked. "You do not seem yourself."

She bit her lip as she often did when she was thinking. Apparently, he was more observant than she had given him credit for. "I am well, thank you," she answered. Thinking quickly, she searched for a new topic to distract him. "How do you find the lamb? Mrs. Jones has tried a new recipe for mint sauce, and she will certainly ask tomorrow if it met with your approval."

Darcy responded, and she was pleased at having successfully diverted him from asking any more questions about her state of mind. In truth, as well as things seemed to be going, she was having a difficult time adjusting to life here at Pemberley. The last thing she wanted was for Darcy to know. It was mortifying that he seemed to be checking up on her. It would not do to give him anything else to be concerned about. The first few weeks had been exciting and challenging, but as they settled into daily routines, the sadness she still felt over her father's death began to occupy her thoughts. Some days, she had trouble rallying her spirits.

"Georgiana has written to ask if she may come home to Pemberley," said Darcy.

"I did not know she needed permission to come to her own home," said Elizabeth staring down at her plate.

"She has been staying in town to give us some privacy."

Elizabeth blushed. There was no reason—at least not so far—for Georgiana to stay away. She also wondered why Georgiana's letter to her had not mentioned wanting to join them. "Did you ask her to stay away?"

"No, it was entirely her idea," said Darcy. "She is still young and has romantic ideas."

"I will write and ask her to come home," said Elizabeth. "I miss her."

"As do I."

"I will be glad for her companionship. I miss my family more than I had expected."

"I am sorry. Have I been neglecting you?" he asked, looking concerned.

"No, but I am accustomed to having my sisters around me. Even though they can be irritating at times, I am bit lonely without them."

Darcy reached out and put his hand over hers as it rested on the table. "I am sorry, my dear. I am used to being on my own much of the time," he said. "I had not thought how different it would be for you here."

"Do not worry about me," she said, trying to sound confident. "I will be fine. There is too much for me to do to be bored. Now are you ready for your coffee?" Elizabeth rang for a servant to clear the table, and they moved into the small family parlor for their coffee. Darcy went to the sideboard and to pour himself a brandy.

"Would you like a glass of sherry?"

"I must confess I am not fond of sherry," she replied as she reached for her needlework.

"Then try this—I think you might like it."

Darcy poured some reddish gold liquid from a crystal decanter into a delicate little glass.

"What is it?" she asked sniffing the contents of the glass. It was sweet and a little fruity.

"Just try it."

Elizabeth took a small sip, held the warm liquid in her mouth for a moment, and swallowed. She could feel the smooth heat sliding all the way down to her stomach. "This is very good. It is not like any sherry I have ever tasted."

"That is not surprising. It is port," he said.

"Hmmm, I have always wondered what port was like. I suspect now after having tasted it that it was men who decided port was too strong for ladies to drink. It is so delicious that they want to keep it all for themselves," she said, taking another sip. The warmth from the potent liquid spread quickly through her body, making her more relaxed.

"If you like it, you should drink it more often."

"What will people say?" she asked, arching her brow.

"What you drink in your own home is a private affair. I promise to keep your little secret," he said. His voice had a vaguely conspiratorial air to it.

"I did not think you were one to throw propriety to the wind so easily."

"There are many things you do not know about me," he said as though challenging her. He sat down across from her and balanced his brandy glass on the arm of the chair.

"You are right, of course. I have a lot to learn," she answered suddenly serious. She cast her eyes back down at her work. So much about Darcy remained a mystery to her. Since she had been at Pemberley, she had seen glimpses of the man behind the perfect manners, but she was learning that it would not be an easy task to know someone who was so complex, not to mention adept at hiding his feelings.

Darcy reached over and took her hand caressing it with his thumb. "I know something is making you uneasy. If you do not wish to tell me, that is your choice, but I would like to know when you have worries or concerns."

Elizabeth wanted to pull her hand away but at the same time, she was enjoying the sensations caused by his touch. He was looking at her so sincerely that for a moment she considered unburdening herself. Where to begin? So many things were on her mind and most of them were directly related to him.

As he continued to stroke her hand, she felt light-headed, and the room began to wobble. Elizabeth pulled her hand from his and put it to her forehead. "I believe the port has gone straight to my head. I think I will retire for the night."

"Are you feeling unwell? Perhaps I should walk with you."

"No, thank you. That will not be necessary," she replied as she walked to the door trying not to reveal how unsteady she felt. Darcy looked concerned, but did not try to stop her from leaving. "Surely, it must be the port," she mumbled to herself.

As Elizabeth walked to her room, she thought about her life as Mrs. Darcy. Why was her emotional equilibrium so easily disturbed? It was not like her to be out of sorts or to doubt herself, but since coming to Pemberley she could not seem to find her place. Each time she thought matters were well in hand, something happened that surprised and unsettled her.

To a great degree, her own happiness depended on pleasing her husband, and even after several months of marriage, she still had no idea how to do that. In reviewing the events of the evening again, she thought she should probably be pleased and not worried that he had expressed satisfaction with her progress in managing the house—and he had reiterated his confidence in her abilities and judgment. Perhaps she should ask him directly what he expected of her. That way, she would know where to put her attentions. Now all she had to do was find the right opportunity to approach him.

TWENTY EIGHT

A week or so later, Georgiana arrived at Pemberley with Mrs. Annesley. Elizabeth had been anxiously anticipating the reunion, hoping it would take away some of the sting of missing her own dear sisters.

When Darcy had been in London the previous winter, he had arranged for the purchase of a new pianoforte as a surprise for his sister. It had been delivered while they were still at Netherfield.

On the afternoon Georgiana arrived home, Darcy and Elizabeth kept her occupied so that she would not have time to visit the music room, which was generally one of her first stops upon returning home. After dinner, Darcy hinted he would like to hear Elizabeth and Georgiana play some music together. In spite of her shyness, Georgiana found that she could not deny her brother any pleasure she might bring him through her playing.

Upon entering the music room, Georgiana discovered her gift. She was completely taken by surprise. "Oh, this is...this is too much, Brother. I do not deserve such a wonderful gift," she said, running her hands lovingly over the smooth wood of the instrument.

"Of course, you deserve it, and you know your brother is never wrong about these things," said Elizabeth.

Tears of happiness came to Georgiana's eyes as she thanked them again and again. "Now would you do us the honor of playing something so I can ascertain if I have made a good investment?" Darcy asked. He gave his sister a reassuring smile.

Although usually shy in front of any audience, Georgiana was so eager to try out the new instrument that she did not have to be encouraged to play. In fact, she played several tunes for them with almost no urging at all. As the sounds of the new instrument drifted through the house, some of the servants came to stand just outside the doors to the music room so that they too could enjoy the impromptu concert.

As they listened, Elizabeth watched her husband's face closely and saw that he looked more relaxed than usual as if the music was a soothing balm. It had not occurred to her to question how he might be bearing up under the strain of everything that had happened over the past few months. While chastising herself for being so selfish and inconsiderate, she resolved to show him more kindness and attention. Perhaps she would suggest taking a walk together tomorrow.

When the little concert was over, Georgiana asked her brother and Elizabeth to step into the family parlor where she had a surprise for them. She presented a book to her brother to add to the library, and to Elizabeth, she gave a picture of Pemberley she had drawn herself.

"It is not very good. My drawing teacher had me work from one of the paintings at Darcy House," Georgiana apologized shyly as she examined the drawing over Elizabeth's shoulder. "He says he thinks I show promise, but I suspect he only says that in order to ensure his employment continues."

"Every proper young lady should learn to draw," said Darcy.

"Must I really continue?" asked Georgiana making a dis-agreeable face.

"Yes, of course, you must," Darcy told her.

Elizabeth noticed how Georgiana was looking down at the floor uncomfortably but the girl said nothing to challenge her brother. Elizabeth touched her finger to her sister's chin and lifted her face. "I think the drawing is very good, and I shall treasure it always," she said, kissing Georgiana on the cheek.

TWENTY NINE

The next morning, Elizabeth arose early and found to her surprise that she was looking forward to walking out with Darcy. Never before had she consciously thought of spending time alone with him as having the potential to be something pleasurable. Perhaps it was just that having been a social creature all her life, she had been feeling the lack of society since arriving at Pemberley. As she was still officially in mourning for her father, she was afforded only limited opportunities to socialize with other families in the neighborhood. The only people she had met from the area were those who attended services at their parish.

Elizabeth missed her sisters most especially Jane and the intimate sisterly talks they had shared all their lives. Although she was coming to think of Georgiana as a sister, it was not the same as the bonds she shared with Jane. Sitting at her dressing table as Margaret fixed her hair, she looked at her reflection in the mirror. The face that looked back seemed both familiar and something of a stranger. She knew she was not Elizabeth Bennet any more—she was Elizabeth Darcy—Mrs. Darcy—but she was still not sure sometimes exactly what that meant.

Descending the stairway to the family dining room, she ran her hand along the smooth wood of the banister that followed the gracefully curving staircase that led to the family's rooms on the main level. Every day she was amazed that she was mistress of all this grandeur. The responsibility was both a great delight and a great weight upon her.

❋

"You look very lovely this morning, Elizabeth," Darcy commented as they walked one of the paths toward the stream that ran down from the hill and into a pond near the house. Elizabeth had chosen one of her favorite bonnets to wear that day. Even though the straw was trimmed in black, she thought it looked less severe than most of the others she had been wearing since her father's death.

"Thank you," she said, pleased he had noticed and made the effort to compliment her. They walked in silence for a while as they often did. Elizabeth enjoyed taking in all the new scenery as they strolled along. Finally, she decided it was time to ask some of the questions that had been occupying her thoughts almost since her first day at the house.

"I would like to talk to you about what you expect of me as Mistress of Pemberley," Elizabeth began a little hesitantly as they neared the pond.

"I am not certain I understand what you mean."

"When you asked me to marry you, you must have had some idea of the role I would play here. I have a great deal of respect for the estate and the importance of the Darcy family in the neighborhood. I want to be certain I am doing the right things."

"First of all, you must know that I did not marry you just to have someone to manage the house and act as hostess here." His voice had an edge of irritation.

"I did not mean to cause offense," she responded quickly. "Every day I discover there is more to learn. I would like to give my immediate attention to what you deem most important."

"You are already involved in much of the household management with Mrs. Reynolds."

"Surely, there are other things you expect of me."

"Eventually, we will be obliged to begin entertaining again. I have been single since assuming responsibilities here at Pemberley, so people in the area have not had the same expectations of me. That will all change now we are married. I am sure many people are anticipating being invited to Pemberley again as they were when my parents were alive."

"I will do my best not to let you down," she said.

"I have every confidence in you," he said. "You have a natural ability for making people feel at ease and bringing out the best in them. I have already seen you applying these talents with the people you have met here."

"Thank you," she murmured.

"In a very short period of time, you have helped Georgiana's confidence to grow. I was always certain she would blossom under your care," he said with some tenderness in his voice. "She is happier and more talkative than I can remember her being in a very long time."

Elizabeth relaxed a bit and sent up a silent prayer of thanks.

"Give me your hand, Elizabeth. The ground is uneven here, and I would not want you to injure yourself."

Although she did not feel herself in any danger, she reached out to him. Darcy took her hand and tucked it under his arm protectively. Peering up at his face, she thought he looked pleased. Sometimes she was amazed at how a small gesture like this from her could bring him such obvious pleasure. It was little enough to ask of her and was it not her duty as his wife to please him?

"Have you thought about asking Jane or the Gardiners to visit us this summer?" he asked.

"I have considered it, but I know Jane is occupied with Mr. Bingley. My Aunt Gardiner says that Uncle's business has been busy this summer and has been requiring more of his attention than usual. I do not think that they will have time to visit," said Elizabeth wistfully.

"Have you written with an invitation?"

"No."

"Perhaps you should," he offered.

"Thank you, I will consider it," she said. And then changing the subject, she began to ask him questions about the trees and the foliage near the pond. Once he started talking about the estate, he was never at a loss for conversation. She knew how much he loved his home by the unconscious enthusiasm he displayed. Elizabeth hoped that some day she would feel as much a part of Pemberley as he did. Until then, she resolved to take things one day at a time and today had been a good beginning.

As Darcy talked about Pemberley, he suddenly became self-conscious about how he was rambling on like a fool. Surely, she could not be as interested in all the details of the estate as she was pretending to be. Still she seemed to be listening attentively and even asked thoughtful questions from time to time. He wondered if her interest was just part her gift for drawing people out as he had seen her do in other situations.

She had certainly charmed Mrs. Reynolds and all the rest of the household staff. They thought she was the best thing that had ever happened to Pemberley and by extension to them. He knew that everyone including Georgiana considered them the perfect couple. He wondered what people would say if they knew the truth about the awkwardness of their relationship. Then he thought of how often the servants knew more about what was going on in the house than even he did.

"I wish you were more interested in riding. There are so many places I would like to show you, but they are inaccessible on foot or by carriage," said Darcy as they walked back toward the house.

"I simply prefer walking."

"You do know how to ride?"

"Yes, but I am hardly proficient. I did not have much opportunity. The horses at Longbourn were generally needed for work on the land. My father did not keep them just for riding."

"You have no objection to horses then?" he asked.

"No, I am not afraid of them if that is what you mean," she responded, "although they do make me a little uneasy because they are so large."

"And you are so small?" His voice was teasing.

"Maybe you could find me a very little horse?" she said, looking up at him through her eyelashes. Then she seemed to laugh at her own comment. The sound of her laughter made it difficult for him to think clearly. It was playful and full of music.

By the time they returned to the house, she had agreed to allow him to begin teaching her to ride although she still did not show much enthusiasm for the project. Darcy wished—not for the first time—that he better understood the workings of her mind.

"Thank you for walking with me today. I enjoyed myself very much," Elizabeth said, sounding sincere in her thanks.

"Elizabeth, I..." He could not find the words to ask what he really wanted to know.

"Yes?"

Embarrassed, he tried to fill the void with something. "I was just wondering if you would like to walk again tomorrow."

"I would enjoy your showing me more of your favorite places on the estate," she replied, flashing her eyes as she spoke.

"Very well, and as soon as you learn to ride, I will take you to a very special place by the river," he said, hoping to give her an incentive to begin her lessons.

"And what do you like about that particular place?" she asked.

"It is very beautiful and peaceful. I have happy memories of time spent there. You will see it for yourself soon, I hope."

After Elizabeth had excused herself to go meet with Mrs. Reynolds about some household matters, Darcy stood in the entryway and watched her walk away. As he did, he thought about all the times he had dreamed of having her here with him at Pemberley. The reality of it was quite different than what he had hoped, but it seemed to him that they were at least making a beginning.

THIRTY

After Georgiana joined them at Pemberley, the household fell into a pleasant routine. Most mornings, Darcy rose early to take exercise on his horse and several times a week, he would join Elizabeth for a long walk. After his morning exercise, he worked on estate business while Elizabeth met with Mrs. Reynolds to review menus, balance the accounts, or deal with other matters related to the house. Georgiana devoted her time to practicing her music, her needlework, or her studies.

One morning as they finished breakfast, Georgiana and Elizabeth lingered quietly reading their books and sipping coffee. Darcy, who had been looking through the paper, pushed away from the table and leaned back in his chair.

"I have to ride out with Adams today to check on some tenants, and then I will be going into Lambton on business." After taking a last sip from his coffee, Darcy rose and kissed Elizabeth on the cheek. "I will see you both late this afternoon, then." He started to leave but then stopped by the door. "I had almost forgotten. I had asked Mrs. Reynolds to find some suitable applicants to fill the post of your lady's maid. She now has several for you to consider."

This was a complete surprise to Elizabeth who was quite happy with Margaret, the young woman who had been acting as her maid since she had arrived. The idea of finding someone new seemed unnecessary. In addition, she felt uncomfortable he had taken it upon himself to speak to Mrs. Reynolds since making decisions about the household staff was her responsibility.

"Thank you, sir, but I will let Mrs. Reynolds know she does not need to bother. I am very happy with Margaret."

"I am sure that Margaret is very pleasant, but she is young and inexperienced. You should have someone more suitable for your position as mistress of the house."

Elizabeth looked down at her hands folded tightly in her lap. "I think Margaret suits me quite well. After all, the mistress of the house is also young and inexperienced." Elizabeth glanced up at Georgiana who was keeping her eyes glued firmly on her book.

"My dear, I do not think you realize the advantages of having someone with more experience attending you. Lady Matlock's maid is a most excellent woman, is she not, Georgiana?"

Georgiana nodded slightly but did not look up. Elizabeth was furious that he would try to draw Georgiana into something that was between the two of them. Most of all, she did not like being told what to do.

"I think it is more important that the person with whom I will be spending so much time is someone I like. Margaret has worked very hard, and I think she deserves this opportunity to prove herself."

"I have already asked Mrs. Reynolds to find other candidates. Please speak with her about this."

Elizabeth's cheeks were warm from the embarrassment that Georgiana should have heard their exchange. She knew she should probably acquiesce and deal with this matter later in private, but her stubbornness would not allow her to leave it alone.

"Of course, I will speak to Mrs. Reynolds if that is what you wish, but I thought we had agreed that I would make all decisions about the household staff," she challenged.

Darcy took a deep breath and let it out slowly.

"I really must be off now. We shall discuss the matter when I return this afternoon if you wish," he said, putting an end to the conversation. Then he kissed her on the cheek again before he left the room.

Although Georgiana did not speak, Elizabeth was certain she had been ill at ease to hear them disagree in front of her. Elizabeth's first instinct was to rush from the room and go off by herself, either to her room or out for a walk, but she did not want Georgiana to know how upset she was at being dictated to in this manner. Although she was fuming, she tried to sip her coffee calmly and act as if nothing was amiss. Finally, she placed her napkin on the table and stood to leave.

"If you will excuse me, I have to see Mrs. Reynolds about the menus for the week. May I come listen when you practice later today?"

"He only wants what is best for you." Georgiana's voice was barely audible.

"I realize that, but I believe in this matter I am the one who is in the best position to decide what I need."

"You have to understand that my brother is accustomed to making decisions without consulting anyone else. It is just a habit he developed from having so much responsibility for the estate thrust on him when he was so young." Georgiana's eyes were pleading for understanding as she looked at Elizabeth.

"I am sure you are correct. There is much for me to learn." She tried to give the girl a reassuring look and then left the room quickly while she still had control over her emotions. Walking back to her room, she wondered what was wrong with her lately. She had never been one to cry so easily. She had cried frequently when her father was ill, but that was understandable. Perhaps the loss was affecting her equilibrium more than she realized. She desperately missed Jane and her calming influence. Contemplating her low mood, she realized that nearly every aspect of her life had changed in the past few months. Maybe it was not so surprising that she was feeling a little fragile.

As she settled in as mistress of the house, it seemed to her like an important time to make her own choices. After all, she was the one most affected by the selection of her maid. To keep the peace, Elizabeth resolved to follow through and consider whomever Mrs. Reynolds recommended. Having complied with her husband's request, then she would tell him that she still wanted Margaret.

The next morning as Margaret was fixing Elizabeth's hair, she seemed to be fumbling a little more than usual with the pins as if she were anxious about something. Looking into the mirror, Elizabeth could see the girl's unhappy face reflected there.

"What is wrong this morning? Are you feeling ill?" asked Elizabeth.

"No, Mrs. Darcy, I am fine." The strained smile on Margaret's face said she was anything but fine.

"I know you well enough by now to be certain there is something on your mind. Please tell me."

"It is nothing, ma'am."

Elizabeth reached up and put her hand on Margaret's arm to stop her work. "I will not allow you to continue until you have told me what this is all about. Please, Margaret, you may speak to me freely."

Margaret kept her eyes down on the floor. "Have I done something to displease you, Mrs. Darcy?" Her voice was so soft Elizabeth could barely hear her.

"Displease me? Whatever made you think that?"

"The gossip below stairs, ma'am. I heard from some of the other servants you are going to hire someone to replace me. I know this has been only a temporary position, but I was hoping you might keep me on permanent-like. I thought we were getting on well."

"I see. You are worried I will be replacing you because you have displeased me?"

"Yes, ma'am," she whispered, keeping her eyes on the floor. "I am so sorry. I should never have mentioned this to you."

"Rest assured that I think you are taking very good care of me. Mr. Darcy has asked me to consider some other more experienced candidates, but I have made my decision. I would like to make this a permanent situation for you. Would that meet with your approval?"

Margaret's face glowed. "Oh, yes, Mrs. Darcy. I am very happy working for you. I do not know how to thank you."

Elizabeth smiled at her. She knew that this was a big moment for a young girl in service. This was a significant promotion to being lady's maid to the mistress of the house. Pleased with her decision, she resolved find a way to deal with Mr. Darcy's disapproval. After all, choosing a lady's maid was very personal matter—a decision only she should make.

※

A few days later, while Elizabeth was sitting alone with her husband after dinner, she considered how best to bring up her decision about Margaret. She spent some time trying to assess his mood and possible receptivity. When he talked about the success he had experienced that day in settling a dispute between tenants, it seemed a good time to share what was on her mind.

"I have done as you requested and reviewed the letters of recommendation from several ladies for the position of my maid."

"And did you find someone to your liking?"

"Yes, as a matter of fact, I have. After considering all the candidates, I have offered the position to Margaret."

His face darkened. "Elizabeth, I thought I had made it clear you must choose someone more fitting your position. Margaret is a nice girl, but she just will not do for the mistress of this house."

"I realize she is lacking in experience, but she seems to be coming along very well, and even more importantly, I have come to trust her."

"I do not want to insist, but I feel very strongly about this. You must choose someone else," he said, continuing to look disapproving.

She smiled sweetly back at him. "I am quite resolved. Is there a reason other than her inexperience that has you so decided against her?" She could not understand his continued insistence about the matter. Now she felt backed into a corner. She had told Margaret she was going to stay, and nothing was going to make her go back on her word. Darcy stood and started pacing restlessly.

"I have nothing against her. I just want you to choose someone more appropriate, not some untested young girl."

Elizabeth bit her lip as she struggled to keep her temper in check. "You told me I would be making decisions about the house and the staff, but when I do something that you do not agree with, you want to overrule me. If you do not trust my judgment, you should tell me now."

He stopped pacing and seemed to be giving close examination to the picture hanging above the fireplace. Elizabeth wondered if possibly there was something he was not telling her. Turning, he fixed her with one of those serious, intent looks she was coming to know so well.

"I do trust your judgment, but I want you to choose someone else. I have given you my reasons, and I expect you to do as I say," he replied.

"Oh, so I may make decisions as long as you approve of them!" Elizabeth was so irritated that she nearly jumped to her feet.

"That is not what I said!"

"I believe that is the essence of it," she replied, unable to keep the edge from her voice.

"I am still master of this house. I am accustomed to having people follow my wishes."

"And I am your wife, not one of your servants. You should not give me leave to make decisions about these matters and then overrule me."

His look went straight through her, but she held her ground. Finally taking a deep breath, he exhaled what seemed a sigh of resignation. "Very well. She may stay on temporarily, but you must choose someone else by the end of the year."

Elizabeth stood. In spite of his disapproval, she did not plan to back down. She walked over to her husband and took his hand. Looking up into his eyes, she said as sweetly she could, "I am sorry to disagree with you, but I have already told her she is staying, and I cannot go back on my word. Now come sit down, and I will read to you."

Darcy looked confused. Although he still seemed reluctant to give up the discussion, she could feel his resistance decreasing a little as she stood there tracing the back of his hand with her finger. "Are you trying to distract me?" he asked.

"Do you object to my holding your hand? I seem to remember a time when you very much wanted to hold mine."

"Yes, I remember it quite well," he said. His face softened. Gently, she led him to the settee. Picking up the book of essays he had left on the table, she opened it at his bookmark and began to read aloud. Elizabeth was not sure if he had decided to allow her to make the decision, or if he was just planning to wait until another time to bring it up again. For the moment at least, she had won the argument quite effectively.

❊

Darcy sat listening to Elizabeth read to him. It was very enjoyable being the sole focus of her attentions. At the same time, he was not sure exactly what had just happened. They had been arguing, and he had told her that he expected her to accede to his wishes, but the moment she had touched his hand, he had lost the will to continue the disagreement. He wasn't certain but he had the vague recollection that he had given in and Margaret would be staying on as her maid.

Elizabeth continued to hold his hand while she balanced the book in her other. Her face was intense as she read, as if she was completely absorbed in the words, and they had somehow carried her away from this place and time. He continued to watch with complete fascination.

After a few minutes, she released his hand and reached up to brush back a stray lock of hair and then to massage the back of her neck while still continuing to read. Darcy felt as if he were viewing something very private. It was that intimate and sensuous. He had always found everything about her slender, graceful neck erotic. As much as he liked her hair down, he also appreciated the advantages of seeing it pinned up. Sometimes, when she was reading or sewing, she would stop to stretch or rub the tired muscles, and he was always mesmerized.

If she only knew the affect this simple gesture had on him. As he watched, he wished it were his hand in place of hers. He thought back to the evening at Netherfield after her father's funeral when she had allowed him to sooth her by massaging her shoulders. It had given him so much pleasure to touch her that way. At the time, he had been hopeful their relationship would become closer, but in spite of his resolve to win her affections, he was unsure if he had made much progress in reaching her.

"May I do that?" he offered.

Elizabeth looked up.

"You look as if your neck and shoulders are tired. May I assist you?"

She examined his face for a moment until she finally seemed to comprehend what he was asking. He wondered if she remembered that evening at Netherfield, too. "Thank you. That would be very nice," she said with a warm smile that made his heart soar.

Darcy gave his attention to stroking the tense muscles in her neck and shoulders as she took up the book and began reading again. Several times, she paused and closed her eyes for a moment before continuing.

"Is this relieving your discomfort?" he asked.

"It feels lovely, but it is beginning to distract me from reading this essay."

Darcy was confused. "Does that mean I should stop or continue?"

Elizabeth reached up and put her hand on his. She squeezed it lightly and said, "Definitely continue although you may have to put up with my missing a word now and then."

A flush of pleasure come over him. Apparently, she was enjoying his attentions. She finished the essay, put a marker between the pages, and closed the book. They sat awkwardly for a few moments.

"I hope you are happy here at Pemberley and are finding everything to your liking," he said when he finally found his voice. The second he said it he knew it sounded trite, but he simply could not think of anything more scintillating to fill the silence. Although he had never been good at conversing with people, trying to talk to Elizabeth frequently made him feel even more awkward and tongue-tied than usual.

"Of course, I am pleased. I would have to say that I am a little overwhelmed, but I am trying my best," she replied.

"What I really meant was are you happy here?"

Elizabeth bit her lip thoughtfully, a gesture that always made him want to kiss her. "I am reasonably content."

He was not sure what he had been expecting her to say, but this non-committal response was a disappointment. "I see. I was hoping for a little more than that by now," he said quietly.

"I think 'reasonably content' is quite a lot at this point."

He could think of no response.

"With your permission, I shall excuse myself and go to my room now." She rose to leave.

He stood too and caught her hand in his as she started to walk away. On impulse, he raised her hand to his lips. Reluctant to break the connection with her, he kissed it again. The soft scent of her perfume was intoxicating. When he turned her hand over and gently touched his lips to the inside of her wrist, he heard her breath catch. The next thing he knew, she had pulled away gently and was making her way toward the door.

THIRTY ONE

One cloudy afternoon when it was too wet to go out, Elizabeth decided it was time to unpack the boxes of books she had brought with her from Longbourn. Most of the books had sentimental meaning for her as nearly all had either belonged to her father or were gifts from him. Margaret had offered to help, but she shooed the young woman away and began the task herself. Just touching the books somehow created a link with her father.

Books went into two piles—those to keep in her own rooms and those to be placed in Pemberley's library. Her few meager titles would not add much to that grand collection, but for some reason, the idea of joining her father's books to the Darcy family library appealed to her. It would be as close as her father would come to visiting the room that would have been like heaven itself to him.

Elizabeth picked up the copy of Shakespeare's "Much Ado About Nothing," which had been a gift from her father a few days before his death. She had read most of it to him during the last days of his illness. The time they had spent together was now so precious to her. She remembered he had been most adamant that she keep this book once they had finished it. After admiring the leather cover, she opened it and inside found a letter written in her father's hand. On the outside it said, *"To my Elizabeth—to be opened in the event of my death."* With shaking hands, she tore open the seal and unfolded the letter.

My Dearest Elizabeth,

As I am writing this, I can feel that my time is coming to an end. I will be glad to be relieved of the pain this illness has brought to my body, but I am also sad beyond measure that I will not live to hold your children—my grandchildren—on my lap and tell them stories as I used to do with you. I can see it in my mind's eye—my arms around a miniature version of you, my love, dark curls tickling my chin and sparkling eyes begging me for just one more story before bedtime.

I have some regrets from this lifetime, as I suppose most men do. I should have been more firm with your sisters when they were growing up. Perhaps they would not have turned out to be such silly girls. I should have planned better for the security of my family. I continued to hope for many years that I would have a son who would inherit Longbourn and provide all of you with the safety you deserve. Instead, I am forced to leave all of you in the protection of Mr. Darcy.

I know that he is not the kind of man you had intended to marry. You always had such romantic ideas of marrying for love, and more than anything I wanted this for you. Instead, for the love of your family, you have accepted the arrangement of this marriage, and I know it has left you with doubts. As I told you on your wedding day, I believe in my heart that the two of you have a chance to find happiness in your life together. He is a match for your intelligence and wit, and you will help him learn to laugh—at life and at himself.

There are also some things about which I have no regrets. One of those would be the many hours we spent together. You have been the light of my life, dearest daughter.

So, Lizzy, please do not grieve too much or too long for me. Think kindly of your dear Papa from time to time and know that I will be with you in spirit always. Your inner strength is so great that I am confident you will be able to overcome any trials or challenges that life puts in your way. Tell your children about me and teach them to love books and learning as I have taught you.

Your loving Father

By the time Elizabeth finished reading the letter, her eyes were so full of tears she could barely read the words on the page. She refolded the precious letter, kissed the paper, and held it tightly to her breast. All of the grief of missing her father that she had been holding at bay for the last few months came rushing out. She crawled into her bed and cried until she was so exhausted that she fell asleep, but even in sleep she could not escape. Her dreams were filled with heart-wrenching scenes of her father, and she awoke hours later more tired than when she had taken to her bed.

✄

Over the next few weeks, Elizabeth continued to have trouble sleeping. After a restless night, she often found it difficult to leave her bed in the morning. The things she had enjoyed about her new home seemed less and less diverting, and she spent more time alone walking. Both Darcy and Georgiana made frequent attempts to cheer her, but their efforts did not meet with much success. She picked at her food and found it too difficult to concentrate on reading. After just a short time, the sleepless nights began taking a toll on her health and humor. Often when she took up her sewing, she would catch herself daydreaming. Without warning she would suddenly realize that she had been staring off into space for five or ten minutes. Then she would reapply herself to her work only to have the same thing happen again.

Although Georgiana repeatedly coaxed her to join in at the pianoforte, Elizabeth had no heart to play. One morning after listening to Georgiana practice for a while, Elizabeth excused herself to go sit in the garden. Her mind kept drifting back to her family. She wondered what her beloved Jane was doing at that moment, but when she started to write a letter, she could not think of anything to say that would not sound melancholy and cause her sister to worry. How could she tell Jane that she desperately missed her, that she was sad beyond belief at the loss of their father, and that her life here at Pemberley was more lonely and difficult than she had ever imagined it would be? As those thoughts swirled around in her mind, she sat watching the bees flying from flower to flower until Margaret came to find her to tell her that Mr. Darcy had returned and was expecting to see her shortly for tea.

THIRTY TWO

After a few weeks, Elizabeth began to feel a little bit more like her old self. Then something happened that deeply shook Elizabeth's confidence and good humor. One afternoon as she walked by the main drawing room, she glanced in and noticed that one of the chairs was not in its place. Just the day before, she had spent hours with several of the maids and footmen supervising a thorough cleaning of the room. Then she had directed them to rearrange the furniture more to her taste. When she investigated, she realized that not only had one chair been moved but also all the furniture had been returned to its original location.

With some agitation, Elizabeth set off to find Mrs. Reynolds to see if she could shed any light what had happened to undo all her work from the previous day. When she arrived at Mrs. Reynolds's workroom, she found the housekeeper going over some bills and paperwork. The older woman looked up and after seeing who had entered, she stood immediately.

"Mrs. Darcy, what brings you here?"

"I wished to speak to you."

"If you had asked someone to let me know, I would gladly have come to you."

"Thank you, I may do that in the future, but I wanted to speak to you immediately, and frankly, it did not occur to me to send someone for you when I could come myself."

Mrs. Reynolds looked down at her papers and then back at Elizabeth. "What may I do for you, mistress?"

"I just walked by the main drawing room and discovered that the furniture has been moved back to the way it was before I changed it just yesterday. I am wondering what happened?"

"Yes, well," she said, clearly uncomfortable with the question. "Mr. Darcy asked me to do that."

Elizabeth was embarrassed that Mrs. Reynolds had discovered she knew nothing of Mr. Darcy's orders, but it was too late to save face now. "And did Mr. Darcy give a reason for this?"

"He just asked me to see that it was moved back."

"Did Mr. Darcy know that the change was my doing?"

"I assume he did, but he did not ask. If I may be so bold as to venture a guess, perhaps he is simply accustomed to having it a certain way. The furniture has been in the same place in that room ever since his mother Lady Anne was alive."

"Yes, you told me change does not happen here quickly. Thank you, Mrs. Reynolds," said Elizabeth shortly and turning on her heel, she started off in the direction Darcy's study.

Whatever had possessed Darcy, she wondered. Several times he had told her to make any changes she wished both in the house and in the management of the household staff. They had discussed this again when he had objected to her choice of Margaret as her maid. She thought she had made her opinions clear.

Now he had countermanded her orders without even mentioning it to her. How must it look to Mrs. Reynolds and the rest of the servants? Surely, they would all be talking about it. Her face grew red with embarrassment. When she went to his study to confront him, she remembered he had gone out for the day and was not expected back until tea. She would have preferred to discuss it while it was still fresh in her mind, but it would just have to wait. Since her agitation at these events was so great, she could not imagine being able to concentrate on any of the work she had planned for the afternoon. Impulsively, she decided to go out for a walk instead. She needed time alone to try and make sense of it all.

As she walked away from the house defiantly, she thought about how hard she was trying to fit in here at Pemberley and could only feel discouraged. How could she ever establish herself if Darcy continued to countermand her instructions? This was not the first time that something like this had happened. There had been the disagreement about who should be her lady's maid and a few smaller ones that were of little consequence but together, they added up to more.

Recently, he had not been happy with the way one of the upstairs maids had been dusting in their sitting room so he had mentioned it to Mrs. Reynolds rather than to her. Just a few days ago he had sent a message directly to Cook requesting a change in the breakfast menu. Perhaps since he had been in charge for many years, the staff thought nothing of it, but Elizabeth felt he should have come to her first. It was a bit like the chain of command in the military.

Each time when she mentioned one of the incidents to him, he apologized but brushed it off saying she should not let it bother her. He was, after all, the master of the house and therefore accustomed to making such requests directly. She had tried explaining to him that now this was her role, but apparently he did not understand. Or, possibly, he understood but had no intention of changing.

The day was very fine, and Elizabeth stayed out nearly all afternoon exploring the woods beyond the lake where she and Darcy had walked several times over the first weeks she had been at Pemberley. As was often the case, the vigorous exercise helped calm her anger and mend her frayed nerves. It was such a beautiful day that she could not bear the thought of being indoors, so after a long walk, she found a quiet spot near a little stream and sat down. Leaning her back against a tree, she relaxed and watched the birds on the water. The combination of lack of sleep and the rush of emotions had left her exhausted. The next thing she knew, she was being awakened by someone calling her name in the distance.

Shaking off the residual fuzziness she felt from sleeping during the day, she cleared her head and, once standing, saw one of the under-gardeners walking along the path in her direction. Raising a hand, she waved at the boy, and he began to run toward her.

"Mistress, we been searchin' for you near an hour now," he exclaimed breathlessly.

"Looking for me? As you can see, I am not lost. I just sat down here for a few minutes and fell asleep, that is all." Seeing the concern on his face, she asked, "What time is it?"

"It is past time for tea, mistress. The Master ordered everyone out to look for you. You was gone so long he feared you might be lost or come to some harm."

Immediately, she was furious with Darcy that he would try to keep such a tight rein on her activities. She had been gone for a few hours, and yet he thought it necessary to organize a search.

"What is your name?" she asked as they walked back toward the house.

"Robert," he told her shyly.

Elizabeth tried to engage Robert in conversation but all his answers were very short. He was clearly uncomfortable that the mistress of the house should be conversing with him so casually. Finally, after some encouragement, he began to tell her about his family. The walk back to the house seemed to take no time at all once he lost some of his fear of speaking with her.

Giving her full attention to Robert and learning about his family had almost kept Elizabeth from thinking about how upset she really was. Eventually, her worries began to intrude again. She had already been upset over the furniture and now would be forced to suffer the humiliation of Darcy's sending out a search party for her when she was barely out of sight of the house. When they neared the house, Elizabeth focused on the young man again and thanked him for his help.

"I will have someone send for you later to collect a reward for your efforts this afternoon. I thank you again."

Robert's face reddened, and he gave a little bow. "There's no need for a reward, mistress. I was just doin' me job."

"Nonsense, young man. You shall have a little something extra for your efforts. I am certain Mr. Darcy would agree."

Robert gave another embarrassed bow and hustled away down the drive. As Elizabeth entered the house, she saw Mrs. Reynolds coming down the hallway toward her in a great hurry.

"Are you injured, Mrs. Darcy? We have all been so very worried about you," she said breathlessly.

Elizabeth shook her head in exasperation. "I was sitting by a little stream and fell asleep for a few minutes. Why is everyone so concerned? I am just fine."

"Of course, Mrs. Darcy. I am pleased to see you are safely returned." Mrs. Reynolds looked relieved.

"I am going to my room now to change. Would you ask someone to send my tea to the small family parlor? I will be down in a few minutes," Elizabeth told her. Then feeling she may have been too short with her, she added, "Thank you for your concern about my well-being, but I am fine—truly. There was no need to worry."

Mrs. Reynolds paused a moment and then replied, "If you will excuse me then, I will inform everyone you have returned safely."

After changing, Elizabeth went down to the small parlor and discovered that Darcy had also gone out to look for her and had not yet returned. Taking up some needlework, she tried to concentrate on the intricate pattern but found it almost impossible. After about twenty minutes, Darcy rushed into the room with clothes disheveled and hair wild. Elizabeth was very surprised as she had never seen him look anything but perfectly groomed.

"Where have you been all afternoon? I returned to find you missing and I was mad with worry! No one seemed to know anything except you had gone out for a walk."

"Yes, I had a lovely walk. Thank you for asking," she said, calmly keeping her eyes focused on her work.

"When you did not appear for tea, I became concerned and sent some men out to look for you." His hands were balled in tight fists as he watched her. Past experience told her this was not a good sign.

"Yes, I know. I am very sorry for the inconvenience, but I simply lost track of the time."

"I had visions of you hurt or lost. Mrs. Reynolds intimated that you were disturbed about something. I did not know what to think." The silence in the room grew as thick as fog. Darcy continued, "Apparently, you have won her loyalty as she would not tell me what had upset you."

"Yes, Mrs. Reynolds is a wonderful woman."

"Well?" he asked.

She looked at him with some irritation. "Well, what?"

"Where have you been? What is troubling you?"

"I simply took a walk around the lake and up into the woods where I found a rather lovely spot by a little stream. I sat down and must have fallen asleep for a while because the next thing I knew, I heard someone calling for me. That nice boy, Robert, one of the under-gardeners, found me and walked me back to the house. That reminds me, could you ask someone to send for him so I can give him a small reward."

"A reward? Elizabeth, I was worried sick."

"Truly, you did not need to worry. I would have awakened very soon in any case and returned. It is not as if I had lost my way. Now may I pour you some tea?" she asked as sweetly as she could.

Instead of taking the tea she offered, Darcy walked over to a small cabinet and poured himself a brandy from one of the crystal decanters. He took a long swallow. "I know how important your walks are to you, but I am concerned about your safety, and this incident has only served to reinforce my fears. I would feel better if you would take someone with you on your excursions."

"I would feel better if I took my walks alone. I use the time to think and having someone with me would be an unwelcome intrusion on my privacy."

"Regardless, from now on you must have someone accompany you."

"Is that a request or an order?" she asked, sharply narrowing her eyes.

"I am afraid I must insist."

"I have always walked out alone," she said. "I cannot imagine asking one of the servants to follow me around all the time. It would be an imposition."

"On you or on the staff?"

"Both, I suppose."

"You are not imposing on anyone. It is their job to take care of Pemberley and our family. Many of these people have worked for the Darcy family since before I was born. In some cases, they are the second or third generation to be in service here. No one would think it strange if I asked someone to accompany you when I cannot go myself."

"Yes, but I think it strange and quite awkward. Would this person walk with me or just...just follow along behind?" said Elizabeth waving a hand in the air. "It all sounds so silly. Why is this necessary?"

"Elizabeth, you are no longer just the second daughter of Mr. Bennet of Longbourn. You are Mrs. Darcy, Mistress of Pemberley. Surely, you must expect some things to change," said Darcy with some irritation.

"Yes, some things must change," she replied, appreciating the irony. Although Elizabeth tried her best to keep her face passive, under the surface her emotions surged. She could not believe he was trying to take away what little freedom she had here. Lately, her walks had been almost her only joy other than the time she spent with Georgiana. As much as she tried to resign herself to accept that her life was not her own now, she still bristled at being so controlled. She thought about trying to talk to him about her objections to his giving orders, but decided it would take more energy than she had at the moment.

"Georgiana always takes one of the grooms along when she rides alone," he added.

She wanted to say that she was not Georgiana, but decided it was useless to argue. "Very well. If you will assign someone to go on longer walks with me, I will confine my solitary rambles to the gardens or at least stay within sight of the house. Would that be acceptable to you, sir?" she said, biting off her words sharply.

"Yes, that will be satisfactory," he said, still looking very uncomfortable. He took another large swallow of the brandy. When she did not respond, he added, "I am only thinking of your well-being."

While she had no choice but to acquiesce to Darcy's wishes, that did not mean she had to like it. Suddenly, being in his presence became unbearable. She knew if she stayed she would inevitably say something regrettable, so she set aside her needlework.

"If you will excuse me now, sir, I am going to my room to read."

"I will see you at supper then?" he asked.

"Actually, I am not very hungry. I think I will just ask for something to be sent to my room."

"You will join me later?" he asked, looking confused.

Suddenly, all the trials of the last few months finally caught up with her, and she found herself trembling from anger and frustration. Still she put on a proud face and answered in as steady a voice as she could. "Not this evening. I am going to finish my book and go to bed early. Please have whoever is going to walk with me ready early tomorrow morning."

"I will be happy to walk with you myself tomorrow."

"Whatever you wish. Good-evening, sir."

"Elizabeth, please, wait." She turned. His face, which had looked angry at first, softened when he saw her tears.

"Another handkerchief?" he asked, reaching in his pocket.

She shook her head. Somehow she just did not want to take anything from him right now.

"What is wrong?" he asked, reaching out to stop her from leaving.

"Please let me go," she said, looking at his hand on her arm. "I just need to be alone." For a moment, it seemed as if he would press her for more of an answer and a part of her almost hoped he would, but then he released her and looked away. As soon as she was free, Elizabeth retreated to her room.

The next morning they walked out, but being together felt awkward. Neither was willing to bring up their disagreement from the prior day, so their conversation was strained and uncomfortable. Darcy looked miserable. After going just a short distance, Elizabeth claimed fatigue and asked to return to the house. As they walked along, she thought about trying to speak with him about the furniture incident, but in the end, she kept silent. Talking about her wishes had not made any impression on him so far. She felt discouraged and confused.

As they passed near the stables, Darcy announced he was planning to purchase horse for her to ride—a small one as they had discussed before, but Elizabeth could not even bring herself to talk about it. She was not sure if it was truly because she was not interested in riding or if her resistance was just a way to exert some control over her life. He could restrict her walks, but he could not make her go riding if she did not wish to.

Later that afternoon she worked on her embroidery in the hope that keeping her hands busy would quiet her mind. There was a certain satisfaction in plunging her needle vigorously through the fabric with each stitch, and she finished a large section of her work without even realizing any time had passed.

When Georgiana joined her later, Elizabeth was certain her sister noticed the violent way she was stabbing the fabric, but Georgiana did not question her or even comment on Elizabeth's dark mood.

THIRTY THREE

Darcy found Elizabeth standing in front of one of the big windows that overlooked the lawns. It was raining, and her face reflected in the glass was as dark as the stormy sky. Lost in thought, she seemed unaware of his presence. He knew she was upset the rain had trapped her inside the house, but there was something else—she appeared trapped inside herself.

At first, when they arrived at Pemberley, she had seemed to brighten with all the new experiences. Everything appeared to be going so well as she settled into her new responsibilities. According to Mrs. Reynolds, she was learning quickly. Everyone loved her.

Recently this had all changed. Although she continued to insist nothing was wrong, she was neither sleeping nor eating properly. When Margaret noticed Mrs. Darcy seemed to be losing weight, she had gone to Mrs. Reynolds with her concerns. Of course, Mrs. Reynolds had come to him.

Elizabeth's unhappiness was evident, but he had no idea what to do to relieve her distress. Darcy was a man accustomed to being in charge. When he saw a problem, he analyzed it and found a way to fix it. Except maybe for being in crowded ballrooms, there was nothing he liked less than this helpless feeling. In some ways, this reminded him of when he had tried to care for Georgiana after Wickham's betrayal.

Just then the notes of a melancholy tune coming from down the hall caught his attention. Georgiana must be in the music room practicing. Why couldn't his sister choose something lighter and happier to practice he thought. If Elizabeth was feeling low, this music was certainly not helping.

Turning back, he watched Elizabeth thoughtfully. When it became obvious that the tears were starting to flow, he went to her. "You have forgotten your handkerchief again, Elizabeth. I fear it is becoming a habit."

She visibly tensed.

"I was only teasing. Whatever is on your mind?" he asked.

"I was hoping to go out for a walk today, but as you can see..." she said, gesturing toward the window. Her voice was so soft he could barely hear her.

"Surely, that is no reason for tears."

"I am fine."

"In spite of what you say, your actions tell a different story. Something is making you unhappy. Please tell me how to help you." When Darcy reached out and touched her shoulder, she pulled away as if his hand had burned her skin.

"You are very kind, sir, but I do not think there is anything you can do. Please excuse me. I feel a headache coming on and wish to go lie down." She left Darcy standing there with a hollow feeling in his chest.

Returning to his study, Darcy found it impossible to focus on his letters and paperwork. He did not want to let this go. Something was making her unhappy, but he had no idea what it could be. How could their relationship improve if she would not share even a little of herself with him? She said she wanted to be alone, but he suspected that might not be entirely true. Then he had an idea. Picking up his pen, he began a letter. Maybe there was something he could do to help her after all.

THIRTY FOUR

A week passed with no noticeable improvement in Elizabeth's mood. She tried to be cheerful, but she was mostly just going through the motions with little feeling or energy. Her moods were unpredictable, and she and Darcy had had words over a few small things that should have been nothing.

Elizabeth still felt the grief sharply over the loss of her father, and the letter from him she had found in the book only seemed to increase her pain rather than relieve it. Without Jane's companionship, all these concerns pressed heavily upon her. Each day was a struggle just to remain on her feet against the weight of it all.

�֍

As Elizabeth sat quietly in the family parlor one afternoon, she heard a carriage pull up in front of the house. A feeling of dread came over her as she wondered who it might be. First she heard footsteps in the hall, and then the door opened.

"Oh, Jane," she cried, jumping up from her chair. Running across the room, Elizabeth threw her arms around her sister. The two stood like that for a few minutes simply finding comfort in each other's presence. "Whatever are you doing here?"

"Lizzy, dear, do you mean Mr. Darcy did not tell you he wrote and invited me to visit?"

"He asked you to come to Pemberley? I had no idea." Elizabeth hugged her again.

"Where is Mr. Bingley? Has he come with you? I am sure he does not want to let you out of his sight for very long these days."

"Mr. Darcy arranged for my travel. Charles is in the north on an extended business trip. He's planning to stop here for a few days next week on his way back to London. Until then, you shall just have to keep me entertained."

Hearing Jane's soft laughter and seeing her reassuring smile made Elizabeth feel better than she had in months. Suddenly, Georgiana burst into the room. Seeing Elizabeth and Jane, she stopped herself and remembering to observe propriety, gave a small curtsey to greet their guest.

"I am so glad to see you, Jane. Welcome to Pemberley!"

"Did you know about this?" Elizabeth asked Georgiana.

"Of course, I knew. I have been bursting to tell you ever since I learned she was coming."

"Did anyone else know about Jane's visit?"

"Just Mrs. Reynolds and a few of the servants, I think. Margaret definitely knew. We had to tell them so they could see that everything was made ready in advance." Turning to Jane, she said, "We have planned the most wonderful room for you. It has a view of the lake and the woods. I know you will love it."

The young girl's face suddenly grew serious. "I hope you do not mind that William and I made plans without telling you. We thought that it would be fun to surprise you, but...you are pleased, are you not?"

"Georgiana," said Elizabeth putting her hand on her younger sister's arm, "I am delighted with your little surprise. I think spending time with my two favorite sisters is just what I need."

✾

Georgiana showed them to a spacious, beautifully decorated room that had, as promised, an amazing view. After a few minutes, Georgiana excused herself leaving the sisters alone to visit. Jane's trunk had already been delivered, and she immediately began to unpack her things.

"Please allow me to ring for one of the maids to do that for you," said Elizabeth.

"I have been packing and unpacking for myself all my life. It still makes me uneasy to be waited upon that way."

"I know what you mean. It is a strange feeling to have servants always nearby. Sometimes I feel as if I am never alone, and I am not quite accustomed to it yet. Darcy and Georgiana do not seem to notice it at all."

"I guess it is something I will have to learn to appreciate after Charles and I are married, but as that has not happened yet, I am quite content to unpack it myself," Jane said happily.

"I imagine that you must be anxious for the wedding. Has mother planned every detail yet?" They both laughed, knowing how their mother loved to plan and re-plan, creating as much drama as possible. Very quickly, the sisters fell into an easy banter exchanging information and gossip about their friends and family.

After a brief tour of the house including Elizabeth's impressive bedchamber, they retreated to her private sitting room to continue catching up on all the news from Longbourn and the neighborhood. Once settled, Elizabeth rang for some refreshments. Tea and gossip about Meryton and the family kept them occupied for more than an hour before the subject turned to the present.

"Lizzy, Pemberley is beyond anything I had expected. The grounds are so vast and the house is...well, I just do not know what to say about it that would be grand enough. How do you keep from getting lost with so many rooms?"

"It has taken me some time to learn my way around, but I have had excellent help from Mrs. Reynolds, our housekeeper.

She has been with the family since Mr. Darcy was about four years old. I could not manage without her."

"Tell me all about married life. Is it what you expected?"

Elizabeth hesitated as she tried to decide what to say. "There has been so much to learn, so much to adjust to," she said, keeping her eyes down as she spoke. "I fear I have been something of a disappointment to Mr. Darcy."

"What makes you say that? Has he said something unkind to you?"

"No, he has mostly been very patient and solicitous. I know it is not like me, but I have been feeling quite overwhelmed of late. I cannot seem to find my footing." What could she tell her sister about her relationship with Mr. Darcy? It was too complicated for her to understand herself let alone explain to someone else. Jane took her hand.

"Something is wrong, my dear Lizzy," said Jane stroking her hand gently.

Elizabeth did not know how to begin. She leaned back in her chair and looked up at the ceiling for a moment, hoping to keep back the tears that were forming. "Jane, I have tried very hard, but I am still quite unhappy and I feel guilty about saying so when I want for nothing. I know marrying Mr. Darcy was the right choice, but I still wonder sometimes what would have happened if I had found the courage to refuse him. I know it would have been hard on all of us, but I have to believe that our situation would eventually have improved."

"Surely, you are not sorry you married Mr. Darcy. He is a good and generous man, and he loves you very much."

"Some days I find that hard to believe," she said with a small sigh. "Although he tries, there are basic elements in his nature that will probably never change. One minute, he is warm and smiling and the next, he withdraws and grows cold. He is so inscrutable; I never know what he is thinking."

"Some people are more reserved than others. I think it is only natural," Jane assured her.

"He is a man accustomed to having his own way, to being in charge. Often when he speaks, it comes out as more of a command than a request. I have to admit that sometimes it makes me resist complying. I guess that is my own stubbornness coming out."

"Yes, you are nothing if not stubborn," Jane grinned.

Elizabeth went on to explain about the furniture and other countermanded orders, and how Darcy had restricted her walks. "Now that I hear myself, I realize how silly I sound. I have no reason to feel sorry for myself. Am I turning into Lydia?" she said with a laugh. Just having someone listen to her made Elizabeth feel enormously better.

"I hope having company here for a few weeks will not be too troublesome for you, Lizzy, but I have to admit that I was glad for a reason to get away from our mother for a while."

"It must be very bad indeed if you are having difficulties with her. You are the most patient person I know."

"I suppose it is only that I am anxious to be married. Waiting is proving more difficult than I had imagined it would be." Jane blushed shyly.

Elizabeth looked at her sister in amazement. "Jane, Mr. Bingley is not pressuring you for favors before marriage is he?"

"Oh, no, that is not it at all. He is a perfect gentleman. It is just that we love each other so much that it is difficult not to...express our affections," Jane said. The blush had now made it all the way from her neck up to her ears. "I am not very experienced in these matters and so I have nothing to guide me in knowing what is appropriate. Oh, Lizzy, this is so embarrassing to talk about, but since you are a married woman, I believe you must understand."

Elizabeth laughed to herself at the irony. She and Darcy were not intimate and while they had all the privacy of a married couple and all the opportunity, there was even less to their physical relationship than apparently there was to Jane and Bingley's.

Elizabeth took her sister's hand and squeezed it gently. "We may be married, but our relationship is still just as new as yours. The engagement period is a time to get to know each other better and to build the trust between you. Mr. Darcy and I have been forced to do that after the wedding. It has seemed a little backwards, and perhaps it is why we so often misunderstand each other. Ultimately, I would say to trust your own heart rather than listen to what anyone else says—including me."

Jane and Elizabeth hugged. As always they found reassurance in each other's company. Elizabeth was the happiest she had been in a long time and promised herself to thank Darcy properly for his thoughtfulness in bringing Jane to Pemberley to visit.

THIRTY FIVE

The following week Charles Bingley arrived. Elizabeth had to admit she was very glad he had come alone. She did not want Miss Bingley or the Hursts there to detract from the joy of spending time with her sister. She and Jane were in each other's company as much as possible. It did not seem to matter what they were doing as long as they were together. Bingley spent time out riding or closeted in the study with Darcy learning more about estate management. He and Jane also took the opportunity to go for walks in the garden by themselves. Although the Darcys acted as chaperones, they allowed the engaged couple had much more freedom than they had enjoyed back at home. Elizabeth noted with pleasure how Jane and Mr. Bingley had grown closer since she had last seen them.

While Georgiana was not accustomed to the kind of easy conversation that went on between sisters, she seemed to revel in it and spent as much time as she could with them. Elizabeth was certain she had never seen Georgiana happier—or more outspoken. The young girl's quiet, gentle nature was much more like Jane's than her own, and she seemed to be making Jane a model for herself.

With each day of her sister's visit, Elizabeth grew more and more at ease. She smiled more easily, laughed more often, and began to feel more like herself again. With Jane and Bingley in the house, even her conversations with Darcy had become a little less awkward. He also seemed to be friendlier and more open, and to Elizabeth's delight, he let his dry sense of humor show from time to time.

❈

One night after a particularly enjoyable dinner and an evening of conversation with Bingley and Jane, Elizabeth joined Darcy in their sitting room for a little while before going to bed. Buoyed by the good feelings created from having her sister near, Elizabeth resolved to thank Darcy again for inviting Jane and Bingley to Pemberley.

"I would like to thank you again for arranging for Jane and Mr. Bingley to visit. Having my sister here means so much to me."

Darcy looked up from his reading. "It is thanks enough for me to see you smiling more often."

"I apologize for my recent behavior and for making you worry about me. How did you know a visit with my sister was exactly what I needed?"

Darcy set his book aside and smiled at her warmly. "You give me too much credit. The truth is that I did not know what else to do. It pained me to see you so silent and withdrawn. I thought if you would not confide your worries to me, perhaps Jane might be of comfort."

"Jane always makes me feel better."

"What would you think of asking them if they would consider being married in London in the fall and allowing us to host their wedding breakfast? It would mean that most of your friends from Hertfordshire would not be able to attend, but it would give your mother and sisters an opportunity to visit London and shop there. I believe Bingley has plans for them to travel after the wedding for while, and by the time they have returned from their honeymoon trip, they could return comfortably to Netherfield to greet friends there."

Elizabeth was astonished at his suggestion. "What a wonderful idea! I can think of nothing I would enjoy more," she said. Then she bit her lip in thought for a moment. "Of course, it would mean having my mother and sisters stay with us for several weeks. Are you sure you are prepared for that?" she asked.

"If it would make you happy, I would endure it gladly."

"I will ask Aunt Gardiner to have Mother and Lydia stay with them, and we could have Jane, Kitty and Mary at our house."

"Before you proceed too far along in your plans, you might want to ask your sister and Bingley what they think about this idea," he remarked with a laugh.

"I think Jane will be very pleased," she said. "Thank you for making such an excellent suggestion and also for your generosity."

"Surely, you know I would do anything to make you happy, Elizabeth," he said, looking at her intently.

Elizabeth's heart stuck in her throat. Hoping to avoid Darcy seeing her emotional state, she set aside her book and said goodnight. As she was walking past him on the way to her room, she gave him a quick kiss on the cheek.

❋

Darcy was left alone wondering at the mystery that was his wife. She had given him credit for understanding her moods enough to know that she needed to see Jane, but in fact, inviting her sister was an act of desperation on his part. He actually did not understand Elizabeth at all.

When they were first married, she had often let him hold her to offer comfort, and she had seemed to enjoy it. When they came to Pemberley, things seemed to be going well at first, but then something had changed. She had grown distant and cool toward him. Having her so close and yet so far away was becoming harder and harder to bear. Daily he struggled with his resolve to wait until she showed some sign of real affection. He wondered if she had any idea of how she tortured him. A few days ago, it had all seemed futile, but now his heart began to hope again.

THIRTY SIX

When Jane and Bingley heard Darcy's idea of hosting their wedding in London, they were very pleased. After that, the two couples talked of it frequently. Elizabeth and Jane concluded they should write to their mother and inform her of the change in plans. This would give Mrs. Bennet some time to become accustomed to the idea before Jane returned home. They both suspected that her excitement at the idea of being in London would offset any disappointment she might feel at not being able to plan everything herself. Their letter had no sooner been sent than they received a post from their mother. The two must have crossed on the road.

"Would you like me to read it aloud?" asked Jane.

"Yes, of course," Elizabeth replied.

Dearest Daughters,

I suppose you are both having such a jolly time at Pemberley that you are not even thinking about your poor mother and sisters here in Meryton. We are managing to keep ourselves occupied although we are not able to enjoy the society of our friends and neighbors as much as we would like. There have been several small dinners at your Aunt Phillips' house to keep us entertained but that is all.

I have been suffering so with having to endure complaints from Kitty and my poor Lydia about how tired they are of wearing black and not being able to go dancing or have any fun. They are quite wearing me down.

"Oh, yes," said Elizabeth, "I can just hear those two now."

Jane, dear, could you ask Lizzy if she has anything to spare for her poor family. We are running a bit short this month. I certainly could use some cheering up. Perhaps we could come visit her at Pemberley. I think that would do us all up quite nicely.
Your Loving Mother

"I cannot believe she has asked for more money. She has been so extravagant in fixing up the new house that she must have gone through most of her allowance for the next few months," said Jane refolding the letter and setting it aside.

"Mother asks me to send money to her with every letter. First, it was new curtains, and then the girls just had to have some new dresses. She thinks because I am married to Mr. Darcy she is entitled to spend extravagantly and he should pay."

"I think she is just feeling sad because she misses Father. After all, she is on her own now with no one to guide her. We are her only protection," said Jane.

"She hardly paid any heed to Father when he was alive. Why is now any different?" Just thinking about her mother caused irritation.

"Oh, Lizzy, we must be more patient with her. She is doing the best she can," Jane told her.

Elizabeth felt a little ashamed of herself for speaking so harshly of her mother. "Of course, as always, Jane, you are right. I will try to be more patient. Now let me find some paper and pens and we will write to her. I have to find a way to break it to her gently that this would not be an appropriate time for her to visit Pemberley."

As she held her pen over the clean white sheet to begin her letter, Elizabeth thought about how ironic it was that she had just promised to be more patient with her mother—almost the same thing she had asked Darcy to do only a few months ago.

✻

A few days later, Jane and Elizabeth sat together working on their sewing projects. It was still early in the day and the light was very good. Although sewing was not Elizabeth's favorite pastime, she was happy to be making some baby clothes to send to Charlotte who was anxiously awaiting the birth of her first child in the late fall.

"Soon we shall be making baby clothes for you, Lizzy," said Jane.

Elizabeth's hand slipped and she pricked herself. Putting her finger in her mouth to keep from bleeding on the fabric, she had to look away so that Jane would not see her face.

"Lizzy? You are not with child already, are you?" asked Jane, her face brightening.

"No, I was just thinking about how much I would like to have one, though. It would keep me occupied. I feel as if I have too much time on my hands here."

"You have always enjoyed your walks and reading. Now you have as much time as you wish for those pursuits," said Jane.

"Yes, but I do not feel useful at all."

"Have you made the acquaintance any of your neighbors?"

"I have met a few people at Sunday services, but it is difficult to make friends. We have attended a few small dinners, but since we are still officially in mourning, I am not able to entertain. I do not mean to complain, but sometimes I should like a little more society and amusement," she said. After pausing for a moment, she added with a laugh, "I cannot believe I said that. I sound like Lydia again!"

Just then, they heard the noise of boots in the hallway, and Darcy and Bingley appeared. They seemed to fill the room with a kind of restless energy.

"Jane, my angel, I have missed you!" said Bingley as he kissed her hand.

"Charles, you have only been away for a few hours," said Jane blushing.

"It seemed much longer than that to me," he said, beaming at her.

"What have you two been doing this morning?" asked Elizabeth looking at the gentlemen.

"We have been riding. It never fails to astonish me how large Pemberley is and what variety it has. There are streams and lakes, fields and woods, and it is all so lovely. I would like to see Netherfield grow to be more like this," said Bingley.

"Just a few minutes ago you were talking about quitting Netherfield and finding a place in Derbyshire closer to Pemberley," said Darcy.

"Charles, is that true? Are you really thinking about finding a house nearby for us?" asked Jane. Her eyes were bright with excitement.

"It would be so wonderful to have you both closer," added Elizabeth.

"What do you think? Would you like to be nearer your sister?" Bingley asked.

"It would make me very happy indeed," said Jane with a glowing smile.

Elizabeth was sure she could see Bingley's heart melt before her eyes at Jane's attentions.

"If you are serious, Bingley, I will begin looking around in the area," said Darcy. "If there is nothing available now, maybe something will come up in the near future."

Elizabeth rejoiced. Suddenly, the future seemed brighter indeed as she imagined frequent visits, pleasant holidays and raising their children together.

Bingley suggested a walk and the four of them set out. Soon Bingley and Jane fell behind, and Darcy and Elizabeth moved ahead in order to give the couple some time alone.

"Your sister and Bingley are very well suited to each other. It was very wrong of me to separate them last fall. I am sorry that my actions caused them pain," Darcy said as they walked along together.

"You have apologized several times before, but I am glad to hear you still agree. He is a kind and generous man. Jane is a very fortunate woman indeed."

"Ah, I think that Bingley is the one who is fortunate. Most of people I know have not been so lucky in finding wives as sweet-tempered as your sister," Darcy responded.

"She is all that is good. Of course, it does not hurt that she is also beautiful."

Darcy glanced down at her. He put his hand over hers as it rested on his arm. "Jane is beautiful in the classical sense, but I happen to prefer your type of beauty. I never tire of looking at you," he said quietly.

Elizabeth was taken completely by surprise. Darcy had never told her that he thought she was beautiful. In fact, he rarely said anything at all about her appearance. She blushed and glanced away at the ground. "I thank you, sir."

"Surely, you are not unaccustomed to receiving compliments."

"You caught me unawares. I cannot recall your ever saying anything like that to me before."

"I have not been certain how my compliments might be received."

"What makes you think I would not appreciate hearing of your admiration?"

"Most women like to hear nice things about themselves, but I have discovered that you are not like most women."

"Your compliments, sir, are most welcome," she said, drawing closer to him. When she looked up, she saw that he was staring at her, his eyes like deep green water.

THIRTY SEVEN

After about a week, Bingley was called away to see to some of his business affairs. Although Jane stayed on for another week, all too soon it was time for her to return to Meryton. After she left, Elizabeth felt her sister's absence greatly but resolved to find some new and useful occupation for herself.

Darcy was obliged to be away for several days on business of the estate, leaving Elizabeth on her own. To her surprise she actually missed his company. Although she and Georgiana spent a good portion of their time together, the young girl had her own routines at Pemberley. Frequently, Georgiana went riding or visited a few old friends who lived nearby. Usually, this was not a problem for Elizabeth but on some days, she felt adrift. With so much time on her hands, Elizabeth thought she should be doing something more productive than just reading, practicing pianoforte, and sewing.

After some thought, she decided to focus her energies on the management of the house. Since she was a quick study, Elizabeth already had a firm grasp of what kept the house humming. With that in hand, she resolved to pay more attention to the finances. The amount of money it took to maintain Pemberley was shocking. One morning as she was reviewing household accounts with Mrs. Reynolds, she noticed something in the ledger that puzzled her.

"Mrs. Reynolds, what is this entry for?" she asked, pointing to a line in the account book.

"That is for baskets for the tenants and families in the area. We put in food, soap, and little necessities. It has been a Pemberley tradition for many years."

"How often do we do this?"

"It varies, but there is a little something for each family about every other month or so. Some families depend heavily upon these gifts to sustain them."

Elizabeth was not unfamiliar with this practice by landlords, but the amount spent at Longbourn was very small compared to the number she was looking at here. "Who makes up these baskets and how are they distributed?"

"I have been in charge of this with help from Lucy, one of the kitchen staff, ever since Lady Anne's health made it impossible for her to continue. One of the footmen has been making the deliveries," Mrs. Reynolds told her. "It was one of the mistress's favorite activities, especially at the holidays. With Lady Anne gone and Georgiana so young, Mr. Darcy's father asked me to see that it was taken care of, and I have continued ever since."

"So this was directly overseen by Lady Anne?"

Mrs. Reynolds nodded.

"If you would show me what needs to be done, I would very much like to help."

Mrs. Reynolds went on to explain how the baskets were made up, who received them and when. As she listened to all the details, she was again struck by the amount of time and money that went into this practice. Elizabeth was thrilled to have found something useful to do with her time. She could only practice pianoforte and do embroidery for so long—neither of these had ever been among her favorite activities anyway. Managing the house and staff was time consuming, but much of that remained in Mrs. Reynolds' capable hands. This meant Elizabeth was free to devote more of her energies to arranging for the baskets and making deliveries. She knew from her experiences at Longbourn that tenants usually enjoyed it when the master's family was directly involved.

First, Elizabeth learned as much as she could about the families on the estate, the number of children they had and their economic stability. Talking to people, drawing them out— this was something that would make the best use of her natural talents. She spent many hours with Mrs. Reynolds, Lucy, Margaret, and others familiarizing herself with each of the families and their needs.

When Darcy returned after a few days, she was glad to see him, but her mind was preoccupied with planning her charity work. Elizabeth never mentioned her intentions to Darcy although she was not certain why she was reluctant to talk with him about it. After only a week, she felt ready to begin although she still had a few concerns to discuss with Mrs. Reynolds.

"I am sure these families will not welcome being surprised by me when I call," said Elizabeth. "Is there an appropriate way to let them know in advance that I will be coming?"

"I do not think that will be a problem, Mrs. Darcy. They probably knew which families you would call on within an hour of your making the decision yesterday. There are very few secrets here. Someone on the staff certainly knows the family or one of their neighbors. Rumors both good and bad spread here very quickly."

Elizabeth smiled.

"I have arranged for Hardy and Jameson to accompany you today. They will take excellent care of you."

"Mrs. Reynolds, I truly do not know what I would do without you. You are simply indispensable."

"I am only doing my job, Mrs. Darcy."

Elizabeth reached over and put her hand on Mrs. Reynolds' arm. "Then you do it very, very well. Thank you for taking such good care of me."

The housekeeper, who rarely showed any signs of being

ruffled no matter what the situation, blushed with pleasure at Elizabeth's words of praise. "If you do not mind my saying so, Mrs. Darcy, I am very glad that Mr. Darcy had the good sense to marry you."

Now it was Elizabeth's turn to glow a rosy pink.

✖

Elizabeth's first call was the Coopers. Mr. Cooper was not in good health, and his oldest sons at ages twelve and thirteen were barely old enough to take up their father's responsibilities. There was also an older daughter who was probably fourteen or fifteen plus two younger children ages four and eight. All of them worked in some way to help sustain the family.

Elizabeth had learned that the Coopers like many farm families were very proud, so she took a basket that contained no more than what they usually received. The difference was that this time the mistress herself would be making the delivery.

Upon arriving at the Cooper's small cottage, Elizabeth found Mrs. Cooper hanging laundry assisted by two of her daughters. When she saw Elizabeth, she wiped her hands on her apron, patted her hair into place, and rushed over to greet her. The two girls followed. The younger one peered out at Elizabeth from behind her mother's skirts.

"Good afternoon, Mrs. Cooper."

"Good afternoon, Mrs. Darcy. You do our family a great honor by visitin' us. This is my eldest, Cathy." Cathy gave a quick curtsey.

"And who is this young lady?" Elizabeth inquired, indicating the little girl who continued to hide her face in her mother's skirts.

Mrs. Cooper smiled proudly. "This is Janie, ma'am, my youngest."

Elizabeth bent down to Janie's level. "I have a very dear sister who shares your name." Janie smiled but hid her face again.

"Would you like a sweet?" Elizabeth asked, reaching out to offer a treat to the little girl. A small hand appeared from behind her mother's skirts and snatched it away.

"Now what do you say, Luv?" asked Mrs. Cooper.

A very small voice muffled by fabric answered, "Thank you, ma'am."

Elizabeth was touched that even in the midst of poverty, this woman concerned herself with her children's manners. Mrs. Cooper offered best wishes on the Darcy's marriage and also expressed her condolences on the loss of Elizabeth's father. Mrs. Reynolds had been correct that very little went unnoticed on the estate, especially when it had to do with the great house. While the two women talked—mainly about the other Cooper children—one of the footmen took the basket into the house.

Mrs. Cooper asked after Mr. Darcy's health. Elizabeth returned by inquiring about Mr. Cooper and learned he was improving slowly. Elizabeth could see that in spite of their apparent troubles, she was a cheerful woman with a wonderful smile. Elizabeth thought she should take a lesson from her. How could she dare feel sorry for herself when she had so much and this woman so little?

"I should not keep you from your work any longer, Mrs. Cooper. It has been very nice to meet all of you," said Elizabeth meaning it sincerely.

"We thank you for your generosity, Mrs. Darcy," said Mrs. Cooper. "Maybe next time you can stay for some tea."

"I would like that very much," said Elizabeth even though she suspected that sitting down together for tea was something that would never really happen.

※

Elizabeth's other calls that day were very much the same. At the next house, she talked with Mrs. Lee—barely more than a girl—who was expecting her first child. In spite of her condition, the young woman was doing all the heavy chores by herself. When Elizabeth asked her if she should not be more careful, she shrugged her shoulders as if to say who else would do it.

All of the women and children Elizabeth met knew immediately who she was and greeted her with warmth and respect. After reporting on her day to Mrs. Reynolds, Elizabeth realized making these calls had helped more to make her feel a part of Pemberley than anything she had done since her arrival a few months ago. Then she began to think about what she could do to help the Lees. Perhaps she could sew some baby clothes or a blanket.

Thinking about Mrs. Lee and the child she was expecting, Elizabeth began to wish that she too would be so blessed. She was still puzzled that Darcy had not come to her room at night. This was not what she had expected would happen. When they were first married, he used to put his arms around her and kiss her. At first, she had been reluctant, but now because of her loneliness she almost wished for that kind of closeness with him. Perhaps it would help her to feel more at ease in her new life if she had a child to occupy her thoughts. Until such time as that happened, she would have to be content with her work on the estate and in the parish.

THIRTY EIGHT

"How do you do it?" asked Georgiana one day when she and Elizabeth reached the end of the piece they had been practicing.

"Do what, my dear?"

"Play with so much...so much feeling! The music seems to flow through you. I watch you and listen, but I just cannot do it. You seem to have the gift of finding the heart of the music," said Georgiana.

"Thank you, but your praise is undeserved."

"Oh, but it is. I may have better technical skills, my fingering may be smoother, but your playing has something more than that. My teacher has always said that what I lacked was passion. I never really knew what he meant until now."

"Georgiana, you give me too much credit. I do not play nearly as well as you," said Elizabeth.

"Tell me how you do it."

"Well, I hardly know."

"What do you think about when you play and sing?"

Elizabeth thought for a moment. "It is easier when the song has words. Then I think about what the words are saying and try to imagine they are my own. I am just telling the story."

"But what if it is not about something you have experienced yourself?"

"Usually, I try to relate it to something I do know about."

"So if it is a song about love and I have never been in love..."

"Yes, but you do know something of love. Just imagine that the song is about the love you have for someone such as your brother or a friend—or maybe your horse?" Georgiana giggled.

"I know it is not quite the same, but often it helps you to relate to the words."

"And if there are no words?"

Elizabeth thought for a moment. No one had ever asked her this before. "Then I guess I make up a story that seems to fit the music."

"A story?" asked Georgiana wrinkling her brow in thought.

"Well, all music has a mood. It may be light and happy, powerful and strong, or sad and mournful, for example. I imagine what the composer might have been thinking about when he wrote it. A happy tune with lots of fast notes could be about a joyful event. Do you see what I mean?" asked Elizabeth.

"I think I am beginning to understand. You have explained it much more clearly than my music teacher ever did. All he could do was tell me what I was lacking. He could not tell me what to do to find it."

"I am very glad if this has helped you."

"More than you know, Elizabeth," said Georgiana. And then she shyly added, "May I give you a hug?"

"My dear sister, you never have to ask permission for that. I always welcome a hug from you."

After their conversation about playing with more feeling, Georgiana's music began to take on a new energy that had not been there before. Even Darcy noticed the difference. When he commented upon it, Elizabeth took no credit but simply said that she too had noticed the change and was delighted.

THIRTY NINE

When Darcy offered again to teach Elizabeth to ride, she was still hesitant. Although she had ridden occasionally as a girl at Longbourn, she generally preferred the security of keeping her feet on the ground. Walking had served her well for many years, and she saw no reason to change. Finally, Elizabeth's desire to get out and see more of the beautiful scenery in the area won out over her reluctance, and she agreed to give it a try.

The day after Darcy returned from an overnight trip to Matlock, he asked her to come out to the stable with him as he had something to show her. Remembering her resolve to think more of his happiness, she agreed. She was rewarded when she saw how pleased he seemed at this small concession from her.

As they walked to the stable, Darcy explained he had found a mare for her that was already very well trained and quite gentle. Inside one of the stalls munching on some hay was a beautiful little black horse with a white blaze on her forehead. "Her name is Sonnet."

"Sonnet?" Elizabeth looked at him in disbelief. "What an unusual name."

"If it does not suit, you may change it."

"No, I like it," she said thoughtfully.

Darcy produced an apple from his pocket and cut it into sections. Elizabeth fed the little horse as she stroked her head and talked to her softly.

"So would you like your first riding lesson tomorrow?" he asked. "Perhaps you might borrow some appropriate clothing from Georgiana until you can have something made up for yourself."

"Oh, my, you have brought me a horse who does not come equipped with riding clothes? Perhaps I should send her back," said Elizabeth with a twinkle in her eye. The smile she received in return made her efforts worthwhile.

Elizabeth thought Darcy would have one of the men who work in the stables teach her, but he insisted on supervising her lessons himself. The time she spent with him turned out to be quite enjoyable. Darcy was knowledgeable not only about horses but also about how best to introduce her to riding. In his teaching, he never tried to rush her or make her do something she did not feel ready for. His constant encouragement helped her confidence to grow more quickly than it otherwise might have. Several times, she almost gave up the whole project, but for some reason, she felt reluctant to disappoint him so she gathered up her courage and continued. Sonnet was sweet and docile just as Darcy had promised and after only a few weeks of daily practice, Elizabeth began to feel comfortable enough to undertake a longer ride.

�֍

One evening over dinner, Darcy announced he had planned a short excursion for them the next morning to one of his favorite places in the estate. It was a little less than an hour each way, and he was certain her riding skills had progressed enough for this short journey. He had already taken the liberty of arranging with Mrs. Reynolds to have a small picnic made up to take with them. When he explained his plans, Elizabeth was intrigued that he would go to such lengths to try to please her.

The next morning the weather was perfect. A few fluffy

clouds floated along on a sea of clear blue sky. The sun was warm but not too hot. Elizabeth had ridden enough now that she knew most of Sonnet's moods, and the little horse seemed to sense she was going to have the opportunity to stretch her legs a bit more than usual. The journey was an easy one, but by the time they finally reached their destination, Elizabeth was ready for a rest. Darcy tied their horses under a stand of trees near the river.

"This has always been one of my favorite places," he said as he helped her down. "I came here often with my mother when I was very young. The water is fairly shallow and the current not too strong, so it's the perfect place for a swim on a hot day."

Elizabeth was flattered he had chosen to share this special place with her. Walking along the edge of the river, Elizabeth wished she could cool her feet in the water but was unsure what Darcy's reaction would be to such informality. Deciding she did not need his permission to enjoy herself, she sat down on a rock and began to take off her boots. Although she could feel his eyes on her, he made no comment while she tried not to notice he was watching her every move. After removing her boots and stockings, she padded barefoot over to the bank of the river. Lifting her skirts just enough to keep them from getting wet, she walked into the water up to her ankles.

"This feels lovely," she said, searching Darcy's face for an indication of what he was thinking. "You should join me."

"I would very much like that, but these boots are impossible for me to remove without help," he said.

"I can do that if you wish. I used to help my father from time to time." The first one came off quite easily but in the process of removing the second, Elizabeth lost her balance and sat down abruptly on the ground. Then she began to laugh.

"Are you injured?" he asked, looking very serious as he reached out to help her up.

"I am fine," she said, still laughing. "Do you think I am so fragile that a little tumble like that would hurt me?"

"Well, I..." he stammered.

Once she was standing, he continued to hold her hand. They stood there for a moment looking at each other before she spoke. "I will need my hand back now, if you do not mind?" she told him gently.

Although he looked away, she could tell that he was blushing. Hiking up her skirt, she waded back in. Tentatively, he followed her into the water until it was just over his ankles. He pretended to be preoccupied with something in the water, but she sensed his eyes following her.

"Shall I tell you a secret that will quite scandalize you?" she offered and without waiting for a response she continued, "When I was younger, I used to climb trees!"

"Somehow, that does not surprise me," he said, following her farther out into the shallow water.

"I spent many hours up in the trees at Longbourn. I would even take a book and read on occasion when I wanted to avoid my mother for a few hours. Once I fell asleep up in a tree. Unfortunately, when I dozed off, I fell out."

"Were you hurt?"

"Only my pride. I have never told anyone that story before. Now I have shared one of my deepest, darkest secrets," she teased, "so you must tell me one of yours." Darcy hesitated for a moment and sensing his reluctance, she prodded. "Come now, Mr. Darcy. I know you must have some secrets."

"Very well, when I was a boy, my cousin Richard and I would often come to this spot in the summer, throw off our clothes, and go for a swim."

"How shocking!" she said, feigning horror at his admission. "Knowing your sense of propriety, I imagine this was his idea."

"Actually, I believe it was mine. Does that surprise you?"

"Yes, but then your actions often surprise me," she responded, her eyes bright with mischief.

"I am starting to like this game. Please tell me another secret," he asked.

"Very well. Yours was actually the third proposal of marriage I had received in my life, but the first I accepted. You know about Mr. Collins, of course, but I had another proposal even before that from a boy who lived in Meryton."

"Oh, really?"

"He was a very handsome lad, and quite charming, too." Darcy frowned but said nothing. After a brief silence, she decided to stop tormenting him.

"Did I mention that we were both seven years old at the time?" she said, putting her hand to her mouth to try and suppress a giggle.

"I think you did omit that detail in the telling," he said, looking clearly relieved.

"He was the son of a man who worked for my uncle in Meryton."

"So you have had some practice with proposals."

Elizabeth smiled at his retort and kicked up some water in his direction with her foot as her reply.

"My proposal to you was my first, as you probably already know," said Darcy, suddenly more serious. "I had planned to ask you that evening at the parsonage, but when I arrived, it was clear that it would not have been appropriate." The silence between them was filled with the sound of the water bubbling over some nearby rocks.

"I was so embarrassed that you found me in such a state, but you were very kind," she said, evading his implied question. "That was the first time you had to dry my tears with one of your handkerchiefs."

"The first of many." He smiled.

"I think I have cried more in the past few months than in my whole life before put together," she said.

"There is no need to explain yourself. This has been a difficult time."

"I just would not want you to think that being constantly in tears is in my nature," she said.

"And what would you say is your nature—generally?" he asked.

Elizabeth considered her words before responding. "I would have to say that I am usually quite happy. I enjoy people and take great delight in the ironies I observe in life. I also believe laughter is an essential part of my happiness. And you, Mr. Darcy?"

"I believe you once told me you thought I had an 'unsocial and taciturn' disposition."

Elizabeth shook her head slowly. "I may have been mistaken in that. You are quiet and prone to stand apart from the crowd, although I believe you enjoy a lively conversation with people you know well. I noticed when Jane and Mr. Bingley were visiting, you talked more than usual."

"I very much enjoyed our visit from Bingley and Jane. I look forward to spending time with them again. Now I am hungry. Shall we see what Cook has packed?" he said.

They spread a blanket under a tree and brought out their picnic. It was a simple affair—bread, cheese, some fruit and biscuits, and two small bottles of cider. Although Darcy had instructed the kitchen staff not to fuss, Cook had been unable to resist adding some tiny cakes to the basket. They sat together comfortably and talked mainly about horses as they ate. She had found that horses was one of the topics on which he would speak at length without much encouragement, and she took advantage of this as often as she could. As a result, she was learning much more about those creatures than she had ever thought possible. As they finished their meal, he slipped out of his coat, which he folded into a tidy bundle and placed under his head for a pillow as he lay back to look up at the sky. This kind of informality was not what she had expected as he rarely even loosed his neck cloth in her presence—let alone removed his coat.

"When I was a child, I used to play a game of trying to figure out what the clouds looked like—a dragon, a horse, a castle. Did you ever do that with your sisters?" he asked.

"Yes, but I believe we saw far different things. We imagined fairies and handsome princes."

"Look up there," he said, pointing to a large cloud overhead. "That one definitely resembles a face."

"Where?" she asked, shading her eyes to look.

"Nearly right above us. You would be able to see better if you were reclining. Here use my coat for your head."

Elizabeth hesitated, a little uncomfortable with the idea, but finally she accepted his offer. "Now where is that face?"

Darcy pointed to a jagged cloud, and she was forced to agree that it did resemble a man with a beard. They looked for other shapes for a while, and then Elizabeth sat up, pulled her knees up to her chin, and wrapped her arms around her legs. "Thank you for bringing me here and sharing this place."

Darcy looked dreamily at the sky. "*In solitude What happiness? Who can enjoy alone, Or all enjoying, what contentment find?*" He turned on his side to face her and rose up on one elbow.

"Milton?" she asked.

"Yes, *Paradise Lost* just before God creates Eve to be Adam's companion."

Elizabeth glanced at Darcy and saw he was looking at her with his unreadable half smile—just a slight curling upward of his mouth as in his portrait in the gallery. She met his gaze for a moment and then looked away pretending to watch the river.

"I am sorry if I said something to displease you, Elizabeth."

"You have nothing to apologize for, but I do think it is time for us to start back," she said as she began putting her stockings and boots back on. "We have a long ride ahead of us, and we have lingered here much longer than we had planned. Georgiana will be looking for us to return. We would not want someone to send out a search party for us." As soon as the words were out of her mouth, Elizabeth flushed. If Darcy noticed her discomfort, he generously did not mention it.

Reaching for his boots, he tugged them on while Elizabeth packed up the debris of their picnic. Then she shook out the blanket they had been using and began to fold it up. It was much too large for her to manage alone, and she struggled for a while before asking for help.

"Would you help me fold the blanket, please?"

"Of course. Tell me what you wish me to do."

Elizabeth looked at him somewhat puzzled. Then it occurred to her he was not accustomed to doing mundane chores like this for himself. There was always a servant around to take care of the details. "You have never shared folding a blanket with someone, have you?" she asked. He shook his head.

"Then what have you done before when you've been out on a picnic?" Darcy merely shrugged his shoulders. "Very well, I shall teach you." As she directed him in what to do, he seemed to be watching her more than the blanket and on the last fold, they each thought the other was going to grasp it, and so it fell back on the ground.

"I believe, sir, you need to learn to follow directions better!"

"No, madam, I think you must be clearer giving the instructions," he responded with mock seriousness, and so they began again. This time, they were able to complete the folding, and while Darcy was packing it away, Elizabeth stood stroking Sonnet's nose as she waited for him to help her up into the saddle.

"I think you have become fond of her," he said.

"She is a sweet creature."

When Darcy put his hands on her waist to lift her up, Elizabeth felt him hesitate. Looking up into his face, she saw such desire in his eyes that she was almost paralyzed. Suddenly, Darcy pulled her to him. Turning her head against his chest, she could hear the pounding of his heart and the raggedness of his breathing. Without thinking, she put her arms around him. His reaction was an audible exhale. Elizabeth relaxed and leaned into him enjoying the sensation of being so close. He smelled of his usual spicy scent, but there were also other smells of horse and sweat mixed in today. It made her almost light-headed.

Darcy bent down and with his lips brushing her hair, repeated her name softly several times. The feel of his breath on her ear sent a chill down the length of her spine. When he began to kiss the sensitive skin on her neck, she heard herself sigh with pleasure at these new sensations.

As he held her, she could feel his hand gently stroking her back. Taking her chin in his hand, he slowly lifted her face and brought his lips to hers. It was a quick, sweet kiss that was immediately followed by a much longer one. It was as if he had tasted her lips and finding them delicious decided to go back for more.

This second kiss was something quite different. Elizabeth experienced a moment of panic at the rush of sensations coursing through her, but she stopped herself from pulling away. He had done so many kindnesses for her over the months of their marriage; certainly she could try to please him by responding to his attentions. It was, after all, proving to be quite pleasurable. Reaching up, she put both arms around his neck. As her knees grew weak and unsteady, any thoughts of irritation about their various disagreements were pushed aside as passion washed over her.

Suddenly, Darcy released her. It all happened so fast that she almost lost her balance. To keep herself from toppling over, she was forced to reach out to Sonnet to steady herself. Darcy walked a few paces away and stood with his back to her. They were both breathing heavily.

Without thinking she heard herself blurt out, "Have I done something wrong?"

Turning back to her, he shook his head. His face, which had been filled with passion only moments before, was now once again under tight control. "I think we should be on our way home now. It is late, and we still have a long ride."

This time when he lifted her up onto Sonnet, he did not look her in the eye. As he walked to his own horse, she watched his back admiring his tall figure and broad shoulders. Her heart continued to race as she asked herself why he had pulled away so abruptly. She began to wonder if she would ever understand him. Darcy had brought her to a place that was obviously special to him, had played in the water with her, and shared a few secrets. He had kissed her passionately, but then the door had slammed shut. Since she had little experience with this, she was very confused. Finally, her confusion began to turn to irritation.

She knew she was finding him increasingly attractive and could no longer deny the power he was beginning to have over her physically. Responding to his kisses was much easier and much more thrilling than she thought it would be. What was happening to her? Elizabeth shook her head to clear out the conflicting thoughts and tried to focus on guiding Sonnet along the path back to Pemberley.

✖

As they rode along, Darcy was furious with himself for nearly going too far. He had been just about to slide his hands down to her hips and pull her closer against him when he recovered his sanity. She was much too tempting—the way she felt, the way she smelled. It was making him crazy. Whenever he was near her, he ached to hold her. What kind of irony was it that the one person with whom he must always be in control was also the one person most likely to make him lose it?

Elizabeth had seemed responsive to his kisses, but then he began to wonder if she was really acting out of love or merely fulfilling the obligation she felt as his wife. While he was exploring his confusion, he nearly hit his head on a branch that was hanging low over the path. Chastising himself for being so careless, he resolved to pay closer attention to where he was going.

FORTY

"We have been invited to Matlock for a visit," announced Darcy reading from a letter he had received from his aunt and uncle, Lord and Lady Matlock.

Elizabeth looked up from her sewing. She had been feeling a lack of society since Jane and Mr. Bingley had left so she was pleased with the idea of meeting another part of Darcy's family—one that might be more welcoming to her than Lady Catherine.

"Of course, if you do not wish to go now, I am sure they would understand," Darcy added.

"I am in favor of accepting their invitation. I would very much like to meet them."

"Excellent! I shall write immediately to make arrangements."

"So may I assume that your aunt and uncle are not of the same mind as Lady Catherine when it comes to our marriage?" Elizabeth asked.

"I think you will find that my uncle could not be more different. If you liked Colonel Fitzwilliam, you will most certainly like his parents. My cousin has his mother's sense of humor."

Letters were exchanged, plans were made and within a fortnight, the Darcys set off for Matlock. Elizabeth was pleased to learn that Colonel Fitzwilliam had been able to arrange a short leave from his regiment in order to join them for a few days. After enjoying many lively discussions with him when they were in Kent, she was looking forward to being in his company again.

✂

Elizabeth suffered from nervous anticipation before their trip but almost immediately after arriving, she discovered that she sincerely enjoyed the company of her new relations. Lord and Lady Matlock were people of refinement, but they were almost wholly lacking the sense of extreme self-importance that Lady Catherine had in such abundance. Although Lord Matlock was clearly a man accustomed to having the world arranged to please him, he still seemed to treat people at all levels of the social stratum with a respect and concern. Elizabeth had observed over the years that you could tell much about people by the way they treated their servants. In a very short time, she was able to observe that both Lord Matlock and Lady Matlock showed consideration toward everyone in their household. Elizabeth warmed to them almost immediately.

Although she was certain that while her new relations must be curious about her, they did not ask embarrassing questions or probe her for information that first evening. Instead, they did all they could to make her feel welcome. Colonel Fitzwilliam, who had arrived the day before, was in fine form and kept them all laughing with tales of his adventures training new recruits. Fitzwilliam's elder brother Viscount Bentley proved to be as pleasant and unaffected as his parents, and his wife Lady Bentley treated Elizabeth with great warmth. The result was a thoroughly enjoyable evening—one of the most pleasant Elizabeth could remember since Jane and Bingley's visit to Pemberley.

✂

When she and Darcy went upstairs that evening to retire, instead of saying goodnight at her door, he followed her into her room, something he had not done before. Her heart began to pound in her ears as she wondered what was on his mind. Much to her relief, Darcy walked over to a small sitting area at one side of her room and made himself comfortable.

"So what is your opinion of my aunt and uncle?" he asked, leaning back and stretching out his long legs. This evening, encouraged by his uncle and cousins, he had consumed more wine and brandy than was his habit. Elizabeth wondered if this accounted for the fact that he seemed more relaxed and animated than usual. She also wondered if it might make him somewhat unpredictable. Elizabeth anxiously perched on the chair across from him and continued to watch for a sign of his intentions. As she studied his face closely, she was reminded that he was indeed a very handsome man.

"Even though they are a good deal as you described, I did not imagine I would like them so very much. As you said, your uncle could not be more different than Lady Catherine. So different, in fact, it is hard to imagine they were raised in the same house."

"My Aunt Catherine is actually the oldest, my mother the youngest with my uncle between them. I think Lady Catherine has always felt slighted that she could not inherit the family title. She certainly thinks enough of herself. I have often wondered if she viewed marrying Sir Lewis de Bourgh as a less than perfect match. Although he was a man of property and great wealth, he was not at the same level of society as the Fitzwilliams."

"I know she can be difficult, but I wish we could find a way to be reconciled with her. Until that happens I will always feel I have come between you and your family," she said. Darcy leaned forward in his chair and reached across the space between them to take her small hand in his.

"Elizabeth, you should not feel badly about a situation my

aunt has created for herself. She is behaving like a petulant child. I believe she will come around soon enough, and if she doesn't...well..." He shrugged his shoulders.

Although Darcy seemed to be quite content tracing the back of her hand with one of his long fingers, Elizabeth felt uneasy. His proximity to her was both exciting and disturbing. Just like the moon pulling the tides, she felt drawn to him in spite of their differences. Darcy must have observed her discomfort. "Elizabeth, is something disturbing you?"

"No, no, nothing. I believe I am just tired," she said, pulling her hand away to rub her temple with her fingers. "It has been a very long day—the travel, meeting your family. I think all the excitement has worn me out."

"But you are pleased we have come to visit?"

She smiled. "Of course, I am. I had a lovely evening. Seeing your cousin the Colonel again is a delight."

"Then I will say good-night." Darcy rose to his feet, and automatically Elizabeth stood, too. When Darcy put his arms around her, her breath caught, and she was sure he must be able to feel her shaking.

"You are cold." He held her closer and rubbed his hand up and down her back as if to warm her. A part of her wanted nothing more than to put her arms around him and relax into his care. When she had done that after their picnic at the river, he had pulled away, leaving her feeling rejected. She did not want to have that same experience again. Although she laid her head on his chest, she kept her arms at her sides. After holding her for a few minutes, Darcy kissed the top of her head and released her. As he closed the door, she thought she heard him sigh.

As soon as she was alone, Elizabeth collapsed back into the chair. Clasping her shaking hands together, she lowered her forehead to rest it on them. She stayed like that taking deep breaths until her heart slowed to its normal rate.

FORTY ONE

The next morning, the gentlemen went shooting. As they planned to go to a neighboring estate for their sport, Georgiana asked if she might ride along to visit with the daughter of that family who had been a friend since childhood. Lady Bentley, who was in the early months of her third confinement, was often indisposed into the afternoon. As a result, she begged their forgiveness for keeping to her bedchamber to rest.

Lady Matlock seemed to be waiting for the opportunity to have Elizabeth to herself. She suggested a stroll in the gardens—an idea that pleased Elizabeth very much. The estate was not as large as Pemberley, but it was easily as grand in its own way. While Elizabeth saw much to admire, she still much preferred the grounds at Pemberley. She was surprised by the proprietary pride she felt when she thought of her home.

As Lady Matlock and Elizabeth strolled down a long, covered walkway, the older woman carried on a running commentary about the plants, especially pointing out the herb garden, a favorite project of hers. As Lady Matlock talked, Elizabeth took the opportunity to observe her aunt carefully. All she detected was genuine warmth.

Finally, they reached a beautiful gazebo where some food had been laid out for them. Conversing with Lady Matlock could not have been more different than being interrogated and preached at by Lady Catherine. Her aunt's interest in Elizabeth seemed more from a genuine desire to know her new niece better than from a wish to pry into her life or pass judgments upon her. At the same time, Lady Matlock was clearly curious about Elizabeth.

"I was very sorry to hear about your father," said Lady Matlock sincerely.

"Thank you for your kind words."

"I believe he passed away not long after you were married."

"Yes, it was less than two weeks. We had hoped that he would rally at least long enough to see my sister Jane married, too, but it was not to be."

"Losing your father must have been devastating."

"I would not have been able to manage without Darcy to help me," she said and as she spoke the words she realized how true it was. The conversation slowed as the ladies sipped lemonade and ate some delicate little cakes decorated with tiny pink flowers.

"You will have to forgive me for being so curious. Darcy has told us so little about you," said Lady Matlock politely. "He has not even told us how you met."

Elizabeth blushed under the older woman's keen eye. What could she say that would not reveal too much? She could hardly tell her the true circumstances of their strange courtship—if you could even call it that. When Elizabeth related the barest details of how they had met last fall and then encountered each other again in the spring in Kent, Lady Matlock did not ply her with questions, although Elizabeth was certain she would have liked to hear more.

"If I am not mistaken you met my son in Kent," said Lady Matlock.

"Yes, I very much enjoyed the conversations we had. Now that I have met you, I can see where he gets his lively wit and charm."

"You flatter me too much. Richard has always been a delightful boy." Then Lady Matlock began to talk about the friendship between Darcy and her sons. "William was always such a quiet child—and so serious. Richard and Henry both loved to tease him because it was so easy to do. There was nothing malicious in the teasing, but it seemed as if he just did not know how to participate in their verbal games," she told Elizabeth.

"Please tell me more about what he was like as a child. I have only Mrs. Reynolds to rely on."

"Whenever he felt uncomfortable in a new situation, he would be silent and watchful. He could pin you to the wall with those big eyes. And such a great observer of people. He took it all in. I came to realize very quickly that he was exceedingly shy."

"Yes, he still has a difficult time talking to people."

"Darcy was also the most honest child I have ever known. When he was about ten, there was some sort of trouble—I cannot even remember what it was now. When I asked Darcy to tell me what had happened, it was impossible for him to lie. I found out later that Richard had also been involved, but my nephew took the punishment and never let on. He is still one of the most honorable young men I know. But I am certainly not telling you anything you have not already discovered for yourself."

"No, in that he has not changed," responded Elizabeth thinking about how much he disliked deception of any kind.

On their walk back to the house, Lady Matlock spoke more of the cousins' adventures as children. Then she suddenly changed the subject. "My nephew has told me that he is very much looking forward to having children."

Elizabeth almost stumbled. "Of course, we are hoping for children...someday...ah, soon," said Elizabeth carefully arranging her face to cover her discomfort.

"You know he is very good with children. Whenever Henry and Diana's little ones visit, Darcy always finds time for them," said Lady Matlock.

Elizabeth tried to keep from revealing her confusion. "We have not really spoken of children in much detail. I have always assumed that he would welcome them—especially an heir for Pemberley—but we have not..." she said her voice trailing off as she did not know how to approach such a delicate subject.

"Again, I have shocked you with my directness. You do not need to explain yourself."

The longer she talked with Lady Matlock the more Elizabeth was reminded of her Aunt Gardiner. She grew more and more at ease and so by the end of their day together, she felt as if she had acquired a new friend as well as an aunt.

The remainder of the Darcys' visit to Matlock passed more pleasantly than Elizabeth could ever have anticipated. Darcy took her out in the carriage to see the local sights, and several times they went riding together. Evenings were filled with family dinners at which both the cuisine and the conversation were of the highest quality.

Elizabeth noticed during their visit that Darcy was very much at ease with his family and she saw a side of him that she had only glimpsed before. As a result, she began to feel a growing closeness between them that she found to be quite enjoyable.

※

On the last day of their visit, Lady Matlock took Elizabeth aside for another private talk. "My dear, when I first heard about your marriage, I must admit I was concerned about my nephew's choice. Now after spending some time with you, I must say that I am pleased—very pleased, in fact," said Lady Matlock smiling.

Elizabeth blushed and looked away.

"Darcy and Georgiana have had so little joy in their lives since the loss of their parents. I can tell you are bringing some light and life back into Pemberley."

"Lady Matlock, I am not sure I deserve such compliments,"

Elizabeth responded uncomfortably.

"Nonsense, my dear. I have seen Darcy three times since your marriage and each time I have been pleasantly surprised at how much he has changed. He will always be reserved, but his sense of humor is returning. He reminds me more and more of his mother."

"Then I am very glad of it. He is a very good man," said Elizabeth.

"I want you to know that when it is time for you to enter society in London, I will be there to help you. It is important to make it clear to everyone that you have the full support of this part of the family at least. The Earl is very taken with you, too. He has promised to confront his sister and let her know we will not tolerate her speaking ill of you."

"I have been so focused on getting comfortable at Pemberley that I have not had time to even begin to think about London society. It sounds completely overwhelming. Thank you for your help. I do not know how I can ever repay you," said Elizabeth as tears formed in her eyes.

At this, Lady Matlock kissed Elizabeth on both cheeks and said, "Just take good care of my boy. He deserves some happiness in his life."

"I will do my best," Elizabeth told her and she meant it.

FORTY TWO

Upon their return from Matlock, Elizabeth renewed her efforts to get along better with Darcy. They frequently went riding because it was something they both enjoyed and it was an activity that did not depend on talking. Because they rode more often, her skills improved quickly. As she became more confident, they wandered farther and farther from home. Darcy was delighted when her riding skills exceeded his expectations. It did not surprise him when she discovered how much fun it was to gallop down a country lane or across an open field. Darcy always stayed close, keeping Hector in check so they could ride side by side.

After following one of their favorite trails, they came to a place where it opened up to cross a road. Suddenly, Elizabeth kicked Sonnet into a gallop and took off up the road. The few seconds it took Darcy to react gave her enough of a head start that she was able to reach the top of the hill first. He saw her slow and look back with a grin on her face.

"That was not fair," he exclaimed, drawing up beside her.

"I need every advantage I can get! Hector is so much faster than my poor little girl." She stroked Sonnet's glossy neck.

During her gallop, Elizabeth's riding hat had come loose and was hanging off the back of her head, held on only by the ribbons under her chin. Darcy watched with wide eyes as she removed the hat and then pulled out the pins holding her hair in place. Once released, her unruly curls tumbled down over her shoulders. As he brought Hector over beside Sonnet, it took all his self-control not to reach out and touch her hair.

"Oh, my God, Elizabeth, you are so beautiful!" he could not stop himself from exclaiming.

She blushed and then her eyes twinkled with mischief. "I wonder what it would feel like to ride with my hair down," she said with a laugh.

Apparently, she was more serious than he had realized as she turned and flew off down the road again with her dark locks waving along behind her. She looked wild and free—so much more like the woman he had come to love all those months ago and more like the Elizabeth who had been missing since that day at the parsonage when she learned about her father's illness.

Darcy followed her, enjoying the view from behind. Usually, he was leading the way, and this was an entirely different and very pleasing perspective. He slowed his horse just enough to prolong the pleasure a few seconds longer before he caught up with her.

Suddenly, she pulled up short. Swinging around, she slid off Sonnet and onto the ground. Even at a distance, he could see the look of distress on her face. By the time he reached her, she was loosening the saddle. A quick examination revealed that Sonnet was starting to develop a sore spot under her saddle. It was clear it would be best for her not to carry any weight for the rest of the way home. Their best option was to walk.

While Darcy was making some adjustments to the saddle blanket, Elizabeth tried to get control of her hair. Since most of the pins were gone, she improvised by winding her hair around several times in the back and then settling her hat on her head to hold her tresses in place. Out of the corner of his eye, he watched in fascination at how her graceful hands moved so quickly and with such certainty in performing their task.

❧

As they walked, the wind increased and the clouds were moving very fast across the sky. Fortunately, the rain seemed to be holding off. Although she sensed Darcy was not inclined to talk, Elizabeth decided the walk might seem shorter if they had some conversation. "I have been acquainted with you for almost a year. We have been married for some months now, and yet there are still so many things I do not know about you," she began.

"Ask me anything you wish."

"I know you spent much time with your cousin Fitzwilliam when you were growing up, but did you wish for brothers and sisters, too? Before Georgiana was born, of course."

"I always wished for a brother to play with. I could imagine him running after me the way I ran after my cousin when I was small. Fitzwilliam is about a year older, and it seemed as if I was always tagging along behind."

"I can just see you two. You must have been quite the terror." She noticed he was grinning.

"My nanny, Mrs. Childs, was a lovely lady, but a bit old to be chasing after us all the time. I think we quite wore her out. She must have been very glad when Fitzwilliam went home after a visit."

"I have always had Jane as my companion and playmate. She and I have different interests, but we could not have been closer as we were growing up."

"You are very fortunate," said Darcy.

"When Georgiana was born, did you wish for a brother instead? I always wanted a brother, but all we had were more girls."

"After my birth, my mother had several miscarriages. I could always tell something had happened when it became dark and still in the house. Then after many years, Georgiana came along. Mother was determined to have a healthy baby that time. She quit riding and often stayed in bed all day. Sometimes I sat with her, and she would read to me when she was feeling well enough. After Georgiana, she never really regained her health."

※

While they talked, they kept an eye on the weather. Soon the sky began to grow dark and ominous. The wind smelled like water and felt alive as it blew across Elizabeth's face. It was quite exhilarating, and all her senses grew alert.

"I think if we do not get back soon, we will get very wet. It might be a bit faster if we both rode Hector," Darcy offered. Elizabeth hesitated but saw the wisdom in his suggestion. "I think it will be easier if you sit astride behind me." Darcy swung up onto Hector and extended an arm to help her up. "Put your arms around my waist," he instructed. When she hesitated, he said, "Elizabeth, I do not bite."

She laughed but did not want to reveal how very uncomfortable she was. Finally, she pulled herself up close behind him, put her arms around his waist and leaned against his back. As they rode along, their bodies moved together in a rhythmic motion in response to Hector's gait. She had never experienced this kind of closeness to any man in her life. Suddenly, she felt warm all over in spite of the increasing coolness of the wind.

Darcy had held her before, but this was different. She was not sure exactly why—perhaps it was the motion—but this was so much more intimate than any time he had ever touched her. With her legs tucked just behind his, there was no way for her to miss the strength of his thighs as they gripped the saddle or the hardness of his back as she leaned against him.

As usual, Darcy did not seem to feel the need to talk, but Elizabeth knew she needed something to distract her from these unsettling sensations. "The weather is certainly closing in quickly." When he was silent, she said, "Now it is your turn, Mr. Darcy."

"What would you have me say?" he asked with a soft chuckle. Clearly, he remembered their conversation at the Netherfield Ball.

"Perhaps you could comment on the wind or the warmth of the day," she offered.

"Very well. I love the way the wind is blowing those stray locks of your hair around so they tickle my neck."

She flushed and sat up straight. This was certainly not what she was expecting. "I think we can be silent now," she said quietly, glad that he could not see how red with embarrassment she was.

"But I was just beginning to enjoy the conversation." Even though she could not hear it, she could feel him laughing.

Elizabeth considered how to respond. Eventually, she decided that talking was better than silence so she decided to try again. "There is something I have been wanting to tell you." At least it was a little easier to talk when he could not see her face. "I believe I owe you an apology for my behavior just before Jane's visit," she began.

"You do not have to apologize."

"I remember one stormy day in particular as I stood looking out the window in the library. You tried to talk to me, but I ran away to my room."

"I could see you were in pain. I just had no idea how to help."

"I know you were trying to comfort me, but I just pushed you away with no explanation. I am sorry."

"Since you could not confide in me, I did the only thing I could think to do. I hoped spending time with your sister would make you feel better."

"It was brilliant, and I am truly thankful for that kindness." She sighed before she went on. "A few days before that as I was going through some books I had brought with me from Longbourn, I found the one that Papa and I were reading the week he died. There was a letter inside it from him. I suppose he thought that reading his words would comfort me, but it only made me feel more alone in the world."

"You loved your father very much. It is only natural that you would feel his loss deeply."

"How did you feel when your parents died?" As soon as she said it, she was sorry she had been so impulsive. The question was much too personal. When she started to apologize and withdraw the question, he surprised her and answered.

"When my mother died, I felt as if I had lost my way in the world, and suddenly nothing was familiar to me. It was as if I had come to a place where I had been before but nothing looked the same. I could not tell north from south. It took a very long time to recover my bearings. When my father died, I had so many responsibilities thrust upon me that I never really had time to think much about his loss. I had no choice but to go on and do the very best I could. So many people were depending upon me—Georgiana, the tenants on the estate, the servants. I have to admit it was a great weight upon me."

She was touched by the sincerity of his answer. "You were very young to have all that on your shoulders. You must have felt so alone," said Elizabeth softly.

"I have always been very independent and accustomed to keeping my own counsel. I am not like Bingley who constantly requires the company of others, but yes, it was a difficult time."

Just then the rain, which had been sputtering, began to come down with more intensity. "Here, take my coat," he said, slipping it off.

"But you will get very wet," she protested.

"I will be fine. Just put this over your head." Elizabeth made a little tent under the coat and pressed herself against his back so closely she could feel the heat emanating from his body. Still, she shivered. Conversation became almost impossible, and so they rode on in silence. In spite of being very wet, she was actually enjoying herself immensely.

By the time they reached the stables, the intensity of the rain had decreased to a mere sputter. Several of the stable boys rushed out to take care of the horses, and one was kind enough to bring some blankets so they could dry off. When Darcy put a blanket around her shoulders, his hands lingered just a moment too long on her shoulders. They stood looking at each other warily for a few moments.

"I really hate that riding hat of yours," he said unexpectedly.

She stiffened. "What do you mean?"

He frowned. "I do not find it...becoming." Elizabeth immediately removed it. Tearing one of the ribbons from the hat, she tied back her hair. She grinned and struck a pose.

"Is that better?"

"Yes, thank you," he said with a nod. Neither moved.

Suddenly, Elizabeth felt the need to step back and put some distance between them. The awkward moment passed, and on the way back to the house, they fell into easy conversation. Although they did not speak of important matters, she had the feeling that some of the closeness of the day still lingered.

❅

That evening Darcy, Elizabeth, and Georgiana shared a pleasant dinner together. Darcy was quiet for most of the meal, but several times she caught him watching her. Georgiana entertained them at the pianoforte, and after retiring to their private sitting room, they read. Still he did not have much to say. Elizabeth wished she knew what he was thinking but was not brave enough to ask. She wondered if the reason for his silence was that he was sorry he had shared so much. Finally, she excused herself to go to her room for the night.

Although she had thought she was tired, once in bed she found sleep eluding her. Deciding it was hopeless, she lit a lamp and looked for her book. As she was searching, she realized she had left it in the sitting room. This caused her no small amount of irritation because now she would have to go retrieve it. After examining her options, she decided to wait until she was sure Darcy had gone to his room. No sooner had she put her ear to the door than she heard footsteps and then the sound of his door closing. After waiting a few minutes to ensure he was not returning, she opened the door a crack and peered in and confirmed that the room was empty.

Elizabeth had just reached the table where her book lay when she heard the door to Darcy's room open. He stood in the doorway watching her. Their eyes held, but neither spoke. Unsure what to do or say, she only knew she was very uncomfortable with the way he was looking at her. Her lightweight summer shift probably left almost nothing to the imagination. Elizabeth felt the heat spreading quickly over her neck, chest, and face until she felt as if she was glowing in the dark. Resolving to keep her dignity, she picked up her book and then looking him squarely in the eye, she said simply, "Good-night, sir."

Walking to her room, she could feel his eyes on her back. Her knees were shaking so hard that she prayed they would not give out before she reached her door. Once safely back in her room, Elizabeth closed the door and leaned against it in relief. It took a long time for the flush that covered her to dissipate and her heart beat to return to normal. It was even longer until she could sleep.

�֎

After watching Elizabeth return to her room, Darcy closed his door and rested his forehead on the smooth cool wood while he tried to regain control of himself. It was all he could do to keep from following her.

Falling asleep that night was almost impossible as he replayed over and over in his mind how amazing she had looked silhouetted against the dim glow of the fire. He had been able to see the outline of her body through her gown from her full breasts to the gentle curve of her hips. He wondered if she had any idea how deliciously tempting she was to him. Keeping the promise to himself to wait to be sure she truly cared for him was becoming painfully difficult. Everything about Elizabeth was intoxicating—her smile, her melodic laugh, her fine eyes. Several times, he had experienced a surge of desire from simply catching the scent of her perfume when he entered a room. How long could he wait? When he finally fell asleep, he dreamed in glorious detail about what would have happened if she had invited him to her room.

FORTY THREE

The warm weather was slipping by too quickly. Elizabeth looked through the window at the beautiful day and knew she must be outside in the sunshine. Opening the double doors of the library, she slipped out and headed down the steps into the perfectly manicured gardens.

She had not gone too far when she heard Georgiana calling her name. Elizabeth suspected she might have something on her mind, as she usually did not show much interest in joining her for a walk.

"Thank you for waiting," Georgiana said a little breathlessly. "May I walk with you a while?"

"I was just going to look at the rose garden," said Elizabeth linking her arm with Georgiana's. They walked in silence for a few minutes before the young girl spoke.

"Elizabeth, I have been thinking about what my brother said recently about starting to plan my coming out season in London—possibly next year." This had been the topic of discussion a few nights ago after dinner. Actually, it had not been much of a discussion as Darcy had talked on the topic, and Georgiana had participated very little other than giving him an occasional sullen look. Elizabeth was not sure he had even noticed.

"And what do you think about it?" Elizabeth asked.

"I think next year would be much too soon. Having to meet all those new people and talk to them and be clever—you know how very much I dislike trying to make conversation with strangers. I am afraid that everyone will think me simple. What if everyone laughs at me? I could not bear the humiliation."

"You are worried about having to talk to people?" Georgiana kept her eyes on the ground and nodded her head. "You are starting to worry nearly a year in advance of the actual event. Much can happen in a year. Do you realize how much you have grown up just in the few months I have known you?"

Glancing at Georgiana's face, Elizabeth noticed the girl's lower lip quivering. She stopped to put an arm around her sister's shoulder. "My sweet, I promise that no one will make you do anything you do not wish to."

"But William says that I must have a season in London and I must find a husband, but I have no wish to leave Pemberley," said Georgiana, her voice betraying an edge of panic.

"That is not what I heard him say. He has said that soon it would be time for you to start meeting people outside our family circle and that does mean following certain rituals, such as a coming out season. Of course, he has hopes you will find someone, but no one will force you to marry if you do not wish to. You are still very young. We just want you to be happy. I think it might be quite pleasant to talk about music and your other interests with some new friends."

"It might be," she conceded reluctantly.

"Some of your new friends will undoubtedly be young ladies. It is not just all about the gentlemen."

"Still, I do not think I will ever be able to talk easily with strangers."

"Then you must do what I once suggested to your brother."

"What is that?" Georgiana asked curiously.

"It is like learning to play the pianoforte—you must practice." Some of the tension left Georgiana's face and she smiled. As they walked on in companionable silence, Elizabeth sensed that her sister had more on her mind.

"Elizabeth, how did you know my brother was the person you wished to marry?"

Elizabeth laughed to herself. "Oh, we are a complicated story."

"Please, tell me. Did you know from the first time you met?"

Elizabeth bit the side of her lip as she thought about what to say. "No, I cannot say we liked each other much at all in the beginning."

Georgiana's eyes grew big. "I cannot believe that."

"Let me assure you it is true. Our paths first crossed at an assembly in Meryton. I think Mr. Bingley forced your brother to come with him that evening, and he was miserable. He was not acquainted with anyone except for Mr. Bingley and his party. You know how he can be when he is not in the mood to talk. Also, the people at that particular dance were not at all the usual kind of society he is accustomed to mixing with. We have much simpler tastes in the country."

"Did you dance together that evening?"

"No, not at all."

Georgiana was truly surprised to hear this. "I do not believe it."

"I assure you it is true. When they arrived, Mr. Bingley immediately requested an introduction to my sister, and then he asked her to dance. Of course, Jane is always considered the one of most beautiful young ladies in any room, and that night was no exception. Mr. Bingley was enjoying himself so much that he encouraged your brother to dance, too. In fact, he of-fered to have Jane introduce us."

"So, Mr. Bingley was interested in Jane from the very beginning. That is so romantic."

Elizabeth laughed thinking about the crooked path that had finally brought her elder sister and Mr. Bingley together. "Yes, I suppose it is."

"You were introduced to William then?"

"Oh, no, when Mr. Bingley pointed me out, your brother refused the introduction."

"That is unbelievable, but how did you find out about this?"

"I was sitting not too far away and overheard their conversation."

Georgiana's forehead wrinkled in confusion. "You must have misunderstood. My brother has always said you are the most beautiful woman he has ever known."

"I think he found I improved upon better acquaintance," said Elizabeth wryly.

Georgiana brightened. "And what did you think of William when you first saw him?"

Elizabeth bit her lip. How could she answer truthfully without telling Georgiana things she would not understand? "I believe my very first impression was that he was quite tall." They both laughed. Elizabeth went on to relate the story of her stay at Netherfield during Jane's illness. She gave only a brief outline of what had transpired and let Georgiana's imagination fill in the details. Elizabeth did not want her dear sister to know the truth of how much she had despised Darcy during the first months of their acquaintance.

"So when did you first dance together?"

"The first time was at the ball Mr. Bingley hosted last fall."

"Did you like my brother better by then?"

Elizabeth smiled as she thought about that evening. "No, I confess I did not, and I was certain he only looked at me to find fault. You know how forbidding he can be. I was quite surprised when he asked me for a dance."

Georgiana looked as if she was still trying to make sense of this new information. "I am confused. If you did not like each other, then how did you form an attachment?"

Elizabeth sighed. From the questions Georgiana was asking, it was clear Darcy had chosen not to inform his sister about the conditions of their marriage. "I guess you could say we became better acquainted in Kent."

"You were visiting your cousin, were you not?"

Elizabeth nodded. "When I received news that my father had fallen ill, your brother gallantly offered his help. I owe him so much for that act of kindness."

"Oh, yes, William is the most thoughtful person I know," Georgiana exclaimed. "He would do anything for the people he loves."

"I was quite amazed when he offered his help. I was not aware of his feelings for me until he came to Longbourn a few days later."

Georgiana looked confused again. "But when he was in London, just before he left for Hertfordshire, he acted as if the two of you had already reached an understanding."

Elizabeth raised an eyebrow. Georgiana suddenly looked a little flustered. Elizabeth gave her a reassuring smile. "Your brother and I had mostly misunderstandings when we first met. Fortunately, we were able to..." Elizabeth let her voice trail off. Georgiana was so absorbed in her own thoughts that she did not seem to notice Elizabeth's hesitation.

"Elizabeth, tell me about love? Is it as wonderful as the novels say?"

Elizabeth was surprised at the directness of Georgiana's questions. "Georgiana, really! This is not something easy to speak about."

"I am sorry, I had no right to pry."

When Elizabeth saw Georgiana's embarrassment, she put her hand on the girl's arm to reassure her. "No, I am the one who should apologize. I should not encourage you to be more open and then chastise you when you are."

"It is just that have never seen my brother look at anyone the way he looks at you. I only hope I can find someone who loves me that much."

Elizabeth sighed. "Marriage is very complicated and our relationship is not without its difficulties. I am trying to be a good wife to him and sister to you. I am also doing my best to learn how to be Mistress of Pemberley, but I am finding there is more to it than I first imagined."

"I think you are wonderful. Everyone here loves you. All of the servants think you are so gracious and kind. They are always saying what a fine choice William made for a wife."

Elizabeth turned to Georgiana. "And how do you know what the servants think?"

Georgiana blushed. "Oh, I hear things. They talk to me sometimes, but do not ask me to say more. I must not reveal my sources," she said with mock seriousness.

"Ah, I can see now if I want to know what is really going on in this house, I must come to you." They both laughed.

"It is late. We should turn back," said Elizabeth. They were silent for most of the way to the house. As they reached the door to go in, Georgiana touched Elizabeth's arm.

"Thank you for talking to me about this. I am resolved to practice more conversation."

Elizabeth gave her sister a hug. "You are a very special young lady, Georgiana. I am very fortunate to have you as my sister."

"Oh, no, I am the one who is most fortunate, Elizabeth. You are everything I had hoped for."

"You go in now. I think I will linger out here a little longer. The afternoon is so beautiful."

With that Elizabeth kissed Georgiana on the cheek. Making her way back into the garden, she found a warm spot on one of the stone benches. As she enjoyed the sun, she contemplated the events in her life that had brought her from Longbourn to become Mistress of Pemberley.

Most of all, she thought about her feelings for Darcy. She respected him for his kindness to her and his support, but there was so much she did not understand. How could he be so generous and protective one minute and so distant the next? He was the most complicated person she had ever known. Nevertheless, she could not deny that she was beginning to trust and rely on him—but that was not love. Or was it how love begins?

FORTY FOUR

The next morning, Elizabeth slept later than usual. As Margaret helped her dress, she thought back to her conversation with Georgiana. How *did* she feel about Darcy? The only thing she knew for certain was that she no longer *disliked* him. The physical effect of his touch was powerful and still very puzzling.

On her way down to the dining room, she heard voices coming from one of the rooms down the hall. Curious, she headed in that direction. The door to one of the guest rooms was ajar, and two of the maids were working there. Although she did not know the girls well, she thought it might be Annie and Betsy.

"That Margaret sure is the lucky one!" Annie said in her high, thin voice.

"Yeah, she went from upstairs maid to lady's maid to the mistress pretty quick, especially considering her family's history here at Pemberley," said the older woman.

"What do you mean?"

"Well, it was quite a while ago back when old Mr. Darcy was still alive—about nine or ten years now that I think about it. Her sister Daisy worked here for a short time. She was a right nice girl and very pretty—turned everyone's eye. The Master and that George Wickham who was always hanging 'round here then, well, I used to see them both watching her. You know how young men are."

"Oh, yes, they can be trouble," Annie giggled.

"The next thing you know, Daisy was packed off to Matlock and married to one of their gardeners, real quick like."

"A baby?"

"Everyone knew it weren't her husband's—born too soon, you know."

"Who was the father?" asked Annie. "Oh, no—you don't think it was the Master, do you?"

Betsy replied, "No one really knows but there was plenty of talk. I shouldn't tell but...well, I heard the Darcy family paid fifty pounds for that man to marry her with no questions asked. Why else would they do that if it weren't the young Master's doin'?"

Elizabeth did not want to hear any more. If this were true, no wonder her husband did not want Margaret as her maid. He probably did not want her in the house at all. Her presence would be a constant reminder. Elizabeth had heard that sometimes wealthy young men took advantage of the servant girls, but she never would have believed Darcy capable of that.

For now, resolving to act as normally as possible, she walked to the breakfast room to join her husband. Taking a deep breath, she arranged her face into what she hoped was a pleasant look before she entered. "Good morning, sir."

Darcy looked up from a letter he was reading and smiled. "Good morning, my dear."

Elizabeth noticed a letter from her sister Jane in the correspondence. Setting it aside to read later, she went to the sideboard for something to eat even though she was not hungry. After poking around in the serving dishes, she decided on some tea and toast to help her stomach settle. Just then Georgiana joined them, and Elizabeth was glad to be relieved of the pressure of having to carry on a conversation with Darcy alone. She was still very distracted by what she had just overheard.

As Darcy was leaving to retire to his study for a few hours of paperwork, he inquired if she would like to go riding that afternoon. Elizabeth invented an excuse not to go. Although Darcy looked disappointed, he left without a comment. After an appropriate length of time so as not to appear in a hurry, Elizabeth excused herself and went off to her sitting room to be alone.

She was so obsessed with finding out what had happened to Daisy that she could think of nothing else. The question was how to do it. After some consideration, she decided against asking Margaret directly. Over the next few days, she found it too difficult to be around Darcy, so she kept her distance. Several times, she found him watching her with a puzzled look on his face. She sensed he knew something was amiss, and her fears were confirmed a few evenings later.

※

Darcy did not understand the sudden change in Elizabeth's behavior. She seemed to be taking great pains to avoid him. Only a short time ago, while riding they had engaged in a rather intimate talk about family. He had been under the impression it had brought them closer together, but now she had pulled back from him again.

"Elizabeth, are you feeling well?"

"Yes, quite well, thank you," she said without looking up from her sewing.

"You have been quiet the past few days, and I thought perhaps you might have caught a chill from being out in the rain?"

"Thank you for your concern, sir, but I am well."

It troubled him that she had started calling him 'sir' again. Darcy was not sure how to discover what was wrong, but it was clear to him something was on her mind. Reviewing the last few days, he tried to remember what he might have said or done, but he could think of nothing. Attributing it to a return of her feelings of grief over her father, he decided to let it go at least for a while.

That evening when Elizabeth announced she was retiring, he tried to kiss her goodnight, but she turned her head. He let her go with no comment. Darcy tried to continue reading but found he was going over and over the same page and still had no idea what it said. When he went to bed, sleep eluded him. After thrashing around for nearly an hour, he rose and began pacing the floor.

Since they had been married, he had thought she was becoming more and more comfortable with him. He knew she did not love him yet, but when he put his arms around her, she seemed to enjoy being held. When he kissed her, she kissed him back, but now something was different. Elizabeth was such a mystery to him. In fact, he had always had great difficulty in understanding most women, but the two who lived in his house—Elizabeth and Georgiana—were the most difficult of all.

❦

Elizabeth found it difficult to concentrate on anything—her sewing, reading, music, and most especially, talking with Georgiana or Darcy. Thoughts came randomly making no sense and having no connection to the one just before. The logic she liked to think she applied to most situations did not help.

She became obsessed with what had happened to Daisy, and the entire matter weighed heavily on her mind. Could Darcy have had a relationship of some kind with one of Pemberley's maids years ago? Could he actually be the father of a child now living on his uncle's estate? Did he still see Daisy or the child? At this point, she would no longer be a girl, but a wife and mother well into her twenties. Elizabeth's mind went over and over each tormenting detail until she began to make herself sick.

At times, she was convinced it was all a mistake, that he would never do something so dishonorable as to take advantage of a young girl in service in his father's house, but then he had been young at the time, too—not more than eighteen or nineteen. She knew that such things often happened. In spite of everything, Elizabeth refused to believe that he would ever have forced himself on any woman no matter her station in life. Was it love or just a youthful indiscretion?

Elizabeth attempted to understand her own feelings. What bothered her the most? Was it that he might have committed such a transgression or that he could still have feelings for either Daisy or the child? If any of this were true, then he had not been completely honest with her. She had asked him directly why he did not want Margaret working for her, and he had not mentioned anything about the girl's sister.

Elizabeth had heard it whispered that gentlemen of his class often had a past. Unlike women, their reputation was often enhanced rather that hurt by their conquests. It was whispered that in the upper strata of society many wealthy men had liaisons with other women, kept mistresses, and had illegitimate children, but all of those seemed out of character for Darcy.

Many times she forced herself to put it all out of her mind, but as hard as she tried, her thoughts kept turning in on themselves until she felt hopeless. Then she began to ask herself why did it matter so much to her? After all, she did not love him. Why should she care what he had done in the past or even what he did now?

Finally, she had to admit to herself that it hurt because she had just been learning to trust him. If he was not honest about this, then what else might he be hiding from her? During her father's illness and after, he had been attentive to her every need—always there for her, listening quietly when she was grieving, and showing kindness when she needed a friend.

On the other hand, since their marriage, his behavior had been somewhat erratic. Although he had often been attentive, he had also overruled her orders to the servants, restricted her walks and tried in many ways to control her. Even though she knew it was his right as her husband, she had been hoping he would treat her as more of an equal. All in all, he was the most frustrating man she had ever known.

After living with him closely for several months, she had learned more about him. For one thing, she recognized that his reserved manner was often more from shyness than arrogance. Lately he seemed to be changing. It delighted her to see him laugh more often and occasionally tease her back. She liked to think that knowing her had softened his heart not only to her but to others as well.

Perhaps the worst part of believing that he might have committed this indiscretion was that it threatened to change the way she had begun to think about him. Over the months they had been married, she had come to respect and care for him in many ways. She had not thought of these feelings as love, but there had begun to be at least the possibility of affection. Now that was in danger of disappearing. Clinging to the small hope that this could all be a mistake, she resolved that somehow she would learn the truth.

❧

A few days later when Elizabeth met with Mrs. Reynolds to go over the menus, the housekeeper handed her a letter from Jane.

"I am so sorry, Mrs. Darcy. This should have been returned to you sooner. I am afraid a grave error in procedure occurred."

Elizabeth looked at the handwriting. Clearly it was from Jane. "Oh, yes, I think I left this on the table in the dining room a few days ago."

"One of the scullery maids discovered it on a shelf in the kitchen. It must have been cleared away with the dishes and then somehow set aside. The footman in charge should have seen that it was delivered to you when they cleared. I have spoken to the young man, and Cook has dealt with the scullery girl who was so careless. I am very sorry this happened," said

Mrs. Reynolds. "Both Cook and I apologize for this lapse in procedure."

Elizabeth remembered setting it on the table on the morning she had been distracted by learning about Daisy. "Thank you, Mrs. Reynolds. It was careless of me to leave it there. Do not be too hard on them for what seems an honest mistake."

"Still, I do not like to have such things happen in my household," said Mrs. Reynolds.

"I am just happy to have the letter back. I have had so much on my mind that I had actually forgotten about it." Although Elizabeth was eager to read her sister's letter, she finished her work with Mrs. Reynolds before retreating to her sitting room to enjoy it.

Dearest Lizzy:

A few days ago Lydia received a letter from Colonel Forster's wife inviting her to Brighton as her companion. Apparently, Mrs. Forster said she misses Lydia's company and just cannot do without her. Of course, Mama immediately told Lydia that she could go. I did not know about it until it was too late. Although I begged Mama to keep Lydia at home, she said she just did not know how she could disappoint her poor daughter.

Lydia has been behaving abominably. Frankly, she is bored. She wants to go out and visit, go to parties and such. She cares nothing for propriety and thinks that mourning is "a silly old rule made up by stuffy old people" to quote her.

This has all happened so quickly. Lydia leaves at the end of the week. I do not even know if there will be time for you to write and tell Mama that she must keep Lydia at home. I can see only bad things happening if she is allowed to go.

Since Mama is bent on willfully ignoring all of my advice, I must apply to you for help. Please write as soon as possible.

Your loving sister,

Jane

Her heart sank. If Lydia was leaving at the end of the week, then it was already too late for her to do anything to stop it. Even if she sent a letter by express it would never reach Meryton in time. Elizabeth decided she had to at least try. The best outcome at this point would be for her mother to insist that Lydia return home as quickly as possible. She had been worried all summer about her mother's unwillingness to curb her youngest sister's behavior. Then something happened that made Elizabeth forget all about Lydia for a time.

FORTY FIVE

Elizabeth closed her book in irritation and tried to restrain herself from throwing it across the room. She had finished but was still wide-awake. Lately, with all that weighed upon her mind, sleep had been proving elusive. Reading was the only thing that seemed to help. Now with no book to read, she had no hope of getting any rest at all.

She would simply have to brave the draughty hallways and go down to the library. Thinking it would only take a few minutes, she simply threw on her dressing gown and slippers and set out for the library. The moonlight was bright enough for her to easily navigate the now familiar hallways without a candle.

The library at Pemberley had proved to be all Elizabeth had expected and more. She often thought of how much her father would have loved to explore the volumes and sit in the big comfortable chairs to read. Sometimes it even seemed as if he was there with her in that room.

The fire in the library had only a small glow from the embers, and the room had grown quite cold. Summer was definitely over. Tying her dressing gown more tightly around herself, she scanned the shelves until she found the volume she was looking for. Unfortunately, it was on an upper shelf just beyond her reach. Pulling a footstool over to the wall of shelves, she stepped up and grasped the book. As she turned around to step down, she froze. Someone else was in the room. Bright light from the moon came through the tall windows creating just enough light for her to see most of the room, but the area by the door from the hall was too dark to reveal anything more than a shadow. Then Darcy stepped into the light.

"Elizabeth, what are you doing?" he asked, giving her what she thought was his disapproving look.

For a moment, she felt like a child caught stealing a sweet from the kitchen. "I finished my book and I am looking for another to read," she said a little defiantly.

When he was silent, she began to wonder if she had done something to cause him displeasure but could not think what it might be.

"Is there some reason I should not be here?" she asked. Darcy continued to watch her but said nothing. "Have I done something wrong?" she said with irritation. "Do I need permission to take a book or move this stool across the room?"

Still without speaking, he walked over, put his hands on her waist, and lifted her gently down to the floor. "I find it strange your first reaction is to assume I am disapproving. I was actually worried you might fall and injure yourself," he said calmly.

"Thank you for your concern," she said, her voice still with an icy edge. "Good-night, sir. I will return to my room now if you have no objection." Before she could take even a step, he took her arm and guided her to a chair.

"As a matter of fact, I would like to talk with you."

"Now?"

"Yes, now. Would you have a seat, please, while I stir the fire?" The last thing Elizabeth wanted to do at that moment was to have a little chat undoubtedly about something she would rather not discuss. She felt vulnerable and exposed. Her nightclothes were thin, almost transparent, and her hair was down. For a moment she seriously contemplated running but that seemed childish, so she decided to let him have his say.

Then he would have to let her go.

He must be planning a long conversation, she thought uncomfortably, as she watched him add a log and poke the fire to stir up some glowing embers. Still without speaking, he brought her a woolen lap robe. As he tucked it in around her legs, he leaned in much too closely. Pushing herself away against the back of the chair, she felt light-headed and unable to breathe. Examining his face, she thought he looked as if he were deciding whether to kiss her or turn her over his knee.

Darcy walked back to the fireplace but continued watching her. His penetrating look made her uneasy. At first, she glared back at him, but that did no good, so she looked away. Darcy started to pace silently back and forth. She remembered he had done that at Longbourn on the day he proposed.

"If there is nothing you wish to say to me, I will return to my room," she said starting to rise. Before she even knew what had happened, he had one hand on each arm of her chair blocking her retreat.

"Elizabeth, I do not know where to begin. I know you were unhappy when you first came here, but I thought things had improved. You seemed to enjoy riding, spending time with Georgiana, and going to visit the family at Matlock, but something happened recently. You have become distant and withdrawn again. Have I done something to make you feel this way?"

"No, I am just having difficulty finding my place here," she responded, trying to sound as if it was only a small matter.

"What does that mean exactly?"

"Oh, there is just so much to learn, so many responsibilities," she said with a wave of her hand.

"Have any of the staff made you feel unwelcome or failed to do their job? I have instructed everyone to follow your instructions implicitly."

"No, not at all. Mrs. Reynolds has been immeasurably patient and helpful. She is lovely. All of the rest of the staff are quite efficient. Like everything else on the estate, your home is very well run, indeed."

"It is *our* home," he said sharply.

Her patience finally snapped. "You have said that I am in charge of the house, but I am not. There seem to be some unspoken rules here you have chosen not to share with me."

His eyes narrowed. "Whatever do you mean?"

"Nearly everything in this house has been done the same way for years and years. Mrs. Reynolds has always managed Pemberley the way she believes your mother would have wished unless she has been specifically instructed otherwise by you."

"Is Mrs. Reynolds not following your direction?"

"She will do whatever I ask. Sometimes she patiently explains why things have been done a certain way forever and ever, but she does her best to see that my wishes are carried out." Elizabeth took a deep breath to try and calm her voice before she continued. "You are the one, in fact, who has been averse to changing anything."

"What do you mean?"

"Several months ago—before Jane and Mr. Bingley's visit—I spent an entire day cleaning and rearranging the furniture in the large drawing room. The next day, you had the servants move everything back the way it was without even speaking to me first. That is not the only time this has happened."

He frowned. "I am sorry. I had quite forgotten. I did not think it was important."

"Not important? The arrangement of the room is not important, but contradicting my directions to the staff—that *is* important. You did tell me to change whatever I wished. You did not say I must obtain your permission first. Although in view of what happened, I will handle things differently in the future."

"So that was why you made the comment a few minutes ago about moving the stool here in the library."

"Yes, exactly."

"That was months ago, but this is the first time you have mentioned it to me. You are usually much more outspoken in your opinions." When she did not respond, he added, "Your ability to think for yourself and speak your mind is something I love about you. I remember at Rosings, you once said, 'my courage always rises with every attempt to intimidate me,' but the woman who used to be afraid of nothing—where has she been recently?"

She hesitated and took a deep breath. "Very well, I will tell you what has been on my mind if you really wish to know. First, it was the furniture; then you denied me the pleasure of walking alone. I never imagined you could be so controlling and un-reasonable. You may be accustomed to giving orders to everyone around you, but I have serious objections to your doing that to me!" She flashed her eyes angrily.

"Elizabeth, I..." he began.

"None of this has been easy for me, but I have tried to make the best of it. My walks were one of my only consolations and after..." her voice trailed off as she felt her throat tighten. "I am sorry. I never should have brought it up." Her voice had become a whisper.

"I had good reasons for not wanting you to go off alone." She raised an eyebrow. "Over the summer there have been several incidents of poaching on the grounds, and I am concerned for your safety. That day you were out so long I was frantic. What if you had stumbled on the culprits while you were walking alone? It could have been very dangerous."

"Why did you not tell me?" she asked.

"I did not want to alarm you."

"I think I would rather have known the truth than to think...well, I thought..." she stammered, not knowing what to say that would not make matters worse than they already were.

"I do not think these are your only concerns. What else has been on your mind?" When she was silent, he asked again, "Well, is there something else?"

"Yes," she said finally, "but I hardly know how to speak of it. Perhaps it would be better discussed another time."

"No, we have left too many things unsaid. I want to know what is disturbing you."

Elizabeth took a deep breath and exhaled slowly. "Very well. When I first came to Pemberley, we disagreed about whether or not Margaret could stay on as my maid. You said you thought I should have someone more experienced, more befitting my position."

"Yes, but you were convinced she was the right person, so I let it drop. That cannot still be bothering you."

"Was that the only reason you did not want Margaret to be my maid?"

"What do you mean?" He wrinkled his brow and shrugged.

"Margaret had a sister who worked here some years ago. Her name was Daisy."

"Why is that relevant?" he asked.

"Daisy got into...well, ah...some difficulties while she was working at Pemberley. Your father made a settlement of fifty pounds so that one of the gardeners on your uncle's estate would marry her."

At first, he looked completely confused, and then his face darkened. "So you think because my father helped her that I must have had something to do with it? Oh, God! You think I took advantage of her?" Elizabeth said nothing, but she blushed deeply and looked away. "Is that what you think of me? That I would take advantage of a young girl who worked in this house?" His voice rose sharply.

Darcy put his hand on the mantle to steady himself. "I thought you knew me better than this. I never had anything to do with that girl. I do not even remember her."

"I did not know what to think. I overheard some talk about it, and knowing you did not want Margaret here...well, it all seemed to fall into place," she responded.

"Why not just come to me and ask?"

"I did not know how," she said, looking away still unable to meet his eyes.

"Did it not occur to you that if something like that were true, I could simply have instructed Mrs. Reynolds not to hire anyone from her family? In fact, you should ask Mrs. Reynolds about this. She of all people probably knows the particulars of what happened."

"How could I? It is not something that one discusses with the housekeeper," she said sharply. All the while she was secretly rejoicing that what she had feared was not true after all.

"So you are convinced it was my doing?" He gave a short laugh and shook his head in dismay. Then he pinned her with a piercing look. "Did you ever consider it might have been George Wickham? Or do you still think better of him than of me?"

Darcy's words shocked her. How could he possibly think she harbored even the slightest preference for Wickham? The sense of relief she had been feeling only a few moments ago slipped away like sand through her fingers.

"After everything I have done for you and your family to save you from descending to a life of relative poverty, you still have such a low opinion of me. I have been dealing with your mother's almost weekly complaints that I do not give her enough money and her complete lack of propriety in keeping your sisters in check—all of this plus the censure of parts of my family I have borne with no complaint because of the promises I made you."

Elizabeth stiffened. Her embarrassment grew into anger as soon as he mentioned her family. Before she could check herself, words flew out. "You sound as if you think I owe you something—as if I should repay you for what you have done."

"You know that is not what I meant," he said. He was red to the tips of his ears.

Elizabeth rose from her chair burning with anger born of the frustration she had been feeling over the past few months.

Something snapped inside her. "What else could you mean? Very well, I know my duty as your wife. Shall we go up to my room now so you can collect on the debt I seem to have incurred?" She gestured toward the door.

Darcy looked stunned as if she had just struck him. Immediately, she wished she could call back the words that now hung in the air between them. "Your duty? Is that what you think I want from you? What kind of a man do you take me for? Do you think I would force myself on you?" he asked.

"I am your wife, and you have every right to..." her voice trailed off unsure what to say.

"I know what I could have demanded as your husband, but I have waited for you out of love."

Darcy was angrier than she had ever seen him. Then the anger in his eyes turned to sadness. As she waited for him to speak, she noticed that the top of his shirt was undone giving her a clear view to the base of his neck—a mysterious place that was always covered by his shirt and neck cloth. Unconsciously, she put her hand to her own throat and imagined touching him there. The thought made her warm.

Finally, he broke the silence, bringing her abruptly back into the room from her thoughts. "So this is why you have been so cold to me of late." He closed his eyes for a moment as if he could not take it all in. "Do you have any idea at all how difficult this has been for me? The torture I endure each day having you so close to me and yet not be able to show you how I feel? But I have learned over the last year that only that which is given freely is worth the having. Recently, I had been deluded into thinking you had begun to care for me. I can see now how very foolish I was." He turned his back and leaned on the mantle for support.

Elizabeth did not know what to say. She could feel the tears of shame and embarrassment starting to rise up and fill her eyes. Her regret at having hurt him was overwhelming. Not only had she injured him tonight—this was just the latest blow—but since their marriage, she could see how much she had hurt him with her indifference. It was true that her feelings for him had begun to grow recently, but there had been so many misunderstandings between them. She felt the need to go to him and put her arms around him, but her feet were rooted to the floor. Her whole body felt as if all the life and energy had been drained from it, and she was not sure her legs would support her if she tried to walk.

The silence in the room was so heavy that the tick of the clock on the mantle sounded like thunder. Then the moment passed and embarrassment returned. The urge to be out of his sight while she still held some semblance of control over her emotions gave her the strength to stay on her feet. "I will excuse myself now if you have no objection," she said quietly.

He did not look up but continued to stare at the fire looking tired and utterly defeated.

"Good-night, William," she said and then she added almost in a whisper, "I am so very sorry for what I said."

Just as she started to leave the room, he called to her, "Elizabeth?"

Turning around to face him, her heart raced in hopes he was calling her back to say that he had forgiven her unkind words. Elizabeth wished he would reach out to her, take her in his arms, and assure her that all would be well.

"You have forgotten your book," he said flatly. For a moment, they held the book between them. He did not let go, and she did not try to pull it away. Finally, he released his grip.

"Good-night," he said softly, turning back to stare at the fire. And with that, she retreated and left him there alone. Once in the hallway, she burst into tears and then set off at a run for her room clutching the book to her heart.

FORTY SIX

How could such outrageous and hurtful words have come from me? What was I thinking? In truth, she had to acknowledge that she had not been thinking at all. The look of pain on his face when she suggested how he might collect the debt she owed was something she could not erase from her mind. Each time she thought of it, she cringed at her own behavior.

Sitting on the window seat in her room, she looked up at the stars in the night sky. These were the same ones she had always seen from Longbourn, but they seemed so different here. Light from the nearly full moon cast shadows across the lawn and the front drive. Pemberley and its grounds were exquisitely beautiful—in many ways more beautiful to her than any place she had ever been. She had come to love it, to feel as if she belonged here.

How could I have let my temper get the best of me? She fumed at her own despicable behavior. At the same time, she rejoiced at learning that what she had feared about his past was not true. How could she have said such terrible things when she actually was relieved?

"What have I done?" she whispered. Examining what had passed between them, Elizabeth acknowledged that Darcy was right about many things especially the behavior of her mother. Mrs. Bennet had always been a source of embarrassment to

Elizabeth from the time she was a child and old enough to recognize the critical looks that other people gave behind her mother's back. Still, it was not pleasant to have someone else point out the faults in your family no matter what you might think of them yourself.

Then she thought back to the time of their first acquaintance. At the assembly in Meryton after overhearing his unkind remarks, she had been unusually wounded. Normally, she would not have cared what such a selfish snob thought of her. Why had his words carried such a sting? Could she have been attracted to him then? Elizabeth began to wonder just how much the experience at the assembly had colored her judgment. When Wickham told her his story, was she perhaps a bit too eager to believe the worst of the man who had insulted her?

Then there was the strange physical attraction Elizabeth was discovering she had for Darcy. It made no sense to her at all. Looking back, she recalled all the times she had been unsettled by those feelings. She had first been aware of it that evening at Hunsford when he reached out to give her his handkerchief. When their fingers had touched accidentally, it had sent an exciting thrill through her body. She was certain he had felt it, too.

She thought about the day he proposed at Longbourn when he had inadvertently put his hand on her leg as he sat beside her. The heat from his touch had found its way up to her face, making her a little light-headed. At the time, she had tried to attribute it to exhaustion and worry for her father, but she wondered now if it had been a sign of something else.

Many times early in their marriage, he had kissed her and though she had kissed him back more out of duty than anything else, he had stirred something deep inside her. At the river, she had been almost disappointed when he kissed her so passionately and then suddenly stepped away. It had felt like rejection. If he loved her, why did he not come to her bed? Was he already sorry he had married her?

Over and over she had denied what these feelings might mean. Could it be possible that when they first met she had looked for reasons to dislike him because she feared falling in love with him, a man she thought she could never have? Had she simply been trying to protect her heart from the pain of rejection?

Tonight in the library when he had lifted her down from the stool, the sensation of his hands through her thin summer dressing gown had both thrilled and embarrassed her. She could not deny that his touch was enough to discompose her. The thought crossed her mind that she might have picked the fight because she was afraid to let him get too close. It had never occurred to her until now that wanting to keep him at arm's length could be a sign of her growing attraction to him.

Elizabeth had grown up having to rely mainly on herself and her own judgment. Her Aunt and Uncle Gardiner had often been a source of advice and information, but as they lived in London, they were not always accessible to consult. Her mother had favored her other children over Elizabeth, and while her father had loved her, she realized now that he was not the kind of strong figure she had needed in her life. True, they had shared the same wicked sense of humor and wit and an amusement at the follies of the world, but he had not offered the kind of constancy she had needed as a child growing up. As much as she loved her father, she saw both his strengths and his shortcomings with equal clarity now.

Darcy had done so much to win her trust and perhaps that was why his suspected betrayal had cut her so deeply. She had just begun to trust and rely on him. Now when she thought the bond that had been developing between them might be broken, she felt alone and adrift with only herself to rely on again. She recalled each interaction between them—at Netherfield, at Longbourn, at Rosings—and she could see the pattern developing. Although she had not cared for him in the beginning, she had never been totally indifferent.

Finally, she saw the truth. All along the strength of her adverse reaction to Darcy had been in direct proportion to the underlying attraction she felt for him. Her heart beat so loudly that it seemed to rattle her whole body. She clasped her shaking hands together over her chest as if this might prevent her heart from flying away.

How could I have been so blind? Why did I not realize this before? I love him! At first, her heart leapt with joy at the thought and then just as quickly, it crashed down again as she acknowledged the reality of what she had done. She had hurt him very deeply tonight with her cutting words. Would he be able to forgive her? Or, had she realized her love for him too late? How strange that it had taken thinking he might be lost to her to make her realize how much she cared.

Elizabeth steeled herself with the belief there must be a way to make amends, to bridge the gap she had opened between them. If he had loved her enough to marry her, knowing she did not return his affection, then surely that love must be strong enough to survive this incident.

Elizabeth stretched out her legs cramped from sitting cross-legged too long and rubbed her calves to bring more circulation and ease the tightness. Leaning back against the pillows in the window seat, she continued to watch the sky as the glow of dawn began to rise from behind the hills.

Just after sunrise, she saw Darcy heading out on Hector. Riding seemed to be his way of sorting out what was on his mind. She suspected today he would be gone quite a long time. Finally, completely exhausted, she fell into bed and slept.

�֎

Elizabeth awoke abruptly after only a few hours of rest. Still exhausted she tried to go back to sleep but when she saw it was no use, she rang for Margaret. Elizabeth asked for a tray so she could eat in her room rather than face going downstairs. Since she had seen Darcy leave to go riding, she was hoping that he was still out. She did not want to cross paths with him until she could form a plan as to how she should approach him to apologize. After eating only a few bites bread, she fell asleep again sitting on the window seat.

The next thing she knew, she heard a discreet knock at the door, and Margaret stepped into the room. "Colonel Fitzwilliam has arrived, mistress. He is in the family parlor with Miss Georgiana. Will you be coming down?" she asked. With all that had happened, Elizabeth had completely forgotten their cousin would be joining them today. Although she was not certain she was fit to meet with anyone, she knew she could not escape her duties as hostess. Margaret brought hot water to wash and sat her down at her dressing table. In the mirror, Elizabeth could see Margaret frown as she examined her tangled hair.

Looking at her own face, she could see the worries of the previous night clearly written there. She only hoped that their guest would not be astute enough to notice. Elizabeth knew she would not be that lucky with Georgiana, who seemed to be aware of everything lately. Margaret's hands moved quickly working their magic with Elizabeth's unruly curls. Before she had much time to think, she was ready.

When Elizabeth reached the parlor door, she heard voices inside and paused for a moment. From what she could hear, Darcy had returned from his ride and joined Colonel Fitzwilliam and Georgiana. She listened as the colonel told a story and from time to time, there was the sound of laughter. As soon as she entered the room, Colonel Fitzwilliam came over and took her hand kissing it in his usual dramatic fashion.

"Mrs. Darcy, you look enchanting this morning. Let me say that marriage seems to agree with you—although I am not sure what you see in this fellow."

Glancing at Darcy, she saw that he was watching her with one of his unreadable looks. "Some would say what does he see in me?" She continued to look at him without blinking. Darcy's eyes slid away to examine his coffee cup.

"You are a very lucky fellow, Darcy, to have won this lady, but then I have always said you have everything—Pemberley, a large income, a beautiful sister, and now an amazing wife."

"Yes, very fortunate indeed," Darcy replied flatly.

She saw a flash of confusion cross their cousin's face, but he recovered quickly and went on as if he had not noticed the chill in the air. Apparently, keeping up appearances in front of people would not be as easy as Elizabeth had hoped. Boldly, she walked over to Darcy, slipped her arm through his and kissed him lightly on the cheek.

"No, cousin, I am the one who is lucky," she said, searching Darcy's face for some sign of hope. Although he did not pull away, she could feel the tension in his body.

"I have been looking forward to this visit ever since we were together at Matlock. I must warn you; I have been saving up my best stories to tell," Fitzwilliam told her.

"I always enjoy your amusing tales," she said, keeping her tone as light as possible. At this point, Darcy tried to move away from her, but she held on firmly to his arm.

"And I hope you will entertain us later with some music. Georgiana tells me that you two have been playing duets," said her cousin.

"Oh, yes, Elizabeth, please," chimed in Georgiana. "I am most anxious for Richard to hear how much my playing has improved."

"I am not sure if I should agree to this," said Elizabeth. "I fear when you hear us both together my poor playing will be exposed. Georgiana far outshines me at the pianoforte."

FORTY SEVEN

After a surprisingly pleasant evening, Elizabeth and Georgiana excused themselves while Darcy and his cousin stayed in the drawing room sipping brandy and talking well into the night. It was a time to discuss what they were reading and often to argue about the politics both of their country and their rather complicated family. Just when Darcy was beginning to relax from the potency of the brandy and the familiarity of being in his cousin's company again, Fitzwilliam began to ask some uncomfortable questions.

"So how are you finding married life, my dear cousin?" he asked, looking at Darcy over the rim of his brandy glass.

Darcy frowned. "What do you mean?"

"It is a simple enough question, old man. I mean how are you enjoying the company of your beautiful, charming wife?"

"My wife?"

"Yes, Elizabeth, Mrs. Darcy—your wife. You do remember her—about this tall," said Fitzwilliam holding his hand out to indicate her height, "dark hair, sparkling eyes…"

"I find your question very impertinent," Darcy responded, wishing he could find a way to change the subject. At one time, he could easily have gone on forever about Elizabeth's beauty and charms, but after recent events, it was not a subject he wished to discuss.

"Is there something you are not telling me, Cousin? Does Elizabeth not find Pemberley to her liking?" He tapped his finger on his cheek. "Hmm...but, of course, no one could find fault with Pemberley so what could it be?"

"I am not sure what you mean, but this is really none of your concern," snapped Darcy. He stood up and walked to the fireplace setting his glass on the mantle so he could stir the fire.

"I seem to have stepped into some quicksand here. Come, come, tell your old confessor what is troubling you."

Darcy turned and shot his cousin a withering glance. "Really, Richard, you go too far," said Darcy hoping to end this line of questioning, but his cousin would not let it drop.

"I well remember how reluctant you were last spring to tell me how you felt about her, but once you opened up, I could not stop you from extolling her virtues. Surely, you are not disillusioned with marriage after so short a time."

"No, that is not it at all." Fitzwilliam waited, saying nothing more. "It is just I am finding women much more difficult to understand than I had imagined." Darcy returned to his chair and sat with a sigh.

"Women—ah, that is a subject I have some experience with, but still I cannot say I am the wiser for it. I have always found them to be a great mystery—but what a delightful mystery! And one I would not mind spending more time investigating."

"You are not thinking of marrying, are you? Have you met someone you have not told me about?" asked Darcy trying to put his cousin off the scent.

"No, I have almost given up hope of ever finding the right woman for me. She must be such a combination of beauty, charm, and capital that I fear I shall be looking for a very long time."

"Oh, come now. There are any number of acceptable young women who would love to join your old family name to their fortunes. If you truly wanted to marry, no doubt there would be countless opportunities," said Darcy.

"Even for a second son with no title and no fortune?" said Fitzwilliam suddenly serious.

"Your charming personality makes up for any other shortcomings you may have," Darcy teased him back, finally feeling somewhat cheered by his cousin's company and the change of topic.

"You flatter me too much. Since meeting your Elizabeth, the bar has been set far too high for most women to measure up. I have no hope of ever finding someone as intelligent, beautiful, and charming as your wife," said Fitzwilliam.

"Yes, she is all that," said Darcy. He thought about how ironic this all was. There was no way he could tell his cousin how badly things had been going. How could he say out loud the fears that plagued him? His heart ached to think that he was even farther from winning her love than he had been a few months ago.

Darcy tried to refocus on Fitzwilliam who continued to ramble on. "...so perhaps when you two are in London next year, you will make some new acquaintances, and Elizabeth will be able to introduce me to a suitable young lady. I never thought I would say this, but I fear I am finally tiring of life as a bachelor. You have inspired me, Cousin."

"Perhaps you should inform Elizabeth you expect her to play matchmaker for you," said Darcy. He raised an eyebrow at his cousin.

"I may just do that."

"I suspect she will probably be very good at it. She seems to excel at almost everything she sets her mind to. I am sure you noticed the difference in Georgiana."

"I did indeed. Sweet, shy Georgiana agreed to play for us this evening without any threats of bodily harm—a minor miracle!" said Fitzwilliam with a laugh. "She also joined in the conversation more easily. I did not have to ask nearly as many questions in order to engage her."

"My little sister is growing into a fine young lady. The

change in her is nothing short of miraculous," Darcy added.

"So you say this is all Elizabeth's doing?"

"Of course. You do not think I could have inspired such a marked difference in so short a time."

"And what other miracles has your amazing wife wrought?" asked Fitzwilliam.

"All of the servants worship Elizabeth, and the tenants think she can do no wrong. I could not have asked for a more perfect Mistress for Pemberley."

"Still, I sense there is something you are not telling me. Are you ready to confess yet or should I pour you more brandy?"

"No! I cannot afford the headache tomorrow morning," said Darcy raising his palms in surrender.

"Then tell me all! You know you always feel better for it." Darcy sighed again as he stared into his glass. "So I am guessing by your silence that things have not gone as you had hoped with Elizabeth. I am truly sorry. Is there anything I can do?" asked Fitzwilliam.

"Do? There is nothing anyone can do to fix the mess I have made of things," said Darcy putting his head in his hands.

"Surely, you just need to give her more time. She has been through so much over the past few months. I believe you said she and her father were very close. She must be feeling his loss exceedingly."

"I wish it were that simple," said Darcy with a touch of irony in his voice.

"Love is never simple, but oh, that I could be as fortunate as you to marry for love," said Fitzwilliam shaking his head.

"Yes, well, it helps when more than one of you is actually *in* love." Darcy had a difficult time keeping the bitterness from his voice.

"I see. So that is how it is."

"Yes, that is how it is. My efforts to win her have failed miserably. Even worse, we seem to misunderstand each other at every turn."

"What has happened?"

"Well, first of all, I gave her a free hand with managing the house, but according to her, I have continued to interfere and have undermined her position with the servants." Fitzwilliam kept silent, waiting for Darcy to tell the story in his own way and in his own time. "It seems I have inadvertently reversed her orders several times."

"Surely, that is a small enough problem."

"She was so upset with me one afternoon that she went out for a long walk and did not return for hours. As you might imagine, I was frantic. I sent out some men to look for her, and that made her even more furious with me."

"Of course, it is only natural that you should be worried."

"We have had poachers in the neighborhood, and I imagined the worst—that she had somehow come to harm. So just at the moment when she was already angry with me, I had to tell her that in the future she would need to have an escort when she went out walking. As you may imagine, that did not make her happy."

"She did not understand your desire to keep her safe?" said Fitzwilliam incredulously.

"I did not tell her about the poachers as I did not want her to worry. I realize now what a mistake that was. She thinks I do not trust her."

"And she is the kind of person who places a high value on trust," Fitzwilliam observed.

"Yes, the highest and I have failed miserably in trying to earn it."

"These do not seem like insurmountable problems. Surely, some time will mend these little misunderstandings. After all, you have only been married a short while," offered his cousin.

Darcy took a large swallow of brandy and set his glass aside. He tried to smile at Fitzwilliam. "Yes, of course, you are right. I will give it a little more time. Now tell me about that new horse you just acquired," asked Darcy attempting once again to change the subject to something a little less dangerous. Much to his relief, Fitzwilliam seemed to take the hint that the subject was closed, and he began to tell Darcy all about his latest purchase.

FORTY EIGHT

Although Elizabeth resolved to speak with Darcy to apologize, finding him alone was proving more difficult than she had imagined. Darcy had managed to elude every attempt she made to speak with him alone. In the evenings, he read in the library or parlor with Fitzwilliam until he was ready to retire for the night, and he never went to the dining room unless he knew his cousin or sister would also be there. Elizabeth had tried every excuse she could think of—household matters, difficulties with families on the estate. There were no more invitations for morning walks or rides. Short of an ambush in the hallway, she had run out of ideas. They had both been putting on a pleasant face in front of Georgiana and Colonel Fitzwilliam, but Elizabeth was sure that at least Fitzwilliam knew something was not right between them.

Perhaps an ambush was not such a bad idea. She would beard the lion in his own den—Darcy's bedchamber. The element of surprise could work in her favor, and perhaps he would hear out her apology this time. Whatever happened, it would be better than the misery of the past week.

That evening after excusing herself to retire, she let Margaret help her get ready for bed and then she dismissed her for the night. She had chosen a dressing gown made of heavily embroidered silk that would cover her with some modesty. After all, her purpose was to talk with him, not to seduce him—although that thought had entered her mind. Unsure how he would react, she decided that ultimately she could not bear it if he rebuffed her.

Elizabeth had been in Darcy's bedchamber a few times for the purpose of reviewing the condition of the draperies and furnishings to determine with Mrs. Reynolds if any changes would be needed to bring the room up to date. She could never recall being in the room alone with him in all the months she had lived at Pemberley. Furnished in dark woods and rich deep-colored fabrics, it was a large room containing his bed and a small sitting area in front of the fireplace with a little table and two upholstered chairs and a footstool. Near the bed were several small bookshelves filled to overflowing with leather bound volumes.

The drapes that covered two large windows on either side of his bed were still open, and the moon lent just enough light for her to find her way over to the sitting area near the fireplace. As she waited, she became aware of a hint of the spicy scent she had often detected when she was close to him. The first time she had noticed it was when they were dancing at Netherfield. Now she associated that scent with him and much to her surprise she found it quite comforting to be surrounded by it as she waited.

More tired than she had realized, she fell asleep after a few minutes. Sometime later she was awakened by the sound of the door opening. Elizabeth was hidden from view by the high back of the chair and when she heard Darcy come in, she was unsure how to alert him to her presence. Finally, she simply stood up and faced him.

When he saw her, all color drained from his face. "What are you doing here?"

"I have tried to speak with you alone all week, but you have made that impossible. I am sorry to invade your privacy, but you really must do me the courtesy of hearing me out."

Suddenly, they both heard his valet moving about in the dressing room next door. At any moment, he would enter to help Darcy prepare for bed. Elizabeth walked to the door and opened it just a bit. "Mr. Darcy will not be needing you this evening, Burke. You may go." Burke looked startled to see the mistress of the house, but in the manner of all good servants, he quickly covered his surprise and disappeared.

"You must have given Burke quite a start appearing like that. This will certainly give him something to wonder about," Darcy told her quietly.

"Yes, we are very fortunate that he and Margaret are discreet, or else everyone would know our little secret." She had a difficult time keeping the sarcasm out of her voice.

"I am sorry to disappoint, but I have nothing to say to you," Darcy told her.

"You do not have to say anything. All I ask is for you to listen." He nodded his head slightly, which she took as a sign that he was willing to hear what she had to say.

"When you asked me to marry you, I remember telling you that I could not promise my feelings would change, but you seemed willing to take the chance. Knowing you as I do now, I realize how much that must have cost you. You have been more patient with me than I deserved."

Darcy stared into the fire, apparently unwilling to meet her eyes. She continued to stand behind her chair, leaning on it for support.

"When my father died, I do not think I could have survived my grief if you had not been at my side to give me comfort. Every day I have leaned on you a little more, and every day my feelings for you have grown," she said, "but it has not been easy for me to acknowledge. For as many times as you have seemed patient and understanding, there have been an equal number of times we have disagreed. The other night, I spoke to you in anger and what I said was insulting and hurtful beyond belief. I am more sorry than you can imagine to have spoken to you that way, but I lost my temper. You did not deserve it."

She watched his face but saw no reaction to her words. "Since then I have thought of nothing else. At first, I did not understand how I could have been so hateful to you. I spent the rest of that night going over every conversation we have had and examining my feelings and actions."

When he still did not acknowledge her, she went over to his chair and perched on the footstool beside him. Placing her hand on his leg, Elizabeth leaned closer. "In spite of our disagreements, I have come to care for you very much." Her mouth felt full of cotton wool, and she had to swallow to clear her voice. "I love you, William. Truly I do. I only wish I had realized it sooner."

Darcy examined at her face for a moment as if searching for something, but then looked away again. Elizabeth took his hand and pressed it against her cheek. "You are more dear to me than I could ever have imagined. I pray I have not killed your love for me. Please tell me it is not too late." Her eyes filled with tears as she fought to keep her voice even. "I know that insulting you as I did was a strange way to show it. I have no excuse for my behavior, but could we not try to begin again?"

Darcy still said nothing. He seemed to find something on the other side of the room more interesting.

"Why must we go on this way? We are both miserable. My greatest wish is that somehow you could just forget what I said."

His eyes were more sad than angry. "How?" he replied.

Elizabeth's heart sank. Her fears were renewed that she had irrevocably ruined everything. She gathered her dignity as best she could. "Yes, I remember now you told me that your good opinion once lost was lost forever," she said quietly, "but I had hoped over time that unyielding part of you had changed. It does not serve us well to dwell on the hurts we have inflicted on each other. If you cannot forget what I said, then I beg you to find it in your heart to forgive me."

Darcy remained silent. "Do you have nothing to say, sir?"

She wanted to take his face in her hands and—what *did* she want to do? Slap him to get his attention? Kiss him?

"I do not want to argue any more. Now please leave me," he said coldly.

Leaning close, she kissed him on the cheek and whispered, "I love you and I will continue to tell you so until you believe me."

Once back in her own room, she crawled into her bed. Too tired to cry any more, she fell asleep almost immediately. Sometime during the night, she dreamed she was trying to tell Darcy how much she loved him, but a storm was raging and he could not hear her. The words came out of her mouth, but they just blew away in the wind.

Unable to sleep, Darcy paced his room. He could not believe he had been so cold to her. Almost from the moment they had met, he had dreamed of hearing her say those words—"I love you." Now she had said them, but he was not certain if he should believe her. She had no reason to mislead him unless she had decided for some reason that her life would be better if she were to play the role of the dutiful wife.

No, that would not be like her. She had always been honest and straightforward about her feelings. He could not believe it was in her nature to be deceptive. Still, how could he be certain? If he confessed his love for her and found out later that she had not been truthful, he knew the pain would all but kill him. Oh, how he wished he had a better understanding of the female mind. He had struggled over the years to grasp his sister's behavior, but it had been to no avail. She, too, remained a mystery to him.

And now Elizabeth. Each time he was in her presence, his heart beat faster. Even now as angry and upset as he was, he had to fight to maintain his composure because a mere look from her could undo him in an instant. He felt almost powerless in her presence. When she sat beside his chair and put her hand on his knee, he could not breathe. And when she leaned over to whisper to him, he had been dangerously close to pulling her into his lap and kissing her with all the passion he had been holding back for months.

He tried to remember how his parents had been when they were together. It was a long time ago, but he had the sense that they sometimes communicated without words. Once he had observed them exchange a look that had said everything about how they felt about each other. Everyone else in the room might have simply disappeared at that moment, and they would never have noticed. Would he ever find that with Elizabeth?

FORTY NINE

The next morning Elizabeth's eyes were puffy. When Margaret clucked over her and tried to apply some powder to hide the dark circles, Elizabeth waved her away. It seemed fitting that she look at least as badly as she felt. After further examining her face in the mirror, she concluded it would be better not to go down as she did not want to face the ordeal of pretending that everything was fine when it was not.

When the maid brought her some tea and toast, Elizabeth found a white envelope on her tray. Recognizing the bold script, she knew it was from Darcy.

Dear Madam,

I have been called to London on business early this morning. Due to the nature of my business, I cannot say how long I will be absent from Pemberley. Make my excuses to Georgiana and please take good care of her in my absence.

Fitzwilliam Darcy

She noticed immediately he had signed his full name instead of just "William" and she wondered if he had done it intentionally to mark a change in their relationship. It seemed so formal and cold. He must have fled to get away from her and he had left the note to be delivered on her breakfast tray. Instead of being hurt, she was angry. In her head, she called him every despicable name she could think of including coward, but still did not feel any better for it.

Unable to face the idea of keeping up a brave face for Georgiana and everyone else in the house in her current state of misery, she resolved to keep to her rooms for the entire day. When Margaret came to help her dress, Elizabeth instructed her, "Please let Mrs. Reynolds know I will staying in my room today with a headache and make my excuses to Colonel Fitzwilliam and Miss Darcy."

"Oh, the Colonel went off this morning right after Mr. Darcy, ma'am," Margaret told her.

Her humiliation was complete. Surely, now everyone would know the master had gone off without saying a word to her. Was he so angry that he could no longer tolerate being in the same house with her? Why had she realized so late how much he meant to her?

❈

Early in the afternoon, Margaret knocked softly at her door. "I have a letter from your sister," she said. "I brought it up straight away. I thought it might make you feel better."

Elizabeth examined Jane's untidy scrawl. How strange that someone who was neat and fastidious in so many ways had the worst handwriting she had ever seen—with the exception of Mr. Bingley, of course. His writing was almost always illegible, too. It was just another way in which Jane and her fiancé were perfect for each other, she thought with amusement. "Thank you, Margaret. It was very thoughtful of you."

"Is there anything I can bring you, mistress?"

"No, thank you. I will just sit here and enjoy my letter."

When Elizabeth read the letter, her heart almost broke. She did not think it was possible to be any more miserable than she was already, but it seemed she was mistaken.

Dearest Lizzy,

Something has happened of the most unexpected and serious nature and although I do not want to alarm you, please be assured that all of us here are well. What I have to say relates to poor Lydia. An express came a few days ago from Colonel Forster to inform us that she has gone off to Scotland with one of his officers. It is George Wickham! It was so unexpected. I did not know Lydia was a favorite of his. Kitty, who you know is always her confidant, did not seem as surprised.

I know you will find this hard to believe, but even I find it difficult to think well of him. We have always known Lydia to be a foolish girl but this is far worse than anything I could ever have imagined.

They were off on Saturday night about twelve but were not missed until the following morning at eight. Although Lydia left a letter for the Forsters saying they were going to Gretna Green to be married, Colonel Forster was not able to find any evidence that they had gone in that direction.

Wickham's friend, Denny, who claims he tried to stop them, informed the Colonel he doubted Wickham ever intended to go there or even to marry Lydia at all. After some inquiries, they were traced as far as London.

As you may well imagine, our mother is greatly distressed at this news. She has retired to her room and will not come out. It is almost worse than when Father was ill, as we all know Lydia to be her favorite.

As there is nothing we here can do to find her, I have written to Uncle Gardiner hoping he can be prevailed upon to make inquiries in London to locate them. I am sure he will come to our aid in this terrible time, as he is the kindest and best of men. With Father gone, he will most certainly act in his place to find Lydia and bring her home or do what needs to be done to ensure that Wickham marries her as soon as possible before our disgrace is known. Charles was called out of town to handle a business emergency and will not return until the end of the week. If she has not been found by that time, I am hoping he will assist Uncle Gardiner in the search.

I am sorry to have to bring you such terrible news, but I thought you would want to be informed as soon as possible. I know it is too much to ask, but perhaps you and Mr. Darcy could also travel to London to help find our poor, foolish sister.

I send my love,

Jane

Even before she had finished the letter, Elizabeth resolved to leave as soon as possible for London. She would go directly to her aunt and uncle's house to be of whatever assistance she could. She felt the need to be near her family during this crisis, and Mrs. Gardiner was just the person to give her comfort.

Elizabeth also hoped there would be a way to keep Darcy from learning about the shameful situation Lydia had created. She just could not bear it that yet again her family should bring such embarrassment to her husband. All the way to London, she prayed it would all be resolved before she would have to tell him.

FIFTY

When Elizabeth arrived at her aunt and uncle's house on Gracechurch Street, she thought she detected some discomfort on her aunt's part at her unexpected appearance on their doorstep. She put this down to her aunt's concern for Lydia but remained alert that something else might be amiss. Much to her relief Elizabeth learned that her uncle had already begun making inquiries in an effort to locate her sister and Mr. Wickham.

Mrs. Gardiner told Elizabeth it was his hope to find the couple and then try to convince Lydia to return to Gracechurch Street with him. It was possible if Lydia was recovered quickly enough they might be able to keep the scandal from spreading too far. Failing that, Mr. Gardiner would try to persuade Wickham—with financial incentives if necessary—to marry Lydia as soon as the banns could be read.

"So Mr. Darcy does not know you are in town?" asked her aunt.

"No, he left Pemberley two days ago to attend to some business," said Elizabeth.

"Lizzy, dear, I know this is not my concern but may I ask why you came here rather than going directly to Darcy House?"

"I have never been to the house here in London. I thought about sending word ahead but I was not comfortable going there for the first time without Mr. Darcy. Besides, I thought I might be of some help to you and Uncle."

"Your place is at your husband's side at a time like this."

"I am not sure I can bear to tell him about this latest disgrace my family has brought upon him," she said as tears welled up in her eyes. "The truth is I do not even know if he is in London at all."

Mrs. Gardiner put her arms around her niece. "Is something else on your mind, Lizzy? This is more than just worry over Lydia."

"I cannot bring myself to ask for his help. He has already suffered so much. With the exception of you and Uncle—and of course, Jane—my family has been a great burden to him. He has tried very hard, but I know he cannot bear to be around Mama, and I cannot blame him for that. And now this!"

"He married you with his eyes open, my dear," Mrs. Gardiner assured her. "I think you must go to your own home and talk to him. Surely, he will understand."

"I cannot face him right now," said Elizabeth unable to look her aunt in the eye.

"Nothing could be so bad that it cannot be resolved. Go home now and when your uncle returns, we will send word to you of any progress he has made."

Resigned to having to face Darcy, she asked for a moment to wash her face and refresh herself before she departed. While upstairs, she heard the front door open and then voices in the parlor. Elizabeth rushed down hoping to hear some good news about Lydia.

"Yes, yes, we have found her, my dear," Mr. Gardiner was saying to his wife just as Elizabeth rushed into the room.

"So you have spoken to them? Are they married yet?" asked Elizabeth eager for some good news. Her entrance was met by a look of surprise on her uncle's face. Then he glanced uncomfortably across the room. Following the direction of his gaze, Elizabeth nearly gasped when she saw Darcy standing alone near the window. After a moment, she recovered herself enough to speak. "Mr. Darcy, it is a pleasure to see you again."

"And you, Mrs. Darcy," he replied formally with a nod of his head. There was another moment of awkward silence before he added, "Mr. Gardiner was just speaking of the search for your sister."

"Yes, I am very anxious to hear the latest news, Uncle," said Elizabeth hoping she did not appear as shaken as she felt. Her mind raced trying to take in the fact that Darcy was here and that he clearly already knew about Lydia and Wickham. As Elizabeth took a chair, Mr. Gardiner began to recount the day's efforts to find her wayward sister. They had uncovered a lead as to where the couple was staying, but when they went there, Lydia and Wickham were out. His plan was to return tomorrow to talk to Lydia and Wickham to assess the situation. They had left someone watching the boarding house to ensure they did not move out.

Mrs. Gardiner surprised Elizabeth by inviting them to stay for dinner, and Elizabeth was even more surprised when Darcy accepted for them before she could respond herself. She wondered what had happened to her aunt's urgency to send her off, but her mind was too full to contemplate it very deeply.

That evening over their meal, Mr. and Mrs. Gardiner kept up some light conversation although they carefully avoided further mention of Lydia. Both Darcy and Elizabeth joined in occasionally, but generally they were silent. From time to time each glanced at the other surreptitiously. Elizabeth could not believe Darcy had involved himself in recovering Lydia without even making her aware of it. Why he would want to keep such a secret was very puzzling indeed. When the gentlemen left the ladies after dinner, Elizabeth accosted her aunt with questions.

"I did not tell you at first that Mr. Darcy was involved because he expressly asked us not to inform you. When the gentlemen returned this evening and found you here, there was no longer any point in trying to keep it a secret."

"But why would he not want me to know?"

Mrs. Gardiner just shook her head. If she knew more, she did not share it. This left Elizabeth to puzzle over the meaning of Darcy's actions.

Shortly after the gentlemen rejoined them, Darcy suggested it was time for them to take their leave. Both men clearly looked exhausted. Elizabeth was unsure how to tell her husband that she wished to stay with the Gardiners, but her aunt stepped in and announced that Elizabeth's trunk was already loaded on the carriage. After that, she had no choice but to go along.

When Darcy took her hand to help her in, Elizabeth's spirits rose briefly as she savored the touch of his hand on hers. Once in the carriage, he stared out the window and did not speak to her.

"I can contain my questions no longer. You must tell me how you learned about Lydia's elopement."

Darcy looked at her gravely. "I received an express from Bingley laying out the particulars. He suggested that I might want to come to London to aid in the search. As soon as I reached town, I called on your uncle to offer my assistance. At first, he was reluctant, but finally, he agreed that it was appropriate since I have more first hand knowledge of Wickham than anyone else."

"When I received a letter from Jane, I decided to come directly to the Gardiner's to see what I could do to help," said Elizabeth.

"You thought you could help?"

"Yes, I know that sounds like a rather foolish idea, but I could not bear just sitting at home and waiting. I thought at the very least I could help by keeping my nieces and nephews occupied."

At this, she thought she saw a smile play briefly across his lips. "No, I cannot see you waiting quietly at home for something to happen," he said.

"So how did you learn so quickly where they were?" she inquired.

"Once we knew from Colonel Forster that they were most likely in London, we had a starting point. I suspected that Wickham's friend from the Ramsgate episode, Mrs. Younge, was living in London again. I believed if I could locate her she would have information about Wickham's whereabouts, and I was correct."

Elizabeth listened, quietly thinking about the toll it must have taken on Darcy to be forced to talk to this woman who had so betrayed Georgiana when she was in her charge.

"After showing the appropriate amount of reluctance to help and extorting as much money as she could for her information, Mrs. Younge directed us to the boarding house where she said Mr. Wickham and your sister are staying. The rest you already know."

"Lydia has always been a rather silly girl, but I never dreamed that something like this could happen."

"We both know how smooth Wickham is with words. Is it any surprise that a young, inexperienced girl would fall for his lies?"

Elizabeth winced at this, thinking of how at one time she had taken Wickham's word as the truth. "No, I suppose not. After all, I am embarrassed to say that I believed much of what he told me once, too."

"Do not blame yourself. I told you before he has always been very clever at convincing people of whatever story he wishes to tell," said Darcy flatly.

Elizabeth's mind reeled as she began to grasp that Darcy had been instrumental in obtaining the information that had led to the couple's discovery. He had taken it upon himself to help find them and now he was planning to go with her uncle to speak to the man who had repeatedly treated him so abominably. She could not imagine what this effort was costing him in terms of his pride.

Even more amazing, he was entertaining the possibility of helping make this despicable man his brother by marriage. Why would he do such a thing? Elizabeth hoped that it was for her, but then she quickly dismissed the idea. Given recent experiences, it had to be more to save the Darcy name than anything else. Of course, he would never allow Georgiana's reputation to be tarnished by association with a scandal.

"Do you think Wickham did this to get revenge on you?"

"Or he may see it as an opportunity to get the money he still believes is due him. I suppose until we talk with him, all we can do is make suppositions," Darcy replied.

"I am indebted to you for your help," said Elizabeth moving across the carriage to sit next to him.

Darcy looked uncomfortable. "That is the last thing I want. You made it quite clear the other night that you do not wish to be indebted to me. It would have been far better, Elizabeth, if you had not come to the Gardiner's today, but I have long since given up trying to tell you what to do."

Overcome with emotion, she took his hand and kissed it and then held it to her cheek. Slowly, he pulled his hand away. "You do not need to pretend feelings for me that you do not have. It insults us both."

"You think I am pretending?"

"When I asked you to marry me, you made your feelings quite clear, but I was blinded by love and refused to listen. I believe now that I made a very selfish mistake."

"What do you mean? A mistake?" Elizabeth felt the walls of the carriage closing in around her, her chest contracted, and she was not sure she could breathe.

"You deserve more. I thought I could offer you enough, make you happy, and that you would come to love me. I know now that it was a foolish hope on my part."

"No, no, I was the one who was a fool. Please William, I beg you. It cannot be too late for us."

The silence between them seemed to go on forever. "I have no answer for you now," he said finally.

Looking at his face, she could see the sadness around his

eyes. "I am so sorry you have to be subjected to this. I know Wickham is the last man in the world you would wish to speak to after everything he has done to you and Georgiana," said Elizabeth.

"That is not important. This is my doing. I knew his true nature, and I chose not to make it known to protect my own privacy. Your father knew the entire story, but I am sure he told no one."

"My father was very good at secrets. I told Jane about his lies but not even she knows about Georgiana."

"As I thought. I should have spoken to your mother. Now your sister Lydia may be paying the price for my silence. Correcting my error in judgment is the right and honorable thing to do."

"Still, I cannot thank you enough for finding Lydia," said Elizabeth fighting down the lump in her throat.

"Someone had to protect the family name. In cases such as this, it is important that things be resolved expeditiously before rumors can spread. As it is, I fear far too many people know already." Perhaps this was a confirmation that Darcy's eagerness to help stemmed more from his desire to safeguard the Darcy name than a desire to help her family yet again.

"Of course, it is critical to protect your family name as we would not want Georgiana to suffer by association." Elizabeth could hear her heart beating in her ears.

Darcy frowned. "I think we should talk about this another time. It is quite late and we are both very tired. I would not want either of us to say something we would regret later," he replied.

Elizabeth refused to return to her seat on the other side of the carriage. After a few minutes, she laid her head on his shoulder, and while he did not try to move away, neither did he put his arm around her or try to offer comfort. Once back at Darcy House, he introduced her quickly to Hawkins, the butler, and his wife Mrs. Hawkins who were instructed to help her settle in. Then he closed himself in his study. Very late in the night, Elizabeth thought she heard him going down the hallway past her door. It occurred to her that even if she wanted to go to him, she did not know which of the many rooms in the house was his.

FIFTY ONE

Elizabeth sat in the church with her aunt and Lydia awaiting the arrival of the groom. He was late, and Elizabeth began to worry that somehow Wickham had changed his mind and fled the city. Finally, the door to the church opened, and the gentleman in question entered flanked by Darcy and Mr. Gardiner. Darcy looked directly at her and shook his head slightly in dismay.

This little exchange was missed completely by Lydia who only had eyes for her intended. When he arrived, she jumped up and started to go to him, but Mrs. Gardiner took her arm and held her back. Lydia gave her aunt a wicked look and pulled away, moving quickly to Wickham's side and taking his arm. They walked up the aisle to the front of the church where the minister was waiting. Darcy stood up with Wickham and Elizabeth took her place beside Lydia.

It was ironic that the only people in the church who were oblivious to the awkwardness of the situation were the two principle characters in the little drama. As soon as the ceremony had concluded and they were officially pronounced man and wife, the couple turned to their guests, unembarrassed by their circumstances, clearly expecting generous congratulations from all. The Gardiners and Darcys both tried to be enthusiastic with their best wishes, but the atmosphere remained uncomfortably strained. Elizabeth watched Darcy to see if she could discern how he was feeling or what he was thinking, but his aloof demeanor gave very little away.

At the wedding breakfast back at Gracechurch Street, the awkwardness continued. The Gardiner's children provided some distraction, but the party was much more sober than any wedding celebration Elizabeth had ever attended. The new Mr. and Mrs. Wickham remained blissfully unaware of what everyone else in the room was thinking. Lydia was still Lydia— untamed, unabashed, wild, noisy, and fearless. The bride laughed loudly, bragged about catching such a handsome husband, and drank entirely too much champagne. Wickham was not at all more distressed than his wife, and his manners were so smooth that no one who did not know the unpleasant history of their situation would have guessed that anything was amiss.

Wickham, who happened to sit near Elizabeth, began inquiring after various acquaintances in Derbyshire with such good-humored ease that she was nearly struck speechless. Both Wickham and Lydia's manner betrayed no awareness of the seriousness of what they had done. The bride simply could not understand why more of her family had not come from Meryton to her wedding!

Most of all, Elizabeth was astonished that everyone played along. Darcy and Mr. Gardiner generously stood to offer toasts to the health and happiness of the couple, and they all raised a glass of champagne to the future. Elizabeth was certain that each person had something different in mind as they drank the bubbly liquid gold.

�֍

"I do not see why Wickham could not have worn his new uniform to the wedding. He looks so well in a uniform, and his new one is a much prettier color," chattered Lydia as she was dressing for the journey to her mother's house in Meryton. "Do you not think my dear Wickham is the handsomest of men?"

When Elizabeth did not respond, Lydia just continued on with her mindless babble. "I remember a time when you seemed to favor him, but the joke is on you. He is my husband now and your husband is such an unpleasant, boring old thing! I am the lucky one!"

Elizabeth, who was occupied with trying to gather Lydia's clothing to pack into her trunk, pretended she did not hear. Marveling at how much chaos one person could create in a room in just two short weeks, she was dismayed to find Lydia's dresses, hats, gloves, and shoes scattered carelessly about all over the room. The only saving grace was that she did not have too many belongings. "You should have packed before the wedding rather than leaving it to the last minute like this," said Elizabeth as she neatly folded one of Lydia's dresses that had been crumpled up in a chair.

"You could have loaned me one of your maids to pack for me, Lizzy, but you are just so selfish!" exclaimed Lydia as she sat in front of the dressing table trying on hats.

Elizabeth sighed but did not offer a response.

"Oh! I cannot decide! Which one of these do you think looks best on me?" asked Lydia.

"You look lovely in both. Just pick one for heaven's sake!"

"There is no need to be such a grump, Lizzy. This is my day. You have had your turn."

Elizabeth was appalled, but then she had never really understood her sister's view of the world. Redoubling her efforts to get all of the new bride's belongings into the trunk as expeditiously as possible, she kept reminding herself that the only way to get a rest from Lydia's foolishness was to finish the packing quickly and send her on her way. Mr. Bennet had been right—Lydia was one of the silliest girls in all of England.

Despite her protests, Elizabeth had been unable to prevent her mother from inviting the Wickhams to visit her before they departed for their new home in Newcastle. Elizabeth was certain the sole purpose of their trip to Meryton was for Lydia to show off her new ring to everyone in town and gloat over what a handsome husband she had caught. She would surely want to visit all of their family and neighbors in order to hear herself called Mrs. Wickham by each of them. Elizabeth winced and concluded that it did not bear thinking about too much. She would be greatly relieved when Mr. and Mrs. Wickham were safely tucked away far from here. With any luck at all, she would not have to see them for a very long time.

❋

While the ladies were thus occupied, Darcy, Mr. Gardiner, and Wickham were closed in the study with the Darcy's solicitor finalizing all of the financial arrangements. The final signing of the papers had been left until after the wedding so that Wickham could not change his mind and flee. Even if he tried to leave Lydia now, at least they were officially married. If Lydia had to return to her family, she would not do so in shame. If a child had been conceived during their illicit time together, Lydia and the baby would now have the benefit of his name.

Wickham, of course, had wanted more than he could get in the settlement, but at length had been reduced to being reasonable. Wickham's debts, which amounted to a little more than one thousand pounds, were to be paid. In addition to Lydia's modest marriage settlement prescribed by Mr. Bennet's will, Darcy had arranged to have a small monthly annuity paid to them, providing the marriage continued. Handing over a lump sum would have been an invitation to Wickham to gamble it all away or abandon Lydia and leave her with nothing. Another part of the arrangement had been the purchase of a commission for Wickham in the regulars. This post offered the distinct advantage of being located at such a distance as to prevent them from visiting family too frequently. There was always the possibility that if the country went to war again, he might be called up.

Ever since Darcy was a young man, he had tried to distance himself from Wickham, but circumstances had continued to put the man in his path. Now Darcy held his breath while Wickham put his name to the papers that tied them even more closely together. In spite of the fact that this situation was causing him great pain, Darcy could not help but appreciate the irony of it.

Even though Wickham should have been embarrassed, he continued to maintain a kind of good-natured congeniality as if what Darcy was doing for him was nothing less than his due. Darcy, on the other hand, had to fight to prevent himself from making uncivil remarks. As a result, he let his solicitor and Mr. Gardiner do most of the talking while he stood quietly at the window, wishing for all the world he could be somewhere else.

Darcy was pleased to have the matter concluded, with the outcome actually far better than he had expected. He was satisfied he had appropriately fulfilled his duty to correct the mistake in his judgment that had contributed to creating the situation in the first place. If only he had been more open about revealing Wickham's true nature, he might have prevented this disaster that was causing pain to so many of the people he loved.

Initially, he had hoped to keep his entire involvement from Elizabeth, but her arrival in London had made that impossible. Even now, although she knew he had helped her uncle, she did not know how much Darcy had paid out to bring this marriage to fruition. She had assumed her Uncle Gardiner was standing in for her father by shouldering most of the financial responsibility, and Darcy had done nothing to correct her mistaken belief. If she knew the actual cost, it would undoubtedly make her feel even more indebted to him, and that was the very last thing he wanted.

When at last their business was concluded and their trunks loaded, everyone gathered to see the couple off. As they watched the carriage drive away down the street, they gave a collective sigh of relief and turned back to the house.

FIFTY TWO

During the two weeks between the time Lydia moved into the Gardiners house and the wedding, Darcy had frequently invited Mr. and Mrs. Gardiner to dine with them at Darcy House. Once the wedding was over, Elizabeth expected these invitations to cease but she was pleasantly surprised when Darcy continued to welcome opportunities to spend time with her aunt and uncle. Strangely, this comforted her. Surely, she reasoned, he would not invest the time and effort to develop a relationship with the Gardiners if he expected to abandon her.

The Darcys also called frequently at Gracechurch Street, giving Elizabeth time to observe how much her husband seemed to enjoy her nieces and nephews. Around the children, he lost much of his formality, and a few times he had actually laughed out loud with them—something she had rarely ever heard him do. Apparently, Lady Matlock had been correct—Darcy was very good with children. While this made Elizabeth happy, it also made her sad as she wondered if they would ever mend their relationship enough to have children of their own. Once as he was reading aloud with two of the Gardiner children on his lap, he looked up over the book and caught Elizabeth's eye across the room. When he smiled at her, she was surprised and thrilled. It was a genuine smile—just a small one but directed at her nevertheless.

To Elizabeth's disappointment, it was an isolated incident. When they were alone at home, Darcy continued to ignore her. Frequently, he made excuses not to be alone with her. On the evenings when they did not dine with the Gardiners, Darcy went to his club and stayed very late. Elizabeth often heard him coming home, but he never stopped to say goodnight even when she knew he could see the light was still on in her room.

�֍

Darcy wanted nothing more than to reconcile with Elizabeth but had no idea where to begin. This was completely new territory for him, as he almost never had to apologize to anyone. As a result, he mostly kept his distance while he considered how to proceed. Finally, he had an idea he hoped would please her. After making all the arrangements, he was anxious to share his plan with her over their morning coffee.

"Elizabeth, I have made an appointment for you tomorrow at Georgiana's modiste, Madam Desiree. I think you should have some new gowns made now while we are in town as I am not sure there will be another opportunity before your sister's wedding. When we begin to entertain or go out, you will need attire that is suitable to your position as Mrs. Darcy and Mistress of Pemberley."

The look on her face immediately told him that his suggestion did not have the desired effect. He heard a loud "chink" as she set her coffee cup down in its saucer. Those beautiful eyes flashed at him in anger, and a lump formed in his throat.

"So now you have taken it upon yourself to decide when I need new clothes? That is very presumptuous of you, sir. Are you saying you are ashamed of how I look?"

"Elizabeth, you misunderstand me."

"Oh, yes, I remember you once said I have a tendency to willfully misunderstand."

314

It took him only a moment to recall saying this during one of their more spirited discussions at Netherfield. "I thought some new things would please you," he offered tentatively.

"I do not object to the idea at all. It is the manner in which it has been presented that concerns me."

Darcy felt his head spinning with confusion. "Then if you do not object, why are we having this discussion?"

"Mr. Darcy, I seem to recall your telling me quite specifically that you would like me to speak up more, so I am simply attempting to comply with your wishes."

"I do want to hear your opinions, but if you already agree..." Now Darcy was truly confused. He looked at the barely warm coffee in his cup and thought perhaps a glass of brandy would be more appropriate given the disastrous turn this conversation had taken.

"How is it you tell me to let you know when I have concerns, and yet when I do, you chastise me? You cannot have it both ways. Either you give me leave to speak my mind or you do not. Which is it?" she demanded.

Again he wondered how what he viewed as a form of apology had gone awry so quickly. "In my own defense, I thought a little shopping would be pleasing to you."

"Very well, if you say so." She gave her head a little shake.

"Then I must ask again—what is this conversation about?"

She sighed. "I am simply attempting to point out that regardless of your intent, it sounded like more than just a suggestion."

"I thought shopping might be a pleasant diversion. My sister seems to enjoy the activity." He shrugged his shoulders.

"And what I am trying to convey is that you have no idea of the effect of your words. Since you do not seem to be aware your suggestions often sound like orders, I believe I must point it out to you." Her eyes flashed warning signals his direction.

Finally, he began to understand what she was saying. She must think I am an idiot to be so slow to comprehend, he thought.

"Very well, let me begin again." He took a deep breath. "Elizabeth, I thought perhaps you might like to take the opportunity to do some shopping while you are in town. I would be happy to make an appointment for you with Georgiana's modiste. I am certain she will be happy to accommodate you even on short notice."

Elizabeth bit her lip as if she was taking her time thinking about his proposal and then to his amazement, she gave him a genuine smile that went all the way to her eyes. "Mr. Darcy, I believe a little outing would be very enjoyable. I will send a note to Aunt Gardiner to see if she would like to accompany me."

By the time they had finished the discussion, he was exhausted with the effort. In the end, she seemed to be happy with the plans, so apparently his idea had been a success although he still was not clear how it had all become so complicated.

❈

One afternoon after returning from a walk in the nearby park, Elizabeth sat down to her needlework in the small parlor where the light was best at that time of day. Just as she was threading her needle with a new color, she heard a commotion at the front door. Although she recognized the voice of Hawkins, their butler, there was another higher pitched voice that seemed somehow familiar. There were footsteps in the hall, and then Hawkins flung open the door. Before he could announce the visitor, Lady Catherine swept into the room. Elizabeth's heart lurched.

Resolving to be as polite as possible, she stood and tried to welcome her aunt with all the deference she knew the older woman would expect. Lady Catherine began without so much as a greeting to Elizabeth.

"I understand my nephew is from home at the moment, but that is just as well as I have been hoping for an opportunity to speak with you alone, Miss Bennet."

"Lady Catherine, you are welcome here. Please sit down. Mr. Darcy should return soon if you would like to wait for him," she said as soon as Lady Catherine stopped to draw a breath.

Waving a hand dismissively in Elizabeth's direction, the older woman added, "I call you Miss Bennet because I will never acknowledge you as Mrs. Darcy. It would simply be intolerable for me to do so."

"May I offer you some tea?" Elizabeth asked politely.

"Oh, no. I shall never sit down to tea with you. You are a fortune hunter and interloper. Your arts and allurements caused my nephew to forget his duty to his family. His mother and I planned the marriage between Darcy and Anne when they were still in the cradle, and you have interfered," she said with a haughty look.

"While I have the greatest respect for family, some people hope and wish for a marriage that is more than just the merging of fortunes."

"Humph! Impertinent girl! I remember now when we first met I thought you spoke your mind too freely. This merely confirms my suspicions. You are an upstart girl with no family connections or fortune. If you think this marriage will raise you in society, you are mistaken."

"In marrying your nephew, I did not consider that I was raising myself at all. Mr. Darcy is a gentleman and I am a gentleman's daughter. So far we are equal."

"True. You may be a gentleman's daughter but who was your mother? Who are your aunts and uncles?"

"Whatever my connections may be," said Elizabeth, "if your nephew does not object to them, then they can be nothing to you."

"I know that one of your uncles is in trade in London. He lives in Cheapside," said Lady Catherine disdainfully. "Oh, how am I to bear this humiliation you have brought upon our family name?"

Elizabeth was losing patience with the woman's dramatic antics. "Mr. and Mrs. Gardiner to whom you refer are people of refinement and good taste. In fact, they are much more pleasant than many people I know who purport to be of the finest families. Certainly their manners are not lacking when it comes to treating people with respect," said Elizabeth tartly.

Lady Catherine colored. Elizabeth's comment slowed but did nothing to stop the verbal assault. "And what about your youngest sister? Oh, yes, I have heard all about her adventures. She ran off with a man who had no intention of marrying her. It must have cost your family dearly to bring them to the altar. How can a girl like that be sister to my nephew and that Wickham person his brother? It is too shocking to be believed! I can only imagine what you did to my nephew to bewitch him as you did."

Implying that she had somehow seduced or entrapped Darcy was more than Elizabeth could tolerate. Her patience snapped, and she was as angry as she could ever recall being in her life—even angrier than she had been that night in the library, if such a thing were possible. She would not stand there silently and allow Lady Catherine's accusations go unanswered.

"Let me make it clear to you that I did not seek your nephew's attentions nor did I do anything consciously to earn his good opinion, let alone his love. It was strictly by his own choice that he asked me to be his wife. And it was my choice to accept him—a decision based upon the kind of man I believe him to be, completely separate from his fortune and connections. I love him for himself alone. He is the most generous and honorable man I know, and he means everything to me."

"Have you no regard for the reputation of my nephew? Unfeeling, selfish girl! Do you not realize that his connection with you must disgrace him in the eyes of everyone in society?" responded Lady Catherine. Her voice became more and more shrill as her agitation increased.

"I do not know what other people think nor do I care. What

I do know is that the only person who has spoken openly against our marriage is you, Lady Catherine. If people have a low opinion of me, it is certainly more from your doing than anything related to me or my family."

For once, Lady Catherine de Bourgh was speechless. She stood in the middle of the room with her mouth open, gasping like a fish out of water, but no words came out.

"Now I will take my leave of you," said Elizabeth. "If you wish to speak to my husband, you may wait for him here. I will have one of the servants bring you whatever you wish for your comfort until then." Elizabeth started to leave the room, but turned to have one final word. "William is the only man in the world to whom I could ever imagine being married. Let me be clear—I will never give him up! Now please accept my best wishes for your health and that of Miss de Bourgh. Good-day to you," she said with a nod of her head.

Elizabeth walked to the door as quickly as possible. She did not want to give that spiteful old woman the satisfaction of seeing that her insults had reduced her to tears. Opening the door, she stepped quickly into the hallway where she walked straight into Darcy who nearly knocked her off her feet. He caught her by both arms, stopped her from falling, and pulled her away from the doorway before Lady Catherine could see that he was there.

Once the door was closed, he did not release her. Instead, he pulled her even closer against him so he could whisper in her ear. "Are you well?"

At this, the last thread of Elizabeth's resolve to maintain her composure broke, and all of the misery of the past few months caught up with her. Grasping the lapels of Darcy's coat with both hands to keep herself from sliding to the floor, she leaned against him as she shook with anger and hurt. Elizabeth felt him put his arms around her and kiss the top of her head.

"I am so sorry she hurt you," he said. "This is my fault. I just never imagined she would come to the house unannounced."

She continued to cling to him for support. Being in his arms was such a comfort that she never wanted it to end. It was the first time he had shown her any real affection or concern since their terrible fight almost a month ago. When she finally regained control of herself, she peered up at him.

Upon seeing her tear-stained face, he offered her his handkerchief. Elizabeth started to decline his offer as she had for once remembered to put one in her pocket, but she reconsidered and gratefully accepted it.

"Thank you," she said. "It seems I am unprepared again, and you have rescued me in more ways than one." Elizabeth could see the pain in his face as he watched her wipe away the tears, but there was also a moment when his eyes softened. This was the look that had been missing from his face ever since that terrible night. As soon as she stopped shaking, Darcy guided her to a chair in his study and helped her to sit.

"Elizabeth, I have a few things to say to my aunt and then I shall return immediately. Will you please wait here?" She nodded. Their eyes held briefly before he broke off and left to join Lady Catherine.

�֍

As Darcy walked toward the parlor, he steeled himself for yet another confrontation with his aunt. Earlier, he had been outside in the hallway for several minutes before Elizabeth had come bursting through the door, and he had heard some of what she had said about him. Could it be true that she really loved him or was that her pride speaking in response to Lady Catherine's insults? He was pleased she had at least regained some of her old spirit and had not hesitated to speak up for herself. Darcy rested his hand on the doorknob and made sure his face reflected only calmness before he entered.

"Lady Catherine, this is quite a surprise. I did not know you were in town," he said as pleasantly as he could.

"I was just speaking to that woman who calls herself your wife. I was explaining to her in no uncertain terms exactly what I think of your marriage."

"You have already conveyed your sentiments in person and also in several letters, but apparently you feel the need to deliver your message in person yet again." Walking over to the fireplace, he rested his arm on the mantle.

"Yes, I wanted to tell that little fortune hunter to her face what I think of her, and now I have a few words for you, nephew," said Lady Catherine tightening her grip on the handle of her cane.

"You are quite mistaken about Elizabeth," Darcy interrupted. "She is no fortune hunter. There are few people I know who care as little for status and material advantages as she does."

"How could you have done this to Anne? You know your mother and I planned your union from the time of your birth," she said, completely ignoring Darcy's comments.

Darcy decided that now was the time to put a stop to her impossible behavior once and for all. "I am sorry for my part in this misunderstanding. Whenever I visited and you spoke of an engagement between Anne and me, I did not agree, but neither did I contradict you. It was cowardly of me. I should have told you a long time ago. Everyone in the family has known for years that Anne and I never intended to marry each other. You must have been the only one who was not aware of it. I apologize for not being more direct about it sooner," he told her.

"You and Anne have spoken of this?" she asked in disbelief.

"We have talked about it many times over the years, and we are in complete agreement. I am sorry if this has hurt you, but it is my hope you will honor my wishes and accept Elizabeth as my wife."

"How could I ever do that? This does not change anything," she said, summoning up her most indignant tone again. "She has taken advantage of you and your family's good name. Look what it has cost you!"

Darcy blanched at the thought that his aunt might know the depth of his involvement in recent matters with Wickham, but then he realized it was impossible that she could have this information. Not even Elizabeth knew the extent of what he had done.

"I have been managing my own affairs for many years now, and I do not require you to tell me what I should or should not do."

"One of her uncles is in trade in London, and the other is a country lawyer or clerk or something like that. Certainly neither of them is a gentleman! Oh, how am I to bear this humiliation?" she said. She was growing more dramatic by the minute and actually seemed to be enjoying herself.

"Elizabeth's aunt and uncle who live in London are the very best kind of people regardless of how Mr. Gardiner earns his living. We have dined at their home many times, and we have returned their hospitality by inviting them here." He watched as Lady Catherine's eyes grew wide in horror, and she gave a little snort of disapproval. "It does not matter to me where they live, and it is certainly no business of yours. After all, my dear aunt, many people we know are only a generation or two away from an ambitious relative who made their fortune in trade. Have you conveniently forgotten about your own husband's father who, though of good birth, had only a small fortune to his name? Did he not greatly increase his wealth through shrewd business dealings? And is that not the same fortune that allows you to live so comfortably at Rosings?"

Lady Catherine gasped audibly. This last statement about the family of Lewis de Bourgh, her late husband, was true, but she clearly did not appreciate being reminded of it. When she turned to give Darcy a withering look, she was quite red in the face with exertion. Apparently, seeing that this argument was only turning against her, she changed tactics.

"And what about her impetuous, misbehaved sister who eloped? How can you bear having that husband of hers—the son of your father's steward—as your brother!" She took a handkerchief from her reticule and waved it delicately to fan her face.

"What happened with Elizabeth's sister is most unfortunate, but she is married now and that is an end to it. Elizabeth is the best person I know. There is more goodness in her than you could ever imagine."

"But...but..." sputtered Lady Catherine trying to form another argument.

Darcy put up his hand to stop her. "In spite of all the terrible things you have said about my wife, she has urged me again and again to attempt reconciliation with you as she believes that the ties of family are of utmost importance. Are those the sentiments of a heartless fortune hunter? I am only going to tell you this once so please pay attention. I expect you to be civil to my wife or you will not be welcome in our home—not here in London and not at Pemberley," he said with finality as he brought his fist down firmly on the mantelpiece, startling both Lady Catherine and himself with the sound. "Now would you like some tea? Or perhaps something stronger would be in order?" he offered in the most pleasant tone he could manage.

As soon as his aunt left the house, he went to his study to look for Elizabeth, but she was gone. She kept to her rooms until the next morning. Although he wanted to talk to her, by the time they met the next day, he had no idea where to begin.

FIFTY THREE

A few days after Lady Catherine's eventful visit, Elizabeth received a letter from Jane describing the Wickham's visit to Meryton in great detail. To no one's surprise, Lydia had paraded around town with her glove off so that no one would miss seeing her wedding ring. Jane was mortified when Lydia had insisted that everyone—including her sisters—call her Mrs. Wickham.

According to Jane, only Mrs. Bennet had wholeheartedly enjoyed the visit. Even Kitty, who usually followed Lydia around like a puppy, was relieved when the newlyweds departed for Newcastle after a tedious week-long stay. But it was the end of the letter that Elizabeth found most curious.

...Today Lydia let slip something that has aroused my curiosity, and so I must set propriety aside and beg you to tell me what you know. Lydia told me Wickham's debts were paid and his commission arranged for and purchased by Mr. Darcy. At first, I could not believe I had heard her correctly. When I inquired, she told me that she had forgotten it was supposed to be a great secret. After that, she would say no more on the subject.

Is this true? We have all been under the impression that our Uncle Gardiner had undertaken to pay off all of Wickham's debts and also to purchase a new commission for him. My dearest Lizzy, please write as

soon as possible and tell me all you know. I am counting the days until
I see you again.
Your Jane

Had Darcy and not her uncle really paid for everything? And
if he did, what was his motive? Was it out of love for her or was
he simply trying to protect the Darcy family name? Elizabeth
resolved she must know the truth and immediately applied to
the one person who might have the information she needed—
her Aunt Gardiner.

The following day, Elizabeth arranged a visit to Gracechurch
Street. As soon as the children went off for naps and lessons,
the ladies took up their sewing. Once they were alone, Elizabeth
asked Mrs. Gardiner to tell her everything she knew.

"He insisted on paying all Wickham's debts and purchasing
his commission, allowing your uncle no part in the arrangement. He said he was correcting what he had failed to do some
time ago."

"Darcy told me once he believed that if he had taken the
trouble of making Wickham's true character widely known last
fall, Wickham would never have been able to make friends in
Meryton the way he did, and his lies would have been revealed
much sooner," said Elizabeth. "I knew he had used his resources
to find them, but I had no idea the extent of his involvement.
How he must have suffered with Wickham's smugness!" If only
she had known, perhaps she could have been more of a comfort
to him during that difficult and humiliating time.

"Your husband is a very honorable man, Lizzy. Of course, he
would want to do the right thing."

"This still does not explain why he would not want me to
know. There was no need to be so secretive."

Mrs. Gardiner set her sewing aside and patted the cushion

on the settee next to her. As soon as Elizabeth joined her, she said, "Mr. Darcy told us he wanted to keep the full extent of his involvement from you, but his reason did not make sense to me at the time. After observing the two of you over the last few weeks, I think have begun to understand."

"What do you mean?"

"The two of you have been very careful not to let anyone see the delicate state of your relationship, but you cannot disguise anything from those of us who know you well," she said. "You are both miserable."

Elizabeth looked around the room nervously. There was really no question of lying to her aunt. "I did not mean to be deceptive. It was just easier to pretend and hope no one noticed than to admit that my own husband can barely tolerate being in the same room with me!"

Elizabeth covered her face with her hands. Mrs. Gardiner remained silent, waiting to hear whatever it was her niece chose to reveal. "I cannot believe the muddle I have made of things. We have had our share of conflict, but shortly before he left for London, something happened. It was my fault entirely. We had an argument. My temper got the better of me, and I said some terrible things in anger. Now I am not certain he can ever forgive me."

"Surely, nothing could be as bad as that," said Mrs. Gardiner laying her hand on her niece's arm.

"You know how I felt about Mr. Darcy when we married, but I have changed or perhaps I should say I have finally recognized what should have been clear to me all along." Elizabeth looked at her aunt with tears in her eyes. "I love him. I love him so very much!" she cried. "My heart is breaking, and because I could not hold my tongue, it may be too late for us. I may have killed the love he had for me. Every time I tell him of my feelings, he does not believe me. He thinks I am just trying to play the dutiful wife."

Mrs. Gardiner put her arms around her, and Elizabeth laid

her head on her aunt's shoulder for comfort. "Darcy said he did not want you to feel indebted to him because of what he was doing," said Mrs. Gardiner.

Elizabeth flinched. "When those angry words passed between us, I said...I said..." she gulped back the lump that had formed in her throat so she could speak, "I can hardly believe what I said!"

"Surely, it cannot so bad."

"It was much worse than bad. I said he was acting as if he thought I owed him something for all he has done for me. The minute I said it, I knew it was not true, but it was too late to take it back."

"That does not sound so unforgiveable," said Mrs. Gardiner.

"That was not all I said. Oh, I cannot bear to repeat the rest. Let me just say I insulted him in the worst possible way."

"Oh, my poor dear girl," said Mrs. Gardiner pulling Elizabeth against her more closely.

"Months ago, I started by despising him and somewhere along the way, I began to love him. I do not know how it happened, but it did. Now no matter what I say he does not believe me." At that, tears began to well up in her eyes, and Elizabeth turned her face into her aunt's shoulder. Mrs. Gardiner said nothing for a few minutes as she gently stroked her niece's hair.

"He wants to believe you, my dear. I am sure of it. Everything he did to find Lydia and bring about the marriage was to ease the pain he knew you were feeling."

Elizabeth sat up and looked at her aunt through reddened eyes.

"It was? I thought he was just protecting the Darcy name."

"You forget that when he and your uncle were looking for Lydia, I had ample time to observe him. I know he loves you still."

"He does?"

"If he did not care, why would he be so hurt?" said her aunt. Elizabeth thought about this for a moment. While she hoped it was true, she could not be certain. "So you think he may still love me in spite of everything?" Elizabeth began to wipe away her tears with the corner of her shawl.

"Why else would he want to keep his actions from you?" said Mrs. Gardiner reaching for her handkerchief to dry Elizabeth's eyes. "Oh, Lizzy, dear, even with a maid to help you dress, you still never remember to carry a handkerchief."

Elizabeth patted her eyes. "This is how it all began," she said, holding up the handkerchief.

"How what began?"

"The evening I received the letter from Jane telling me about Papa's illness, I cried, and Mr. Darcy offered me his handkerchief. That was the first of many I have collected over the past few months from him. I do not know why but I kept them. They are all washed and folded in a drawer by my bed. I believe he has had to order new ones from his tailor," she said, recalling his remarks. "He is too much of a gentleman to ask me to return them."

FIFTY FOUR

Although Darcy never brought up what had happened during Lady Catherine's visit, Elizabeth began to notice subtle changes in his behavior. He dined with her on evenings when they were not with the Gardiners and went to his club less often. When he did go out in the evening, he returned home earlier. Whereas before, he would not speak unless he had something specific to tell her or a question to ask, now he seemed willing to carry on a conversation. The talk was strained, but she could tell he was trying.

That night after the discussion with her Aunt Gardiner, Elizabeth lay awake, trying to decide if she should speak to Darcy about what she had learned. At first, she had thought to keep it to herself but then realized she had to say something. To carry out her plan, Elizabeth asked Darcy if he would like to accompany her on a walk in the park and was thrilled when he agreed. Going down the front steps, he offered his arm, and she gladly accepted, heartened by even this small contact. At first, they merely talked about the weather. Finally, Elizabeth found the courage to speak.

"Mr. Darcy, I have something I must say to you," she began. "I can no longer keep silent. I must thank you for everything you have done for my undeserving sister, Lydia. I cannot tell you how much your kindness means to me."

Darcy looked away and did not speak for a moment. "You have already thanked me for helping to locate them. It was little enough," he replied.

"I am speaking about the other ways in which you assisted. I know you paid Wickham's debts and purchased his commission. Without those concessions, I am sure the marriage would never have taken place."

He frowned. "I am very sorry you found out," he said. "But how? Who told you?"

"Lydia slipped and mentioned something to Jane when they were in Meryton, and Jane wrote asking me what I knew. I applied to my aunt for the truth. We have all been under the impression that Uncle Gardiner had undertaken the financial arrangements."

"And I was glad to let you think that," he said. "I did not think Mrs. Gardiner was so little to be trusted."

"Please, you must not blame her. Once I knew part of the story, I would not rest until I knew all of it. She would never have told me, but when I asked her directly, she could not lie to me. She is not capable of deception."

Darcy smiled wryly. "No, of course she is not. Your aunt and uncle are very honorable people. I would be glad to count them as friends even if we were not related."

"They have come to care a great deal for you, too," Elizabeth told him quietly.

Darcy looked away self-consciously while they walked in silence. "When exactly did you learn of this?" he asked suddenly.

"Just yesterday," Elizabeth told him.

"Yesterday?"

"Yes, I received a letter from Jane the day after Lady Catherine's visit and I spoke with Aunt Gardiner after that," she confirmed.

"So you just became aware of this yesterday?" he inquired.

"Yes, that is what I said. Yesterday. Why do you want to know?"

"It does not signify. I just curious; that is all," Darcy told her. A small self-satisfied smile played across his lips as if he knew a secret he did not wish to share. Elizabeth thought about questioning him more but decided to leave it there. Pulling herself closer to him as they walked, she tried to content herself with hoping that a new beginning might be possible.

FIFTY FIVE

That evening, Darcy surprised her by inquiring if she wished to return home to Derbyshire. Elizabeth eagerly agreed. Although she had not lived at Pemberley for very long, it had already become her home. Time away from the city with its noise and bustle would be a welcome balm to the stresses of the past few weeks.

The journey proved to be more pleasant than Elizabeth had imagined it would be. As they traveled, she and Darcy talked of possible changes to the gardens and some other improvements to the house. They also talked of plans for Jane and Bingley's wedding, which was just around the corner. Elizabeth had been concerned that he might change his mind about having her family stay with them in London and giving the wedding breakfast for the couple. She was relieved to discover that he seemed to be looking forward to these events with pleasure. In the silent moments as they rode along, she examined his face for some sign of his feelings. Was he softening toward her or was it just her wish to believe it so? Sometimes she thought she detected a change in his manner and at others, he still seemed to be coolly indifferent.

At the point in the road where Pemberley could first be seen, Darcy ordered the carriage stopped. They both walked to the lookout with its amazing view of the house and valley.

Quietly, Elizabeth slipped her arm through his and stood as close to him as possible. Although he did not acknowledge her, she was certain she saw a look of pleasure upon his face. She hoped it was not only for seeing home again, but also that she was by his side.

Once back at Pemberley, their lives generally returned to the patterns and rhythms they had established before their fight and Lydia's elopement. Elizabeth took up her charitable work again, making deliveries to tenant families and calling on those in the parish who were sick or injured. From something Mrs. Reynolds said, she knew that Darcy was aware of what she was doing, but he said nothing about it to her. At one time, this would have made her uneasy, but now it made her smile. At least he cared enough to take an interest in her activities.

Elizabeth thought she saw some improvements in their relationship but hesitated to trust it. Darcy made no efforts to seek her out, but when they happened to find themselves alone, he did not make an excuse to leave as he had before. Although most conversations focused on mundane matters, Elizabeth sensed he was going beyond what was required to simply make a show of normalcy in front of Georgiana.

After they had been back a week, one rather urgent issue remained unresolved, and Elizabeth was unsure how to handle it. She knew they had to talk but was reluctant to risk disagreeing with Darcy on any matter lest it disturb the fragile truce they seemed to have established between them. It had to do with how and when they would tell Georgiana about the real reason for their sudden trip to London.

Elizabeth was of the opinion they should talk with her immediately, but Darcy favored keeping it from her for as long as possible. Elizabeth stood her ground on the matter. It had to be done. With Wickham married to her sister, the danger was too great that Georgiana might learn about it accidentally. After several uncomfortable discussions, he finally relented. Once that was decided, then they had different opinions about how to tell her. At first, Darcy thought he should speak to her alone, but finally Elizabeth convinced him it would be better to do it together. Several times, Darcy postponed, saying the time was not right yet, but after stalling for a week or so, he ran out of excuses.

�֍

"Georgiana, Elizabeth and I have something we need to speak with you about," he began as they sat together in the family parlor one evening.

Georgiana frowned and set aside her needlework. "You sound very serious. Have I done something to bring you displeasure?"

"No, it is nothing like that," Elizabeth assured her.

Georgiana's eyes widened. "Is there going to be a baby?"

Both Elizabeth and Darcy blushed. Darcy recovered first. "No, this concerns the matter that took Elizabeth and me to London last month," he said.

"I did wonder what had happened when you both left with hardly any explanation," she replied.

"There is no easy way to tell you this, my dear. It involves Mr. Wickham," Elizabeth began. Georgiana's eyes widened but she said nothing. "He attempted to elope with another girl about your age," said Elizabeth.

"Oh, no! That poor girl," said Georgiana, her face full of concern.

"The outcome was better than we had first hoped," Darcy explained, "and they are now married."

"I see, but why did this concern you, Brother. He has no connection to us any longer."

"That is the more delicate part of the matter. The young lady to whom he is now married is Elizabeth's sister, Lydia."

As Darcy mentioned Elizabeth's name, he reached over and gently put a hand on her arm. She was completely taken by surprise by this easy, intimate gesture and she laid her other hand over his. Georgiana moved over to sit beside her brother putting her head on his shoulder. He placed his arm around his sister protectively.

"I am so sorry that you ever had to hear his name again, let alone learn that he is now related to us by marriage. It is the last thing I wanted," said Elizabeth. She reached across Darcy to take her sister's hand, and Georgiana squeezed back. After that she sat up very straight and drew her shoulders back. When she spoke, she sounded so grown up that Elizabeth would forever mark this day in her mind—Georgiana was no longer a little girl.

"Elizabeth, you are not responsible for the foolish actions of your sister. I am so very sorry for dear Lydia, but at least they are married. That is something," said Georgiana.

"The truth is he never intended to marry Lydia. It was only by your brother's doing that they were discovered and Mr. Wickham persuaded to agree to the marriage."

Georgiana sighed and shook her head sadly. "Will we have to see him?" she asked hesitantly.

"No, he has a new commission in the regulars, and his post is way up in Newcastle. In fact, he and Lydia will not be attending Jane's wedding," he said, trying to reassure her. Georgiana took a deep breath and let it out slowly.

"Poor Lydia. I cannot imagine being tied for life to a man such as that." After another sigh, she said, "Now I think I will play some music for you. Would you like that? I have been working on a new piece I think you will enjoy."

As they listened to the soothing melody, Elizabeth moved closer to Darcy on the sofa. Instead of moving away, he put his arm around her. As she felt the heat radiating from his body and then spreading through her, she realized she had not been truly warm in a very long time.

❋

The day following their little talk with Georgiana, Darcy surprised her with an invitation to go riding, and she accepted with pleasure. She took great care to dress in her smartest riding outfit and made Margaret fix her hair three times before she was pleased with the outcome.

When they reached the stables, Elizabeth felt a bit uneasy. She had not ridden Sonnet in some time and wondered if the little horse would remember her. As if he knew what she was thinking, Darcy produced an apple for her to feed to Sonnet. After rubbing the little horse's nose and talking with her for a short time, she could hardly wait to ride again.

Reaching a favorite look out point on the hill, they stopped. They were looking down at the house from a point on the opposite side of the valley from the one they always stopped at when they journeyed home. The view took her breath away every time she saw it.

"I have been receiving reports about your charitable work on the estate," he began.

"I hope I am doing some good," said Elizabeth.

"You are doing more than that," he said. "Your efforts are strengthening our relationship with our tenants. Although the baskets and gifts continued after my mother died, it was not the same as having a member of the family involved. Everyone speaks very highly of you."

"I see the hard life these people have and I want to do what I can for them," she said.

"Elizabeth, I thank you for what you are doing. I know that your concern for these people is sincere, and so do they. That is what makes them care so much for you."

Elizabeth was pleased to hear his words of praise and she hoped when he said the tenants cared for her that he might be expressing how he was feeling, too. "What is done from love needs no thank-you. This is my home now." As she said it, she felt it in her heart. Pemberley had become a part of her. It was more her home than even Longbourn had been.

Darcy looked at her as if he was going to say something but then thought better of it. Still, Elizabeth sensed he had something more to say so she waited quietly. "Elizabeth, I wanted to tell you that you were right in insisting we talk to Georgiana about Wickham and Lydia. I thank you for your good advice."

"I am happy I was able to be helpful," she replied.

"I knew she needed someone like you." As he turned his horse back toward the stables, she thought she heard him add, "We both did," but his voice was so soft that she could not be certain.

FIFTY SIX

After they had been home at Pemberley for a few weeks, Elizabeth received a message that little Janie Cooper had been injured. Generally, in a case like this, the mistress of the estate was not expected to attend, but Elizabeth had developed a special connection with the little girl over the course of her visits. The last time she visited their house before going to London, Janie had presented her with a small stick doll with little scraps of cloth tied on to make a gown. The idea that this little angel could be hurt tore at Elizabeth's heart.

She sent a message to Cook who packed up a nice piece of roast beef, some potatoes and fresh bread for her to take along. The last thing Mrs. Cooper needed to be concerned about was making dinner for hungry children. One of the young footmen, Hardy, who often accompanied her on her visits, was dispatched to bring the curricle around.

As soon as they were out of sight of the house, Elizabeth insisted on taking the reins. She had begun learning to drive even before her trip to London, as it pleased her to do more than just sit and be carried from place to place.

Hardy had protested at first, but acceded when he saw there was nothing for him to do but let her have her own way. He insisted on lessons, telling her that if she was going to handle the horses, at least she should know how to do it properly.

Upon reaching the Cooper's cottage, she was relieved to see the doctor's horse already tied outside.

�֍

"She climbed one of the tall ladders when no one was looking and tried to help with the apple picking," said one of the other children as soon as Elizabeth reached the door. Mrs. Cooper looked surprised to see the mistress of the great house but seemed glad to have the supplies Elizabeth had brought.

Janie was lying on a small cot in one corner of the room. It was clear at a glance that her arm was broken. Since the doctor and Mrs. Cooper seemed to have things well in hand, Elizabeth began talking to some of the other children to distract them. Rounding them up, she took them outside for a little picnic, and kept them entertained with stories of when she was young.

When it was time to say her farewells, Elizabeth asked to speak with Janie for a moment. Kneeling down beside the bed, she gently brushed some strands of damp hair back from the little girl's tearstained face. In spite of being groggy from the laudanum the doctor had given her for the pain, Janie's face brightened when she saw her friend. Elizabeth whispered to her for a minute, then Janie managed a small smile. She kissed the little girl on the forehead and stood to leave.

As Mrs. Cooper walked her out, she asked, "What ever did you say that made her smile, Mrs. Darcy?"

"I told her the little doll she gave me on my last visit had been to London and had accompanied me to several very nice parties and a wedding."

Mrs. Cooper shook her head. "You certainly have a way with the little ones, ma'am. I was just about to shoo the other children away when I saw you had already distracted them. I thank you."

"I am glad to see that she is feeling better," said Elizabeth.

"You were more help than you know. It left me both hands

to help the doctor without any of the others in the way. If you will forgive me speaking plainly, I think you will be a wonderful mother someday."

Tears sprung to Elizabeth's eyes as she thanked Mrs. Cooper and took her leave. The only thing on her mind was returning home and talking to Darcy about her day.

Although exhausted, Elizabeth still wanted to take the reins on the return trip. She and Hardy went through their usual routine—she asked, he declined, she insisted, and he gave in. When they had left on their errand in the early afternoon, it had been unseasonably warm for November. On the way home, it suddenly began to grow colder. A bitter wind whipped up the trees and a storm seemed imminent. The rain began as a steady drip and finally a downpour. In just a few minutes, they were both soaked to the skin.

Hardy begged her to allow him drive and finally she agreed. Just as she was in the process of handing over the reins, a streak of lightning flashed very close-by. It was immediately followed by a loud crack as a tree was struck by the lightning. Almost simultaneously, they heard booming thunder. The horse, terrified by the light and the noise, bolted dragging the curricle along behind at a frightening speed. Elizabeth pulled on the reins as hard as she could, but it was beyond her strength. By the time she tried to pass the reins over to Hardy again, the situation was already out of control. They careened along until the wheel hit a rut in the road. The next thing she knew, she was on the ground. Elizabeth lay very still, checking herself over for injuries. While nothing appeared to be broken, she ached all over and was shaking.

Through the rain, she could see the curricle nearby was a twisted mess. Hardy, who by some miracle had jumped clear of the wreck and was unhurt, ran to check on her. Although she tried to assure him she was not seriously injured, she could not miss the panicked look on his face as he stared at the right side of her head. Reaching up to check what he was looking at, she located a large bump on the side of her head. Pulling her hand down, she saw it was covered with blood.

"Do not look so worried! I just need something to stop the bleeding. Do you have a handkerchief?" Hardy did not look convinced. "Head wounds always bleed excessively. Truly, I feel just fine."

It was immediately clear that despite her protestations of being "just fine," she was unable to stand on her own. Scooping her up, Hardy carried her to the shelter of the overturned curricle. Taking off his coat, he draped it over Elizabeth to help keep her warm and dry. He tied the nervous horse to a tree and took off at a run for the nearby stables.

The thunder was in the distance, but the bitter rain showed no signs of letting up. By the time Hardy returned with some men and a wagon, Elizabeth was so cold that she wondered if she would ever be warm again. Just a few minutes after that, Mrs. Reynolds arrived carrying her special basket filled with ointments, salves, and bandages. The motherly housekeeper examined the bump on Elizabeth's head and pressed a fresh cloth on the wound. Although Mrs. Reynolds tried to hide her concern, Elizabeth could tell she was worried.

"Margaret will not be happy with me for getting blood on my gown," Elizabeth said, trying to make light of the situation. Mrs. Reynolds said nothing as she kept pressure on the wound. "Do you think the blood will come out?" Elizabeth asked through chattering teeth.

"We must take her home as quickly as possible. She needs to be out of this miserable weather and warmed up," ordered Mrs. Reynolds taking command of the situation as if she were drilling a military unit.

Hardy took the wagon and transported Elizabeth and Mrs. Reynolds to the main house. As soon as they arrived, one of the footmen carried Elizabeth to her room where Margaret was waiting. Hot water was already being poured for a bath. They stripped off her wet, bloody clothing and helped her into the tub.

Between the efforts of Margaret and Mrs. Reynolds, Elizabeth found herself washed, dressed, and tucked into bed almost before she knew it. Fortunately, her head had stopped bleeding before they returned to the house. Dr. James arrived soon after Elizabeth was in bed. Upon examining the wound, he pronounced it was not serious and no stitches would be necessary.

Then he checked her over very thoroughly and found no broken bones. As the he was completing his examination, he coughed into his hand nervously. "Mrs. Darcy, is there any chance that you are with child?"

Elizabeth could feel the heat of embarrassment radiating from her face. She lowered her eyes. "No, that is not possible."

"I only ask because if you might be, then my examination would be a bit more, ah...extensive."

Elizabeth did not look up but shook her head "no" again. Just at that moment, Darcy arrived out of breath. His usual good manners seemed to have abandoned him, as he had rushed into the room without so much as a knock.

"How is she? Is she injured?" he asked directing his questions to Dr. James.

"She is just fine," Elizabeth said firmly. "I am not unconscious and you may address me directly."

Darcy looked at her with wide eyes. Movement in the doorway to her dressing room caught his attention, and he glanced over just in time to see Margaret picking up the sodden, blood-covered clothing that had been carelessly dropped to the floor in the rush. Darcy went completely white. The young woman apologized and scurried off with the soiled items.

Turning back, he asked, "Elizabeth, is that blood all over your clothing?"

"She had a cut on her head. It was small but deep. The bleeding has stopped, and the wound will not require stitches as long as she rests and stays quiet for a few days," the doctor assured him.

"So much blood," Darcy repeated.

"Head wounds always bleed excessively," Elizabeth told him, but the color did not return to his face.

Although the doctor told him repeatedly that the injuries were only slight, Darcy did not seem comforted by the news. After giving further instructions to Mrs. Reynolds and Margaret, who had been hovering nearby, the doctor excused himself saying he would call the next morning to check on his patient. With just a look from Darcy, everyone cleared the room leaving them alone.

"I cannot believe Hardy was so foolish as to let you go out in that storm!" Darcy began.

"Hardy is not to blame. We were on our way home from visiting one of the tenants when the rain started. We were almost back to the stables when there was a lightning strike near us in the woods, and the horse bolted. It all happened so quickly," replied Elizabeth. "The next thing I knew I was on the ground."

Darcy paced nervously near the bed. "Nevertheless, I have already given the order to dismiss him."

"Please, you cannot do that!" Elizabeth sat up, shocked at his response.

"I can and I will." Darcy scowled at her.

"It was not his fault," she insisted again. "It was mine. I was driving when it happened."

"Elizabeth, you should not try to take the blame."

"But it is true—I was driving. I have been practicing taking the reins on my trips to visit the tenants. Hardy always protests, but I leave him no choice but to do as I ask. So it's not his fault; you cannot dismiss him."

Darcy's face, which had been pale, now grew red, and his hands were balled into fists at his sides—not a good sign. "What were you thinking? What if something more serious had happened to you? I do not know..."

Too tired to be polite, she interrupted him mid-sentence. "I did not think you cared enough about me to be concerned," she snapped. With that, she fell back on the pillows and put her hands over her face. Darcy started toward the bed.

"Elizabeth, you misunderstand me. I simply meant..."

"Oh, so I have misunderstood you yet again," she said between sniffs.

Before he had a chance to explain, Georgiana burst into the room. "Oh, Elizabeth, are you injured?" she began and then seeing that something was not right, she stopped and looked from Elizabeth to Darcy and back again. Georgiana went pale.

"I am sorry. I have forgotten myself. I did not mean to rush in without knocking, but I was so worried when I heard about the accident."

"Where have you been?" Darcy asked his sister.

"I just now arrived home from visiting the Newlands."

"You were out in this storm as well?"

"Yes, I..." she began and then seeing the look on her brother's face, she continued, "You have never objected to my visiting friends before as long as I take one of the grooms with me."

"You should exercise better judgment about going out when the weather looks threatening."

"The sun was out when I left," Georgiana replied calmly, "and I know the same thing has happened to you many times."

As Elizabeth listened to their exchange, she used the time to regain her composure. The last thing she wanted was to worry her sister or put her in the middle of their disagreement. Georgiana sat on the bed and put her arms around her sister. As they hugged, she whispered something in Elizabeth's ear.

"Yes, I was driving," Elizabeth responded. She looked over Georgiana's shoulder at Darcy and said rather pointedly, "It was no one's fault. The horse was frightened by the storm."

Darcy's eyes grew wide. "Georgiana, you have been aware that Elizabeth has been taking the reins? How long has this been going on—and why am I the last to know?" he asked his eyes darting between them.

"Please, do not blame Georgiana. I swore her to secrecy," said Elizabeth.

"I cannot believe you would take such a risk!" Darcy's voice grew louder with each word and before Elizabeth could speak, Georgiana came to her defense.

"You should not raise your voice, Brother. She is only trying to please you!"

Darcy furrowed his brow. Then Elizabeth saw him put on his distant, impossible-to-read face—the one she detested. Apparently, the subject was closed.

"Very well, we will revisit this at a later time when you are feeling stronger. If you will excuse me, I am going down to my study now as I have some work to do. Should I send Margaret in to you?" he asked.

"I was hoping you would sit with me," said Elizabeth softly brushing an invisible speck of lint from the counterpane, "but of course if you have work to do, I am sure Georgiana will stay."

Darcy hesitated, and for a moment, Elizabeth thought he might change his mind. "I shall leave you in Georgiana's hands for now, but I will return to check on you later."

After he left, Georgiana asked, "What was that all about?" Elizabeth rubbed her eyes and said nothing. "Oh, I am sorry to have pried into private matters again. It is just that I care about both of you so much," said Georgiana taking Elizabeth's hand. "What can I do for you? Does your head hurt?"

Margaret and Mrs. Reynolds both came in several times to check on Elizabeth. Each time, she was able to report that she was feeling better but still very tired from all the excitement.

❧

When Elizabeth awoke in the night, she lay quietly in that misty place between the worlds of sleep and wakefulness. Although her head still ached, at least it had subsided to a dull throb. As she became more aware, she remembered Darcy had come to sit with her late in the evening after everyone else had retired. She must have fallen asleep as he was reading to her.

Opening her eyes, she saw that he was still in the chair, but had leaned forward and was asleep with his head resting on the bed beside her. Elizabeth could not resist running her fingers gently through his curls. Seeing him like this made her love him all the more. "I am so sorry, William. I was in such a hurry to get home to you," she whispered. Just as she was tracing his ear lightly with her finger, he stirred. She withdrew her hand quickly.

Darcy sat up and rubbed his eyes as he shook off sleep. "Have you been awake for very long?" he asked.

"No, not long."

"You are feeling better?"

"I have a bit of a headache, and I am sore all over, but I suspect I will live," she said with a smile.

"I was more tired than I thought," he said, rubbing his neck and stretching his arms.

"Yes, it must be exhausting to have such a trying wife."

At first, he looked serious, and then a warm smile spread across his sleepy face. "You are a trial, but a lovely one." He surprised her by kissing the top of her head.

"Must you go now?" she asked.

He hesitated a moment. Her heart began to beat more quickly under the intensity of his gaze. "I think it is best. You need rest, but I will come first thing in the morning. Do you need anything before I go?" Elizabeth shook her head. "Everyone has been so concerned about you that it would not surprise me to find Margaret, Mrs. Reynolds, and Georgiana all asleep in the hallway waiting for news."

"Tell them I am fine," she said. "And thank you again for sitting with me."

Darcy took her hand and kissed it quickly before he left. Almost as soon as he had stepped into the hallway, the door to her dressing room opened and Margaret appeared.

"I have a sleeping draught Dr. James left for you," she said, but Elizabeth waved it away.

After fluffing the pillows and fussing over her mistress for a few minutes, Margaret put out the lamp. Elizabeth lay awake thinking about her exchange with Darcy. How she wished that he had stayed just a little longer. In fact, she would not have minded at all if he had laid down beside her and held her the rest of the night. She fell asleep, imaging what would have happened if he had.

FIFTY SEVEN

Elizabeth healed quickly with no lingering effects from her accident. Georgiana brought word that the Coopers had learned of her accident and had asked after her health. Georgiana was also able to report that little Janie was doing well. The Coopers were not the only tenants concerned about Elizabeth. Wherever Darcy went on the estate, people inquired about Mrs. Darcy and expressed their wishes for her speedy recovery.

During her convalescence, Darcy remained solicitous. Several times while she was still in bed on doctor's orders, he brought her tray himself and stayed to eat with her. Elizabeth was not sure why he came, but she was glad for it. They talked of everything except what was really on their minds.

After just a few days of bed rest, Elizabeth was beyond bored. Once released by the doctor, she went downstairs for meals and then began to take short walks in the garden. After a few more days, she asked Darcy if he would accompany her the next morning on a longer walk. The late fall day was cool but clear when they set out in the direction of a small wilderness area near the lake. The leaves crunched under their boots with every step. Over time, Darcy had learned to shorten his long stride to match hers in order to remain by her side. Some things about being with Elizabeth were easy; others were more difficult and taking much longer than he had hoped.

As he was rehearsing what to say to her, she asked him, "William, please tell me more about your mother."

"What is it that you would like to know?"

"I am not sure. What was she like? She must have loved you and Georgiana very much."

"Yes, she did," he responded.

"And?"

He thought for a moment. "Both my parents loved me but they showed it in different ways." She gestured for him to continue. "My mother was more demonstrative than my father. Of course, as I grew older, as with all boys, I pretended not to want hugs or kisses from her but secretly I missed it."

"You were too young to be left without your mother," said Elizabeth.

"It was not easy for me. When she died, there was no one to show me that kind of affection." He thought back to the loneliness he had felt after his mother's death and not for the first time wondered how it had changed him. He was not really certain why he was telling Elizabeth about this. It was something he had never shared with anyone, including Georgiana. "My sister had her nanny and then her governess. I suppose Mrs. Reynolds became like a mother to me, but it was not the same. Father loved me in his own way. He taught me how to be a gentleman, to be responsible, and run the estate."

"I am sure your father must have been very proud of you."

"Yes, of course, but being proud is not the same as affection. I missed that special love my mother gave me." He paused for a moment before he continued. "I am only beginning to understand how much."

"And were both your parents as serious as you are?" she asked. One side of her mouth turned up.

Darcy shook his head. "Father was usually very stern and serious; Mother loved to laugh. I remember she knew just how to make him laugh, too." He inclined his head to the side a bit and looked up at the sky as he tried to remember his parents more clearly. "As I think back, I realize now that after my mother died, the only person who made my father laugh was George Wickham."

"That must have made you more than a little jealous."

"Many times I would have liked to have his charming way of talking to people, of knowing the just the right thing to say." There was a silent moment before he continued. "For example, had I greater facility with words, I would have talked to people at the dance in Meryton that first evening. How I envied Bingley his easy manners and friendly speech that night. Instead, I kept to myself."

Elizabeth laughed, "I seem to remember thinking you a snob that first evening. What was it you said about me? 'Tolerable, but not handsome enough to tempt me,'" she said, imitating his deep voice. "That stung more than I liked to admit at the time."

Remembering that evening brought him pain. If he could go back to that night and start over, he would have asked her to dance. "Elizabeth, please, you must forget I ever said such a thing. I behaved like a fool."

"Now that I know you better I can see how your actions were more from shyness than anything else."

Here he stopped and turned to face her, "I saw you laughing with Mrs. Collins that night and I secretly wished I could talk and laugh with you like that. I just did not know how to begin."

"Then you should have asked me to dance. We would have found something to talk about, and I might have formed a different opinion of you from the very beginning," she said. Darcy wished he was better at reading people. Could she be flirting with him?

"Ah, but there was another evening not long after the assembly. I did ask you to dance, and you declined most vehemently," he said.

"Sir William Lucas suggested it so I assumed you were just attempting to satisfy him. That is not the same as asking me yourself."

"Usually, at such affairs, I was hesitant to dance with anyone outside my party lest people get the wrong idea. Everywhere I went mothers would throw their daughters in my way hoping to catch my attention. My only defense was to withdraw into silence."

She shook her head thoughtfully. "Yes, I can only imagine how my own mother would have acted if she had perceived any partiality for me on your part. Her behavior regarding Jane and Mr. Bingley was embarrassing enough. I understand the need you felt to protect yourself from such unpleasantness."

Darcy was suddenly overcome with a desire to tell her how much he loved her, how much he wanted her, but he had no idea how to begin. As if she were reading his mind, at that exact moment, she reached up and took his arm. Her touch, light as a feather, sparked something in him. How he had longed for that feeling, longed to touch her in ways that made him blush. He wanted to make her blush, too.

Just as these thoughts were whirling around in his head, Elizabeth interrupted. "Are you well, William? You seem flushed. Is the walk too strenuous for you?"

Embarrassed at being caught out by the very object of his daydreaming, it took him a moment to realize what she was saying. "I believe you are teasing me."

She flashed him a devilish look.

"I like it when you do that," he admitted.

"I am glad for I dearly love to tease you. It makes you somehow less formidable." She hesitated and then added, "It also closes the distance between us a little, I think."

Darcy's breath caught. Had he understood her correctly? Was she giving him an opening to speak to her? He stopped and took her hands in his. "Please, Elizabeth, do not tease about something as important as this. In spite of everything that has happened, you must know how much I feel for you. Do not say you want to be closer if it is not true. I could not bear it. I have been waiting for you to..."

She silenced him by gently caressing his face. He watched her carefully, and her eyes seemed to give permission. Leaning over, he kissed her lightly on the lips and then looked at her face to read the result. At first, her eyes remained closed. Finally, she looked up, her luminous eyes focused intently on him.

"My feelings have been so confused. I think it might help if you did that again," she said.

"You want me to..." he stammered. Before he could finish his sentence, she stood up on her tiptoes and kissed him again. When they separated, he tried to speak, but she put a hand behind his head and pulled him close to whisper in his ear, "Shh, this may be one time when it would be advantageous *not* to talk."

Needing no further encouragement, he touched her lips with his again. As they kissed, this time much longer and more deeply, she reached up and wound her arms around his neck. He felt Elizabeth lean into him, and when he released her mouth, she turned her head and laid it on his chest. He knew his heart must be beating wildly.

"So you have forgiven me," she said quietly.

"I forgave you weeks ago."

"Why did you not tell me?" she asked.

"I was still uncertain of your true feelings."

"And now?"

He took her face in both hands and kissed her again.

FIFTY EIGHT

That evening Elizabeth sipped a small glass of port as she read. Looking up from her book, she watched as Darcy held his brandy glass in one hand and carefully balanced his book in the other. An errant lock of hair fell across his brow and from time to time he set his glass aside and brushed it back into place only to have it tumble down again. She marveled at how much she enjoyed watching him when he was unaware of it.

She still felt the glow of what had passed between them on the walk that afternoon, but as with most things between them, nothing was ever simple. Although he had kissed her and then held her hand, the closer they got to the house, the more self-conscious he seemed to grow. Eventually, he had released her hand, and his reserved manner had returned.

Elizabeth sighed. After refocusing on her book for a while, her eyes grew heavy. Setting her book aside, she stood up and stretched.

"Are you retiring now?" he asked. She studied his face but found no clues as to what he was thinking.

"Yes, I believe I shall."

"Very well, good-night and sleep well." She heard what she hoped was a note of regret in his voice, but he made no attempt to kiss her or follow her to her room.

Once in bed she found she was no longer sleepy; her

thoughts naturally turned to Darcy and the complexities of their relationship. Since their walk that afternoon, they had been dancing around each other, both watching for some sign, but neither willing to make the first move. Wasn't it his responsibility to come to her? She thought she had made it clear enough he would be welcome, but as time passed there was only silence on the other side of the door.

Finally, after about an hour, when she had given up all hope he would join her, she decided to light a lamp and read. Unfortunately, she had left her book in the sitting room—again—and she would have to retrieve it.

The room was almost dark now with just a small glow from the embers in the fireplace. Darcy was asleep in the big chair, his long legs resting across a large upholstered footstool. He was still dressed but had removed his boots and loosened his neck cloth.

Elizabeth smiled at his sleeping form. How different he looked asleep and unguarded. His hair was tousled and all the lines of worry seemed to have left his face. Elizabeth knelt down beside his chair. As she studied his sleeping form, she began to wonder if this might be her opportunity. Although she wished he had taken the initiative to come to her, for some reason he had not.

Elizabeth gently pushed back the recalcitrant lock of hair that had fallen across his forehead again. She wondered what he would think of her being so forward. Would he be pleased? Or would he be uncomfortable with such wanton behavior? She trembled as she tried to imagine what might happen if he accepted her advances. She placed her shaking hand on his chest so she could feel the beating of his heart. Its steady thump brought a smile to her face and warmth to her hand.

Could she give herself to him completely and with no reservations? She had never been one to be afraid of the unknown. As a child she boldly climbed trees, investigated the fields and woods, and followed her natural curiosity. This is just a different sort of adventure, she told herself. On the other hand, she was risking the mortification of possible rejection.

After months of struggle, Elizabeth knew she loved him, loved him with an intensity she had not believed possible. How strange that when she had first met him, she had not thought him handsome at all. Now to her eye, he was the best looking man she had ever known.

Yes, he still had difficulty remembering that he should seek her opinion more often rather than make decisions on his own and that his requests sometimes sounded more like orders, but his heart—the one she felt beating beneath her hand—was good and loving. He had shown her he was willing to try to change. At least it was a beginning.

Running her fingers lightly along his jaw, she felt the roughness of his beard contrasted by softer skin as her hand trailed down his neck. Reaching the top of his shirt made her think about that awful night in the library when she had been so distracted by seeing the hollow at the base of his neck. Gently, she unfastened one more button on his shirt until she could see the place that so fascinated her. Just as she started to reach out to touch him there, he stirred a little but did not open his eyes. Startled, she automatically pulled her hand back and watched until his breathing evened out.

Reaching out she ran her fingers lightly along his cheek again. Then with even more boldness, she cradled his face with her hand and kissed his cheek. Slowly turning his face to her, she touched her lips lightly to his. Without opening his eyes, he responded, kissing her back. Elizabeth quickly forgot everything except the sensations in that moment. Then suddenly he pulled away, looking startled and confused.

"I thought I was dreaming," he said still not fully awake.

"I hope it was a good dream," she whispered.

He smiled sleepily and kissed her again, this time more deeply. Heat began to build inside her. As she responded—tentatively at first, and then with more passion, all of her fears were quickly forgotten, and she made a decision about what she wanted.

Elizabeth stood up and holding his gaze, untied the ribbons on the front of her dressing gown. Lowering her arms, she let the garment fall to the floor in a silky puddle behind her. She knew her nightdress would leave little to the imagination. Although she blushed with the thought of what he could see, she did not look away. Elizabeth was quite sure she heard Darcy's breathing quicken. Then she crawled onto his lap and put her arms around his neck.

Darcy pulled her close and began to place small kisses starting just behind her ear and moving down to her bare white shoulder. Then he ran a finger along the path he had just kissed. Elizabeth heard herself sigh with pleasure at his touch. Next he turned his attention back to her mouth. Just as she was having difficulty catching her breath, she felt him untying the ribbon that held her hair. Once the ribbon was removed, he slowly combed his fingers through the length of her braid. She shook her head until her hair fell freely over her shoulders and down her back.

"I have wanted to do that for a very long time. You have no idea," he whispered hoarsely as he gathered up a handful of her hair inhaling the scent. "You always smell so wonderful," he said. "Intoxicating."

Elizabeth's heart raced wildly. The heat inside her was continuing to build. Although she did not understand what was happening, she only knew she did not want him to stop. She gasped aloud as he ran a finger along the sensitive skin at the top edge of her nightdress and then kissed the trail of fire his fingers had left.

"Oh, God! You are so soft, so tempting," he said. Closing his eyes, he let his head fall back. "Elizabeth, I...I should not," he began.

"Please do not pull away from me now. I do not wish to be alone tonight," she whispered with as much dignity as she could manage. She felt him tense.

"Is this truly what you want or do you just think this is your duty?" He looked at her with hope in his eyes.

"I love you and want to be your wife in every way," she said, sounding bolder than she felt. Elizabeth felt his body relax, and he pulled her tightly against him burying his face against her neck.

"Oh, Lizzy, my love," he sighed. "I have been waiting to hear you say that for so long."

More kisses, more heat, and suddenly the chair seemed very small and cramped. "Should we move to a more comfortable situation? Would you prefer your room or mine?" he asked.

"Definitely yours," she said.

When he looked at her, his eyes were so dark with longing that she almost panicked, but the desire for more of his kisses quickly pushed away any second thoughts. Darcy scooped her up in his arms and started for his room. Elizabeth buried her face in his chest and held on to him tightly. Seizing the opportunity, she put her hand inside his shirt and ran a finger slowly along his collarbone from the shoulder to the base of his neck. Her reward was a small groan of pleasure in the back of his throat. For a moment, she thought he might drop her.

"You are distracting me, my love."

"That is exactly my intention," she mumbled into his shirt as she stifled a nervous giggle. Setting her down on the bed, he stood back, looking at her as if he could not believe that she was really there.

"Tell me this is real," he said as he ran his eyes over her with an intensity that only turned up the fire inside her even more.

"My love for you is very real. Now come here and put your arms around me again. I am cold without you to warm me."

As he started toward the bed, she suddenly put up a hand to stop him. "Wait, take your coat off first, please."

He complied, letting it fall to the floor.

"And your waistcoat," she added.

He grinned showing the dimple in his cheek. "You look as if

you enjoy telling me what to do."

"Yes, I think I do," she said. Her eyes twinkled as she looked boldly into his. Then she hesitated and cast her eyes down. "But very soon we shall be at a place where you will have to tell me as we will be beyond my experience."

Stretching out on the bed beside her, Darcy pulled her into the warmth of his arms. "I think I can manage to show you, my love." His mouth found hers and he kissed her with all the passion that had been building up over the past few months. Her whole body tingled with pleasure in response.

She pushed his shirt back and began to kiss his neck starting at the base and working her way up to just below his ear. In spite of being breathless, she could not resist teasing one more time. She whispered into his ear. "Mr. Darcy, what will Burke say when he finds your beautiful coat tossed on the floor in the morning?"

"At this moment, my love, that is definitely the last thing on my mind."

FIFTY NINE

Elizabeth lay with her head on her husband's shoulder, an arm across his chest, and her leg entwined with one of his. Resting quietly, she remembered all the tender words of love and desire he had whispered to her and how his arms had felt around her as he had given her pleasure beyond anything she could ever have imagined. She was his now—completely and totally—and she had never been happier in her life. So this was the great mystery that no one wanted to talk about. The thought made her laugh out loud.

"What is it, my love?"

"It is nothing—just, well, I had no idea."

"No idea of what?"

"How wonderful this could be! This part of marriage is so rarely spoken of. It was always implied to me that a woman must put up with doing her wifely duty, but I knew that could not be the entire truth. Aunt Gardiner tried to tell me, but I had no idea it would be so...so pleasurable."

Darcy tightened his arm around her. "I have always said your aunt is a very wise woman."

"So you did not think my behavior was...was wanton?" Suddenly, she felt shy and uncertain of herself.

Darcy put a finger under her chin and lifted her face. "Lizzy, my sweet, what you did was exciting to me beyond anything I could have imagined. Your gift of yourself was truly the most wonderful I have ever received. You have my permission to be the same every time we are together."

"I so wanted you to know how my feelings have changed over the few past months," she told him.

"Then you expressed yourself very well indeed."

A small smile flitted across her face as she blushed and cast her eyes down. Darcy kissed her on the forehead and pulled her closer. She languidly stretched out her bare leg running it down his. "I feel so deliciously content here with you," she said softly.

"That is an improvement. Months ago, when I asked if you were happy, you told me you were just 'reasonably content.'"

"Oh, I am *so* much more than that now—I am *exceedingly* content! I feel as if I am glowing all over. Can you tell?" she laughed, tossing her hair back so he could better see her face.

"Let me look." Darcy examined her face very seriously and then peeked under the covers at the rest of her body. He grinned. "Mmm, yes, I believe you are glowing—'*Celestial rosy red, Love's proper hue...*'"

She smiled. "You do love Milton."

He whispered in her ear, "'*Awake, My fairest, my espoused, my latest found, Heaven's last best gift, my ever new delight!*'"

"Ah, yes, my paradise is here with you," she replied just before he silenced her with a kiss.

❈

Later when she was able to speak coherently again, she said, "You have called me 'Lizzy' several times tonight. You have never done that before."

"You have been 'Lizzy' in my dreams for a long time."

"So you have been dreaming about me?" she asked coyly.

Now it was his turn to blush. "Constantly."

"And when did this begin?"

"I believe it was when you were staying at Netherfield."

"Ah, so you stared at me all day and dreamed about me all night? Is that it?" she teased.

"I have made love to you in my dreams so many times, but no dream could possibly compare to the reality of this night."

Her eyes danced as she laughed. "And you said you are not good with words! That was the nicest thing you could have said to me. I believe you have just been forgiven for all those months of taking liberties with my person without my knowledge."

"It is true. Being with you has exceeded my expectations by so much—so very much." He kissed her forehead.

"When did you begin to believe me?" she asked.

"Believe what?"

"You are tormenting me! Surely, you know what I mean."

He grinned but then grew serious. "When you came to my room to apologize, I began to hope again. I wanted to believe you, but I think I truly started to take you seriously the day Lady Catherine came to call."

Elizabeth propped herself up on her elbow to better see his face. "Lady Catherine? I do not understand."

"I overheard some of what you said to her," he confessed.

"You were listening at the door?" Frantically, she thought back trying to recall what he might have overheard.

"You told her you loved me for myself alone, and that I meant everything to you. You had no reason to say that if it was not true."

"You heard that? Then you were outside the door when she was being such a beast to me and you did not help! How could you do that to me?"

Darcy jumped as she poked him in the ribs. Laughing, he playfully fumbled to catch her hands to prevent her from doing further damage. "Very well, I apologize! I am sorry for not coming to your rescue, but you seemed to be doing a very fine job of defending yourself."

"What else did you hear?"

"Hmmm...there was something about my being the only

man in the world to whom you could ever imagine being married. I believe that stunned me in such a way that I could not move."

"And that is your excuse?" she asked, tilting her head to one side. He shrugged. "You were paralyzed?" Again, he answered with just a grin. "I told you the day I accepted your proposal that I would not pretend feelings I did not have. Did you forget that?" she asked suddenly very serious.

"I did not forget—I was just afraid to trust it."

"Still I cannot believe you did not come to my defense!"

"Truly, I was about to rescue you. I only listened for a moment, and then you came bursting into the hallway."

"You know what they say about people who listen at doors?"

"I know I should have interrupted, but I have rarely heard anyone who was more equal to the task of putting my aunt in her place than you were that day."

Elizabeth took a deep breath and exhaled with resignation. Then suddenly, in a flash of inspiration, it all made sense to her. She sat up and looked him in the eye.

"So that is why you were so curious to know the exact timing of when I learned the extent of your role in helping Lydia. You were trying to determine if I had discovered this before or after your aunt's visit." She took his silence as confirmation. "If the discomfort your aunt inflicted upon me helped to convince you of my love, then perhaps I should send a letter thanking her."

Elizabeth conjured up an image of Lady Catherine's thunderous countenance at reading such a letter. Her amusement began as a giggle and grew into a full-blown fit of uncontrolled laughter. At first, Darcy did not understand what had given her such delight, but then the cause dawned upon him, and he immediately succumbed to laughter himself.

"I do not know why I find it so funny," she said, wiping the tears away.

Darcy recovered, too, and shook his head in amazement. "I do not think I have laughed this hard since...well, I am not sure when, but it has been a very, very long time."

"If you do not remember, then it has been far too long. I shall have to make it my mission to ensure you laugh on a regular basis. I am certain it must be good for your health."

Darcy reached out, pulling her into his arms and held her tightly against him. Elizabeth gently placed her hand on his chest to feel the steady beating of his heart.

"Oh, my love, I do not know what would have happened to me if I had not found you. You have brought my poor heart back to life," he said.

"I am only sorry it took me so long to recognize my feelings."

"So when did you begin?" he asked.

"I think I had loved you for a long time, but I did not truly know it in my heart until I thought I had lost you. I remember you once said that your good opinion once lost was lost forever. I was terrified I had ruined everything with my cruel words."

Darcy put his hand under her chin so he could look her in the eye.

"But you never lost it—I could never stop loving you even if I wanted to. When you apologized and said you loved me, it was everything I had hoped to hear."

"But why were you so cold to me?" she asked.

"I wanted so much for you to return my love, but I was afraid to believe it was true. If it wasn't, I could not have survived the pain of losing you yet again. My coldness was my only defense."

"Oh, my poor dear. I am so sorry to have caused you pain. I will just have to find a way to make it up to you."

"I can think of several things you might do," he said, raising an eyebrow and giving her a suggestive grin.

Elizabeth laughed and poked her finger at his chest. "You, sir, can be very wicked—but I will do my penance with pleasure." She rolled on top of him and happily began her atonement.

※

Lying together in contentment, they talked until dawn, sharing and sorting through many of the things that had remained unspoken over their months together. Eventually, they began to hear the servants starting their morning routines to prepare the house for the day.

"I should feel tired after being awake all night, but I do not," she said.

Darcy sat up and threw his legs over the side of the bed. "Last night has left me weak with hunger. I require something to eat."

Elizabeth sat up, putting her arms around her drawn up knees. "If we ring for a breakfast tray, we could have a picnic right here," she suggested.

Suddenly, she put her head in her hands. "Oh, no!"

Darcy turned back to her, looking concerned. "What is wrong, my love?"

"I think I should return to my room before Burke finds me here. I suppose Margaret already knows I have not slept in my own bed. Oh, this is so embarrassing. Everyone knows that husbands and wives should sleep in their own rooms." Elizabeth pulled the counterpane over her head to hide how red her face had grown.

Darcy gently lowered the covers and gathered her into his arms. "I am not embarrassed you are here. You have made me the happiest of men. In fact, I am not planning to let you sleep alone again for a very long time." Then he added quickly, "Of course, if that is acceptable to you."

Elizabeth finally saw the humor in the situation and kissed him. "It is more than acceptable. In fact, I demand it."

SIXTY

It took all of Elizabeth's will power not to interrupt Darcy in his study that afternoon. She found that she could think of nothing else but the feel of his body against hers. Finally, she could wait no longer. The look in his eyes when she entered his study made her warm all over.

"Mr. Darcy, I have been feeling very strange all afternoon," she said playfully.

"Are you feeling ill, my love?" he asked, a look of concern on his face.

"I have been unable to concentrate, in fact, to even think clearly. When I was talking to Mrs. Reynolds about the menus, my mind kept drifting away. Georgiana had to ask me the same question several times before I even knew she was speaking to me. What is happening to me?" she asked, raising an eyebrow dramatically.

Darcy pulled her onto his lap. "Let me check to see if you have a fever."

As he reached out to touch her forehead, she caught his hand and kissed it. Then she laid her head on his shoulder and began to run a finger along his jaw line and down his neck. She was pleased when she felt him shiver under her touch.

"All I have been able to think of is last night and when I think about it, I lose track of everything else. Tell me it was not just a dream," she said.

Darcy pulled her close and began to kiss her in a way that would leave her with no doubts.

"Is that better?" he asked a little later.

"It is a good beginning," she told him as she reached for him again.

After a few minutes, she felt him hesitate and then gently push her away. "Elizabeth, we must stop. We are in my study. Anyone could come to the door."

"I am not sure I really care right now," she said with a devilish grin. Then she went back to tempting him by running her hands gently through his hair. He caught her hand and kissed her palm.

"What am I going to do with you?"

Boldly, she told him just exactly what she had in mind. Darcy shook his head and laughed.

"You amaze me!"

"Perhaps, like conversation, this part of our relationship also requires practice. Since we are just learning about each other, do you not think we should practice now?" she asked with an impish grin.

"What will the servants think if we retire to our room at this time of day?" he teased.

"Tell them your wife is tired and wishes to take a nap before dinner, or tell them she cannot wait to be in bed with you again. I do not really care what you say as long as you come upstairs with me."

Darcy laughed. "Is this ordering me about going to become a habit?"

Elizabeth grinned and shrugged her shoulders. Then she took him by the hand and led him to their room.

SIXTY ONE

Elizabeth awoke slightly disoriented but then quickly remembered where she was—the big bed in Darcy's room. The past few days—and nights—had been perfection. Their first night together, their afternoon nap, dinner by candlelight, and then more nights of new experiences and revelations—this kind of intimacy in a relationship was so much more than she had ever dreamed of. At last, she was truly his wife and although her face reddened at the thought of what transpired between them, her body tingled and her heart rejoiced.

As she lay quietly taking time to enjoy becoming more fully awake, she sensed she was alone in the big bed. It seemed strange to her that Darcy could have arisen without waking her, and she began to wonder how late she had slept. The clock told her it was only eight in the morning, not so late as she had first thought. Reaching her arms above her head, she stretched out fully and thought about her plans for the day.

Just as she started to sit up, she realized she was missing something very important—her nightdress. In the rush to be together last night, Darcy had pulled it off and tossed it into the air. It must have landed somewhere on the floor near the bed. Scanning the room, she saw it was now neatly draped across a chair along with her dressing gown. She groaned. Two things came to her mind—how did it get there and more importantly, how was she going to retrieve it.

It was a long way from the big bed to the chair. Reclaiming her nightclothes would necessitate walking eight to ten feet across the room completely naked. She would die of embarrassment if one of the servants should choose that exact moment to come into the room! Or what if Darcy returned? It was one thing to be with him under the covers, but it would be something different altogether to be caught out in the open. Just thinking about it made her face warm.

Finally, acknowledging she might be forced to wait for a long time if she did not brave the walk, she took a deep breath and made a dash for the chair. She had just slipped the gown over her head and was starting to reach for the robe when there was a knock on the door. Startled into action, she dashed back to the bed and leaped in pulling the covers up around her.

The door swung open, and Darcy entered carrying a tray with coffee and scones. "I have brought your breakfast, Mrs. Darcy. Ah, I see you have been up already," he said, nodding toward the chair.

"Did you..." she trailed off, waving her hand anxiously in that direction.

"No, your things were there when I awoke."

"So someone came in while we were asleep and..." her voice trailed off again. Elizabeth groaned and pulled the covers over her head. Darcy laughed as he set the tray down on the bed. Gently, he uncovered her face and kissed her forehead.

"Most likely, it was Margaret since your dressing gown was on the chair as well," he said as he began pouring coffee into the delicate china cups.

"I do not think I shall ever become accustomed to having servants around me all the time. Does it never disturb you? Sometimes, I feel as if I am never alone."

Darcy shrugged. "I do not think about it. Their presence is just a fact of life. Of course, there are times when I wish to be alone. Everyone knows not to come into my study without knocking, and usually no one enters my bedchamber in the morning until I ring. Perhaps, you might tell Margaret the same."

"I am not sure if I shall ever be completely comfortable. They must know everything we do."

He raised an eyebrow. "Well, not *everything*, but I suspect Margaret and Burke were well pleased to know you were here again this morning."

Darcy added milk and sugar to the cup before handing it to her. Reaching up, he fingered a stray lock of her hair and watched her intently. She blushed under his gaze.

"My love, if you are going to turn red every time I look at you..." he began as he stroked her cheek with his thumb. She leaned her head against his hand.

"I cannot control it. It just happens," she told him.

He gave a short laugh. "Strange, isn't it that this is the one sort of situation in which you are the one who is shy and instead of me."

"Do not tease." She set her coffee aside. "Now I feel very much in need of hearing again that you love me." At that, he smiled.

"You must know you are my whole world. I do not think I truly lived until I met you." Starting just below her ear and working his way down to her shoulder, he placed light kisses on her sensitive skin.

She shivered. Tipping her head back slightly, she closed her eyes, lost in the sensations.

When he reached the obstacle of the strap of her nightdress, he gently slid it off her shoulder. "Lizzy?"

"Hmm?" Dreamily she opened her eyes and found him watching her.

"I love you," he said softly.

Putting her arms around his neck, she pulled him down onto the bed with her. Slowly, taking his time, he made sure his lips communicated exactly the extent of his regard.

❋

When the last of the water was poured into the tub, Margaret shooed the maids from the room and then followed them out. Elizabeth slipped into the warm water with a sigh of pleasure. This was just one of many details that continued to amaze her about living at Pemberley. The bath water was always just the right temperature; the food arrived at the table warm and delicious; and fires were lit in precisely the rooms she wished to use. Everything was always perfectly arranged to meet the needs of the Darcy family. In spite of her involvement with the household management, Elizabeth continued to wonder at the thoroughness and efficiency of Mrs. Reynolds and the staff. Nothing was missed. Many times she had wondered if the housekeeper could read her mind. It seemed as if all she had to do was wish for something and it appeared.

Letting the warm water relax her, she began to daydream. As she turned over the events of the past few days in her mind, her thoughts turned again to her husband. He had been so gentle with her, and yet she could feel the strength of his passion that burned beneath the surface. More than anything, she had been very surprised at her own behavior. There was something thrilling about the adventure of trusting in him and simply allowing herself to do whatever felt good. It seemed her body knew what it wanted. Thinking too much simply got in the way.

And when he had casually left the bed to pour her a glass of water, he had been completely unselfconscious as he walked around naked. Although she blushed to think of it, she had barely been able to take her eyes off his perfect body. He had broad shoulders and was muscular in a sleek, cat-like kind of way. She guessed it was from riding and fencing and also the physical work he did on the farms. In spite of the fact she had tried to hide her interest, he had caught her watching him. Instead of being embarrassed he had grinned at her in the most devilish way. There was so much to discover about this man.

Closing her eyes and thinking back to last night, she could almost feel his touch. As she put a hand to her neck and throat, she relived the experience. Her face flushed from just the thought of it. Of course, Margaret chose that exact moment to knock at the door. Elizabeth prayed the young woman would assume her high color was from the hot water.

"I am not ready yet, Margaret," she called.

"Yes, ma'am, but Mr. Darcy has sent a note for you. May I bring it in now or would you like to read it when I dress your hair?"

"Please bring it to me now," she said. Wondering what could be so urgent that he would send a note, she dried her hands and took the folded paper from Margaret.

"Please return in five minutes, and I will be ready to dress." As she opened the letter, she noted the Darcy family seal impressed in the wax. She smiled. My family seal now, she thought.

My dearest, loveliest Elizabeth,
"Doubt thou the stars are fire;
Doubt that the sun doth move;
Doubt truth to be a liar;
But never doubt I love."
Hamlet II.ii.116

With all my heart,
W.

Elizabeth was astonished at the depths of feeling that lay behind Darcy's quiet ways. Although he was becoming more open in telling her about his feelings, there would always be things he could never say in words. Here he had let the quotation speak for him.

SIXTY TWO

After dinner one evening, Darcy, Elizabeth, and Georgiana retired to the music room so Georgiana could play her newest
piece for them. "She has improved so much," Darcy leaned
close to whisper.

Elizabeth smiled as she felt the softness of his breath against
her ear. Giving herself over to the enjoyment of the music, her
mind turned back to the perfect afternoon they had spent together. Unfortunately, the weather had been too inclement for
walking so they had retired to their sitting room to spend time
together reading in front of the fire. In truth, they had only
been alone for a matter of minutes before Elizabeth had moved
to Darcy's lap, and one thing had led to another. Her cheeks
warmed with pleasure as she recalled the softness of her husband's touch, the feel of his lips upon hers, and the passion
they had shared. Suddenly, Elizabeth was brought back to reality
as Georgiana's piece ended. She joined Darcy in appreciative
applause,

"What a wonderful performance! You seem to be improving
every time I hear you play," Darcy told her.

Georgiana flushed at the praise. "You are too kind."

"You yourself told me that your brother never exaggerates
nor gives praise where it is not deserved," Elizabeth reminded
her. Both Georgiana and Darcy smiled at her, and for a

moment, she thought she saw a hint of family resemblance.

"There is something I would like to discuss with both of you," said Georgiana suddenly serious.

"What is on your mind, my dear?" Darcy inquired.

"You know how very important music is to me. Playing brings me such great joy, but I would like to do more."

"More?" Darcy gave her a questioning look.

"I have begun to compose music," she said shyly. "The piece I played this evening is one I wrote myself."

"You wrote that yourself!" Elizabeth exclaimed. "It was lovely!"

"Georgiana, it was truly beautiful! I knew that you were very gifted, but I had no idea," her brother told her.

"Thank you. I have been working on it for quite some time." She smiled. "This brings me to what I would like to discuss. I would like to have a special music tutor to teach me more about music theory and composition. All of the best music masters are in London." She hesitated and then added quickly, "Of course, I am not anxious to leave Pemberley. I do so love being at home with you both."

Darcy frowned. "I am not sure about..." he let his voice trail off for a moment and then he began again. "Georgiana, dear, I applaud your eagerness to learn. Elizabeth and I would like to discuss this between us before we make a decision."

"Of course, I understand," Georgiana replied, looking from one of them to the other.

Elizabeth smoothed over the awkward moment by suggesting that Darcy might enjoy hearing the duet they had been practicing.

※

Later that evening when they snuggled down under the covers of the big bed, he pulled her close. She lay in the crook of his arm with her head on his shoulder. "Elizabeth, what do you think about Georgiana's request?" he asked.

"I believe she should have the opportunity to explore her natural talents."

"I am concerned it might be too much for her right now. After all, she will be coming out in the next year or two, and there is still much she must do to prepare."

"This seems very important to her," she replied.

"Hmm," he murmured thoughtfully, kissing her on the top of the head.

Elizabeth burrowed closer against him. "Is there any reason why she should not further her music studies?" she asked.

"No, of course not. She has a marvelous talent and should develop it if she wishes."

"The piece she played this evening was lovely. I think she may truly have talent."

"I agree," he acknowledged.

"Perhaps you are hesitant because these studies could take her away from us," Elizabeth suggested.

"Being here at Pemberley with the two women I love most in the world is very special to me. I am reluctant for this idyllic time to end," he said.

"She is a young woman and, as you have pointed out, will be coming out soon and eventually getting married. This is what you want, is it not, or do you plan to keep her here at Pemberley forever?"

"I want her to be as happy as we are," he said, kissing her cheek.

"This is a dilemma then. You would like her to pursue her interests, but also stay at Pemberley with us for a little longer." Elizabeth let her words hang in the air for a few minutes. She took the opportunity to place a few kisses strategically on his throat and face as she waited.

"You are distracting me, my love."

"Oh, I am so sorry!" Elizabeth said with a giggle, but she did not stop.

Later as they lay together in mutual contentment, Elizabeth realized she was becoming accustomed to her husband's protracted periods of silence. She was learning it did not necessarily mean that something was wrong. It just took him time—sometimes a long time—to think things through before he spoke.

"I have been considering Georgiana's request."

"Do you mean that while we were making love, you were thinking about something else?" Elizabeth could not resist teasing him.

"I did not hear you complain!" he said, feigning indignation.

"Very well, so you began thinking about Georgiana's request after we..." she stopped, completing the rest of the sentence with a flourish of her hand.

"Seriously, Elizabeth, I think I have reached a solution that will solve the problem quite nicely."

"Ah, a solution?"

"I shall offer to engage a music tutor to come here to Pemberley at least until spring. Then we can reevaluate if she should move back into town. What do you think?"

Elizabeth had already concluded that this would be the best solution but had been hoping he would think of it himself. "It is a splendid idea. We could suggest it to her and see what she thinks. I believe it is also her desire to stay here with us," she said. Elizabeth rose up on one elbow and kissed him lightly.

"What was that for?" he inquired.

"Do I need a reason to kiss you?"

"Of course not. I suppose I am just not yet accustomed to having you at my side all the time."

"I am not going anywhere," she said as she kissed him on the cheek again.

"I have also been giving some thought to what you said about Georgiana not feeling ready for her coming out," he said.

"You have been very busy thinking. Are you quite certain you were giving me your undivided attention earlier?"

"Of course, I was!"

"I believe I have need of further assurances," Elizabeth suggested coyly, and he readily complied, making sure to overlook no detail until he was certain she could have no further complaints.

SIXTY THREE

Very soon their idyllic existence was interrupted, as it was time to leave for London to prepare for Jane and Mr. Bingley's wedding. As much as Elizabeth wanted to give her sister the very best wedding day possible, she was loathe to do anything that might disturb the delicious harmony she and Darcy seemed to have achieved. At Pemberley, there was so much time for them to be together. They took rides, went for walks, and lingered in bed sometimes into late morning. This was a very special time, and she wanted to savor every moment. Reluctantly, she acknowledged that if they did not leave for London soon, she would never have time to make all the preparations for the wedding.

�֍

Once in London, planning for Jane's wedding occupied nearly every moment of Elizabeth's waking hours. She was almost obsessed with making everything perfect. Arranging the food, the church, the flowers—those were the easy things. What was difficult was balancing all of the diverse personalities involved in the event.

Shopping for the last few items of Jane's trousseau had been the subject of much interest to all of the Bennet ladies. Before they even reached London, Mrs. Bennet had spent hours instructing Jane what to buy and where to find it. Unfortunately, Caroline Bingley believed that everything related to style fell in her province, as she and only she knew all the best places in town to shop. Of course, not wishing to offend anyone, Jane invited everyone to go on the shopping excursions.

Elizabeth convinced her mother that in order to be polite to Jane's new family, they should go first to all the places Miss Bingley recommended, and then Mrs. Bennet could arrange additional trips if they did not find everything on their list. Reluctantly, Mrs. Bennet agreed. It was a tenuous compromise held together with not much more than pretty ribbons.

❧

When Darcy arrived home on the afternoon of the ladies' shopping trip, he met Jane just coming out of the parlor. "Hello, Miss Bennet. May I enquire how your..." he stopped mid-sentence when he saw the look on her face.

"What is wrong? Has something happened?" he asked.

Jane, who always had a sweet smile on her face, looked distressed. "Do not worry, Mr. Darcy. All is well. Lizzy and I were just talking about Caroline Bingley's rather unpleasant behavior while we were shopping. I was trying to tell Lizzy not to let it bother her."

"What did Miss Bingley say?"

"I think you should ask Lizzy about it yourself," Jane told him. "Now if you will excuse me, I will retire to my room."

As she started to walk away, he inquired, "If I may ask, what are Miss Bingley's plans for after you are married?"

Jane smiled sweetly and paused on the stairs. "Charles and I have agreed it is time for Caroline to spend more time with the Hursts—and less with us."

Darcy smiled as she walked away. Perhaps he had underestimated the quiet Miss Bennet.

MR. DARCY'S PROPOSAL

✻

When Darcy entered the sitting room, Elizabeth was standing at the window. Crossing the room in a few quick steps, he put his arms around his wife. It was something he was learning to do when she was out of sorts. At first, he had tried offering solutions to her problem and he could not understand why this sometimes made her even more upset. Finally, he discovered quite by accident that simply putting his arms around her and listening was all that was generally required.

"What has happened, my love? What has upset you so?" he asked, already knowing full well at least part of what was causing her discomfort.

Elizabeth buried her face against his chest and mumbled two words, "Caroline Bingley."

"Oh, I see," he said, sitting down and pulling her onto his lap.

"She is so insufferable!"

"You sound as if you have only just discovered this."

Elizabeth scowled at him. "She insisted our family knew nothing about where to find the best fabrics and the most fashionable dressmakers in London—as if we had never shopped in the big city before. She treated us like country bumpkins—as if she were the queen of style."

"Did you or your mother have words with her?"

"Fortunately, my mother was too busy looking at fabrics and ribbons and instructing the modiste. She was not attending enough to understand all the implications of what Miss Bingley was saying. Jane tells me that worrying about Caroline Bingley is not worth my time, but I cannot let it go. How could she behave so meanly?"

"Elizabeth, this is not the first time she has done this sort of thing."

"Yes, but it has been much worse recently. She seems to despise my family even more since you and I married." He wrinkled his brow and looked at her questioningly. "You must know she has never forgiven me for becoming Mrs. Darcy. She believes I stole you away from her."

"Stole me? But that is nonsense. I never gave Miss Bingley any reason to believe I held any special regard for her."

"I do not doubt that, but nevertheless, she saw things quite differently. I am certain she expected your declaration every day. I know I should not repeat gossip, but Charles told Jane that his sister was so upset about our marriage that after we left Netherfield, she shut herself in her room for days afterwards. Then she went around slamming doors and berating the servants until Charles had to insist that she get hold of herself."

"But Charles never mentioned this to me."

"Can you really imagine dear, sweet Charles Bingley ever bringing up such an unpleasant subject with you?"

"I suppose not," said Darcy thoughtfully. "Bingley has never liked conflict and almost always chooses to ignore anything unpleasant."

Elizabeth rested her head on his shoulder. After a while, he could feel her breathing even out and her agitation subside.

"Are you feeling better, my love?" he asked.

"Yes, but I have something to confess."

"Confess?"

"It happened some time ago before we left Netherfield last spring." Elizabeth sighed and slipped her arm around his shoulders snuggling closer. "Miss Bingley and I had a little conversation over the breakfast table. When everyone else had left the room and we were alone, she said some rather pointedly rude things to me. I knew she was suffering, and I did not want to be unkind to her, but it was almost impossible to resist!"

"Exactly what did she say?" Darcy asked.

"I do not want to repeat it as it may make you think less of her."

"I believe it is already much too late for that," he said, raising an eyebrow.

Elizabeth smiled wryly. "If I tell you, you must promise never to repeat it."

"I would never..." he began before she cut him off by kissing his cheek.

"You are so easy to tease," she said with a laugh. "Very well, if you wish to know, Miss Bingley intimated that I must have known in advance you would be visiting Rosings over the Easter holidays. She truly believes I somehow set a trap for you."

"If anything it was quite the other way around." Darcy laughed and shook his head.

"Then she told me straight out she did not think I was capable of being Mistress of Pemberley."

"Perhaps you misunderstood her," suggested Darcy.

Elizabeth threw him a look. "I do not think so. She was very clear."

"But that is not her business. I am the only one who has the right to make that judgment."

"Still, that is what she said, and at the time her words stung me."

Darcy pulled her to him again, and she buried her face against his chest. "Oh, my poor love. Surely, you do not believe everything Miss Bingley says?"

"Oh, but I do," said Elizabeth with an edge in her voice. "She is an expert on every topic imaginable, especially fashion, beauty, and style."

"And how do you know this?" he asked.

"Why she has told me so herself!" said Elizabeth.

At first, Darcy's shoulders begin to shake, and finally, he burst out laughing. Elizabeth poked him in the arm.

"I know it is humorous in retrospect, but at the time, it was very hurtful."

"So what did you say to her?"

"That I hoped some day when she visited Pemberley I would be able to return in equal measure the hospitality she had showed us at Netherfield."

"And how did Miss Bingley respond?"

"That quieted her for the moment, but now clearly she has forgotten herself again."

"My love, if you make it your mission to change Caroline Bingley, you are in for a big disappointment."

Elizabeth answered by covering his face with kisses, and very quickly they both forgot about Miss Bingley.

SIXTY FOUR

Elizabeth awoke on the morning of the wedding with anxious anticipation. With so much on her mind, she had barely slept and knew that only checking and rechecking her lists would provide her with any comfort. Just as she was starting to inch toward the side of the bed to arise, Darcy woke and pulled her back against him.

"Mmm, you feel wonderful this morning," he murmured into her ear.

The feel of his body touching hers and his breath on her neck was almost enough to make her forget why she had been so anxious to be up and about.

"As much as I might wish it, I cannot linger in bed today. There is so much to do before we depart for the church," she said although her will to rise was being seriously compromised by the exquisite sensations of her husband's hands stroking her back.

"You and Mrs. Hawkins have been over every item at least a dozen times. I cannot believe there is any detail that you have missed."

"You are very wicked tempting me this way," she said as she tried to wriggle loose, but Darcy held her all the more tightly.

"You know Mrs. Hawkins is very capable of seeing to anything unexpected that arises. You should relax and enjoy yourself on your sister's wedding day." As he planted kisses down the back of her neck, Elizabeth felt her resolve weakening.

"I want everything to be perfect for Jane."

"I think perhaps you want everything to be perfect for this wedding because it was not so for yours," Darcy observed.

She frowned. "William, our wedding was lovely."

"Oh, yes, everything was excellent except for the small matter of the bride wanting to be anywhere else in England other than in that church."

Elizabeth turned in his arms and lightly ran her finger along his jaw. "That is not fair. You know my feelings are different now. I love you more than I can say," she said, snuggling against him.

"I might need more convincing. Perhaps, if you stayed here just a little longer ..."

As she distracted him with a kiss, her fingers found their way to his ribs, and she began to tickle him. She had only recently discovered this weakness and planned to take advantage of it at every opportunity. When Darcy rolled to the other side of the bed to escape, Elizabeth moved quickly to pin him to the bed with her body, and her fingers continued to search for his ribs.

"No, stop! Stop!" he cried breathlessly.

"Only when you tell me how much you love me," she teased. As she looked down into his dark green eyes, her heart melted, and she forgot everything else. No longer able to resist, she lowered her head and kissed him deeply. When she laid her head on his shoulder, he whispered in her ear all she had been wishing to hear and more.

❀

During the ceremony, Elizabeth sat very close to Darcy. She knew it was not acceptable for even married couples to display affection for each other in public, but she risked putting her hand in his. Without looking down, he closed his hand around hers, and she saw the shadow of a smile play across his lips.

Jane looked aglow that morning. Her dress was perfect. Her golden hair was swept up and held with her special wedding gift from Elizabeth—pearl covered hair combs that were a perfect match to the necklace Charles Bingley had given her the night before.

As the bride and groom exchanged their wedding vows, Elizabeth thought about repeating those words at her own wedding. Now with everything so different, the words held new meaning for her. At one point in the ceremony, tears came to her eyes. Sensing her discomfort, Darcy offered his handkerchief. Patting her eyes, she thought about the small stack of fine linen handkerchiefs she kept in the drawer by her bed. She had saved every one Darcy had given her. Somehow they were symbolic of how their relationship had grown. Smiling at the thought, Elizabeth looked over at her husband. Watching his face was something she knew she would never tire of. Darcy chose that exact moment to glance in her direction. He returned her smile and squeezed her hand gently.

❇

The doors of the church opened to a world that had been covered by a light snow while they were inside.

"The snow is wonderful! Just enough to make the city beautiful, but not enough to cause difficulties with our travel," said Elizabeth taking Darcy's arm.

"In a few hours, I fear it shall all be a gray mush."

"Then let us enjoy it now," said Elizabeth. "I think it is a good omen for their marriage."

"Ever the optimist!" said Darcy as he lifted her hand, kissed it, and then tucked it back under his arm as they descended the steps of the church and waited for the others to emerge.

Mr. Gardner exited with his wife on one arm and his sister on the other. Mrs. Bennet's shrill voice cut through the quiet caused by the snow as it muffled the sound of the carriage wheels on the street.

Although Elizabeth had carefully warned her mother to maintain a certain amount of decorum at the wedding, the occasion quickly went to Mrs. Bennet's head.

"Oh, is my dear Jane not beautiful! Was she not the most beautiful bride you have ever seen?" exclaimed Mrs. Bennet.

"My dear sister, our Jane is the perfect bride. No one could be lovelier," Mr. Gardiner said in a much softer voice than normal, hoping she would follow suit.

"Jane's beauty is only exceeded by her sweet and gentle nature," added Mrs. Gardner also in a low voice.

Miss Bingley and Mrs. Hurst were right behind them on the arm of Mr. Hurst. Elizabeth cringed as she saw Caroline Bingley roll her eyes whenever Mrs. Bennet opened her mouth. Instead of trying to diffuse the situation, for once, Elizabeth turned her back and left it for someone else to manage.

❊

The Darcys hosted the wedding breakfast in magnificent style. No one could fault any of Elizabeth's plans. When the double doors to the main dining room were thrown open, the guests almost gasped at the splendor. The table was set with snow-white tablecloths and the Darcy family's finest china, crystal, and silver service. The sun streaming through the windows reflected off the crystal glassware throwing rainbows around the room. Elizabeth had arranged to have fresh flowers sent from Pemberley's green house, and the large bouquets on the tables were clusters of white, yellow, green, pink, and lavender.

Guests streamed into the room and began to search for their place cards on the table. Elizabeth had lost more sleep over the seating arrangements than any other detail. She had taken great care to keep certain personalities apart.

When it came time for toasting the bride and groom, their Uncle Gardiner again stood in for Mr. Bennet. On this occasion, Elizabeth felt her father's absence exceedingly and knew Jane must be having similar thoughts.

"I have known our dear Jane all her life. She has grown from a sweet little girl with golden curls into a truly beautiful and gracious young woman. This is a most joyous occasion for us to see her joined today to this fine young man. May they always be as happy together as they are today. To Mr. and Mrs. Bingley," he said, raising his glass and winking at his niece.

Jane blushed at the compliments. Charles Bingley took Jane's hand and kissed it. No one could miss how much they loved each other.

SIXTY FIVE

When all the guests had departed except the bride and groom, the two sisters slipped away to Elizabeth's private sitting room to share a few moments alone. Both knew that it could be several months before they saw each other again.

"Oh, Lizzy! I could never have dreamed of being so happy! This is the most wonderful day of my life. Thank you so much for everything you have done for Charles and me."

"It was our pleasure."

"I can never repay you. Your husband is generosity itself. He is such a good man," said Jane.

"Yes, he is the very best of men," said Elizabeth with a smile.

"Lizzy, I have observed that something has changed between you and Mr. Darcy. Since I have been in London preparing for the wedding, I have noticed you both seem different."

"Oh, dearest, I cannot even begin to tell you. Let me just say that I am no longer sorry to be married to Mr. Darcy. In fact, I now believe that we are very well-suited for each other. I have even discovered he has a sense of humor although he generally keeps it for when we are alone."

"Hearing you say that makes my joy in this day complete. To see you happy has been my most fervent wish."

Suddenly, Jane blushed and lowered her eyes. "Lizzy, what is it like...hmm...being married," she stumbled through the question with some embarrassment.

Elizabeth put her hand on her sister's. "I can only speak for myself, but it is more wonderful than anything I could even have imagined."

"I confess to being a little nervous about tonight."

"I believe our Aunt Gardiner gave me the best advice. She said to trust my own feelings and my husband, and she was exactly right. If you have enjoyed Mr. Bingley's kisses, then you may look forward even greater happiness tonight."

Although Jane's face was still flushed, she looked into her sister's eyes and tried to smile. "Will you come to the house this evening and help me prepare for bed?" she asked.

Elizabeth squeezed her sister's hand. "It would be my pleasure to return the favor you once did for me."

�֎

While the sisters talked upstairs, Darcy and the groom shared a glass of brandy together in the study. Bingley, who had barely stopped grinning all day, still glowed with happiness.

"You are a very fortunate man, Bingley, to have found a wife who is so sweet-tempered and beautiful," said Darcy. "It is not often that you find both qualities in one woman."

"She is an angel, is she not?" Bingley looked dreamily into the fire, and Darcy, never one to say too much, simply sat with him as they drank their brandy in companionable silence. Finally, Bingley spoke. "Thankfully, my sister Louisa and Mr. Hurst will be staying on here in London, and Caroline will be joining them as she wishes to stay in town."

"I am certain you and Jane will be very happy to have some time to yourselves." Darcy swirled the brandy around in his glass and held it up to the light as he thought about how pleasant it was to be alone with one's wife.

"You will be interested to know I finally found the courage to tell my sister to hold her tongue. After Jane told me about the ladies' disastrous shopping excursion, I felt I could not ignore Caroline's rude behavior any longer. She was so shocked that she was actually speechless. I think that may be the first time in my entire life that I got the better of her. I am not certain I would have been able to do it without the encouragement of my dearest Jane. It is something I should have done years ago."

"Then Jane truly is a remarkable woman," said Darcy smiling to himself.

"Once you and Elizabeth were married, I was hoping Caroline would begin to look elsewhere for a husband. At first, she was too angry, but then she settled down. In fact, much to my surprise, she snapped out of her black mood much more quickly than I had expected."

"She is an intelligent woman. If she spent as much time being kind to people as she does being spiteful, she would find life much more pleasant."

"My sister is her own worst enemy when it comes to attracting a husband, but I am pleased to say that it appears she finally has a serious suitor."

"Who is he?" asked Darcy. This was indeed good news for a variety of reasons.

"His name is Wilson, Edward Wilson. He is a little older, a widower from a good family, not of the first circles but accepted by most of society here in London. His first wife was very wealthy, and he was able to use her money to make much needed improvements to his estate. After about ten years, his wife died, and now he is looking for another wealthy wife to improve his position even more."

"What kind of man is he?"

"I do not know him well, but he has a good reputation. He is as eager to advance in society as Caroline, and he believes that her money will help him in that endeavor. Needless to say she is delighted to find someone whose social interests so closely coincide with her own. I am simply pleased to find anyone who will take her off my hands!" Bingley's eyes glowed with mischief as he looked at Darcy over his brandy glass.

"To the happy couple then," said Darcy raising his glass.

Bingley returned the salute with a wicked grin.

SIXTY SIX

When Elizabeth returned from settling Jane in at the Bingley's townhouse, she found Darcy in his favorite chair in the study. He looked up from the book he was reading and smiled when he heard her enter. With a sigh, she sank into the chair next to his.

"It was a wonderful wedding breakfast. You should be proud of yourself for all you did to make things so perfect," said Darcy setting aside his book.

"Thank you, my love. Of course, I could never have done it without the help of Mrs. Hawkins. She is such a gem."

Darcy suddenly looked quite serious. "My dear, I know it may not be proper to ask, but how was your sister feeling when you left her?"

"I know she is nervous and I tried to talk to her, but even as well as I know her, it was difficult. I made sure she looked beautiful, and now the rest is up to them."

"Ah, as it should be. Bingley is a good man. He will treat her very well I am sure," he said. "Would you like a sip of my brandy?"

Elizabeth made a face. "A small glass of port would not be unwelcome."

Darcy poured her drink and settled back into his chair. Elizabeth took a sip of the sweet liquid and smiled contentedly.

"I am so very glad you introduced me to port. This is divinely delicious." After another small sip, she sat watching her husband. Even after all these months, she never tired of looking at his handsome face. Once again she thought of how very glad she was that he had persisted in his pursuit to win her love.

"When we return home, I have a special present waiting for you," he said, breaking the silence.

"You do? What is it?" she asked, sitting forward in her chair.

"I am not sure I should say. It might be better if you were surprised."

"But my love, if you did not want me to know, you should not have mentioned it at all," said Elizabeth, her lips forming a sweet little pout.

"Perhaps I might be convinced to tell you," he teased.

"You do know how relentless I can be once I make up my mind about something."

"Very well, I will tell you if you come here," he said, patting his knee.

She threw him a look, which he answered by patting his knee again. Elizabeth sighed, knowing that the only way she would get more information was to cooperate. Of course, sitting on his lap was really no hardship to her. When he pulled her closer, she laid her head on his shoulder. Darcy kissed the top of her head and then began working his way down her neck tantalizing her with more sweet gentle kisses in all the places he knew would increase her pleasure. Elizabeth could feel the familiar heat building inside her.

As she began to relax, he started to pull at the ribbons on her dressing gown. At first, her mind was occupied with the sensations his kisses were invoking in her. Then suddenly, she realized what he was doing and she tried to sit up.

"Wait just a moment. You promised to tell me about my present if I came over and joined you," she protested.

"Yes, but I did not say *when* I would tell you."

As Elizabeth tried to push herself away in protest, he held

her all the more tightly to him. "You are a most infuriating man!"

Darcy made no comment but returned to moving his lips slowly across the delicate skin at the base of her neck. Elizabeth shivered. "We are not in our own room you know. Someone could come in at any time." She attempted to push him away again, but she was not really trying very hard.

"I have taken care of that," he told her as he ran the tips of his fingers across her collarbone. "I dismissed all the servants for the evening with the understanding that no one should come into this part of the house unless specifically called."

"What about Georgiana and Kitty?"

"My aunt and uncle are in town, so I obtained an invitation for the girls to stay with them for a few days."

"And my mother and Mary?"

"The Gardiners have taken them off our hands. Lizzy, you really are talking too much." Darcy continued to torment her with little kisses, but she squirmed in his arms.

"So you had this planned? All the servants must know why you dismissed them! Oh, William, this is too embarrassing!"

"I distinctly remember a time when you declared you did not care what the servants thought."

"I may have been under a spell," she said with a twinkle in her eye.

"Sweetheart, the servants are so overjoyed to see us happy that they do not care what we do. Now tell me you are not enjoying yourself, and I will stop," he offered.

"You know I cannot say that."

"Then be silent," he said, taking her face in his hands and putting his mouth over hers.

Elizabeth gave herself over to the pleasurable sensations invoked by his touch. After a few more minutes of this exquisite torture, he lifted her up and carried her over to the rug in front of the fireplace. After gently putting her down, Darcy pulled a pillow from one of the chairs to put beneath her head. Then he stretched out beside her and began to kiss her face and nibble on her ears.

Elizabeth rolled onto her side to face him and snuggled close. "While Jane and Bingley were reciting their vows today, I was thinking about our wedding," said Elizabeth.

"Hmm," Darcy murmured, burying his face in her hair.

"You are not listening, my love," she said, pushing herself back to look into his face. "I am very serious."

He sighed knowing she would not rest until she had talked about what was on her mind. "Of course, I am listening," he said, rolling over on his back. Elizabeth moved closer and laid her head on his shoulder.

"Do you think we should repeat our wedding vows to each other again—now that things are so different?" she asked.

"Is this truly important to you?"

"At our wedding I tried to take the vows seriously, but now they mean so much more to me. It would be as if we were starting over knowing that we truly love each other."

Darcy faced her again. "You forget. I loved you then," he said, tapping her nose lightly with his finger.

"I know you did. I am sorry I was so slow to recognize my own feelings. Clearly you are much wiser than I." Elizabeth ran her fingers through his curls, brushing them back from his face.

"If we were to repeat our vows, there is one that would have to change if you are to have any hope of keeping them," he told her.

"And just what is that?" she asked frowning.

"The 'obey' would need to be removed from part about 'love, honor, and obey'. Experience tells me that you never obey anyone, let alone me."

"I see what you mean." As she pretended to be thinking seriously about his comment, her eyes twinkled. "Could I say 'try very hard to obey'? Would that count?"

He shook his head and kissed her. "There is no hope. You are simply too stubborn."

"Ha! If we argued over which of us was the more stubborn, that discussion would go on for a very long time, and I fear nothing would be resolved."

"Yes, but you must know I did not marry you to change you. *'Love is not love Which alters when it alteration finds...'*" he began as he slowly slid his hand from her shoulder down to the small of her back, pulling her against him. She responded with a little shiver.

"You know that is one of my favorite poems."

"If you remember, it is one I marked in the book I gave you on your first night at Pemberley."

"So even then you were trying to tell me something?" she asked, rising up on her elbow to watch his face.

"I am not very good with words, so I thought I would let the Bard speak for me," he replied with a grin.

"I had no idea you were such a romantic," she whispered, intentionally letting her breath tickle his ear.

"I cannot reveal all my secrets at one time! How would I keep your attention if you knew everything about me?"

"Somehow I do not think you will ever have to worry about that." She threw him a saucy look.

Darcy took her face in his hands and gave her a lingering kiss. He had just returned to the ribbons on her dressing gown when she put a hand on his chest to stop him. He sighed. "What is it, my love?"

"Seriously, do you think we should consider repeating our vows? Perhaps on our first anniversary?"

"I have one vow in particular on my mind at this moment."

Elizabeth wrinkled her brow. "And which is that?"

"I remember promising to love...and...cherish," he breathed, planting a kiss on her neck with each word.

"Hmm, cherish? And in what way do you plan to cherish me, sir?"

Darcy silenced her effectively with a kiss. This time when he reached for the ribbons, she made no attempt to stop him.

EPILOGUE

Elizabeth walked up the hill ahead of Darcy, almost pulling him along. "Why are you so slow? At this rate, we will never reach the top," she said.

"Should you be walking so quickly?" he asked.

"You worry too much, my love. I am accustomed to walking and I feel very well, thank you. Now come along. I am anxious to see the view."

"Are you certain it is good for you to be out in the summer's heat?"

"It is early—the sun is barely up. We will be home well before it becomes too hot."

Darcy sighed. He worried constantly about Elizabeth and the child she was carrying. His child. Just thinking about it almost made him light-headed. This was not what he had expected. The child was not yet born, and he still felt as protective of it as he did of his wife.

Upon finally reaching the top, they stood together looking out over the valley. In the distance, they could see Pemberley with all its grandeur. She was reminded of another time when they had stood just this way, looking out the window of her old bedroom at Longbourn on the day of her father's funeral. That seemed so long ago now. At the time, she had not loved him, and every touch of his had felt strange and awkward. Now having his arms around her seemed the most natural thing in the world.

Elizabeth leaned back against her husband's strong frame and relaxed. "So much has changed in the past year," she said. "I lost my father. We married and moved to Pemberley. Now my dearest Jane is married, and she and Bingley have moved closer to us in Derbyshire."

"I know you must still miss your father."

"Yes, every day, but my grief is not as sharp around edges as it once was."

"Now there is a new life to occupy your thoughts," he said, laying his hand gently on her stomach.

"It is difficult to think of much else when the evidence is right in front of me," she said, placing her hand on top of his. Darcy's lips tickled the back of her neck causing shivers all through her. "Now tell me again when you first knew you were in love with me," she asked.

"There is no specific starting point I can name. I was in the middle before I even knew I had begun," he replied.

Although she could not see his face, she knew he was smiling. "I love to hear you say that. I am so thankful you were patient and waited for me to catch up."

"It took you long enough," he teased.

"Some things are worth the wait," she responded.

"Indeed they are."

Finis

ABOUT THE AUTHOR

You might be surprised to learn that when Ms. Mason-Milks read *Pride and Prejudice* for the first time in the eighth grade, she was not impressed. That changed when she saw the now famous 1995 mini-series version of the story. Deciding to give Austen another chance, she read all of Austen's novels and fell in love.

About five years ago, she was delighted to discover that there were dozens of web sites devoted to everything "Jane." After reading the fan fiction posted on various web sites, she decided to try her hand at writing a story herself.

She says, "Writing stories inspired by Austen's books offers a way to spend more time with the characters I've grown to love. Just because the book ends, it doesn't have to be the end of the story." Her favorite Austen book is *Pride and Prejudice* with *Persuasion* a close second.

In addition to writing, her other loves include singing in a women's *a cappella* chorus, reading, and yoga. She currently lives in Seattle with her husband and four very naughty cats.

You can visit her blog at:
http://www.austen-whatif-stories.com/

Made in the USA
Lexington, KY
10 October 2011